Intrigue

Cecil Denney

Acknowledgments

Those who read my first novel, *Intruder*, found it interesting enough to encourage me to continue. One reader, Donna Meinhard, read drafts of *Intruder* and *Intrigue* and made helpful suggestions. I am indebted to Larry Zeigler for creating fantastic covers for both books. Vera Haddan has been a most skillful editor. My wife, Janice, has endured the many hours I stood at my computer writing, rewriting, and living with the characters in my stories. As I daily expounded or she read story's progress, Janice patiently listened and proofread my creations.

Writers in the Woods. Mary's Woods, and the Jottings Group, a weekly column in the Lake Oswego Review, encouraged me to write.

Introduction

A National Public Radio show inspired Kyle Tredly's story when I lived in Maple Grove, Minnesota. The announcer interviewed an author who said he did not work from a cast of characters or a plot; an initial spark started a story, and the story wrote itself. That sounded interesting. It would be like starting to read, in this case, write, a novel, not knowing how it would turn out. And, by writing it, the author gains a couple of things. First, the story would turn out exactly as intended. Second, it would entertain longer than reading a novel. In my first novel, *Intruder,* I began by wondering what it would be like to wake up with an intruder in my house. As I worked on multiple drafts, I came to like the main character, Mr. Tredly, and wondered what additional adventures he might experience.

In this second story, *Intrigue* moves Kyle to Portland, Oregon, to escape Houston, Texas, after a disastrous hurricane. He applies to several companies for a programmer's position. During his invitation to interview, he runs into a former girlfriend, Laura McLaughlin, who offers him a ride. When he steps into the car, he meets Richard Meisner, the CEO, and owner of Meisner Industries, his future boss. Before his interview, Meisner has a private meeting with Kyle, which begins his new adventure and leads to love and danger involving an international conspiracy.

Chapter 1

~ Intentional Coincidence ~

Kyle had not been at the bus stop five minutes when a black SUV with darkly tinted windows pulled over to the bus stop. When the front window on the passenger side rolled down, he was shocked to see Laura McLaughlin, his ex-girlfriend from Houston. He had not seen Laura since she moved to Dallas and sent him a "Dear John" letter breaking off their relationship.

Kyle allowed an hour and a half to get downtown even though projected to take only forty-five minutes. He could not afford to be late for the interview appointment at Meisner Industries. He carried several additional copies of his updated résumé and descriptions of software projects he worked on in Houston in a small leather folder. Rain was predicted, so Kyle took his umbrella with him. Two other people were waiting for the bus but did not appear to know each other. As an introvert, Kyle did not try to engage in conversation. He would learn that although people thought of the South as being more friendly, Portland had Houston beat on that score

When Laura rolled down the window, Kyle could only stare for a moment, puzzled, then blurted out: "Laura? Is that you? What are you doing in Portland?" He paused, expecting answers to his questions.

"Hi, Kyle. Long-time-no-see. You headed uptown?" Laura responded, ignoring Kyle's questions.

"Yeah, but, uh—" Kyle responded, and then his brow involuntarily wrinkled in sheer puzzlement.

"Hop in. We can give you a ride." She continued as though nothing happened over the last couple of years, but with a manner that betrayed a particular disconnected tone.

Having caught his breath after being so surprised, he declared, "I can't hop in right now, Laura. I have a job interview downtown. I am on my way there. Could I get your number or something? Could we catch up later?"

Ignoring Kyle's comment, Laura repeated, "Kyle, wherever you are going, we can take you. Hop in!"

"You don't understand. I need to get downtown for an important job interview. I am out of work. I just moved here. I need work. I don't have time to chat right now. Couldn't we meet someplace later?"

"Kyle, we are headed downtown, near Lloyd Center. We have you covered. And besides, it will be a lot quicker than taking the bus. Are you going to be your normal stubborn self? Get in!"

The other two people at the bus stop had not spoken, but when Laura called Kyle stubborn, they looked at each other quizzically, and one of them rolled their eyes as if to say, "You are an idiot. Take the ride!" Then both of them simultaneously looked up the block for the bus with mixed feelings. They were there to catch the bus, but not yet. Not until Kyle got in the car, and the car moved. They did not want the bus to pass by because a car was in the way. Laura's insistence reverberated through his head, and he thought, *Yes, that was one of the issues Laura always complained about. She complained that I was stubborn, too set in my ways, "like an old man," she used to say when I hesitated to take action. So, what would be the harm in accepting the ride? She had always been the helpful type. She could not pass a Houston panhandler without giving them something, even though she did not have all that much from waitress tips. Although she thought I was stubborn, she usually got her way when we were together, and things turned out better than they would have otherwise. So, why not take her up on the offer? After all, we might get back together.*

His thoughts turned. *Who is driving the car? Her new boyfriend? Well, maybe I can find out what the competition is like? Obviously, she is doing okay, or at least her boyfriend owned a car, a BMW at that, which I lack at the moment.* He realized he was slow to react when Laura chimed in again.

"Well?" Laura asked with a bit of flirting impatience.

Shaken out of his mental gymnastics, he responded, "Okay, Lloyd Center. That's close to where I need to be." He moved off the curb toward the car. When Kyle opened the back door of the car and started to get in, he hesitated. There was already someone in the backseat. But he was committed now, so he climbed in, nodding to the other well-dressed passenger.

"Hello, Kyle. My name is Richard. Glad we could give you a lift." Preoccupied with the surprise of seeing Laura, Richard's comment went unacknowledged.

Kyle's mind went into an overdrive of curiosity. The driver did not introduce himself. Judging by his cap, Kyle surmised he was the chauffeur, not a boyfriend. So, who was this guy in the backseat? Laura turned around as the car pulled off.

"Kyle! So good to see you. How have you been doing?" Laura said with apparent sincerity as though nothing had happened between them. Kyle used to be able to tell when Laura was playacting. She was always playing tricks on him when they were together. Kyle remembered how much fun they used to have. Now, she was acting as if she had never written that damn "Dear John" letter.

"Uh, fine. And you?" Kyle asked before he realized that was a stupid question, given she was riding around in a BMW with a chauffeur. But before he could add anything else, Laura jumped in.

"Now? Well, now, I am doing fine."

"So, how is your mom? I was expecting to hear from you, and how your mom was doing rather than the letter I did get?" Kyle said with a tinge of sarcasm that he wished he had not intoned.

"Kyle, I still have trouble talking about it. She passed away about a month after I got home."

"Oh. Laura, I am so sorry. If you had let me know, I would

have dropped everything and come up to Dallas to support you. Why didn't you call?"

"I don't know. I was confused about our relationship, my Mom, my life in general. I was depressed and could not do anything for a while. I know I should have called, but then as time passed, I began to think about our relationship. I decided I was not ready to be a good partner. Sorry about the letter." Laura had already been thinking she would have to lie. Though trained to lie, with Kyle it seemed somehow very wrong.

"Sounds like things are doing better now?" Kyle interjected.

"Kyle, other than a year of depression after Mom died, things have been going well. I missed you a lot that year. Sorry I did not call when Mom died. Oh, I said that, didn't I. And, Kyle, you may not believe this, but I regret the letter I wrote. It was a deplorable decision. Well, then when I came to my senses, and I realized we could still be good friends, I tried to look for you, but you moved."

Kyle had moved to a different apartment in Houston after he received the "Dear John" letter.

Laura continued uninterrupted, "That's about the time I met Richard on one of his trips to Dallas, and well, you know. We seem to have hit it off. I know that is not a good excuse, but there it is"—long awkward pause when no one said anything— "Forgive me?" she asked in an almost begging tone. That answered a question for Kyle. It was Richard, not the chauffeur she was hooked up with. So now, Richard was of more interest to him. Kyle assumed he was the one who owned the car but was confused. If Laura was Richard's girlfriend, why wasn't she sitting in back with him? Why was she sitting in front?

"So, how did you and Richard meet?"

"After Mom died, I got a job with a catering company. We catered high-profile events at the Dallas Golf Club. A Dallas software company was having a dinner to celebrate the sale of their company to Richard's company. It was a nightmare. I dropped a plate right behind Richard's chair. As if I was not embarrassed enough, Richard helped me clean it up. I thought for sure I would lose my job, but Richard put in a good word. Later he looked me up, and well, one thing led to another. He invited me out for drinks. When I met Richard, things began to turn around for me, and you know how it goes."

"To be honest, Laura, I don't," Kyle said before he could take it back. "I am glad you are okay now, and I guess Richard is the lucky guy."

Richard jumped into the conversation, "Yes, Kyle, I am a lucky guy, but I guess you understand that. Laura has said a lot of good things about you too. Don't take all of this the wrong way. If it is as she describes it, she has moved on now."

They had been heading toward town for several minutes in moderately heavy traffic. Kyle didn't tell Laura where, precisely, he needed out.

"So, who do I tell where I need to go? You could drop me off at Lloyd Center if that works for you. I have a job interview downtown that I can't afford to miss."

Richard answered. "Kyle, we already know where you are headed. Sorry for the intrigue. I am Richard Meisner, CEO of Meisner—"

"Meisner Industries?" Kyle interrupted in surprise. "Oh my God, what a coincidence. That is where I have an interview at 11:30. I take this as a good omen." It did not immediately occur to Kyle that Richard had said he knew where Kyle was going, and by implication, knew he was going there for an interview. There was an awkward pause while Kyle's comment fell like a lead balloon rolling around in the car. It took Kyle a moment to realize he was the only one surprised that he had an interview. Richard waited and watched the series of expressions on Kyle's face until it reached the point of recognition. Then he spoke.

"Sorry, Kyle. We seem to be getting off on the wrong foot— my fault. As you may have guessed, I knew you had the interview. Laura told me you were very punctual, and I found out you had no car, so we were waiting for you to come to the bus stop."

"But why?" Kyle managed to squeeze in between breaths Richard took. "And how did you know where I live?"

"It was on your resume, Kyle. Hopefully, I can make things clear when we get to the office. I want to spend time with you before you do your interview. I think you will find you can be a great asset to Meisner Industries. Let me tell you about my company on the way downtown."

Kyle's curiosity was piqued, and to tell the truth, his mind wandered a bit as Richard tried to fill Kyle in on Meisner's. Obviously, this was not a standard interview process, and he did not know whether to be concerned. It sounded like Kyle had the job already by the way Richard was explaining things to him. Much of what he said about the company, Kyle already knew from the research he did to prepare for the interview. But there were aspects of it he did not know, so he tried to pay attention.

Laura's part in this was still confusing to him. She had turned around, so it was he and Richard facing each other as the chauffeur guided the car efficiently through traffic. Kyle became self-conscious as his face contorted trying to be attentive to Richard, and at the same time, puzzling about Laura. He realized he was adding lots of "uh-huhs," as Richard talked. Fortunately, the ride did not take long, and they were pulling into the garage and Richard's private parking space. The chauffeur got out of the car and opened Richard's door first. He came around to open Laura and Kyle's doors, but both had already exited the vehicle.

Richard spoke to the chauffeur, "Bill, I will need the car back here at 1:30 as we planned."

Laura caught up with Richard, and Kyle followed. They walked toward an elevator door marked Private.

"Kyle, when we are through, you will come back down to this floor. Turning around and pointing toward the adjacent stairwell, he said, "You will go down one flight and walk across the garage, and there is an elevator to the street level. Come back to the front door of the building and take the elevator up to your interview. Did they tell you which floor?"

"Yes," Kyle answered, "the letter and the phone call told me to take the elevator to the eighth floor, and the receptionist would point me to Human Resources."

~ Move to Portland, Oregon ~

The first serious response to multiple applications since Kyle came to Portland, Oregon was encouraging. He was scheduled for an interview and determined to present his best self. He shaved, pressed his newest Dockers, and put on a clean white dress shirt and a navy-blue tie. He wore his polished brown leather shoes—no sneakers today. Kyle could not afford to be late. Lacking a car, he had to take the bus. Fortunately, Kyle managed to secure a reasonably priced apartment in Tabor Hill Terrace on East Burnside between 60th and 61st Avenues. There was a TriMet bus stop across the street on the corner.

Before coming to Portland, Kyle worked for Softtek, a Wilson and Brodrick Company. Softtek was a successful software engineering firm in Houston, Texas, before the storm. Harvey, a Category 4 hurricane in 2017, dumped massive amounts of water on Houston. The storm knocked out a power-station that fed the buildings around Softtek headquarters. It took over three weeks to restore power. Restoring the company's water-damaged computer server farm took another six weeks. In retrospect, the server farm should never have been located in the basement of the building. The backup pumps could not keep up with the storm's deluge. The backups, stored off-site in Conroe, Texas, were also damaged. The prognosis for a rapid recovery was out of the question. The company laid off almost thirty percent of the staff to avoid declaring bankruptcy. Softtek customers, mostly in the greater Houston area, were also harmed in the storm-related flood and were not in a position to pay for partially completed software systems.

Kyle lacked enough seniority to make it through downsizing. It was an unfortunate circumstance, not his fault, although he was suspicious the layoffs were not fairly administered. The prospects for another job in the area were slim due to the slow recovery of other business enterprises and the abundance of workers. He tried unsuccessfully to find another position in Houston. Kyle was concerned he would run out of funds before the recovery opened up the Houston job market for programmers. After six months, he decided to move.

Lacking any clear idea of where to go, he emailed an acquaintance, A.J. Stentz. He met A.J. at the University of Houston in computer engineering classes. A.J. moved to Portland, Oregon, with his wife and daughter, before the

Houston storm. Job prospects in Portland attracted A.J. In an email, A.J. informed Kyle the prospects for work continued to be promising, better than Houston. Kyle, although not usually an impulsive guy, decided to try his luck in Portland. He was always intrigued by the stories he had heard about the verdant Northwest. It suit his liberal leanings. His experiences in the Midwest had certainly given him problems.

Kyle's car was submerged by the floodwaters and needed work. So were a lot of other vehicles. Getting his car in for repairs involved waiting in queue while it rusted. Even if he repaired it, he was not sure "Old Faithful" would make it to Portland, so he sold it for almost nothing and bought a bus ticket. To help plan the trip, Kyle ordered a map of Portland from Amazon. Apartments-Online helped him qualify and secure an apartment on East Burnside. The bus ticket cost him $165.

Kyle packed the few belongings he had into a suitcase and a large cardboard box. He packed a change of clothes, toiletries, and his laptop in a carry-on backpack. It was not clear there would be an opportunity to change clothes for the two-and-a-half-day trip. When the bus left Houston, it was full—a lot of people anxious to get out of Houston. Kyle found two empty seats together. He took the one by the window. Soon after he stowed his backpack in the overhead bin and was seated, an older woman asked if she could take the aisle seat. She was carrying two large plastic bags. Kyle helped her stuff one of them in the overhead bin, and she sat down with the other one on her lap.

"Where you headed," Kyle asked.

"Dallas, I'm heading to niece in Arlington. She says I can hang with her."

"My name is Kyle," Kyle said.

"I go by Sue. You know, Kyle—that is my grandkid's name. "Where you headed?"

"Portland, Oregon."

"You live there?"

"Oh, no. I am from southwest Texas. I am hoping to find a job in Portland. A friend of mine said the market was much better than here in Houston."

"Yeah, Houston's crap, right? I was laid off right after storm. Don't imagine I'll find work here.

"You don't have family here in Houston?"

"A no-good husband."

"Uh—huh," Kyle did not know what else to say.

"He worked at Shell refinery east a town. He scared of storms, so he took off before it got'em. No idear where he is to."

"Scared of storms?"

"Yeah, sure as hell. He was prisoned in Huntsville when big tornado hit. They was all hunkered down when roof blew off. Sucked a guy right out of his cell. Found his body da yard.

Scared shit out-a Huey. He's all big guy till a storm comes along, then he's like a kicked puppy. Nothing I can do him for. Imagine he'll find me ventually."

"I don't much care for tornadoes either," Kyle said to be sympathetic. Kyle figured this could be a long ride to Dallas. Fortunately, it was already 8:00 PM, so it would not be that long before he could rest. He endured a few more stories before a restroom stop. He pretended to sleep as soon as it began to get dark. They made it to Dallas-Fort Worth around 12:30 AM. Sue got off. The seat next to Kyle was vacant the rest of the way to Portland, much to Kyle's relief.

The rest of the trip was uneventful, and Kyle managed to keep to himself as people got on and off during the trip. When he arrived in Portland, Kyle was tired and took a taxi to the apartment. Kyle had the foresight to order an inflatable mattress from Amazon and have it delivered the day he arrived at the new apartment. He slept well for the first time that night. Kyle brought his meager curated clothes with him. It took only a few minutes to get the key to his apartment since he had already paid online. The mattress was there waiting for him. He would need to get sheets and a blanket as soon as he was settled. Some of his clothes had been ruined, wading through storm-related water. It made decisions about what to bring to Portland relatively easy, hence the reduced wardrobe in one suitcase and a large cardboard box. It did not take him long to get set up in his apartment with furniture and access to the internet.

Wilson & Brodrick Softtek at least made him feel like they hated to lose him. They had written an excellent introduction and recommendation. They provided him with a document that explained the nature of the storm-related layoffs. Kyle applied online to several companies in Portland before he left Houston. A.J. Stentz sent an additional list of possibilities after Kyle had packed his computer and canceled his internet service in Houston. He had to wait until he arrived in Portland to follow up on those suggestions. As soon as he could, Kyle located a copy center. He made additional copies of his resume with a cover letter and mailed them to the list Stentz sent him. The list included Meisner Industries. To his surprise, within two weeks, he received several invitations to interview, including with Meisner Industries. According to his research, Meisner Industries had an excellent reputation. He called and arranged a time to interview.

~ The Private Meeting ~

It was a short walk from the car to the elevator. Richard passed a ring on his right hand in front of a pad next to the private elevator. The doors opened. They all went inside, and Richard passed his hand in front of a pad inside the elevator. The doors closed, and the elevator began to rise. There were no numbers on the panel. When the elevator stopped, everyone emerged into a large executive suite that looked west over Portland's Willamette River.

"Give me a moment, Kyle. I will be right with you. Have a seat." Richard pointed to the couch across the room. He walked over to his desk and pressed a button.

"Yes, Mr. Meisner?" his personal assistant Charla Roshken answered.

"Charla, Laura and I came up on the elevator. I need a few minutes to talk to her about a private matter. Please make sure I am not interrupted."

"Yes, Sir. I have a few calls for you. Do you want to wait for your messages?"

"Yes, I will let you know when I am available for business. Otherwise, no interruptions, and certainly no one coming into the office."

"I understand," Charla responded.

Kyle would have understood if Charla had said: "I understand" with a "knowing" tone that implied she understood what Richard and Laura would be doing that made it so important not to be interrupted. There was no such tone, just a purely professional response.

As Richard spoke, Kyle went to sit on the couch. Laura led the way and sat in the easy chair on the left that looked out the windows. She squinted. Richard followed them both and sat in the chair to the right of the couch with his back to the window. To look at Richard, Kyle had to squint because the light from the windows was bright. Noticing Kyle's squint, Richard smiled, and turned to speak to no one in particular, and said, "Alice, close the screens, please," and a sun-screen lowered from the ceiling.

"Impressive," Kyle noted to himself, but unconsciously, he said it out loud.

"After all, Kyle, we are a tech company, among other things, and one of the best. Now let's get to the reason you are sitting here before you go to your interview."

It could not have been soon enough for Kyle. He gave Richard his full attention.

Richard continued, "First, Kyle, I need to be clear on one thing. You are not guaranteed a position at Meisner Industries. I have a practice of not getting involved in the hiring process. Let me revise that statement. I have a practice of not getting involved in the hiring process *directly*. The culture of Meisner Industries is critical to our success. A person must fit in to be a successful part of the team here. In our interview process, you will meet with several individual members of the team who, if you are hired, will have to work with you. So, you can expect questions that extend beyond the normal, work-related questions."

"Like what?" Kyle interrupted without thinking.

"I will get to that. But first, I need to explain my particular interest in you. I do not usually meet potential employees unless they are hired for a team leader or director position. But I do have overall responsibility for the company's success, so I have a keen interest in the people we hire. In that regard, the Human Resources team leader, Tom Bosworth, who you will meet, screens all applications, and I have a list of hot topics. Tom lets me know when a potential candidate shows up who has experience in one of these areas. In your case, your work in multi-spectral analysis was the hot button. That alone would not have developed into an interview had it not been for two factors." Meisner turned to point at Laura. "I happened to mention your name over dinner a few days ago, and Laura had many positive things to say about your integrity and how you treated her when you were together. That led me to believe a pre-interview might be useful."

"What was the other factor? You said there were two."

"The fact that you had worked for Softtek. Meisner Industries happens to own a fourteen percent share of Softtek, and I sit on their board. I know the CEO very well, so I was able to ask him about you casually."

"Winston Clarkson?"

"Yes."

"I don't think I ever met him personally, just saw him occasionally at large staff gatherings."

"Well, Kyle, he sure knew you. He spoke very highly of your work and expressed regret that you were one of the people caught up in the layoffs. He was hoping things would turn around more quickly than they did, and he would be able to attract you back to the company."

"That seems strange to me." Kyle said, "He never said anything to me; never let me know in any way of his interest. Although I was pleased and interested in the work that Softtek was doing, I don't think I would have gone back there."

"Why is that?"

Kyle hesitated, unsure how he should answer. He decided to be upfront and honest. After all, Meisner Industries was not the only place he had applied. "Well, to be honest, I thought the layoffs were managed unfairly. It appeared that some of the staff who were not making contributions were retained, ones that had a personal connection to the director of their HR Department. Several of us who were let go; at least, I thought so, were essential to the projects we were working on. I realize that an employee doesn't necessarily have the big picture, but that is the way it looked to me and a couple of others."

"Fair enough. I don't think you will find that kind of behavior here at Meisner Industries, at least I hope that the culture here prevents it. Let me get back to questions you will be asked that are not directly related to your professional skill set. Laura tells me you are a runner. You will find several people you meet are competitive runners in local and national races. You may receive questions in that area. She also tells me you are interested in science topics outside the scope of the work you do. You may find questions in that area. Finally, she tells me you are a religious person. You can expect questions that, while not directly asking about religion, are designed to invite you to share those beliefs."

"That might be a problem area," Kyle answered hesitatingly.

"How is that?"

"Well, although I am interested in religion, I would not call myself a believer in the general sense. I am not a fundamentalist; I am progressive compared to many religious people."

"Don't worry about expressing that. I can tell you it will be compatible with many people who invite discussion in those areas. Of course, none of these questions will be direct. We could be in trouble if people perceived that our hiring practices were discriminatory in religion or other protected areas. You need to be listening for these so-called invitations, usually by a person disclosing something about themselves that naturally evokes similar responses."

"Oh, I see. I can handle that."

"Again, I need to assure you there are no guarantees here, but I am confident that if you are yourself and listen for the invitations to volunteer information, you will do fine. There is one last thing. We seriously consider an applicant's references. Their responses to our inquiries carry a lot of weight. We do them confidentially and verbally, never anything in writing, to avoid potential lawsuits. You stated on your resume that references would be provided on request. Am I right about that?"

"Yes. I have a list in my briefcase in the event a list was requested."

"I need you to hold that list. I would like you to add a

particular name to it. It will not be a problem if you say you will bring the list tomorrow. Would you be okay with that?"

"Holding it and bringing it tomorrow, yes. But first, you need to tell me who you want me to add. You have not seen my list; maybe I already have that name on my list."

"I doubt it. I want you to add the name of Gene Mattorky of Softtek. Did you ever meet him?"

"Yes, once, but I doubt if he knows much about me?"

"On the contrary, he knows a lot about you, your work, your value to Softtek, and how the layoffs were mishandled. He would be a wonderful reference. I have discussed this possibility with him, and he would be happy to be included. I assume he was not on your list?"

"No, but I would be interested in why you would want me to include him?"

"That's easy. Gene is well known by the engineers and developers working here. They are familiar with his work, and they have a lot of respect for him. He has provided references for others who have turned out to be good additions to Meisner Industries. Assuming you do well in the interview process yourself, this should seal the deal for you, no guarantees."

Kyle had other questions, but he felt they might have been a bit confrontational. In his research of Meisner Industries, he found no financial information because it was a privately held company. Additionally, the full scope of Meisner Industries working units was not on the web, at least not under Meisner

Industries' heading. They were probably incorporated under different names. He would have to wait on his other questions if he was hired. Kyle did not want conflict with the "big boss," especially now. But this whole process seemed fishy, curious, highly unusual. He typically felt he owed a boss his allegiance, but this was different, like a personal owing. But, on the other hand, he needed a job, and the position did sound interesting. He did like to work in a team environment, and if the people were likable to boot, what could be the harm. He held out hope that working for Meisner Industries might keep him in contact with Laura.

"Did you have any other questions, Kyle?

"No, what do I do now?"

"Well, I would prefer that our conversations here never be mentioned. I need to know if you can manage to keep this secret?"

"No problem." Kyle blurted out despite the fact it was a cause of concern.

"As I said, I try to avoid direct influence in the hiring process, and in a way, I am not influencing how your interview goes. If they decide you are not the fit, although I think you will be, that will be the end of things. If they do approve of you for the position, then where is the harm. In the unlikely case you do not get the job; Laura will contact you, fill you in, and provide some suggestions and assistance in getting interviews with other firms. Now to the privacy of this meeting."

It suddenly dawned on Kyle how he had been compromised. He would keep the meeting private because he wanted to see Laura again. He would need all the help he could get if he did not get this job. He realized Meisner was a manipulative guy. He wondered how that might affect his work here if he did get the job.

Meisner continued, "You will go back down my private elevator, down the stairs one flight, catch the parking garage elevator to the ground floor, and then come in the building from the front entrance, making no reference to having been here. There is a small Starbucks coffee shop on the ground floor. You could wait there until time for your interview. At some point in the process, if they decide to hire you, we will be introduced, and I would appreciate your treating that as a first introduction. Do you think you could do that?"

"I see no reason I couldn't." *There I go. I compromised so easily.* "So, here is hoping I get to meet you," Kyle said with a jocular tone to cover his concerns. Richard led him to the elevator, and the door opened. Kyle walked in, and Richard reached around and touched the pad with the same ring. After he retracted his arm, the doors closed, and the elevator descended.

~ Laura and Richard's Secret ~

Meisner turned to Laura as soon as the elevator door closed and began to descend.

"Well, did that go as you hoped?" Laura asked Meisner.

"Interesting fellow," he answered. "Time will tell how he handles himself in the interview. If he is as reliable as you think, things will be fine. If not, no harm will come of my subterfuge. I will want to review the video of the interview, of course, before deciding. You like him, don't you?"

Laura ignored his question, instead saying, "I hope I am right. Kyle certainly was honorable as far as our relationship was concerned. I still feel guilty about how I broke it off with Kyle. He didn't deserve it. I hope he does nail the interview." Laura reflected this as much to herself as to Richard.

"You are too hard on yourself, Laura. Unless you have been successful in hiding things from me, and I seriously doubt it, you underestimate your skills and ability. Your help in this endeavor could be quite beneficial to Meisner Industries. Who knows, you and Kyle might restore the good relationship you had in Houston. You don't have cold feet, do you?"

"No, it's not that. Laura said. "I am in one hundred percent. But, to be honest with you, I do still like Kyle," she finally confessed. "He was very decent to me, maybe a bit too innocent, but a fundamentally nice guy. You will have to be very careful how you use him. The experience of being accused of murder back in St. Andrews may have made him a generally skeptical person. He has learned how to read behind a person's declared intent. He has a strong sense of doing the right thing. However, I do think he will cooperate so long as he thinks your requests promote good and just outcomes."

Meisner added, "That makes him the better employee. I am counting on you, too, you know. I could not do this without your assistance. I will ask you one more time, and then I won't question it again. Are you sure you can go through with this?"

"Richard, if you keep questioning my commitment, I might show you my angry side. You know you can ruin me financially, professionally, and socially if I double-cross you. Besides, I think this is the kind of project I have been missing in my life. Need I say more? You can count on me. Can I trust you?" Laura lied. It was not her first lie to Richard nor her last. It came with the job.

"Okay, okay, we are set. Now we have to hope Kyle aces his interview and gets hired. You better get out of here. We don't want Charla's imagination to get too vivid. Let her know I am ready for the day's business as you leave."

Laura picked up her jacket, checked her appearance in the reflective glass of a picture, and headed out the door, stopping to have a friendly chat with Charla.

Kyle and Laura dated seriously two years ago in Houston. Laura was a hometown kind of girl who everybody liked. She was tall and shapely with a very fair complexion and jet-black hair; she was striking. Whenever they walked into a room together, everyone's eyes landed on Laura. Kyle did not mind that. He felt a certain kind of personal pride that someone as beautiful as Laura was his girlfriend. They had been intimate, rooming together for eight months. It was hard for him to let her go, but that was when he was working, and she moved to Dallas to tend to her sick mom. Laura's dad passed away several years earlier, and her mother lived alone. She made the move sound temporary, but there was more to it than she shared. Not long after she moved, she broke off the relationship in a "Dear John" letter. She put no return address on the letter and changed her cell phone number. Kyle did not have a clue how to contact her. He still had a soft spot for her despite the abrupt "Dear John" letter.

Chapter 2

Kyle left the parking garage as instructed and went to the coffee shop to wait until it was time for the interview. As he sat there looking out the window, he noted that it had started to drizzle. He saw Laura pass by. At first, he thought she was going to come in, and he started to get up, but she didn't. She just looked in the window briefly and walked on.

He could have sworn she was coming in. It looked like she was and then changed her mind at the last moment. Had she seen him? She stopped at the door and reached for the door handle, then backed away. His first reaction was to look around to see what else might have changed her mind. All he could see were two guys huddled at a table by themselves, heads close together in quiet conversation. He could see the one almost facing him was wearing a badge around his neck. It was purple with large letters "MI" in the center. Possibly it was a Meisner Industries badge. The other fellow was facing the glass door to the coffee shop. Perhaps he too had a badge that Laura saw. Maybe she recognized the fellow and did not want him to see her greet Kyle. It was puzzling, but made sense if Laura was well known. It would not be good for her to be seen greeting Kyle, at least not yet.

The curious experience in Meisner's office had made him suspicious and uneasy, a kind of déjà vu of past experiences in St. Andrews. He had been framed and then came close to being prosecuted for two murders. He did not relish going through an experience like that again. The meeting with Richard Meisner made him feel uneasy. He could not imagine that Meisner pulled this on every employee that he hired. What could be his interest in Kyle, and what did Laura have to do with it? He was beginning to have second thoughts about a position there. But, hey, a job is a job; he had been out of work for almost a year. His savings was running low. He did not want to dip into funds he had saved for his retirement. As brief as his time was at Softtek, he already had a reasonable nest egg in an IRA. He could always quit if it became too weird at Meisner Industries. He did want to explore the possibility of getting to know Laura better. He still felt she owed him a thorough explanation of what happened in Dallas.

When he finished college and began earning money, he laid out a plan to save twenty times his annual salary by the time he retired. He did not have to save a lot because interest would continue to compound during his working life. With luck, that would be at least forty years. Then, with a five percent return on his savings, he figured he could maintain his standard of living. So, he could take this job at Meisner's, provided he got it. He would have to be alert.

He was still puzzled about Laura and Richard Meisner. Maybe he was a bit paranoid after the meeting with Meisner.

As his thoughts became random, time passed. He finished his coffee and got up to go to the interview. He was fantasizing about what his future would hold.

~ The Interview ~

Kyle made his way up to the eighth floor to HR. He was about ten minutes early, so he was asked to wait in a small room with a conference table. He had a view out a window overlooking Rose Quarter. Before long, Tom Bosworth, HR team leader, came into the room and introduced himself. He explained the interview process, repeating some of what Meisner had told him. Bosworth asked Kyle if he had references with him. Following Meisner's private recommendation, Kyle agreed to bring references first thing tomorrow. Bosworth said the interview team would be in shortly and made small talk with Kyle while they waited.

One by one, Joe Walker, Josh Smythe, Dennis Andersen, and Jeneen Jenkins came in, introduced themselves, and took a seat across from Kyle. Tom introduced each person again, identifying Joe as the team leader. He pointed to a camera and told Kyle all personnel interviews were recorded to avoid any possible misinterpretations. Tom asked Kyle if he had any objections to the session being recorded. Kyle had never had an interview video recorded before. Meisner Industries did not leave much to chance, he noted. Kyle nodded is assent. Tom turned on the video recorder and asked Kyle again for the record for his willingness to have the session recorded. Kyle again agreed. Tom, having fulfilled his chore, left the room. Joe

Walker identified each person in the room for the record and began the interview process.

"Kyle, it is good to have this chance to discuss the possibility of joining our team. Each of us had an opportunity to review your resume, and we have a few follow up questions for you. Don't know if you have been in this kind of interview before, but we have a short script, guidelines that we follow. We ask each applicant we interview the same basic questions. It helps us compare the candidates fairly. Of course, we don't want it to be too formal, so feel free to ask questions about anything of interest to you. Furthermore, since team compatibility is vital to us, we are all good friends, there will be informal discussions and we will tell you about ourselves. Before we finish, you will have a chance to ask any final questions you have. Does this work for you?"

"Yes, of course. Fire away," Kyle answered with a lightness in his tone. *I hope that did not sound too familiar. I hope I can answer their questions.*

Joe started with general background information type questions, including questions related to his employment history. It got uncomfortable when Joe pushed him to tell more about his work in St. Andrews and why he left. Kyle omitted the kidnapping and jail experiences. They might have already read about that in material Bosworth prepared for them. Joe also grilled Kyle on his electrical engineering knowledge, mainly electronic hardware-software integration. Kyle felt he would only give himself a passing grade on those questions.

Dennis had specific questions about his knowledge of the software tool they used at Meisner's to develop their products. Kyle was familiar with the software but had not used it. He told them about the tool used at Softtek. He was unaware that Meisner Industries had designed the software tool they used in-house. That had not shown up in the research about the company. The depth of the questions worried him, but Kyle answered honestly. He had always been a quick study of software tool sets and was more or less competent in five currently used tools and languages of the industry. Kyle was confident but also humble, self-assured, but not a braggart. He took opportunities to demonstrate the depth of his knowledge without sounding like a know-it-all. When Joe finished, Kyle felt confident he had adequately and accurately reflected his skill level.

Jeneen's questions were more general. What were his interests outside of work? Here he talked about his interest in running as well as drawing cartoons. Jeneen was a runner herself, so he seemed to make a hit with her. She asked Kyle if he knew about the Hood to Coast run. He had not heard about the run, another research failure. She told him that several people from Meisner Industries formed a team every year. The run consisted of a particular kind of relay race that started at Mount Hood and ran to the coast. Unfamiliar with the distance, Kyle did not know how much to be impressed. He had run marathons, so hundred-mile runs impressed him. Jeneen assured him that as a runner, he would hear much more about the Hood to Coast Run in the coming months. The conversation was cordial, but there was a sense of competitiveness in her questions. How many marathons had he run? What was his time? Had he ever run the Boston Marathon? The New York Marathon? When? It was hard for Kyle to imagine that these questions were on the script.

Josh asked questions about finances and the stock market. Kyle was not as competent in understanding how a hedge fund worked over and above general knowledge, but he was confident he could pick that up if that were part of the job. Based on what Meisner had told him, he thought his job was more technical than economic. However, Kyle had worked on many financial systems in his previous positions and was well versed in accounting practices. Josh made it known that Sunday's were off-limits for him. He played drums in a band for his church. Kyle asked him where he went to church. He was not familiar with the church or what it might be like, so he didn't ask any more questions. Josh asked Kyle if he had ever attended a church. Kyle let everyone know he was a Christmas-Easter kind of guy. A couple of the group verbalized similar, making Kyle a bit more comfortable. Josh was reasonably brief, but he felt Kyle had done an adequate job answering his questions.

Now it was Kyle's turn to ask questions. How did their team function? Did they enjoy their assignments? How did they handle the pressure? Did they have any hobbies outside of work? Had they ever increased the size of the team before?

(Yes.) Was that successful? (Yes.) How many teams were there at Meisner Industries? (More than 25.) Where did they work? (Various locations besides Portland area including Denver, Chicago, and New York.) Kyle avoided questions around compensation, vacations, time off, and so forth. All that could be dealt with if he was offered a job. They all participated in answering his questions and seemed cordial and warm.

When they were done, Joe told Kyle that Tom Bosworth would be in touch. Kyle knew he still had to deliver the list of references to Bosworth. Joe said it would be, at the most, one week before a decision was finalized, and gave Kyle his card in case he came up with additional questions. He let Kyle know they were only interviewing three candidates, had already talked to one of them, and the other was scheduled the next day. Kyle was given directions to the exit, and the team stayed to debrief his interview. He wished he could be a fly on the wall of that discussion. Kyle wondered if the debrief was also recorded and if he would ever get to see it.

Kyle left the building and walked to the bus stop. It was only five minutes till the bus arrived, and Kyle was home in less than 30 minutes, in time for a late lunch.

On the bus, Kyle reflected on the interview, Dennis, in particular. Dennis was a funny guy. He was continually squirming around in his chair. When Dennis introduced himself, he spent a long time telling about his various interests outside of work. He talked about his girlfriend and how long they had been together. Kyle had wondered if Dennis would ever ask him a question, but he finally did, asking about multi-spectral detectors, pushing Kyle to dig into rather technical details. That engaged Joe. Dennis and Kyle got so deep into technical discussions that Joe finally closed out the interview.

As best he could tell, Kyle felt the interview was successful. Time would tell. He prepared the list of references he promised to deliver to Bosworth, Adding the reference Meisner suggested. After his lunch, he spaced out, watching a Netflix movie. He did not want to obsess over getting the job. After all, there were other places he had applied, and he fully expected to get another interview. If Meisner Industries did not work out, Laura had promised to help him find another job. He did not expect to wait long to hear back.

~ Kyle's Reflections ~

Kyle woke up early Thursday morning after a relatively restless night. He assumed it was anxiety about the job. He had been out of work too long. Without easy access to all the software tools he had on his last assignment, he felt a bit rusty. It made him anxious. The computing field tended to change quickly. Twelve months was a long time to be out of the loop. He had tried to keep up with the literature since the trade magazines were still willing to cut him a break on subscription prices, but forwarding magazines from Texas was slow. The information they contained was useful but did not help him keep up his skill level. Without an active project to work on, it was hard to keep a sharp edge.

Maybe the insomnia was brought on by the amazing ride yesterday, meeting Laura again. Apparently, she was close with Richard Meisner. When Kyle learned that Meisner Industries was a privately held company, he wondered whether Richard had any partners. If not, Richard, as the owner, could sell the company at any time. It raised a question on how secure a job there would be if Meisner sold the company. Many times, a sale also meant staff was downsized. The net worth of the company was confidential. Kyle imagined it was in the hundreds of millions of dollars.

He was reminded by the encounter yesterday how attractive Laura is, so it was no surprise that Richard would have noticed her. Fortuitous, he thought, getting Meisner's attention at the banquet, dropping a tray of dishes. Richard was good looking himself, probably better than Kyle, so the story they gave about how they met was credible. When Kyle and Laura were dating, Kyle had no indication that Laura's attention was focused on anyone but him. He could understand why Richard would like her. Richard was a good catch for her too. Kyle and Laura had only been together for eighteen months, and no matter how close they were; eighteen months was not that long. Kyle's parents were married fifty-two years, and he recalls his Dad telling him a few years before he passed away that he was still discovering things about his mom. He could understand why. His mom was always a stranger to Kyle. He never got along with her.

Kyle took his revised reference list to Meisner's and left it in an envelope addressed to Tom Bosworth. When he returned home, he fixed a sandwich for his lunch and turned on the small TV he had purchased. As he tooled around the channels, he ran across a debate on CSPAN about a bill to improve voting participation. If he had known what his future portended, he might have paid more attention. Kyle had a high-speed data connection for his computer. He occasionally streamed movies, but mostly he tried to keep up with friends and computer technology. Kyle decided to do additional research on Meisner Industries, Richard Meisner, and Laura.

Searching for Laura McLaughlin, he could find no social network links for her on any of the popular sites. Nor could he find any links on any professional sites. He had expected to find her on LinkedIn, but she was not listed. He did not have access to any of the fee-based databases other than LinkedIn, so he ran into a dead end on Laura. He was not too surprised.

In Houston, when they dated, she did not seem very interested in computers or technical devices. She kept her life very private. He never met her mother and didn't know her mother's address, although he did know she lived in the Dallas-Fort Worth area. Laura had a cell phone, but it was not one of the latest models. After the "Dear John" letter, he never got her cell number to respond. She did not send or receive text messages, best he could remember, she just used the phone as a phone. Given the power of a modern cell phone, Kyle thought that it was a waste to ignore its capabilities. Still, he had a fondness for her anti-tech sweetness, but it did limit their conversations to non-technical things. That put him at a disadvantage, but he liked having his knowledge of music and movies broadened. She could never work all the remotes to operate his TV, DVD player, sound system, and Internet interface box. Her helplessness was somehow endearing to him, too, as frustrated as he got when she tried to operate them and got everything out of sync. It never occurred to him that her ignorance of technology was faked.

On the other hand, Richard had made the news several times and had somewhat of a social life before Laura came on the scene. He also had a reputation of being a tough negotiator, usually coming out ahead. His company had acquired several smaller shops, and successfully integrated most operations, laying off only a few. One thing caught his eye. Meisner Industries had been investigated once for a possible case of patent infringement. Meisner had sold software to a company that claimed that it did not work as promised in the sales agreement. A Meisner's competitor jumped on the publicity to claim patent infringement. The attack was quickly resolved and there was no follow-up information about the investigation. Kyle supposed it was resolved much like an out of court settlement. Perhaps it was rumors created by one of his competitors in an attempt to gain market share.

Although he obtained very little information about Laura, Richard, or Meisner Industries, he felt somewhat satisfied there were no skeletons, at least not any that were easily found. He thought he could work for Meisner Industries, although he did worry about that initial meeting and what it could mean for his future.

~ Kyle gets the Job ~

Monday afternoon around 3:00 PM, Kyle's phone rang. He had been reading a technical paper on the internet. The sound startled him.

"Hello.

"Is this Kyle Tredly?"

"Yes"

"This is Tom Bosworth from Meisner Industries. Meisner Industries would like you to come down and discuss a possible job offer. How about tomorrow, at 1:00 PM? Would that be possible?"

"Yes, where do I go?"

"Come to the office, eighth-floor reception desk. Same place you came for the interview."

"Okay, who do I ask for?"

"Introduce yourself at the reception desk. They will let me know when you arrive, and I will come to meet with you to discuss the possibility of a position."

"Do I need to bring anything?"

"Yes, we will need a photo ID, preferably your passport if you have one."

"I do have a passport."

"Do you have your Social Security Card?"

"No. But I do have a Social Security Number."

"We can work with that. If the arrangements work to our mutual satisfaction, there will be forms to fill out. We will want to start you right away. I will need to know if that works for you, assuming all things work out to our mutual satisfaction. About your parking pass ..."

Kyle interrupted, "I won't need a parking pass, at least not for a while. I will be using public transportation."

"You understand, this is not an offer yet. There will be additional questions. Assuming we can agree, there will be a contract. We will allow time for you to review the contract in detail and ask and resolve any questions you have. You should allow three or four hours for the process. If we can't complete the process in one session, we can continue the next day. We will need you to take a drug test, sensitive to any drugs you have taken in the past week or so. If you are taking prescription medication, you will need to bring those bottles with you. Our lab will take one pill at random to verify and match it to the prescription list. As you can see, we are very cautious in our hires. Again, all this is assuming we can come to a mutual agreement."

"Not a problem. I am not on any medications. That's tomorrow, 1:00 PM?"

"That's right. See you then."

Kyle hung up the phone and made a fist-up gesture and shouted, "YES!"

Kyle came down to the area of the Meisner Industries building early and had a quick lunch at Panda Express at Lloyd Center's food court. It was in the low 50s with a brisk western wind, so the walk over to the office was a bit cooler than he expected. He arrived at the eighth-floor reception desk at 12:50 PM, ten minutes early, and introduced himself. The receptionist told him that Mr. Bosworth would be meeting with him, but that Bosworth was out at the moment. She asked if he had his photo ID, which he presented. The receptionist asked Kyle to stand in front of a computer connected camera. She put the passport on a mat under another camera. She indicated that their system used facial recognition to verify that he matched the passport photo and then used an internet application to check his history. She took a couple of pictures that displayed on a screen facing him. The passport photo was five years old, so Kyle wondered how the facial ID software would manage that. Kyle assumed they had an internet service that could find virtually everything about him, including any traffic tickets he had or arrests he had like the ones he had in St. Andrews. He hoped they had already reviewed the time he was arrested for murders in St. Andrews, but if they had not yet done that, he wondered if it could tank his job prospects.

Surely Laura had told Richard Meisner about that before they talked to him.

The receptionist handed Kyle a small jar with a lid and a packet that could be sealed. She called someone who turned out to be from security. She told Kyle he could use the bathroom at the end of the hall to provide a urine sample in the jar. The fellow from security would accompany him. In addition, the security guy would pluck out one or two hairs from Kyle's head and include that in the envelope and seal it. Kyle did as he was directed, and the security guy took the samples. He was told it would be about an hour wait as the samples were tested, and a report was received. The receptionist offered Kyle a cup of freshly made coffee, which he accepted. Kyle sat again in the reception area, sipped on his coffee, and picked up a recent *Time* magazine. Before he could finish an article on the Occupier Movement, Tom Bosworth showed up and ushered him back to his office.

Before long, A young woman entered the office and handed Bosworth a folded sheet of paper. Bosworth opened it and read it. It was a long note as he did not look up as he read. Bosworth did not indicate the contents, just nodded as if to say things were okay. As he gave his attention back to Kyle, he indicated the background check and drug tests were satisfactory. Bosworth slipped the sheet he read into a folder and handed Kyle a thick folder of material, warm, as though recently printed. Bosworth did not let go of it. He said the folder contained information about his background check, a questionnaire, W-2 forms, an I-9, and a multi-page contract.

Tom held the folder looking at Kyle. "Things are in order for us to continue. First, you need to complete the questionnaire, W-2, and I-9. Then I will take you to a private room, and you can read the other materials. The background check includes a final page on which you must acknowledge it is accurate and complete; that there are no other records we should know about. If anything is missing, we will have to obtain that before we can continue. Your honesty is essential to your success here at Meisner's. The work we do here is considered highly confidential and proprietary, and you will have a Meisner security status based on your background and modified only by Mr. Meisner. Finally, the contract. It does not include your salary, but all other benefits of the position. It includes your agreement to security restrictions as well as patent ownership agreements. You don't sign until the salary has been negotiated. We run a very tight ship here at Meisner's, so I suggest you read very carefully. When you are ready, let the receptionist know, and I will come to answer any questions you have. Take your time. We don't want to rush you. Finally, we can discuss the issue of salary."

Bosworth showed Kyle to a room where he could review the contract in private and fill out the necessary paperwork. The background analysis was complete, including details even he had forgotten. The background contained the details of his arrest for murder in St. Andrews. He completed the forms and studied the contract in detail. Everything was standard. Security protocols were tighter than he had experienced. The only thing strange, to him, was the section on Meisner Security and on patents. If he signed the contract, he agreed to several invasive actions at the discretion of Meisner Industries. He agreed to have his living quarters electronically monitored (bugged as he interpreted the effect of it) and not to disable them. He would also be agreeing to pass through electronic detection devices when he entered or left Meisner Industries. That feature puzzled Kyle. He had seen none of that on his visits to Meisner Industries. He speculated they were well hidden, maybe in the lobby, on the elevator, or in the office walls. He thought he would have to ask about that. He also agreed to have his workstation, both at work and home, electronically monitored and recorded. It was intrusive, almost paranoid, but since he was an honest person, he saw no harm. A lot of companies these days permitted employees to use company computers for personal use. As he read the documents, that was not allowed at Meisner Industries. He took note that this security protocol was the second compromise he would make to work here. The first was the agreement to keep the initial meeting with Meisner confidential.

On patents, he was expected to acknowledge that any intellectual property developed by him at work or home, even the completion of projects he might have previously begun, must be disclosed and would become the sole property of

Meisner Industries. There was a technical question he had to ask Bosworth about the work he did at Softtek that had not been patented. He couldn't see how this work could be included in the contract with Meisner Industries. The contract, in this regard, was almost standard, except for proposed ownership of prior ideas.

There was also a non-disclosure and non-compete clause that struck him as very severe. He agreed neither to work in the industry for five years after leaving Meisner Industries nor to disclose or develop any idea or product he might have originated or thought about developing while at Meisner Industries. This made him pause. If he thought about an application, even in detail, but never wrote anything down nor discussed it with anyone, how could this patent clause apply? Additionally, how could this apply to every product Meisner produced when he did not even know them all?

Although it was somewhat standard to have non-disclosure and non-compete clauses, this one seemed very onerous. What if he was hired and then laid off six months later? Would that then make him ineligible to work in the field for five years?

Kyle decided to check with an attorney friend in St. Andrews. He took out his phone to get in touch only to learn he had no signal. Since he had bars outdoors, he assumed the cell service was somehow blocked inside Meisner Industries. It made him wonder if he had already been electronically scanned when he entered Meisner. "Oh well," he thought, "I need this job, and given the current market, I can't afford to back out unless the salary offer is too low." He went back to the reception desk, and Bosworth was notified. He was escorted to Bosworth's office.

"Any questions?" asked Bosworth.

"There are two items in the contract that I find difficult to accept. It is the five-year non-disclosure and non-compete clause. Given that I have been out of work for a year and understand that the market is not that great, I want to know what guarantee I have I won't be fired or downsized soon and then be ineligible to apply my skills for five years?"

"What would you think was a reasonable time frame?"

"Hmm. About one year, maybe?"

Bosworth took the contract, crossed out the five, replaced it with one, and then initialed and dated it. He passed it over to Kyle for his initials as well. "Any other questions?"

"Yes. The limitation on work after leaving Meisner's, does it apply to every project I work on at Meisner's? I don't think I even know all the products. I only know what is already in the public domain."

Tom thumbed through the contract to the page Kyle was referring. He crossed out the line and wrote it so it only applied to projects Kyle worked on or had direct knowledge of. Then he asked Kyle to read what he had written. "Will that clear it up for you? Good catch. I think I will get the contract revised to be clearer in the future."

Kyle read Tom's scratching and said, "Yes. That clarifies it for me." Kyle added his initials alongside Bosworth's.

"Anything else?" Tom asked.

"There is a paragraph about patents. I do not see how that can apply to things I think about but do not document. How can that be legally enforced? It seems to be more of a threat than something that could be proven. Is there any way we could revise that paragraph?"

"Hmm, let me see that paragraph," Tom said. "I think I see what you mean—another good catch. The intent is to prevent former employees of Meisner Industries from developing or offering to another company things developed while working for Meisner's. Let me rephrase this one sentence."

Bosworth scratched out a couple of sentences and rewrote them in the margin. He handed it to Kyle to read. "Does this new statement resolve your concerns, Kyle?"

Kyle read Bosworth's new paragraph and nodded, "Yes, that helps a lot," and initialed the changes.

Bosworth asked again, "Is there anything else of concern?"

"Not in the contract. I would be able to sign that as we have altered it. However, I noticed my cell phone does not work. Is that a permanent feature of working in this office?"

"No. Once you are employed, your phone will be fully functional. However, our security system will monitor it. I know this sounds a bit heavy-handed, but Mr. Meisner has had unfortunate security problems and insists on tight control of information going in and out of the company. I am sure you understand."

"Sure," Kyle answered, but he was a bit disturbed by the excessive sense of distrust Meisner Industries seemed to have with its employees.

"Okay. We are ready to talk about salary. I hope you are not shocked by our salary offer. Mr. Meisner places a high premium on his employees having more than ample resources. He pays us all about twice what the industry pays and expects a high degree of loyalty. I assume you read in the contract the section on privacy of company salaries?"

"Yes. That is not too uncommon. Softtek had a similar requirement."

"Okay, here is the figure we are proposing for you to start. Bosworth handed Kyle a contract addendum. Assuming things go well, you can expect a fifty percent increase in one year and, after three years, an annual bonus based on the company's success."

Kyle was shocked to see the figure. It was substantially more than he expected. It was significantly more than he received at his last job. "This seems more than fair. I would even say generous. To be honest, I am surprised." It caught Kyle off guard. He had intended to ask how the success of the company was calculated as it applied to salary bonuses, but the thought escaped him as he looked at the generous salary offer.

"I take it you are ready to sign the contract then?"

"Yes."

Bosworth called in the receptionist and asked her to witness the signatures and initial all the places changes had been made. Finally, Bosworth signed the last page, Kyle signed, and the receptionist signed as a witness. The receptionist then took the contract to make a copy of the summary page and the last page with the signatures for Kyle. Bosworth made a point of calling attention to the confidentiality clause in the contract. He noted that the contract stipulated that the terms of the agreement be confidential. Bosworth reemphasized the details, including confidentiality of each person's salary. It was not to be shared with anyone inside or outside the company. The clause was enforceable in a court of law. The clause even stipulated the size of monetary damages. Again, Kyle felt uneasy. There were aspects of Meisner Industries that were outside any norms of which he was aware. Kyle wondered if anyone had been taken to court over this clause or if it was an act of intimidation to encourage people to self-enforce. Bosworth continued his monologue.

"You can report for work tomorrow, around 10:30 AM. I will conduct an orientation to Meisner Industries and review our policies. You will have lunch with Mr. Meisner. Someone will escort you to Mr. Meisner's assistant, at 12:15. After lunch, around 2:00 PM, you will have an orientation that includes selections for your health benefit and retirement package choices. There will also be an abbreviated tour of Meisner Industries headquarters and a security orientation. By this time, we will have everything we need, and you will get your electronic badge and instructions. You will start with your team the following day. Welcome to Meisner Industries. We will see you tomorrow at 10:30."

~ First Day at Work ~

Kyle arrived at 10:30 AM sharp. He had to wait for about 20 minutes before they were ready for the orientation to begin. By the time the orientation was finished, and he provided additional information, it was time to meet with Richard Meisner for lunch. Kyle wondered what kind of lunch it would be.

Bosworth escorted Kyle to the top Meisner Industries floor, where he met Charla Roshken. "Charla, this is Kyle Tredly, a new employee. Kyle, this is Charla Roshken. She guards access to Mr. Meisner, who is a very busy man." Kyle was now able to put a face to the voice he had heard the day he secretly met with Laura and Mr. Meisner.

"Glad to meet you, Charla," Kyle said.

"Kyle, welcome to Meisner Industries. Mr. Meisner is not quite ready for you. It will be a few minutes. Why don't you have a seat? Do you need coffee, water, or anything?"

"No, I am fine, Charla," Kyle answered and took a seat in the reception area, which was around the corner from Charla's desk behind a glass door. He decided the glass door was there to prevent him from overhearing any conversations that might take place. It was only about four minutes when Charla stuck her head in the door, "Mr. Meisner is ready for you now. Come this way." She led him a couple of steps down the hall from her desk, knocked on the door, and opened it without waiting for an answer. She motioned for Kyle to enter ahead of her and followed him.

"Mr. Meisner, I would like to introduce you to Kyle Tredly, our newest employee. Kyle, Richard Meisner, Chief Executive Officer and owner of Meisner Industries."

Richard Meisner stood up from his desk and came around to greet Kyle as if they had never met. Good actor. He extended his hand, and when Kyle took it to shake his hand, Richard also grasped Kyle's hand with his left hand in a very cordial handshake. Richard kept holding on to Kyle's hand as he talked. Kyle had an eerie feeling Richard was saying, "I own you now."

"Kyle, it is my pleasure to meet you. I have read the background information Bosworth provided me, and I must say, I expect you will be a great asset to Meisner Industries. So glad to have you aboard."

To Charla, he said, "Thanks Charla, the meal you arranged sounds delicious. We could use more new employees." closing his remark with a slight wink. He let go of Kyle's hand.

"Is there anything else I can do for you?" Charla asked.

"No, we are fine."

Charla left the office and closed the door.

A small table that had not been there the last time he was in the office was placed near the fireplace between the couch and chairs. It was covered with a linen table cloth and had two place settings. The lunch plate was covered with a cloche, one of those silver looking domes to keep the meal warm. Richard motioned Kyle to a seat facing the window, but this time, the shade was already drawn, so the glare was minimal even though the sun was out and bright, shining slightly into the room. Richard sat opposite and removed his cloche, so Kyle did the same to observe a delicious, generous looking salmon steak with a pilaf of rice of assorted colors and several shoots of asparagus. A spinach salad with fresh grape tomatoes, green onions, blueberries, and cucumber slices was beside the plate. Two pieces of key lime pie decorated the table. It made Kyle's mouth water. He had been skimping on his food bill to conserve his resources lately, so this meal was better than he had enjoyed for quite a while.

Richard began the conversation. "So, you made it through the HR maze, I see."

"Yes, it was a fascinating process. Will I be working with the same team that interviewed me?"

"Absolutely, but you will find a great deal of fluidity among the various teams here in the building, so before long, you will know almost everyone in the building on a first-name basis. How were the terms of your contract?"

Kyle was not sure what Richard was fishing for. "Are you referring to the salary? If so, I was quite surprised and very pleased. If I can inquire, is this the way all employees are compensated? The confidentiality clauses in the contract seem to prevent me from asking anyone else but you."

"Good point. We are cautious about our privacy, but yes, I have found several factors that tend to make my work teams more effective than my competitors. Salary is an important component. It helps ensure my employees are not stolen away for better salaries. Few of my competitors are willing to pay what I pay. But the other perks of working here are also important. Hours are flexible; sick leave is generous. If you read your contract closely, you may have noticed there are very few restrictions on leave. I find that if I remove the distractions and give people work that they can enjoy and can be proud of, work that is meaningful, I get loyal, dedicated employees, at least for the most part."

"Most part?"

"Yes. Not all employees appreciate my hands-on management style. I get feedback via the rumor mill that I am a perfectionist, that I can be too demanding, and that at times I expect the impossible. That is probably all true. And, oh yes, sometimes too paternalistic, and have high expectations. Kyle, that will apply to you as well, but when you have done the impossible, you will experience what many of my employees experience, great pride in your accomplishments. Meisner Industries develops the best damn products in the business, and our customers can attest to that. We have made many a company prosperous using our products, both software and hardware. Our customers are loyal, but I don't want them to hire my well trained and highly experienced staff away from me. When they purchase from us, they enter a partnership like relationship. Their purchase contracts also prevent them from hiring our employees unless we approve. Does this make sense to you?"

"Yes sir," Kyle answered as he savored the salmon, salad, and asparagus anticipating the key lime pie. *But very restrictive.*

"Kyle, I depend on the best scientific knowledge about developing a productive, efficient workforce. You may think you got this job because of Laura's recommendation. That is partially true because she was the reason we looked at the resume you sent. However, that is serendipity. I have to believe we would have discovered you in any event. Kyle, I have high expectations for you and the special assignments I will be discussing with you. They will require a high degree of confidentiality. I need someone I can trust, and your profile fills that bill. Do you think you can handle working on the side, on a project for me? I need to know your thinking now rather than later."

"I am sure I can manage that. I am by nature, a private person, as you have probably already figured out. I am up for a challenge, and you can count on me to be a hard worker. I want to ask you a question, however."

"Sure, anything. Now is the time to get things cleared up. We will not be having meetings like this in the future. I keep a hectic and tight schedule."

"I found the security features of the contract a bit unusual. Is this business that competitive?"

"You can't imagine. As you know, many companies use computer systems to do automated business deals. They might make a thousand deals an hour. The ones who make the most money have the best software. It takes real talent to be the best and to prevent industrial espionage from stealing your best ideas or best people. In the case of hardware, companies would like to reverse engineer our products and manufacture competitive products to capture our market share. That is why I place a priority on treating my employees well. I don't want them stolen by my competition. I also don't want my best systems stolen either, and that takes a significant effort to secure the ideas and work of Meisner Industries. Unfortunately, all this cloak and dagger stuff plays havoc with trust.

"Your team is working on a project related to public sector voting. It requires error-free processes, both software and hardware. It must resist manipulation by forces who would like to disrupt our elections. It requires a high level of security."

Kyle was quiet for a moment after Richard finished talking, taking time to savor the key lime pie. Then he said. "I guess this is an aspect of working here I will have to get used to. As you probably know from your research about me, I have a history of working with several groups on open source applications. I take it from the contract that will not work anymore. Am I correct?"

"Yes. I am afraid that will be one of the casualties of working at Meisner. You do have freedom to do volunteer work as long as it does not include software development. In fact, we encourage it. You will be asked from time to time to engage in a community project. Meisner hesitated and then, in a serious tone, asked Kyle, "I need to ask you an important question. Did Bosworth adequately stress the importance of confidentiality? Have you mentioned to anyone that we met here in my office once before?"

"He did. I have not mentioned that we met."

"Good." was all Meisner said about the meeting. "We need to finish up here. I don't want to take more time than I generally take with employees. But I will want to talk to you further. I will let you know when and where we can do that.

Sorry to be so secretive. This, too, has to do with a security issue that I will need your help with."

"Okay," Kyle said as he finished his pie. Security issue? *Am I getting involved in a subterfuge that will compromise my integrity?* As Kyle's thoughts briefly wandered, Richard got up and extended his arm to shake hands with Kyle. The lunch was over, and Kyle was out the door. Charla greeted him and let him know that he was to report to Bosworth. She gave him directions to Bosworth's office on the eighth floor.

Kyle took the stairs down to the eighth floor. There was a reception desk near the stairwell exit, so he asked for Bosworth's office. The receptionist had him take a seat and sent a message to Bosworth. It only took a couple of minutes before Bosworth appeared and ushered him into his office. Bosworth's office was neatly arranged. There were several file cabinets against one wall. His desk was clear except for a few folders on one corner. Over to one side of the office was a small conference table with four chairs. Kyle was asked to sit in a chair on the opposite side of the desk from Bosworth.

"Welcome to Meisner Industries, Kyle. We all go by our first names here, so you should call me Tom. I wanted to give you an orientation to Meisner's and let you know about the initial orientation sessions you will need before you begin actual work. We do not hire many people at a time, so most of your orientation will be individual. That means they will be scheduled at times convenient to the session leader. Your first will be at 11:00 AM tomorrow with our benefits specialist, where you will select your benefits package. It will help you determine medical benefit choices, retirement benefits, and work schedule particulars. At 1:00 PM, you will meet with the head of security, Frank Storch, to make sure you understand security protocols and arrange for your home security system installation. You will then meet with the Projects Manager, Jessy Northrund, to get your particular assigned project team. After that, you will be done for the day. Jessy will let you know when and where to report for work. Any Questions?

"No, that seems clear enough. Anything else?"

"No. I think that takes care of things. Report here tomorrow, and I will see you get headed in the right direction."

Kyle thanked Tom and left his office. He was done for the day, so he took the elevator down and headed home to revel in his new job at Meisner Industries and puzzle over the "secret" meeting with Richard Meisner on the day he first interviewed, and to think about the non-coincidence of meeting Laura.

Laura had an apartment in the Pearl District. She realized the flame that she was instructed to snuff out in Houston was not completely extinguished. All the good memories were not easy to forget. She was assigned to keep Kyle safe in Houston, but she made a classic mistake and fell for him in the process. It is easy to fall for someone. It is not so easy to erase that mistake. The FBI pulled her off her Houston assignment and sent her to Dallas because she needed to take care of her mom. Laura worked a lot of undercover jobs. She was, therefore, not allowed to tell Kyle she worked for the FBI. Since she had cover as a waitress, she never had to lie to Kyle about the FBI specifically. But when the FBI made her sever ties with Kyle in the move to Dallas, she reminded herself that falling for Kyle was something she might have made an effort to prevent. That was painful. She did not know what it had done to Kyle, but it was painful for her. What if the FBI changed her assignment again, and she had to move? Working with Kyle put her in the position to abandon him a second time. She wondered what she could do to keep things in balance and avoid getting "involved" again. Could she do it?

Chapter 3

Laura graduated from Southern Methodist University with a BA in criminal justice. She went on to get an MBA and took the LSAT, considering a degree in law. It wasn't that being a lawyer was all that attractive; she was not aware that other options fit her interests. She passed the LSAT with flying colors when her exceptional abilities came to the attention of the FBI. She was offered a position as an FBI agent utilizing her skills and knowledge. It was not a hard decision for her to abandon the idea of a law degree. She already had a large student loan. The chance to earn money and do interesting work won out. The FBI knew her physical attractiveness would affect men from which she sought information. She began work in the Houston office. After six months of training, she was asked to go undercover in a Houston restaurant frequented by a man under investigation by the FBI. She worked as a waitress. It also happened to be a restaurant frequented by Kyle Tredly. The FBI from St. Andrews notified the Houston FBI when Kyle Tredly moved out of St. Andrews to Houston. They gave Kyle a positive recommendation and helped him get a programming job at Softtek. They indicated he might need protection until the trials of the people who tried to kill Kyle were complete, and the criminals he had fingered were incarcerated. The Houston office assigned Laura to keep an eye on Kyle.

Kyle had no idea the FBI had anything to do with his position at Softtek. Neither did he know his role in Laura's life. Because she was attractive and subject to being asked out often, she needed a significant other to augment her cover. The request from St. Andrew's office fit the bill. As planned, Laura made sure she and Kyle became a pair. Laura and Kyle developed a genuine affection for each other, against her FBI training. That was not part of the plan. The FBI had not intended to be a matchmaker. As long as Laura could convince the FBI her involvement with Kyle was strictly by the books, they did not suspect it was, in fact, more. The FBI had trained Laura in the art of strategic lies, and she was good at it. When Laura's mother became ill, her mother asked Laura to move to Dallas to help her. She and Kyle communicated briefly, but the local FBI, not realizing Laura had a crush on Kyle, something she could easily lie about, insisted she make a clean break. Laura did not want to break it off with Kyle, but her FBI boss in Dallas insisted. Kyle, lacking information, never understood. Laura was instructed to write Kyle a "Dear John" letter and "disappear."

~ Laura, the FBI, and Richard ~

Laura's mother was in Hospice. She passed away not long after Laura had been instructed to write Kyle a "Dear John" letter breaking off the relationship. She even moved from Dallas to Fort Worth using an unlisted phone number to prevent Kyle from finding her. It was depressing at first. Then the FBI in Dallas called on her for another undercover assignment. It was arranged for her to work for a catering company that covered high profile events. Posing as one of the servers, she was to carry out surveillance of certain persons of interest and the connections they made with others at catered events. Keeping track of contacts and the degree of interactions was an important analysis tool. When Richard Meisner was scheduled to attend the Dallas Open Golf Tournament Banquet, the Portland, Oregon FBI office contacted the Dallas FBI office. Dallas arranged for Laura to be assigned to Meisner's table. Richard Meisner noticed Laura when she strategically dropped a tray of food behind him and managed to douse him with a pitcher of iced tea in the process. In the exchange that transpired, Laura gave Richard her phone number. She offered to pay for Richard's cleaning bill. Instead, Richard suggested they meet for drinks and dinner. Richard had an eye for class and thought Laura might be able to fill a need he had in Portland. Better yet for Laura. Acting embarrassed and hesitant, she finally agreed. That led to a work arrangement with Richard and a move to Portland, Oregon. The Dallas office reluctantly agreed to the move. This relationship was better than what the Portland FBI office planned. Having Laura working with Meisner allowed Laura and the FBI to get inside information on Meisner Industries and Richard Meisner in particular. Richard had been involved in a lawsuit that caught the FBI's attention. When the lawsuit mysteriously disappeared, it came to the attention of the FBI. Laura had to be careful about how things developed. However, unlike her work with Kyle in Houston, Richard Meisner did not stir any positive emotional ties. Her solicitations had to be faked. But Meisner did not seem to be attracted romantically to Laura, which made things easier. Meisner's arrangement with Laura was strictly business. He needed a female companion for business reasons. The FBI did not initially know that Richard was looking for someone to be a personal escort to events to hide his gay preferences. Although the social clique suspected Richard might be gay, that knowledge became apparent to the Portland FBI over time with Laura's help.

In Portland, Laura had to manage what seemed like multiple personalities. Today, Laura was an FBI agent and needed to visit the local FBI office on NE Cascades Pkwy near the airport. Laura went to the third floor to use the computer pool reserved for undercover field agent visits. She wrote her report on the most recent meeting with Richard Meisner and Kyle Tredly.

Laura was confident neither Richard nor Kyle was currently aware of her relationship with the FBI. Laura exhibited such a professional air that Richard determined she could help him more as an aide than an escort to social affairs. Richard, aware of her college degree and LSAT score was somewhat suspicious of her work as a timeshare salesperson. Nevertheless, he asked her to help uncover a leak in his company. He wanted to plug the leak. Richard did not disclose which project had the leaks. Since Laura had a previous relationship with Kyle, he reasoned, the pair could help him.

He would be able to discover who was responsible and the process they were using. Laura's FBI job was to keep Meisner under surveillance without his knowledge. Richard's suggestions supported the FBI's interest placing someone inside Meisner Industries. Today she had little to report except Richard Meisner's developing plan for her to reestablish a connection with Kyle to uncover a leak. As a competent systems programmer with special interests in systems security based on personal experience in St. Andrews, Kyle was positioned to gain access to crucial information about Meisner's developments and investments; she reasoned. The files on Kyle indicated he was a straight shooter, a person of integrity. Laura outlined her plans to reengage with Kyle, gain his trust, and hopefully obtain information the FBI was seeking. Personally, she had concerns about how Kyle would interpret her interest in working with him on Meisner's agenda. Laura recorded the bare necessity of details. Completing her report, she planned to visit the timeshare business office, where she worked as a cover for her FBI relationship. After all, she needed to successfully sell a few timeshares to maintain her cover. This way, she could hide the salary she got from the FBI. The timeshare properties she was assigned were in Hawaii and turned out to be advantageous in her assignment to monitor Richard.

Before she left, she went to check in with Kameron Wilson, her FBI supervisor. To provide cover for her assignments,

Kameron arranged for Laura to be hired by a local travel agency that marketed timeshares in Hawaii.

Laura made such a powerful impression on Richard that he decided to use her services in a variety of ways. Her talent and knowledge of business and legal issues made her useful above and beyond a companion at social affairs. It did not take Laura long to become one of Richard's most trusted friends. On occasion, Richard would use Laura to test out an idea or check on the advice he planned to give. Laura was the only person he truly trusted. But he did not tell her everything.

~ Richard and Meisner Industries ~

Richard was a tech wonder. After undergraduate work in computer science and a PhD-level MBA (without the PhD.), Richard Meisner formed Meisner Industries with money he inherited from his father, Phillip. His father made his money in the stock market by creating a popular and successful hedge fund. Richard's father had a killer instinct about the stock market and had been hard on Richard growing up. He gave his guarded approval to Richard's venture into high tech hardware and software dependent products. Within five years after his father's death, Richard turned the inherited investment into a multi-million-dollar enterprise. Being privately owned gave Richard considerable freedom to take on risks that investors in a public company might have rejected. His inheritance was significant; he did not need to borrow money to expand. Borrowing always required disclosures he liked to avoid. Besides, being a public company might slow down development. Alarmed by his successful ventures, some of his competitors accused him of patent infringement and threatened court relief. Unlike his first skirmishes with competitor attacks, these threats materialized into lawsuits. The word on the street was that Meisner Industries had resolved these lawsuits with financial settlements in confidential agreements, a way of avoiding long public disclosure and legal battles. The threats of his competitors, combined with private agreements, got the attention of the FBI. They consequently uncovered his secret friendship with U.S. Senator Rolfe Corning. Meisner Industries was a tight operation. So much so, the FBI had been unsuccessful in getting an inside man working there. Getting Laura into a relationship with Meisner was good, but not good enough. They counted on Laura, Richard's seeming trust of her, and her prior relationship with Kyle to discover whether there should be any concerns about Meisner Industries activities. Should his relationship with Senator Corning be of concern? The FBI Washington Bureau had made inquiries when Richard's name came up in one of their investigations.

Meisner was considered by many in the tech industry as an enlightened leader. There had been numerous attempts by competitors to hire his staff away from him, but they were never successful. None of the competitors were willing to pay the salaries a Meisner employee garnered to compromise their loyalty to Richard. Employees who reported the details of attempts to bribe them for information were handsomely rewarded. On the other hand, Meisner's personnel contracts that forbid working in the field for five years if they ever left Meisner Industries made it unfruitful for his competitors to steal employees. The exception made for Kyle was to be temporary. Kyle had missed the implications in his initial contract that required a new contract to be drawn after a one-year probation period.

Meisner was an enigma. On the one hand, he was very personable and well-liked by almost every employee of the company. On the other hand, he was a taskmaster. It was not unusual for him to tell an employee that the product of their work was not acceptable, that they could do much better. In particular, programmers were both fearful of Meisner's critique of their work and pleased when they accomplished what was generally considered the impossible, or at a minimum, exceptional. Recognition by Meisner was highly appreciated, especially after they were pushed to excel. As much as employees appreciated working at Meisner Industries, it was, at the same time, a stressful place. The workers, at all levels of the company, were exceptional employees. Meisner sold the idea that everyone's job was constantly at risk by corporate espionage. As a result, they did not question security and the way he managed to compartmentalize work. No one wanted to jeopardize the exceptional salaries by crossing Richard. Yet, few seemed to have a complete picture of how their work fit into the big picture at Meisner Industries. The rewards of working for Meisner kept most people from seriously challenging Meisner Industries' secrecy.

~ Kyle's Background ~

Kyle was pleased to have a job at Meisner Industries and especially happy at the salary. He had not had an easy time in the last few years. While the recent loss of his job in Houston, due to the storm, had not been pleasant, it did not compare with the experience in St. Andrews. Kyle inadvertently and unknowingly was involved in tripping up the governor and a major crime boss. He had taken pictures while camping that happened to reveal a financial exchange between the governor and a crime syndicate boss. He did not know he had these incriminating photos. Still, the governor's aide happened to notice him taking pictures. The aide was concerned about the potential disclosure such pictures might do to the governor's plans, tried to retrieve the images, and eventually set Kyle up as the murderer of two innocent women Kyle knew and with whom he had been intimate. It almost worked. The governor had Kyle kidnapped to make it appear he had run away rather than turn himself in. The experience had shaken Kyle. He decided to move away from St. Andrews and start a new life. That is how he got to Houston. He had received excellent references from his former workplace as well as law enforcement in St. Andrews. He did not know the local FBI office was secretly helping.

Kyle did ponder his good fortune in getting a job at Meisner's, primarily since much of this past was known by

Richard Meisner and Laura McLaughlin. It was his past experiences that made him especially cautious. He had a version of Post-Traumatic Stress Disorder, which he was able to hide very well. Laura was an interesting question. She had helped him with his PTSD by being such a good girlfriend in Houston. He wondered whether they could be friends again, given the way Laura had dumped him. Could he trust her? He wondered if it was going to continue to be awkward if and when she was around?

~ A.J. Stentz ~

Kyle had not contacted A.J. since he arrived in Portland. Other than being classmates at the University of Houston, they had not been close. Nevertheless, he thought he needed to express his appreciation for A.J.'s suggestion that he move to Portland. He might enjoy having other friends in Portland not related to Meisner Industries. He gave A.J. a call.

"Hello?"

"A.J., This is Kyle, Kyle Tredly.

"Oh ... Hi ... What's up?"

"I wanted to call and thank you for your suggestion. I am now in Portland, and have secured a job, so things are looking up."

"That's great! So, Kyle, where are you working?"

"I got a job at Meisner Industries. Have you heard of this outfit?"

"Heard of them? Of course, I have. Everyone in application development in the whole damn state has heard of them. How the hell did you get a job there?"

Kyle stuttered, "I don't know. Just lucky, I guess."

"Shit, Kyle. I would give my eye teeth to work there. They have a reputation for treating their staff great and producing amazing software and hardware. A lot of it is by reputation because it is hard to get any inside information from that outfit. When did you get into town? How long have you been working there?"

"I got into town approximately three weeks ago. I just got the job, so I have not started work yet. I go into work tomorrow. I was wondering if I could take you and your family to dinner? I am indebted to you for your suggestion, and anyway, it would be good to catch up. You're married now, right?"

"Yup! Sheila and I have a little girl. She is six months old, and already she can get me to do anything she wants. She may not be walking or talking yet, but she can sure let you know what she likes and dislikes. Let me talk to Sheila and see what we can work out about getting together. We have never left Lindsey with anybody. Can I call you back and let you know?"

"Of course," Kyle responded, and gave A.J. his phone number and Gmail address. "You can reach me almost any evening. I don't have much going on these days. I would like to know how things are going with you and your family."

"Okay, got it. Listen, I have to go right now. You know, chores. And I need to get Lindsey ready for bed. That is my job and pleasure, I might add. I will call you after Sheila and I have worked out possible dates and times we could meet, and see if we can match your availability."

Kyle responded, "I doubt there will be any problem getting a match. I don't have a thing on my calendar yet. I will be waiting for your call or email. Great making contact."

"Great. I will be in touch soon. Thanks again for looking me up.'

Kyle finished the phone call and hung up. He was looking forward to meeting A.J.'s family and learning about his work in Portland. The phone call was brief. It was possible A.J. didn't care that much about getting together. Kyle guessed time would tell.

~ Meeting with the Team ~

Yesterday was his first official day at Meisner Industries. Tom Bosworth had arranged for all the administrative things that Kyle needed to take care of, such as benefits choices and security training. Today began his work with the software team. While their hours were somewhat flexible, the team needed to have times they could all be there to coordinate their work. Kyle showed up at 8:00 AM. Joe Walker, the team leader, was already at work. When Kyle showed up, Joe dropped what he was doing to greet Kyle.

"Great to see you, Kyle. I am looking forward to working with you. Let me show you where you can work." Kyle's name was already posted by the entrance to a ten-foot-wide by ten-foot deep cubicle. Kyle was pleased to have more space than Softtek gave him in Houston. It had an L-shaped counter-top attached to five-and-a-half-foot high cubicle partitions with a two-drawer file cabinet to one side and a pencil drawer to the other. A three-shelf bookcase unit sat across the cubicle. The bookcase appeared populated with several manuals and three-ring binders. He assumed these were the tools and documentation he would need. What looked like a small stereo radio and a wireless headset was on top of the shelves. There were two computers under the desk and three large-screen monitors to facilitate his work. One monitor was centered in the elbow of the L shaped desk with the other two monitors on either side. There was a multi-button phone on the desk. Kyle was impressed. A small round table with two chairs was in the corner.

"Somebody from security will be by today to get you set up on the company network. They will also talk to you about security issues here at work, and your ...," Joe hesitated because he did not know where Kyle lived.

"Apartment," Kyle finished Joe's sentence.

Next, Joe showed Kyle the break room that included a couch large enough to nap on if necessary, something Joe pointed out to Kyle.

"Kyle, we do not expect—do not want—you to spend so much time here that you need to sleep overnight. However, there will be occasions where that might be needed. Sometimes a short nap can be helpful. We try to avoid that kind of last-minute pressure with accurate tracking of our progress on various modules. I think I mentioned we all used software to coordinate our work. Fortunately, we are at the initial design and prototype stage, so the real pressure will not occur for several months. The company provides snacks and various cold drinks, so you need not worry about feeding any kitty. Use whatever you want, anytime you want. The company puts RFID tags on all the goodies they supply. If you start taking lots of the goodies home, it will be tracked by security, and you will hear from them." Joe made a sardonic smile, trying to communicate that he knew this from first-hand experience. Still, Kyle did not put two and two together. Finally, Joe showed Kyle the restrooms and labs. Joe noted that the labs were only used when they had to test their code with actual hardware. That did not come up too often, he noted. However, Kyle should expect to be one of the team that would need access before long. When they worked their way back to Kyle's cubicle, Joe showed him a folder that was on his desk.

"Kyle, it will take you a while to get oriented and working on an actual project. It is always a process to get up and running. Be patient. There will be plenty of times you can't be patient. In the meantime, you can do background research."

Joe handed Kyle the folder. "Your first project is in this folder. Take your time, and then if you have questions, come and see me. The materials you will need and their location are outlined in the folder. Of course, you can't work on them until you are set up by security. Plan on expecting a few interruptions today as people arrive. They will want to reintroduce themselves and chat. We will get to know each other better in an informal get-together on Friday afternoon at City Tavern over on Grand. Any one of us can give you directions."

With that said, Joe left Kyle to look at the folder. In it were several pages describing the project Kyle was to work on. Much to Kyle's surprise, it was a problem in hyperspectral analysis. He realized that his knowledge of hyperspectral analysis listed on his resume had been relevant in securing this job after all. There was a prototype machine available in Lab 3 that he could use to experiment, once a new hyperspectral component was installed. Joe had not taken Kyle into Lab 3 or 1 or 2 for that matter. In Lab 3 was a test instrument developed by Meisner Industries to produce a digital readout of a hyperspectral analysis. Kyle was intrigued and could not immediately imagine what purpose the device had. In due time, he reasoned. Kyle determined he would need to do additional research on hyperspectral analysis. Kyle would have to check with Joe to see if Meisner's had a research library or had access to an online resource for him to do additional research.

Before he could check with Joe, Dennis Andersen came to greet him. Dennis's cubicle was next to Kyle. Behind the opening to both Dennis and Kyle's cubicles was a window that looked over Lloyd Center, so it got the morning sun. The window had an automatic window screen sensitive to external light. It was down when it was in direct sunlight and when there was internal lighting after dark. That meant that it went up in the afternoon and back down at dusk, all automatically. However, there was an override control beside the window. Kyle wondered if it automatically went up in cloudy weather. He had been told there were many cloudy, wet days in the winter. Dennis was friendly and welcoming and encouraged Kyle to feel free to interrupt with questions he had about virtually anything. Dennis asked Kyle lots of questions about his experience with electronics. Kyle was able to answer most of his questions. Dennis, however, was not familiar with hyperspectral imaging.

Kyle estimated that Dennis was in his early thirties. Dennis did not burn bridges. He maintained his old apartment in SE Portland where he kept his electronics workshop. He had dreams of inventing something that would make him rich. Currently he was living with Jill Haung in the Pearl District. From there, he could bike to work most days to leave his car for Jill to use. Jill had been married before and had a three-year-old girl named Tabi.

It was not long before Jeneen Jenkins, and Josh Smythe came in. Both dropped by Kyle's desk and greeted him, offering to help him get started. Jeneen offered Kyle a challenge. She said she was able to break any code Kyle wrote of more than two hundred and fifty lines. Jeneen's job was quality control, and she specialized in finding errors in everyone's code. Neither took more than five minutes and headed off to their cubicles. Their cubicles were in the same room on the other side of Kyle and Dennis's cubicles. It was not long before Joe dropped by again, and informed Kyle of a team meeting at 1:30 PM. Kyle asked him about research, and Joe wrote down a service they used. It was a private Meisner service. All communications with the service were encrypted over a virtual private network that prevented Meisner Industries' research from being tracked by their competitors. Kyle guessed that his use of it was monitored. If what you needed was not immediately available, you could put in a request. Within a day, additional resources would appear. Kyle was intrigued by the degree to which Meisner's went to protect their work from prying eyes.

~ Meisner's Legislative Interests ~

Richard Meisner did not leave things to chance. Neither did Rolfe Corning. Corning was chair of a critical U.S. Senate committee, Commerce, Science, and Transportation. This committee had legislative jurisdiction on matters related to science and technology, oceans policy, transportation, communications, and consumer affairs. Meisner worked with Corning to get legislation drafted that provided funds to local jurisdictions that wanted to adopt mail-in ballots for federal elections. It had been referred to Corning's committee and scheduled for hearings in a couple of months. Meisner kept a lobbyist on retainer to track hearings and progress on any legislation that might impact Meisner Industries. Meisner also had an internal company lobbyist to deal with local and state politics. The lobbyist was a lawyer that wore more than one hat. The Oregon legislative situation in Salem was more favorable to businesses, especially ones that paid taxes like Meisner Industries. Money lubricated the political process, and Richard was not stingy with his support for the things he wanted. Meisner Industries was the primary financial support for the American Commerce Council PAC. The ACCPAC was a significant contributor to Corning's reelection. Corning was keenly aware of how much ACC had contributed to his reelection and how much Meisner supported it. Corning was attentive to Richard Meisner whenever Richard asked for help with legislation favorable to Meisner. In fact, over the past few years, Meisner and Corning had become more than close friends. They sought legislation that might benefit them both.

Richard was careful to avoid activities that might fall in the purview of public information laws. Communications with legislative personnel were always in person, never in writing. His internal public relations guru carefully vetted emails. He did not think of his work as illegal; at least that is what he paid his lawyers to tell him. His public relations guru was extraordinarily talented in framing communications to avoid the appearance of lying in any written or recorded communications. In technical matters, lying could be disastrous. Technical specifications needed to provide detailed, accurate information. False information in business communications could result in a lawsuit, something Meisner was eager to avoid.

Meisner made frequent trips to Washington. Meisner Industries maintained a Meisner Industries' office in a house he owned near Washington. The office covered for his trips that included nonbusiness activities. As an accomplished pilot, he could fly to Washington in his personal jet. However, Meisner Industries retained a pilot used on routine trips. On a recent trip, Laura accompanied Richard. Richard and Laura stayed in a Washington hotel, in separate rooms, on different floors. He and Corning were scheduled to meet in person at a social event that Laura also attended. Richard suggested that Laura go back to the hotel since it was getting late. He and Corning had a private conversation in her absence. Laura left them, but on the way, she passed information about the meeting to an FBI colleague in Washington. Neither Meisner nor Corning wished to have the content of their conversation on the record and made considerable effort to ensure what they had to say was private. They utilized a room Richard had booked an hour before they met. Although the FBI would like to have known the content of the conversation, they were unable to make the necessary arrangements to overhear them on such short notice. Laura was surprised the next morning when Richard did not answer the phone in his hotel room.

While in Washington, Meisner also made contact with a lobbyist working for K & W manufacturing, a company in Taiwan that provided a critical component that Meisner wanted for an important project. K & W was owned by Tao Li, a person Richard had met at Stanford University when they were both students. Richard wanted an updated progress report on the development and production of the component. He was assured that everything was on schedule, and the prototype would be available in the next ninety days. Meisner noted that there would be financial and political consequences if there were delays delivering the prototype.

Chapter 4

Kim & Wong, (K & W Manufacturing) in Taiwan was the firm that Meisner used to acquire critical components for a number of his projects at Meisner Industries. Richard Meisner and the CEO and principal partner of K & W, Tao Li, attended Stanford University and developed a working relationship. Since Li went back to Taiwan and became the primary partner of K & W Mfg., Meisner had depended on Li to supply specialty parts for Meisner Industries. Li has given Meisner competitive prices and excellent service and entertained Meisner on his occasional but rare trips to Taiwan. Li and Meisner had a mutual understanding of the importance of careful communications.

Meisner wanted to prevent his competitors from stealing proprietary technology. He tried to stay clear of any probes from law enforcement agencies or the press. Technical details were generally delivered to Li in person by Meisner or a trusted employee. In recent months, Meisner came to appreciate the talent and discretion of Laura McLaughlin and had entrusted her to make deliveries to Li, and return with prototype devices from K & W.

Meisner, however, was not aware that Li was subcontracting some of the work for Meisner to Xiazhen

Manufacturing in Shenzhen, China. Li was able to provide products to Meisner at considerable savings to Li and his Taiwan company. This was Li's secret. Unknown to Li and Meisner, the CIA was aware of this ruse, and was interested in precisely what was being manufactured, and how that was to be used by Meisner. When the CIA learned that Laura was making trips to Taiwan to visit K & W, Li's company, their interest was piqued. The CIA and the FBI had a history of territorial conflicts. So, when the CIA discovered that Laura was working for the FBI, they sought a working relationship with the Portland FBI office to learn anything that Laura uncovered. The local FBI office reluctantly agreed to cooperate so long as it did not compromise their investigation into Meisner's activities and his relationship to Senator Rolfe Corning.

The latest product order from Meisner to Li was for a specialized hyperspectral read-head that Meisner needed as part of a project of interest to Corning. There was a strong popular push to move away from voting machines and toward paper ballots, and Meisner intended to be the prime supplier of all the equipment needed to tabulate paper ballots. Since Oregon had been using mail-in paper ballots for a long time, being in Portland was ideal. With Corning's influence in Washington D.C., Meisner expected to gain a significant portion of the U.S. market. He felt he had influence over Corning by permitting Corning to secretly purchase, at discount, private issue stocks in Meisner Industries. Meisner's hyperspectral read-head was a key to Corning's aspirations.

~ Kyle and the Team ~

As the days passed, Kyle became comfortable with the Meisner development team. He learned they had adopted an unofficial name for themselves; "The Miracle Workers." Richard Meisner referred to them as the "Close Team" because of their location in headquarters. There were other software teams in Meisner Industries, located in various parts of Portland. The teams in various locations had different functions. However, at times, Meisner liked to give the same assignment to two different teams and have them compete for the best solution to a particular problem. He did this only on high-value jobs where exceptional quality and innovation were vital to the overall project's success. Usually, both teams designed great solutions and both were integrated into the final product.

Kyle especially appreciated the *camaraderie* of his team. Although Joe was the designated and recognized leader of the group, every person on the team was a professional, proud of their skill and work products. Kyle was developing and integrating his code to take advantage of the hyperspectral read-head based on the specifications provided. He was told that additional specifications would be forthcoming to provide information on other needs and features. During these early days of coding, Kyle did not know how his work on hyperspectral read-heads would be utilized. As a new employee, he knew better than to ask too many questions. So far, he did not need to know any more than the specifications. Based on the weekly reports provided to Bosworth in HR, Bosworth called Kyle in for an early performance review. The review made Kyle nervous since he was still in a probationary period. He went to see Bosworth as directed.

"Kyle, good to see you. Please have a seat." Bosworth pointed to a chair at a side table. "I have been reviewing the weekly reports you have provided, and I want to put you at ease. Everything seems to be going well."

"That's a relief," Kyle sighed.

"Sorry if it worried you. No need. Your work and progress are beyond acceptable at this point."

What does that mean, "at this point?" Are they anticipating things won't be okay in the future?

As Kyle's alarms were quietly rising, Bosworth added, "It is not uncommon for Mr. Meisner to have a chat with key employees after they have been on the job for a few weeks. Mr. Meisner sent me a note that your work on hyperspectral processes was of interest to him, and he wanted to get an update on the technology as you learn new things. He would like you to drop by his office this afternoon at 4:00 PM. Were you planning on being in the office at that time?"

"Sure," Kyle answered. He typically did not leave work until 5:30. The bus was less crowded after 5:30.

"I will let him know that you will drop by his office upstairs at 4:00 PM. That's all I have for you today, Kyle."

"Great, I can get in additional work," Kyle answered, and went back to his cubicle. Kyle did not tell anyone on his team about Meisner's request to meet. He had not heard that anyone else on the team had met with Meisner except, perhaps, for Joe, team leader.

At 4:00 PM, Kyle reported to Charla, Meisner's assistant. She announced his appearance and indicated he should enter Mr. Meisner's office. Kyle entered the office and closed the door behind him. He had brought a thumb drive with him in case Meisner wanted a personal update on the hyperspectral work he had been doing.

"Kyle, good to see you again. I trust your experience here at our company has been a good one. No need to sit, I have a question to ask you."

Kyle stood awkwardly in front of Meisner's desk, holding his thumb drive. "Kyle, Laura, and I would like to invite you to have dinner with us this evening. Would your schedule allow that?"

"I have not been in Portland long enough to be involved in many activities, so my nights are usually spent studying technical manuals. I would love to take a break from that." Kyle said, trying not to sound too enthusiastic. Yes, he had been studying manuals, but he also had been watching Netflix movies.

"Good. Good. I have reservations at Andina Restaurant, NW Glisan. I hope you like Peruvian food. How about you meet Laura and me there this evening at 7:30 PM. It is not a formal place, so work attire is fine."

"Anything I should prepare for?" Kyle asked, not knowing for sure what Meisner had in mind.

"No. This is an informal get-together. I want to follow up on our earlier conversation about how I might need your assistance with a special project. I will explain everything this evening."

With that, Meisner dismissed Kyle. Kyle decided to head home to clean up the day's grime. He was both looking forward to a good dinner and learning more about the "secret" project Meisner had for him.

~ The Secret Project ~

When Kyle arrived at the restaurant, he was directed to a small private room. Laura and Richard Meisner were already there having cocktails. Kyle wondered at first if he had misunderstood the time, but Meisner resolved that question immediately.

"Laura, you are right. Kyle is a very prompt person. Just in time, Kyle." Richard offered.

"Oh, I thought at first I had misunderstood the time. Hello Laura."

"Hello, Kyle. It is always good to see you. How has work been going so far?"

"Pretty good, well, actually very good. I like the team and am having a ball learning new tools and ways of developing systems. How have you been? I have not seen you around for the past three weeks. What are you doing anyway?"

"Kyle, I hope you don't laugh. I am selling timeshares in Honolulu. I work for a local real estate outfit that owns property in Honolulu, and I help with marketing. The upside is I get to go to Honolulu every few weeks. I was over there last week."

"I should have known you would find such a plush gig." Kyle bantered.

"Plush my eye! Timeshares are not that easy to sell these days. I am lucky if I make a couple of sales a month. And to do that, it takes talking to lots of potential customers, many who were not serious to begin with. It can be a drag on any given day. So, no, this is not a plush gig!"

"My bad," Kyle responded. Before he could say anything else, Richard signaled for everyone to take a seat. Almost as if on cue, a waiter appeared with wine and another with their meals.

"Kyle, I took the chance and ordered for you. I think you will like the food here," That was an understatement as the three of them enjoyed the evening conversations over several courses and ample wine. At last, Richard got to the point of the evening.

"Kyle, Laura has told me how much trust she has in your ethics, your concern for doing what is right and just. I have had hints of that myself since I met you. That is why I hope I can entrust you with a task for the company. I am concerned you might find the project awkward. So, let me finish before you make up your mind."

"Here is the issue, Kyle. Meisner Industries does very innovative and creative work. It results in jealousy among those who want to be competitors in certain lines of work we do. It is a constant pressure to be at the top, and when an employee shares too much information with a competitor, knowingly or unknowingly, it is detrimental to the company. Recently, I have learned that key proprietary information is being shared with one or more competitors. I don't know the reason. It could be money, but I pay Meisner employees well to reduce that source of temptation. I realize, however, that for some people, there is never enough money. I try to screen new hires for that, but the process is imperfect. It could also be dissatisfaction with some aspect of working for the company. Still, Meisner Industries gets top ratings on places to work in the yearly *Oregonian* newspaper poll. I can't divulge my sources, but it does not include identity about who or where the leak is occurring. At this point, I do not know precisely what has been leaked. One thing I highly suspect is the team the leak is coming from. Can you guess which one?"

Kyle responded, "Well, since I only know one team, mine, I assume you suspect it comes from our team. That's hard to believe, frankly. Everyone seems so ..." Kyle paused, looking for the right word. "It is hard to believe. You don't think I am the one, do you? Did this start after I was hired?"

"Oh No, Kyle. I had this problem before you were hired. I was hoping the team hired you. You couldn't be of help to me if I had not let the team hire you. I believe Laura. I believe what she tells me about you." Kyle smiled at Laura. "I needed someone new on the team who can help me discover where and how the leak is happening. I need your eyes and ears. How would you feel about doing undercover work to help solve this problem?"

Kyle did not answer immediately, and he mulled over the implication of being a spy. In a way, it was a trigger reminding him of his experiences in St. Andrews. He certainly did not want to end up in jail again.

Before he could respond, Laura jumped in, "Kyle. I know you. You have been involved in things far more dangerous than what Richard is asking of you. I hope you don't mind, but I shared the details of your St. Andrew's experience with Richard, things that were not part of his pre-employment research. I told him he could count on your discretion regardless of your decision about helping with this problem. Please, consider this seriously."

Kyle wanted to believe he could count on Laura too. Laura had always seemed to shoot straight and care about professional ethics. They had discussed that more than once, when they were together in Houston. He felt that if Laura believed what Richard was asking was ethical and right, it probably was. Finally, Kyle decided he owed it to himself to do the right thing, and in this case, it meant trying to uncover unethical behavior in his team. He answered Richard, "Okay, I am not sure what I am getting myself into, but I am willing to help find the source of the sabotage you suspect is coming from my team. What is the next step?"

Richard seemed to relax and filled Kyle in with the nature of the leak. Kyle was not sure his team was the only one involved, but he did not know that much about other teams. Kyle asked Richard if it was possible the problem was coming from a different team. Richard did not reject the idea but wanted Kyle to focus on his team for now. Kyle asked if that meant he would be able to look at other teams in the future? Richard answered affirmatively. Richard left it up to Kyle and Laura to work out the plan to uncover the source of the leak. He allowed it might be another team, so encouraged Kyle and Laura to investigate wherever it might lead. That gave Kyle a good feeling; he would see more of Laura, someone for whom he still held affection. Working with Laura also avoided having secret meetings with Richard. He still could not figure out why Richard seemed to be so trusting of Laura. Perhaps Kyle had a lot to learn about Meisner Industries.

~ Laura and Kyle ~

Not long after the secret meeting with Meisner and Laura, Laura reached out to Kyle and arranged a time they could meet. Laura invited Kyle to come to her apartment in the Pearl District. The apartment was a far cry better than his. Not aware Laura was working for the FBI, he assumed her residence was secured the same way as his, with hidden mics, cameras, and internet taps. Of course, it was, but not by Meisner Industries. The FBI had cleverly installed a system that fed false data to Meisner Industries and directed actual information to the FBI local office that kept active surveillance whenever Laura gave the signal.

Kyle came over as directed on a Saturday evening promptly at 8:30 PM. Laura buzzed him into the lobby, and he made his way up to her apartment. He looked for a doorbell or knocker, but none were apparent, only a small flat panel to the right of the door handle. He pressed on it, but nothing happened. He assumed it required a dongle or card to open the door, so he knocked. A moment later, the door clicked and opened an inch. Kyle carefully pushed the door open and called out.

"Laura? Are you here? This is Kyle."

"Yes," came a loud call from the back of the hallway. "Come on in, down the hall. I am in the kitchen."

Kyle shut the door and went down the hallway past two closed doors. At the end of the hall was a spacious living/dining room adjacent to a small kitchenette. Windows along the exterior wall of the living area looked South East toward the tall buildings of Portland. There was a bar with three stools between the living/dining area and the kitchen. Laura was taking something out of the oven. The unmistakable rich smell of chocolate chip cookies wafted through the apartment. Kyle took a stool.

"I am running late, sorry. I have a couple more trays to cook. Maybe you could help me. Here is a spatula. I need these cookies taken off the cookie sheet and placed on the wire rack to cool. Okay?"

"Of course," Kyle answered. "However, I cannot guarantee that they will all make it to the wire rack." Laura laughed.

"Help yourself. If you need something to drink, you can get it out of the fridge. If you don't mind, pour me a glass of milk. The glasses are in the cupboard next to the fridge."

Kyle smiled. She was not serving alcohol, but milk. Just like her. Was her cordiality a performance or genuine? *Time will tell.* He challenged, "Laura, did you go to all this trouble making cookies for me?"

"Of course not. It is my special torture technique. The smell alone has been known to break the toughest crook. Of course, I made these for you, for old times. Remember?"

Kyle did remember the times she made chocolate chip cookies for him in Houston. He always ate too many. Memories of the good times they shared flooded in. *Maybe this IS an attempt to torture me.*

"So that is what you were doing to me in Houston, torturing me? If that was torture, I can take all you dish out, no pun intended. But I assume we have work to do tonight." *Why did I say that?*

She teased, "I don't know why we can't mix business and pleasure, do you?"

This was going to be an unbearable evening if she continued to tease him. He assumed Laura was in a relationship with Richard, so he decided to ask.

"Laura, I have been confused ever since that day you and Richard picked me up at the bus stop. Are you two in a relationship? Is it serious? You are confusing me."

"Kyle, I am sorry if I have been confusing you. I thought you knew that Richard is gay. I guess in a way, I am his cover, the girl on his arm. Don't get me wrong, I do like him, and I do work for him. My main job is with the timeshare in Honolulu."

Kyle interrupted, "Work for him? Exactly what do you do? That is if you can tell me."

"I describe it as research. I try to get information on Meisner Industries competitors for him, so he knows what to expect before it happens."

"And precisely, how do you do that?"

"Kyle, some things will have to be left to your imagination. Okay?" Kyle did not like where his imagination immediately took him. "But I also do tasks like the one you and I are going to work on tonight. And, furthermore, I suspect this to require several semi-secret meetings like tonight. By the way, are you cool with working on a secret project for Richard?"

"Cool? I don't know that I would use that term. I feel pressured into something that I don't fully appreciate. If you were not involved, I would be looking for another place to work. You sure this is all on the up and up?"

"No question at all," although that was partially a lie. The FBI was very interested in Richard Meisner. "You are still willing to work with me, aren't you?"

Kyle nodded as if he understood. Although he expected to focus on the task at hand, it would be a form of torture if his relationship to Laura were strictly business. The fact that Laura was not Richard's girlfriend was interesting and gave Kyle a warm feeling. As soon as all the cookies were baked, they sat down in the living room to develop a surveillance strategy to discover who or what was leaking information. They knew there was no need to monitor phone calls or electronic transmissions because Meisner Industries' security was doing that. Of course, if necessary, he could watch for any corruption of the surveillance system. That was something he had experience with when he worked in St. Andrews. However, his access at Meisner Industries was considerably different than St. Andrews.

It appeared that Kyle was going to have to be sociable to become better friends with each member of his team. Laura and Kyle agreed that the process would start with Kyle regularly joining the team when they went to the bar after work instead of begging off. Kyle needed to make a note of who he socialized with, and let Laura know so she could research them.

Of course, Kyle had no idea how she did the research. Laura did not share the fact that, among other things, she used FBI resources for research. He did not know Laura worked for the FBI and therefore had significant resources available. Nor was he aware that she was also keeping an eye on Richard Meisner for the FBI.

Kyle was distracted by his returning affection for Laura. The "Dear John" letter was long forgiven but not forgotten. They finished up around 10:30 PM, and Kyle headed for home. It took a while to get to his apartment since he had to transfer from one bus to another. Kyle looked forward to owning a car, although traffic in Portland could be congested like Houston. Maybe he could find an apartment closer to work. Perhaps he could bike. It seemed like lots of people in Portland used bikes.

~ The Homeless Encounter ~

A couple of days after meeting with Laura, on his way to work, he wanted to finish a book he had started the night before. It distracted him from work and secret projects. He took the book with him on the bus. He was so engaged, he missed his regular bus stop and had to walk back three blocks. He had not personally encountered the number of homeless people on the streets before. Typically, the bus stopped virtually in front of his office building. As he was walking along, he spotted a somewhat disheveled woman pushing a baby carriage. Not knowing what possessed him, he stopped to look in the carriage at a fussing baby. He expected to see her daily supplies, but instead, he saw a baby that could not have been six months old. He stopped.

"Your baby?" He asked.

"Yeah," She responded warily.

"How old?" Kyle asked to be friendly, as was his nature.

"Five months," She answered, suspicious of a young man that would be attentive to her and her baby.

"You live around here?" Kyle asked, not thinking about how he got into this conversation.

Sensing Kyle's warmth and genuine interest, the woman opened up to Kyle. She told him she was from Helena, Montana. She shared how her husband was a drunk and was threatening her and the child. She had heard that there were jobs in Portland, so she used her last few dollars to catch a bus. When she got here, people told her there weren't any jobs. She found a shelter in Gresham, but they would not let her stay there during the day. They gave her a TriMet pass, so she came downtown to look for a job.

Kyle did not know why, but her heartbreaking story touched him. He decided to give her a boost with a few dollars. He intended to give her twenty, which would give her and her baby food money for the day. He indicated he wanted to help and took out his wallet. When he looked in it, there was only one bill, a fifty-dollar bill. He had forgotten to refresh his cash supply. Since he had committed to help, being a man of his word, he went ahead and took it out and gave it to her. He could always get more cash from a cash machine. Now that he worked for Meisner Industries, he was flush with funds.

It surprised her when she looked at the fifty-dollar bill. Spontaneously, she reached out and put her arms around Kyle, hugging him tightly and sobbing. Kyle felt tears come to his eyes too. He put his arms around her as if to comfort her. It was hard to imagine how as little as fifty dollars could cause such an emotional response. When she finally stopped crying and wiped her eyes on her sleeve, she again thanked Kyle, and he wished her luck in finding a job. Kyle left deeply touched by that experience, knowing the job prospects were very poor for a woman with a baby and no child care to lean on.

At work, the experience continued to pop in and out of focus, making it hard to concentrate. He wondered what it would be like to have no resources, stranded in a strange place with a small child dependent on you, and have no way to support the child. This would not be the last time he felt compelled to help someone.

Chapter 5

~ Taipei Taiwan ~

Dr. Tao Li, the owner of K & W Manufacturing in Taiwan, was a successful businessman in a very competitive market place. Li relied on relationships he had developed when he went to school in the U.S.A. His labor costs were substantially less than those in the States but still more expensive than those in mainland China. When he could, he outsourced work to several different firms in China, but this was his secret. Most of his customers in the U.S. only cared about the price and the quality of the finished product, not the physical factory that made it. His customers assumed Li manufactured all their contracted items in Taiwan. It never occurred to them K & W might subcontract work on the mainland. Most of his customers could have sourced in China themselves, but they preferred to source in Taiwan. Li manufactured parts for all kinds of technical equipment that required an embedded electronic component. He did a lot of work for an elite electric car manufacturer, mostly screens for their cars. For an aerospace firm, he supplied critical electronics used to monitor and manage injection nozzles. Based on the capability for custom manufacturing of quality parts, at a reasonable price, and delivered on time, he did not lack customers wishing to avoid Chinese entanglements.

He met Richard Meisner in an electrical engineering class when they were students at Stanford. They studied together and became good friends. In Taiwan, being gay was not an acceptable lifestyle, but in the U.S., at Stanford, it was acceptable. As a result, Richard and Tao became very close. Since Tao became the principal owner of K & W manufacturing, he had supplied Meisner Industries with several technically sophisticated parts for Meisner Industries products. These products were successful, so Li and Meisner both did well financially. Li was comfortable in Taiwan, but he also liked the states. Li was forming a subsidiary corporation in the U.S., and he needed Meisner's Washington connections. Meisner had connections in Washington in addition to Corning, so he offered to help Li establish a U.S. corporation.

Li was willing to set up shop in Oregon and liked the idea of doing it in Portland, close to Richard Meisner. It was Li's dream to spend as much as half his time in the states, Portland, to be specific. He imagined continuing his relationship with Meisner. In contrast, Meisner preferred to keep his sexual preferences confidential, hence the use of Laura McLaughlin for a cover when he attended social events. The ruse mostly worked, but it was generally known in private circles that he was gay. As much as he liked Li, he did not visit Taiwan because he loved him. Meisner was all business when in Taiwan. That frustrated Li.

Anxious about his vote-counting machine applications, Meisner asked Laura to go to Taiwan to deliver new specifications and pick up a hyperspectral read-head prototype he could test. Laura told Kyle she had to be out of town for a few days, going to Honolulu to follow up on her timeshare job. Kyle did not know she would only be in Honolulu long enough to catch a flight to Taiwan. While deception was sometimes essential for her work at the FBI, she did not like it when it was necessary to deceive Kyle. She did not feel it was an acceptable way to relate to someone you worked with closely. Deception with Kyle nagged her conscience.

~ Laura in Taiwan ~

Laura's layover in Honolulu was a tight forty minutes. She left Honolulu at 11:00 AM arriving in Taipei at 4:00 PM the next day after an eleven-hour flight. She managed to get a couple of hours sleep on the plane, so she was okay to stay awake for most of the evening in Taipei. Meisner had let Li know through an encrypted communication that Laura was coming to bring specifications, and get the prototype hyperspectral read-head. Li had a car and driver waiting for her at the airport and took her to the Hilton Taipei Sinban Hotel. It was almost 5:30 when she got to her room. She was not particularly hungry. She had eaten and snacked on the flight. She stepped into the shower to freshen up before going down to the bar for a drink. As she came out of the shower with a towel wrapped around her, she saw that someone had slipped a note under her door.

"Meet me in the bar tonight at 7:30. H"

She recognized the "H." It was Huang. She decided to wait until 7:30 to go down. Huang was her CIA contact, which she referred to as her handler much to Huang's chagrin. She finished blow-drying her hair, putting on makeup, a white blouse, and gray slacks. Laura did not want to stand out. She was not surprised that Huang had been alerted to her arrival and hotel arrangements. The Portland FBI office had agreed to keep the CIA informed when Laura made a trip to Taipei. Laura meandered through the lobby to the bar. Looking around, she saw Huang in a booth near the rear of the bar. She noticed as she sat down, he had already ordered her a beer. Laura was careful with alcohol. It had ruined a lot of good agents who thought they could handle alcohol.

"Hi Huang," Laura said as she sat. "Good to see you again. Do you live here in Taipei?"

Huang smiled. "Hello to you too," he replied.

Huang answered very few questions unless they directly applied to his current assignment, and then only what was necessary. Despite his Chinese origin in rural China, Huang had spent most of his life in the U.S. His parents left the mainland and moved to Taiwan when Huang was three. After three years in Taipei, his father moved to the U.S. to work for a Taiwanese firm. Huang grew up in the Los Angeles area, where he learned impeccable English. Most of what he knew about China came from things he had read and stories his parents told him. He did well in school, majored in mechanical engineering and drama. He imagined himself a celebrity actor, doing many walk-on parts, but he never got a leading role. He got stereotypical roles, usually as a bad guy in TV crime shows. After playing "the part," his interest in real crime developed. He went back to school to get a master's degree in criminal justice, where he attracted the eyes of a CIA recruiter. Native-born Chinese now U.S. citizens were in demand. He was forty-two, the same age as Meisner. He worked out creating his muscular build, which he liked to flaunt with tight-fitting shirts. He was unusually tall, almost six foot one.

"Not going to answer my question, are you?" Laura challenged him, "Sometimes, you are impossible."

"I think we need to talk about why you are here and what you can do for me," ignoring her question. Huang knew she would say something smart back. She always did.

"That's for me to know and you to figure out. Why don't you tell me why I am here? I know—do you know, or are you just fishing?"

"My bait, dear lady, is irresistible, so don't bite unless you want to get reeled in."

"Okay, you win. What is it worth to you to know my plans for the next couple of days?" Laura quizzed.

"I would settle for a good word to my boss back home. I am easy, are you?"

"Depends on what you mean by that. I think I am easy to work with, but I don't bed easily if that is what you had in mind." Laura always suspected Huang would like to screw her, but he never made any moves. He was always professional and proper. Laura paused and turned from banter to serious. "I am here on business. By the way, did you check to see if I was followed in the bar? I don't want to be questioned about my associations by Li or Meisner. Also, do you have any other agents assigned to this visit? I don't want to be looking over my shoulder when it is not necessary."

"Only me, but I plan to keep out of sight. Also, no one followed you in here. Our main interest is in the dealings that Li has with people in mainland China. I can't tell you anything, but if you do get any hints of mainland China connections, please pass them forward. Do you have an FBI contact here in Taipei?" Huang asked.

"FBI here in Taipei? You know better than that. No. I am here on Meisner Industries business. I deliver specifications, and they are to provide me with a prototype component for testing back in the States."

"I would like to see the specs," Huang ventured as Laura interrupted him.

"Sorry, I have strict instructions. I don't share any documents or items with you directly. I can talk to you; I can answer questions. I can tell you where I am going and what I am doing. If there is any sharing to be done, that will be done back in the states, first by the FBI, and then your buddies."

Huang started again, "I was about to add when I was so rudely interrupted, I would like to see the prototype too. Is that off-limits as well?"

"I think I was clear. Communications but no items. Share words privately, things never."

"You want to dance?"

"What? Here?' Laura knew what he meant, but liked to tease Huang.

"There is no danceable music I can hear, and even if there were, the answer would still be no.

Ignoring the tease, Huang parried, "Wrong dance lady. I meant; do you want to continue to dance around this?" Huang responded.

"No. I think I made my case. When do you want to meet again?"

"After you meet with Li. Do you know when that will be?"

"Yes," Laura hesitated then stopped dancing. "I meet him tomorrow afternoon briefly. Then I am scheduled to fly back the next morning."

"Ah, then the dance is not over. You want to meet here or someplace else?" Huang questioned.

Laura ignored the dance reference. "If you think this place is secure enough, it is fine with me."

"It's good. How about 10:00 PM? Too late for you?"

"No, that is fine. I don't expect to find out anything of interest to you, but I will keep my eyes and ears open." With that, Laura got up and sauntered out of the bar while Huang watched the swinging hips dance after all, just as Laura had intended.

~ The Exchange between Laura and Tao Li ~

Laura knew she needed to sleep, and her internal clock told her it was very late, maybe 1:00 AM. Even though it was only 7:00 PM local, she was drained. Getting sleep on the plane ride helped, but adjusting had always been difficult for Laura. She needed to be at her peak. When she hit the bed, she fell asleep immediately. When she woke up, it was 4:00 AM in Taipei. She could live with that. She got up and checked the email on her phone. The only emails were advertisements and spam. She opened her secure files and keyed an encrypted note about her evening with Huang: Not much of interest. She decided to go down to see if it was too early for breakfast. By the time she was dressed and primped, it was 6:00 AM. The breakfast bar was open, so she found a seat, ordered coffee, and helped herself to the buffet. She kept the documents she needed to deliver to Tao Li with her at all times according to directions from Meisner, and unbeknownst to him, the FBI. The documents were contained on a micro S.D. card encased in a protective metal case. She carried it in a zippered pocket between her under and outer garments. Meisner was taking no chances that his valuable proprietary information was hijacked. As a ruse, Laura also carried a small briefcase that contained a sealed envelope. The envelope contained false specifications on a second S.D. card, and a letter addressed to Li. The specifications included a complex process that would work but unrelated to any work of Meisner Industries. In case someone was going to try to steal his secrets, Meisner would feed them incorrect information. He expected the thieves would assume it was real intelligence, and the diversion would give Laura extra time for the actual exchange. No one made any attempt to take the false envelope at breakfast, so Laura signed the bill and went back upstairs to her room.

Laura took the elevator down around 9:30 AM. The elevator stopped the floor below hers. A gentleman looked in the elevator hesitatingly, then got on. Laura was tense, alert to a possible altercation. It spiked when the gentleman walked over to the elevator panel. Laura braced for him to halt the elevator, so she reached into her bag and grasped the knife that was in there. The man did not stop the elevator, however. He punched the button for the mezzanine. She breathed in relief as the elevator descended empty of other passengers to the main floor, where she waited for a car to take her to Li. She did not wait long. Li sent a driver to bring her to his offices next to the factory. Traffic was heavy, and it took almost fifty minutes to arrive. Laura always enjoyed Taipei's streets, a vibrant, busy city with lots of walkers, bikers, and cars. Traffic thinned out a bit as they neared Li's office. The driver drove into the building's parking garage, stopped, and opened the door for her. He pointed to the door she was to enter. This was not the first time she had visited Li, but the driver did not know that. It was not the same driver she saw the last time she was here. She entered the building and climbed the stairs to the lobby, where the receptionist greeted her.

"Greetings, Ms. McLaughlin," the receptionist was expecting her. "Dr. Li will be with you, momentarily. He is finishing his review of the factory floor. Could I get you anything? Coffee? Tea? Water?" Laura shook her head. The receptionist spoke perfect English with only a tinge of an accent. In the States, no one would even notice. "No, thank you. I had coffee at the hotel. Is there a ladies' room close by?"

"Yes, the first door down the hallway to the left."

Laura took the opportunity to remove the metal case with the specifications while in the restroom. She made it back as Li returned.

"Laura McLaughlin! It has been a while since you honored me with your presence. I pray you had a pleasant trip." Li ushered her into his office and suggested a chair at his conference table.

"Routine," she answered. "You appear to be in good health." Laura offered. "And your family?" Li was married, had three children, one son, the oldest, and two daughters. With a wife and family, no one suspected his gay preferences. His son was currently in the U.S. studying at his father's alma mater, Stanford. "Do you get to see Chao often?"

Li closed the door before he sat down. "No, not recently. He is a good student and won't take a break to come visit. But we do hear from him on Skype every once and a while. He tells us he is doing fine. He found a girlfriend at Stanford who is also from Taiwan. We have not met her yet in person, just via Skype."

"Possibly, he does not want to be away from the girl?" Laura suggested.

"Hmm, possibly, but surely she will come to visit her parents soon. Then I think he will come too, and we can meet her and her parents. I assume you have something for me?" Li asked, changing the subject.

"Yes, and I think you have something for me?" Laura responded. She removed the S.D. card from its metal container and handed it to Li. Li took it over to his desk and slipped the S.D. card into a slot on the side of his keyboard. He perused it for several minutes as Laura observed all the ornaments on Li's office wall. The degrees and honors would impress anyone who visited this office. On his desk was a nameplate which emphasized his status. "Dr. Li Tao," said it all, matching his diploma from Stanford mounted on the wall. Laura noted that Li had several piles of documents scattered over his desk and credenza. He was not as neat as she imagined an engineer of his stature should be. It looked more like the desk of a forgetful professor. She knew he was far from forgetful.

"Looks like what I needed. Thanks." Li breathed a small sigh of relief. "I had a factory line downstairs that was shut down because I needed these spec changes." This was a lie that Laura did not notice. These specifications were needed for the factory in China that would produce Meisner's special read-heads.

"Good," Laura answered, not sure what else to say. "What do you have for me?"

"Let me get it for you." Li got up and went to a safe hidden behind a hinged picture on the wall. Entering the push button combination, he opened the safe. He withdrew a box and closed the safe. He brought it to the table."

"This is interesting," Laura said quizzically. "you keep toothpaste in your safe?"

"No, no, no. Your prize is inside the box."

"You have disguised whatever it is as a box of Colgate toothpaste?"

Li smiled. "Take a look at what is inside."

Usually, Laura would not inspect items for Meisner, but in this case, Li insisted she look. Laura opened the end of the box carefully and slid out a tube of Colgate toothpaste. "Are you kidding me, Li? No one told me you were a practical joker." Li was not known for making jokes or playing tricks, so Laura was puzzled. She continued, not knowing what else to say, "All you want me to take Meisner is a tube of toothpaste, or is this a tube of magic goo? I can tell you he will not be pleased if this is a gag."

"No gag," Li said gleefully with a grin from ear to ear. "It does not contain toothpaste, but a non-toxic, static suppressing jell and a special electronic component. The tube is the old fashion lead tube, so its contents will not show up on x-ray machines. Just tell Richard to be careful. He should open it on this end." Li pointed to the end opposite the screw off top. "He will have to unfold the end, remove the contents, and clean the jell off. He will know how to do that safely."

"Ah, very clever. I will let him know," Laura responded. Now she mused how this would complicate either the CIA or the FBI from checking the contents before she delivered it to Richard. "Do you have a decoy for me as well, in case someone has ideas of snatching Meisner's product?"

"Of course, I do. Richard and I worked this out a long time ago. Here is a small box that contains a circuit and chip-set that will keep someone busy for a while. Even the box is booby-trapped to make it appear the contents are of special importance."

"I will never try to fool you, Li. You and Richard are sly dogs, but I love you both. Anything else? My return trip leaves early tomorrow morning.

"My driver can take you to both hotel and airport," Li answered.

"No need to come back to the hotel in the morning. I can get a cab to the airport."

"Not a problem for my driver. Besides, I like to ensure my delivery if you know what I mean."

"Okay, fine. That makes sense," Laura concurred. She was thinking ahead. How would Huang be contacted if the driver hung around till morning? Huang would want to be debriefed? She could not let the driver see that. She would have to figure that out on the drive back to the hotel. She could dismiss the driver and catch a cab in the morning.

Laura and Li continued conversations demanded by courtesy. After those exchanges, Laura left with Li's driver. He said nothing on the drive to Li's factory, and she suspected he would not change that on the way back. He surprised her.

"You live in the states?" The driver asked.

Laura did not want to engage in a conversation. She answered only, "Yes."

"Whereabouts?" Two could play this game.

"Portland," she answered.

"I have been to the states myself," he said, adding, "San Francisco and once in Houston, Texas."

Laura did not respond. She pulled out a piece of paper from a folder and opened it pretending to read. She was counting on the driver seeing her in the mirror and leaving her alone. It worked. The driver dropped her off at the hotel and indicated he would pick her up in the morning in time to get her to the airport. Laura made it clear she did not want a ride in the morning. She wondered what Li would think when the driver reported he was not needed to go to the airport. She hoped that would not alarm him.

Laura went to her room to freshen up. There she noticed her phone flashing a message. She punched the message button. It was from Huang, asking that she come down to the bar as soon as possible. She brushed her teeth, freshened her makeup, and headed down. In this case, she could not hide the goods in her clothing. She put the package in a purse she brought for such an occasion. She checked to see if Li's driver was in the lobby or the bar. Since he was not, she looked for Huang and saw him in the same back booth as last night. Laura looked around the bar once more and headed Huang's way. As she sat, a waitress came over. Laura ordered a Coke.

"Hello again," Huang greeted Laura. Laura returned the greeting and filled Huang in on her meeting with Li.

"So, where is the item?" Huang asked.

"It is in my room in my carry-on bag of toiletries," Laura whispered, leaning close to make sure no one overheard her. That would have been a logical place for a tube of toothpaste, but Laura could not take any chances. She needed the item with her at all times.

"Given the circumstances, I can't loan it to you. I seriously doubt you could remove it from its packaging without it becoming evident. It would be tricky to handle quickly even back in Portland before I get it to Richard." Laura described the package.

"How about this? We have an excellent lab in Honolulu. I could get your layover flight delayed for a day. That would give our Honolulu lab time to investigate the item," Huang suggested.

"I am not sure my boss would like that," Laura countered.

"Already approved and arranged with your boss."

"Oh yes, and which boss might that be?" Laura retorted.

Huang ignored her snide remark. "I assure you; you will not be able to tell the item has been tampered with. Do you need to call your boss, or can you trust me?"

Laura did not want to call her FBI boss and create a telecommunications record. She decided Huang had to be trusted until she reached Honolulu. She could contact the local FBI office, and make sure Huang was correct. Given the circumstances, she agreed with the plan. Laura again exchanged a content-free conversation with Huang until she finished her Coke. Then she left. Huang went back to his CIA office and finalized the arrangements.

The Plan: A customs officer in Honolulu, a CIA plant, would remove the toothpaste disguised item from her luggage or person on arrival, and a TSA CIA plant would place it back in her luggage when she went through security to board for Portland. There was confusion in Honolulu since she did not keep the item in her luggage. But it worked out when they scanned her purse and found it there. Since her flight would be delayed a day, it worked out okay. She even had a chance to check on her timeshare job. Laura arrived back in Portland a day late, but with rest from the layover in Honolulu.

~ Kyle and A.J. ~

A.J. called back with proposed dates he and his wife could meet with Kyle. They settled on a restaurant on West 23rd that was not too far from A.J.'s apartment. The restaurant did not take reservations. It was first come, first served. Kyle took the bus to a close stop and walked to the restaurant four blocks away. A.J. and his wife, Sheila, arrived about two minutes before Kyle.

"Hey, Kyle, over here," A.J. yelled over the clamor of the waiting crowd. We just got here, but I put our names on the list. They said the wait would be about forty minutes."

"A.J., so good to see you." Kyle surprised A.J. with a big hug and a pat on the back. A.J. responded in kind after a brief hesitation. "No problem with the wait," Kyle said.

"Kyle, I don't think you ever met my wife. Honey, this is Kyle Tredly. Kyle, meet the love of my life, Sheila."

"Sheila, I am pleased to finally meet you. A.J. used to talk about you all the time when we were taking classes together. Glad to finally put a face to the name. Is A.J. treating you right?"

"Nothing to complain about. I think I will keep him," Sheila responded with a smile as A.J. made wrinkles between his eyebrows."

A.J. turned to Kyle and shrugged his shoulders. "Sheila is in charge of chores. With Lindsey's arrival, there are lots of chores, but in Lindsey's case, they are chores with rewards." Then he hesitated, thinking of diaper duty. "Well, mostly rewards if you know what I mean. There are a few nasty chores too." It took a moment for Kyle to understand what he meant by that.

Kyle, A.J., and Sheila traded banter about what life was like, single, married, and married with children. Kyle would love to be in A.J.'s place, even with all the extra work marriage and children could be, according to their list. It was clear to Kyle, as A.J. and Sheila tried to one-up each other with who had the most chores, that it was effused with lots of love. It did not seem like forty minutes before they were seated, had ordered, and were served. The evening passed quickly.

A.J. had lots of questions for Kyle about Meisner Industries. Kyle had restrictions about what he could tell A.J. He was able to tell A.J. enough about the restrictive contract for A.J. to appreciate that Kyle could not be forthcoming on every question. Kyle, however, encouraged A.J. to ask anyway. Some people might have stopped asking questions about his work, but A.J. was relentless. Kyle was able to tell him about the interview process, the number of people on his team, and the security rules imposed on all employees. He could not share what he was working on or what training and educational topics he was assigned. He dared not share the unusual nature of his relationship with Richard Meisner. Generally, Kyle was positive about the work environment, salary, and benefits without disclosing details. Sheila wanted to know about his love life. There was little he could share there except meeting Laura McLaughlin again. Pressed, he confessed he still felt something for her but doubted it was reciprocated. A.J. was surprised that she worked with Meisner Industries.

Kyle confessed that he had not met anyone in Portland other than workmates, and Laura, of course. Sheila jumped in and suggested they introduce him to a few of their friends. A.J. agreed. A.J. worked for Intel and knew quite a few people there. Sheila volunteered at a local food bank; at least she did a lot more before Lindsey entered their life. They all agreed to meet again before too much time passed. Kyle was outwardly agreeable. However, he was not too enthusiastic about being the object of matchmaking. He preferred to make his own matches, and right now, he liked to imagine that he and Laura might get together again, maybe.

Chapter 6

~ The Hyperspectral Read-head ~

Laura delivered the read-head in a Colgate toothpaste tube to Richard personally. At first, he looked puzzled and frowned, suspecting Laura was about to play a trick on him. He had a sense of humor, but not so much around things that were important to him or when it came to Meisner Industries. Seeing his confusion, and realizing Li had not told him the form of delivery, Laura was quick to explain.

"No joke here, Richard. The read-head is inside the tube. Li used it because the tube is made of a lead alloy. The contents are not visible on airport security X-Ray machines."

"Oh?" Richard shook the tube. There was no sound of anything; it did not rattle. It was heavy, however. Li was always full of surprises. Richard pulled a small pocket knife out of his pants pocket to open it.

"Wait! Wait! You don't want to do that! There is also gel in the tube. I think Li said it was a special non-static and nontoxic goo that could be cleaned off the read-head with alcohol without damage. Caprice?" Laura smiled."

Richard closed the knife. "I know how to clean components, thank you." he said as though he had been slightly insulted. "Laura, I do appreciate you running this errand for me."

Laura thought, "Errand, like a trip to the drugstore? Since when is a trip halfway around the world just an errand." But she quipped, "No problem. Any time Richard."

"Laura, did Li say that all two hundred thousand read-heads would be delivered this way?

"No. He did not say, and I did not think to ask. Would that be a problem?"

"A bit. Okay, I will follow up with Li myself," Richard said.

After Laura left, Richard called one of his trusted technicians to his office, gave him the tube with instructions to remove the read-head, clean it, and install it in the machine in Lab 3 on the eighth floor. Richard didn't wait for the technician to notify him that the read-head was installed. He called Joe Walker to his office to get the ball rolling.

"Joe, one of the techs will install a new prototype hyperspectral read-head in the machine in Lab 3. As you know, Kyle has been developing code based on his experience with multispectral devices in Texas. I would like him to do some testing with his code on the machine. You have given him the specifications for the interfaces to the modules the team is working on, haven't you?"

"Yes, we all have the interfaces well defined. We meet weekly to assess each other's progress. Things are going according to plan. Do you want me to double-check Kyle's code?"

"At some point, we will need to check all your modules with each other. For now, let us see what Kyle is capable of. Let him run with it. You will be able to track his work, won't you?" Joe nodded. Richard continued, "If you see anything that concerns you, let me know. I don't want to slow you down with a supervisory task, but I need to know soon if Tredly has the skills to utilize the read-heads capability. I think it will be clear very quickly whether Kyle can cut it or not. However, if he does ask for help, please jump in. Can you work with that for a while?"

"Sure. My plate is full, and I have a few issues to get my code to play nice with the interface. I might have to call on other team members for assistance if I don't resolve my issues quickly." Joe regretted having admitted any weakness to his boss.

"Joe, you are too hard on yourself. That is my job," Richard admitted as he smiled. Richard was aware of his reputation of expecting too much. "You are one of the best coders I know. I am confident you can master any problem that comes your way." With that, Richard excused Joe. Joe returned to the eighth-floor team suite.

When Joe returned to the team suite, everyone was in the break room, waiting for a report. On previous rare visits, Joe was called to Richards office, and returned with either compliments or complaints from Richard. They were anxious to learn, which it would be this time. Instead, Joe said it was neither, and explained what had transpired. As a recent hire,

Kyle was surprised he was selected to test the read-head all by himself. The others found that only slightly odd since none of them were experts on hyperspectral theory.

Kyle explained that when any radio-spectrum waves interacted with some physical items, some reflections tended to break down into multiple wave-forms. Everyone knew how this worked with a prism and light as it was broken down into different colors. But Kyle explained this also occurred on electromagnetic frequencies above and below the visible spectrum. The team members understood the basic idea that hyperspectral readers were designed to read these invisible reflections. They also knew that interpreting the analog results and converting them into useful digital readings could be tricky. There was not one result but a multitude frequencies, multiple effects to read, and interpret. Picking out the critical frequencies from the chaotic jumble was not trivial. Kyle knew how that should work. They were all okay with leaving that to Kyle, even while being a bit jealous of his unique talent that Richard seemed to respect. Joe told Kyle he would notify him when Lab 3 was ready.

~ Ministry of State Security, China ~

The Ministry of State Security of the People's Republic of China is analogous to a combined United States FBI and CIA. Its powers include espionage both domestically and abroad. The MSS is partitioned into seventeen bureaus. The Taiwan - Hong Kong - Macau Bureau does intelligence work in Taiwan. The Science and Technology Investigative Division manages science and technology projects. The Imaging Intelligence Bureau includes satellite imagery technologies. These three bureaus had a particular interest in Tao Li in Taiwan, his son Chao Li attending Li's Alma Mater, Stanford in Palo Alto, California, and the work Li outsourced to a factory in Shenzhen on a project for Meisner Industries. Although headquarters is located near Tiananmen Square at No. 14 Dong Chang'an Jie, MSS had offices throughout the country as well as secret ones in major manufacturing centers in the U.S. masquerading as international import-export businesses. There was considerable competition among the various bureaus and some resistance to sharing information when projects crossed bureau boundaries, much like the FBI and CIA in the states. Human nature, and the desire for power and influence it seems, is the same everyplace. Discipline, however, varies by culture.

Although Li would not have been surprised by mainland surveillance, he was unaware of the nature of the MSS's particular interest in Meisner Industries and his work for them. Due to one of their sources in the U.S., the MSS was aware of Meisner Industries' interest in hyperspectral imaging hardware and software and how Meisner intended to use them. The Chinese also had projects utilizing hyperspectral imaging, but theirs was mostly used in satellites. They had limited information about how Meisner would use Li's read-heads. They needed more information. Meisner had not told Li how the read-heads would be used. The MSS believed the reports that Li was unaware of the purpose Meisner had for the read-heads. They knew about Meisner's association with Senator Corning and were close to obtaining intelligence on the precise purpose of meetings between Meisner and Corning. An effort to obtain critical information was in progress. However, the MSS did have a person they communicated with in Senator Corning's office.

The MSS viewed Li's use of a Chinese firm to manufacture hyperspectral read-heads as a useful opportunity to learn more. It would be a coup if MSS could embed a component into the read-heads that would allow them to discover their intended use. To that end, they placed agents in the factory Li was using to manufacture electronic equipment for Meisner. The MSS had been successful getting an agent inside Meisner Industries, but that agent had so far been unable to uncover the purpose of the read-heads. Meisner's security was too tight. The MSS had another approach. Chinese scientists had previously developed a micro-meter sized component that could be controlled remotely and surreptitiously. The Chinese scientists were working on similar components that could be integrated into any electronic part. Integrated with the read-heads, they would be able to capture data. These micro-components were not only able to transmit data passing through the read-heads, they could also hijack the data and alter it on the fly from a remote-control location not far from the device. That meant they could impact the operation of the read-heads. The design of the prototype hyperspectral read-head manufactured by Xiazhen Mfg. in Shenzhen contained one of these micro-components. The current version of the MSS altered design of Li's read-heads had the ability to eavesdrop, but not yet to influence the operation itself. That was still being tested by MSS engineers. Knowing how aggressive Meisner was in producing products for his customers, MSS placed a high priority on completing the development of the upgraded device. On the manufacture of the final version, the MSS expected to modify Meisner's design, adding their enhanced microscopic component so they could actually influence the read-head operation, not just read what it read.

The modification of the read-heads was one of the MSS operations. Until the MSS learned the purpose of these read-heads, it remained an important but relatively low priority project. Meisner's plan was much more devious than the MSS realized. Because of the way Meisner partitioned work, even their inside source did not discover how the system would be used. Neither was the MSS able to get a copy of the software, which was key to Meisner's design.

The MSS was not aware of Meisner's intended use for the hyperspectral read-heads. Li was not aware that the MSS was modifying the design and production of components Li ordered from Xiazhen Mfg. in Shenzhen. Li was not even suspicious, although he should have been. The MSS was unaware Meisner was using someone to sniff out the source of a leak, a leak

Meisner thought came from Kyle's team, a leak that could expose their espionage.

~ Joe Tells Kyle about Lab 3 ~

Team leader, Joe Walker, stopped by Kyle's cubicle to inform him the new read-head prototype in Lab 3 was ready for Kyle's testing.

"Knock, knock," Joe said as he walked up to Kyle's cubicle. He did not want to startle him. "You have a minute, Kyle?"

Kyle swiveled around in his chair to face Joe. "You want to sit?" Kyle offered Joe a seat.

"Not necessary," Joe answered. "This won't take but a moment. I heard from Mr. Meisner, and he informed me that the latest prototype hyperspectral read-head was being installed in the machine in Lab 3. Richard told me it would be ready to test tomorrow. He would like to get a report by the end of the week. Think you can do that?"

"I don't know if I can get it to work flawlessly, but I can sure get some preliminary information. Am I supposed to report this to Meisner?"

"No, keep me posted and write up your report. Give it to me, and I will make sure it is in the form Meisner likes. I will get it to him," Joe responded. That suited Kyle. He had other directions from Meisner related to leaks that still needed lots of work. Kyle wondered if he should include something in the report that would determine whether Joe was the source of the leak in the office. Kyle could not figure out how to accomplish that since Joe would be passing his report along to Richard.

"Okay. I will get right on it. I think my software is in good shape if the prototype meets its technical specifications. If my report needs modifying, will you let me see what you have done to it? That will help me get reports in better form next time."

"Sure. It is not all that complicated, but I will show you what I do to your report, that is if it needs anything done to it at all. As I said, not that complicated."

Joe let Kyle know Lab 3 was ready the next morning. Kyle quickly finished and saved the work he had been doing before going to Lab 3. He realized he did not know if the lab was locked and if his badge would open it. When he tried to open the door, it would not open. He went back to the team room and reported his problem to Joe. Joe picked up the phone and called security. They answered promptly.

"Good afternoon to you too. Hey, Meisner asked that Kyle Tredly work in Lab 3, but his badge won't open the door." Kyle could only hear Joe's end of the conversation as Kyle listened to silence. "Meisner, the boss," another silence. "Yes, he tried it," another silence while Joe listened to security personnel. "No, this is not my request, Mr. Meisner asked me." Brief wait. "Yesterday." Another pause for security to talk to Joe. Joe looked at Kyle with a frustrated look on his face and raised one hand in the air, palm up as if to say, "Can you believe this?"

Joe continued on the phone, "I did not call you yesterday because we did not know yesterday that Kyle's card does not work. Mine works, but you know I am not supposed to open the lab so someone else can use it!" Then Joe lowered the phone to his chest and turned to Kyle. "I am on hold now. Sometimes security is a bitch to deal with."

Kyle wondered if it was just sometimes. So far, as it concerned Kyle, it was every time. Joe put the phone back to his ear. It seemed like ten minutes but probably was less than three. "Yes, I am still here," Joe said, meaning, "Of course I am still here, you idiot." But you would never say such a thing to security. You don't mess with that group. After another brief silence, Joe answered, "Ten minutes? That will work. Thank you," and he hung up the phone.

"Got that, Kyle? Ten minutes he said, but I would allow thirty. Security is always optimistic about how long something will take when they are supposed to do something FOR you. They expect you to jump when they want something FROM you. I guess that is the nature of their work. They can be tough to work with when they need to look at your code to declare it secure. I suppose that is understandable since they don't deal with code all the time. To tell the truth, I don't know if they have enough expertise to know if the code works like it should or not."

It suddenly occurred to Kyle that if security reviewed code, they could be a source of leaks. That would complicate things. In fact, it sent an involuntary shiver up Kyle's back.

Kyle thanked Joe and returned to his desk, checked the clock, and mentally noted when thirty minutes would be up, and he could try Lab 3. Since that would fall during his lunch break, he decided to take lunch now and go to Lab 3 after lunch.

~ The Read-Head Test ~

After lunch, Kyle tested his badge on the Lab 3 door. It opened. Kyle stepped in and looked around the room. There were all kinds of test equipment in the place and a computer he could use to test the software. The techs had already connected the machine to the computer, and he could see the cables between the two. He would have to port his software to the computer in the lab to run his tests. He wondered what the preferred method was. Should he try to connect to the team's software development server, or should he bring a thumb drive over? First, he checked to see if he could log in to the computer in the lab. He couldn't. Now, he would have to call security himself.

Kyle went back to his team's room and looked for Joe. He had not returned from lunch yet, so Kyle knocked on Dennis's cubicle.

"Hey, Dennis. I have a problem. Wonder if you know how I connect my software module to the computer in Lab 3 so I can test the device in there?"

"Above my pay grade, Kyle. I have never had to use a lab before. You will have to ask Joe. Oh yeah, I think Jeneen used the labs once, maybe she would know."

"Thanks anyway. Sorry I bothered you," Kyle offered.

"No problem, guy, anytime," Dennis answered.

Kyle checked to see if Jeneen was at her desk. She was, so he asked her the same question. Her reaction puzzled Kyle. At first, she looked alarmed. Then she looked around to see if there was anyone else with Kyle. Then she blushed and told Kyle she did not know how to access Lab 3. She had never been in Lab 3. However, she had been in Lab 2 next to it. She was blushing because she had entered Lab 2 without permission. At Meisner Industries, exploring various places in the building was not encouraged. Kyle checked Josh's cubicle, but he was not there. He gave up and decided to wait for Joe to return. He left a note for Joe.

When Joe returned and read the note, he came over to Kyle's cubicle and told him how to access his software module in Lab 3. With that, Kyle followed up and ran tests. He was pleased to have his code execute without error. This did not provide much information. His code reported hyperspectral data from the new read-head, but it was mostly static. He noticed an unopened ream of multi-colored paper in the lab that he could use to calibrate the read-head with his code. He spent the rest of the afternoon running various tests adding a data matrix to his code to compensate for small deviations between values for the same color paper. He managed to adjust the test equipment and his code, so there was minimal deviation from expected results.

It was 6:00 PM before he knew it. He felt he had run all the tests he could. The only thing left was to write up a report for Meisner. He could do that in the morning from his notes and code changes. The peculiar situation in the testing was a background radio-spectrum signal from the machine in which the hyperspectral read-head device was installed. It was present only when the machine was on. It was steady and did not vary when he applied different parameters to the read-head code, so he assumed it was coming from the machine rather than the read-head. Perhaps a malfunctioning transformer in the host machine. It did not occur to him the anomaly was coming from the read-head itself. As a result, Kyle ignored it.

The next morning, when he finished his write up, he took it to Joe. The report did not mention the RF noise anomaly. He needed to do more testing before he could track it down. Joe looked it over and found it thorough, so he took it up to Mr. Meisner's office without modification. Meisner's administrative assistant offered to give it to Mr. Meisner, but Joe declined, said he was to deliver this report personally. She offered to call him as soon as Mr. Meisner was available. Joe had returned to his desk when she called him back up to Meisner's office. He delivered it directly into Meisner's hands.

~ Meisner Calls Laura ~

Meisner let Joe know he would read the report after lunch. When Meisner read the report from Kyle, he was impressed with its thoroughness. He sent a note to Joe with a simple "Thank You." Joe would know what it was for. Although he counted on Joe as the team leader, Meisner still had to be careful. Fortunately, the leaks were minor so far. Meisner was concerned they could become serious if he did not figure out where they were coming from. If they did, he might have to make a more thorough investigation. He hated the idea his good working environment could turn bad. He also had in mind having Kyle visit several Meisner Industry sites, to see with fresh eyes how things were going. He had a strange trusting view of Kyle.

Everyone on the software team knew Kyle was testing in Lab 3. Meisner hoped Kyle was not providing too many details to the rest of his team. Only Joe knew what Kyle was doing and had read the report. Perhaps, if these leaked about the tests, only Joe or Kyle could be to blame. But the leaks began before Kyle joined the company. He was certain it was not Kyle. He needed a way to communicate with Kyle directly without drawing attention to his secret task hunting for the leak. He could not regularly invite him to dinner. Eventually, that might be discovered. He called Laura on a line that bypassed security, one he had set up, unaware the FBI was also listening on Laura's end.

"Someone special calling me?" Laura answered the vibrating phone.

"Laura, how is the hunt going?" Meisner said without any other introduction.

Laura responded, "I have only had one meeting with Kyle so far. You sent me on an errand, remember?"

"Yeah, yeah, I know. I want to push this thing along. With the package you brought me, I need to get things moving, and I can't let someone leak this. It is essential to have a resolution to the leak."

"Hear you, boss. I will get on it right away." Laura answered, annoyed. Meisner could push alright. Sometimes she wished she were on a different FBI assignment.

"Give me an update by next Monday," Richard said and hung up, not waiting for an answer.

How annoying. Laura resolved to set up a meeting with Kyle again this week. She sent him an encrypted text message. "Need to meet. Tonight?"

Kyle got the message and answered, encrypted, "Okay, Your place? 8:00 PM?" He was pretty sure security could not decode encrypted text messages. However, the encrypted messages did raise red flags and reports to Meisner. When Meisner saw it, he realized it was probably Laura's fault. He would talk to her next time they communicated. He did not want security to throw him a curve by exposing the work he had for Laura and Kyle. He told security they should alert Kyle that this amounted to a security breach. He figured Kyle and Laura would need to work out a different way to communicate. Security let Kyle know violations are reported to Meisner, and any future such communications could result in possible disciplinary actions. It shook Kyle up a bit, and he resolved not to communicate this way and to ask Laura when he saw her, not to text him unless it was an absolute emergency. Better if she just called Richard.

~ Laura and Kyle meet ~

Kyle and Laura met at her place. As he entered the apartment, he smelled something baking. Laura was putting the frosting on a German Chocolate cake, one of his favorites. He noticed she had placed a couple of cake plates on the counter.

"You remembered!" Kyle said, and his mouth began to water in anticipation. "I suppose you want something in return?"

"Of course. I am a practiced slayer of men-giants," Laura announced with a mischievous smile.

"So, you think of me as a man-giant?"

"Well, yes, but I don't plan on *slaying* you—you idiot."

"Good. If so, you better not text me or call me at work if I am supposed to be doing undercover work for you and Meisner. Security called me on the carpet for receiving and sending encrypted messages."

"I know. Richard was on my case to hurry up. Sorry," Laura opined and finished with the frosting. "Done! Are you ready for a piece?"

"Or two or three," Kyle hinted.

"Tell you what. I will cut you an extra-large piece and a piece to take home. Will that work?"

"What is the plan for the evening?"

"We need to make plans. Based on your encounter with Meisner security, we also need a way you can safely report results. I have some ideas we can evaluate. After all, you will be the one doing the surveillance," Laura continued, "We need a way to signal each other that does not involve Richard's supervision. I was wondering about a drop at the newsstand next to the bus stop. Every evening as you leave, you could check the bulletin board, and you and I could exchange notes there."

"How would that work? Wouldn't anybody be able to pick up one of the notes?" Kyle wondered.

"Here is my idea," Laura laid it out. "I will make a small 'Apartment for Rent' sign with a nonworking phone number on it. The phone number will have a four-digit extension. The first two digits will be the day of the month we should meet. The second two will be the time in twenty-four-hour notation. For example, to meet on the twelfth of the month at 7:00 PM, the four-digit extension would be x1219. If the extension is x3200, it means no meeting is scheduled.

If you need me, draw a heart on the sign, and I will know you got the message and agree to the date and time. If you can't meet at the suggested date and time, put an X through the heart. If you place an arrow through the heart, I will know you need to meet, and I will put up a new sign with a suggested date and time. Got it?"

"Okay, so long as you don't happen to use a real phone number. Somebody might get multiple calls and be suspicious. What did you want to meet about tonight?" asked Kyle as he got a mouthful of cake.

"Have you made any progress with the team. I mean, got any ideas yet about how the leaks are happening?"

"No, haven't had a chance. Richard has had me working on the prototype read-head. Oh—is it okay for me to discuss these things with you?" Kyle suddenly realized he and Laura had never had a conversation about security protocol as it applied to them. He turned to look at her more intently.

"It's fine, Kyle. You can consider me as secure as Richard himself," She lied. Not only was her apartment bugged by the FBI, but she also had to make reports about meetings related to Meisner Industries. Even though Laura was a well-trained FBI agent and lied many times before, for her work, she did not like to lie to Kyle. She hoped Kyle was never asked to do something illegal for Richard. She had to protect her cover because she had a separate FBI based agenda tracking Richard. Getting information from Kyle was an important part of her assignment. She had to be careful, asking Kyle about Richard. She was expected to keep her FBI relationship secret. Yet, Laura felt protective of Kyle. She took notice of a familiar feeling, a conflict between her work and her—she was not sure what to call it. She realized she never got over her affection for Kyle. She guessed that was not abnormal, but she did not want to hurt him again. Her FBI boss in Dallas told her she had to cut her relationship with Kyle off. Her objections were overruled. She came out of her momentary daze as Kyle was talking.

"I thought so," Kyle said, "but I needed to ask to be sure. I would hate to get you in trouble with Richard, especially over a security breach. I like the fact we get to work together. Are you okay doing this?"

"Kyle, you know full well I don't do anything I am not okay doing. Right?

"Right!" Kyle responded assuredly.

Laura let Kyle know he needed to be quick and efficient in his search for the leak. Then for the rest of the evening, the conversation sounded more like a date than a strategy session. Kyle's hopes were encouraged, and Laura's affection for Kyle was stoked. Kyle needed to socialize with his workmates and know more about their ambitions, personal values, and family relations. This was not a natural thing for Kyle, but he promised to do his best. Turned out, he was not that bad at it.

~ Kyle's Night with the Team ~

It was only three days after meeting with Laura that Joe dropped by Kyle's cubicle and informed him that the team was planning on having drinks together at Red Robin over on Grand. They planned to meet around 5:30 PM. Kyle said he would love to go with them.

Kyle walked over and got there around 5:35. The rest of the team was already there and had reserved a place for him at a large round table. It was noisy, so Kyle had a hard time keeping up with the conversations. Jeneen was talking about her trip last month to Hawaii with her significant other, Roja. Kyle had seen Roja's picture on her desk, a handsome guy, dark complexion and hair, and good build. He was in shorts, shirtless, obviously taken at the Oregon coast. Could he have connections in Hawaii sharing information gleaned from Jeneen? Jeneen did not mention her mother. Joe had told Kyle Jeneen's mother did not have long to live. She had cancer. It struck Kyle strange that Jeneen would leave her mother and take a trip to Hawaii. But who was he to judge? After all, he had skipped out on his family once.

Joe was complaining about diaper duty at his house. His baby girl, Sara, was only three months old. His wife worked, but Kyle did not know what she did or where she worked. He ventured a question.

"So, Joe, diaper duty? We all need a little shit in our lives to give us perspective. I assume your wife also does duty."

Joe jumped on that, "Of course. She works from 4:00 PM till midnight, so mostly my duty is in the evenings. She does hers in the daytime. A neighbor takes over until I get home. Even the neighbor gets diaper duty sometimes if I am lucky." he said with a silly smile."

"What kind of job works 4:00 PM till midnight?" Kyle probed for more information.

"She works for a telecommunications company tracking international calls. It is a combination of accounting and bill collecting and supervision of international call volumes. She claims she loves it, and by the good humor she seems to maintain, I believe her. Not my cup of tea."

Kyle involuntarily raised one eyebrow, and he stored the fact Joe's wife had access to international communications.

Jeneen observed, "Those hours seem awkward, Joe. When do the two of you ever have time together, if you know what I mean?"

Amused, Kyle noted that everyone else at the table was keenly attentive to Joe now. They had probably wondered that themselves.

"Pardon me, Jeneen, but morning sex is the best kind. We communicate well in the mornings, not every morning, of course. Fortunately, Tabi sleeps until 8:30 AM. Tabi takes a nap in the afternoon so Jill gets to rest then too. I get to play with Tabi in the evenings until she goes to bed around 8:30 PM.

"What?" Jeneen teased, "You don't think I know about sex? I get my share of inspiration in the evenings," Dennis gave her a "there she goes exasperated look again."

Don't look so shocked, Dennis," Jeneen interjects as she elbows him.

"Dammit Jeneen, why do you always pick on me? You think I don't know all about your kind of hanky-panky. I get my share. Plenty!" Dennis defended himself.

"Ah, of course, I forgot about hanky-panky," Jeneen continues to tease him. "And how often do you have to pay for it?"

"That's enough, Jeneen!" Joe reprimands. "Why do you always have it in for Dennis? What did he ever do to you? Don't answer. Kyle, you will get your turn to be roasted by Jeneen before long. It's all in fun, you know." Although, from Kyle's observation, he was not too sure.

Kyle responded, "Can't wait." After a brief pause when everyone at the table was silent, he added, "I see I need to be prepared for repartee to survive this group."

Kyle learned that Dennis was cohabiting with someone named Jill Haung, but not what she did. Josh was married to a life coach who worked from home via phone mostly with occasional trips around the country to make presentations to help workgroups survive working together. Kyle would have to learn more about all these suspicious significant others, more about their ambitions, values, and relationships. Kyle wondered how he might get to know his team better. He needed to engage with them one to one rather than in a social setting. He would see if Laura could give him any advice in this area.

Chapter 7

~ New Read-Head Ready ~

K & W Mfg. in Taiwan received the final specifications for a hyperspectral read-head from Laura McLaughlin on her last visit to Li's company in Taipei. Li's mechanical and electrical engineers had been busy transforming the specifications into a producible product. It had been a month of careful work, and the design was ready to send to Xiazhen in Shenzhen. The MMS had a spy in Li's engineering department making adjustments to drafts to enable mainland engineers to place their modifications surreptitiously on the read-heads. Mainland engineer's tasks were to re-engineer the specifications in a way that Li's team would not detect, and include the transceiver into the circuit to enable them to control its function. This was no easy task. Li, who was confident of his engineer's abilities, sent the specifications to Xiazhen once the engineers released them. Li did not inspect the specifications. It had been several years since he personally reviewed the work of his engineers.

The MSS intercepted the specifications so they could be modified. The delay in delivery was not that unusual as bureaucracy in China was notorious. Earlier, Li had told Meisner that he could not meet the deadlines, so he had a comfortable cushion time-wise. The MSS worked quickly and delivered the modified specs to Xiazhen without anyone being aware of anything other than the standard surveillance that manufacturing requests from Taiwan typically received. It was only a month from the time Li sent the specs until a prototype was received for testing. The testing was successful, so Li sent Meisner a wire that said, "Ready when you are. Li."

Meisner asked Charla, his assistant, to arrange a dinner meeting with Laura. It turned out that Laura had gone to Honolulu to deal with a timeshare client. Charla sent her a text that Richard wanted to have dinner with her as soon as possible. Laura agreed to meet Richard in three days. When they met, Richard asked her to go back to Taiwan to fetch the updated prototype from K & W Mfg. in Taipei. Laura was able to arrange the trip for Monday, the following week. Before she went, she would need to check in with her boss in the FBI. Her boss told her that the CIA believed the MSS was interested in Li and the work he was doing for Meisner.

"Laura, thanks for coming in on such short notice," Laura's boss, Kameron Wilson, greeted her.

"Good to see you too, Kam. How's Vera?"

"She is doing fine. Her Knee surgery went well, and the physical therapy seems to be working well too."

"Good to hear. What's up?" Laura asked.

"We got a lead from the CIA that Tao Li has become a person of interest to the MSS. He has been using a manufacturing plant in Shenzhen. Were you aware?"

"No! Does Meisner know this?" Laura asked.

"How am I supposed to know? That's why you are working for him. The CIA does not want Li or Meisner tipped off about the MSS or CIA or FBI involvement. I trust you, Laura, but I want you to be very careful what you say to either Li or Meisner."

"And I assume this includes Tredly as well?" Laura inquired.

"I would think that was obvious, Laura. You are to tell no one. However, if you learn that Meisner or Tredly know about the parts being made in the Peoples Republic, please alert me ASAP. By the way, how do you get along with the CIA handler in Taipei? Are you getting any information from him?"

"He is as tight as a snare drum. He won't answer any questions. He only wants information from me. I try to avoid answering him, though. The CIA seems to have me watched. He shows up looking for information every time I hit the hotel. You knew the reason for the delay on my last trip from Taipei, didn't you?"

"You mean the CIA getting a chance to look at the device in Honolulu? Yes, they were good about letting us know. They did not share much information, however. I think they view us as their lackeys. Just be sure you keep me in the loop if they try to pull anything over on you."

"Of course! Listen, I have to go. Meisner is expecting me to do another pick up for him. I have to make arrangements with the timeshare business to cover for this trip. I just got back yesterday. We done?"

"Sure. Keep the reports coming, as usual. I appreciate your work on this. How's the relationship with Tredly going?"

"What are you getting at? I am keeping things professional. I don't think he has a clue about the FBI's involvement. I believe he thinks I am Richard's girlfriend."

"Be careful to keep it professional, okay?"

"No problem here," Laura said, although it was a problem since she still cared for Kyle.

Laura left the FBI office and went to the timeshare office to make arrangements to cover her trip to Taipei. She managed to get a flight arranged to Honolulu Monday with connections to Taipei.

~ Laura and Kyle Confab ~

Laura rushed over to the newsstand to post a new message. It proposed Kyle meet her that evening at 9:00 PM. She would have to check to see if he got the message after he got off work, which she hoped would not be too late. When she did check, she found his little heart, indicating he had read the message. She stopped by the Quick Mart and picked up some beer, a pie crust, chocolate pudding mix, and a can of Reddi Wip whipped cream. Tonight, she did not have time to bake, but she could make a quick cold chocolate pie. Kyle arrived promptly at 9:00 PM.

"Hello, Mr. Tredly," she greeted him at the door.

"And hello to you, Ms. McLaughlin. No cookies or pie tonight? The air is devoid of the wonderful fragrance of home-cooked goodies."

"No time tonight. And anyway, don't expect goodies every time we meet."

"Why not?"

"Just because. Listen, I have to go back to Hawaii again Monday. It might take a few days. One of my timeshare arrangements is in trouble," Laura did everything she could to keep from wincing because she was lying to Kyle again. Fortunately, she had been trained about how facial expressions could give one away. In Kyle's case, it was a problem because she cared for him. Otherwise, she would not feel so guilty. *I am a professional;* her thoughts continued. *It's necessary. If I ever get past this job at Meisner Industries, hopefully, I can confess and, more importantly, be forgiven. Sometimes I hate the FBI work as necessary as I know it is.*

Kyle broke her reflections, "Just kidding, Laura. If you wanted an update, I don't have much to report yet. I have had only one opportunity for social time. Looks like lots of possibilities with spouses, but for now, they are things that need to be followed up on."

"Maybe I could help. Maybe ..."

Kyle interrupted her, "How? The minute you showed up, the team would turn quiet. They are not going to say much in front of the boss's girlfriend."

"I don't mean help that way. I know somebody who does detective work on the side. She has a lot more experience looking into people's private lives than you and I do. Maybe she could get us leads to help figure out who to concentrate on. What do you think?"

"Hmm," Kyle mumbled as he *thought, Detective, huh. I wish George were here.* Kyle continued, "We could use help. Hey, did you have her look into my background too?"

"Of course not," Laura lied. The FBI had done a background check on Kyle in Houston when they arranged for Laura to meet him. Laura wished there was a way she would not jump so fast into a lie, at least where Kyle was involved. She needed to talk to an agent friend to get advice. "I already know about you. Remember, you told me all your dirty secrets back in Houston?"

Kyle remembered how helpful George Lockit, a private investigator in St. Andrews had been when he was in trouble. *I wonder how George is doing,* he thought. He and George had only communicated a few times since he left St. Andrews.

As Kyle was musing over historical events, Laura said, "Well?"

Kyle snapped back to reality, "Well, let's give it a try. Can't hurt. I suggest you start with Angela, Joe's wife, and Roja,

Jeneen's significant-other. I am still working on getting more info about Josh and Dennis. Dennis, however, seems high strung. At least Jeneen seems to have his button. She teases, and he doesn't like it."

"Okay, I will add him to the list for now. Meanwhile, you need to push to get more social time. Maybe you could initiate a get-together at a local pub. Look into it, and I will get back to you when I return. I will see if my detective has any information," Laura responded, winding up this part of their conversation. Then she turned the conversation to the good times they shared in Houston, confusing Kyle.

"Laura, is there a chance we might meet socially? Or are you Meisner's official escort?"

"I could take offense at that, Kyle. I am not an escort, period! I help Meisner when he needs someone to keep other women from making passes at him in social settings or other propositions. He may be a master business owner, but socially, he is awkward. I don't love him; I don't sleep with him. I run errands, and okay, I guess escort is a good word as long as you are not referring to those businesses called escort services. I am his escort for certain social occasions. We are not a thing. I told you he is gay and wants to keep people guessing about that, so don't you dare suggest I am an 'escort' to anyone. Okay?"

"Okay, okay, I get it. But you did not answer my question. Is there a chance we might get back to where we left off in Houston someday?" Kyle said, shyly.

"We'll see." was all Laura would say.

We'll see? That is what his mother used to say, which usually meant "no."

To appease him, Laura served him a piece of chocolate pie and boxed up another he could take home. When they finished, Kyle left, feeling a bit more pressure on his special task for Meisner. He was not sure he was going to be successful. He was sorry he got into this secret assignment. He hoped Laura would be able to get information from her detective friend that would help. After all, she too needed to please Meisner.

Laura closed the door with very mixed emotions herself, conflicts with work, Meisner, and her slowly returning affection for Kyle. And she was living a lie with him like she did in Houston. Laura realized it did not bother her in the least to be lying to Richard, just Kyle. She wondered how it would all develop. She had an excellent resource for help, the FBI, but she could not tell Kyle who her special FBI detective friend was.

~ Baker, Lockit & Rogers ~

Baker, Lockit & Rogers was a legal partnership in St. Andrews, Texas. Kyle had worked for AHS, Andrews Health System before he moved to Houston. Baker and Lockit had been instrumental in exposing criminal efforts to frame Kyle for the murder of two women. Mobsters had kidnapped Kyle contributing to his arrest and incarceration for the murders. Kyle owed Baker and Lockit his freedom and possibly his life. They were friends he could count on in the most challenging circumstances. It occurred to Kyle they might help him in what seemed to be his dilemma at Meisner Industries. He liked his job and the people he worked with. He did not like keeping secrets, especially ones that seemed likely to alienate him from his co-workers. Calling St. Andrews was complicated with the surveillance from Meisner's security team. He had to purchase a long-distance card and call from a phone booth. He called the office in St. Andrews.

"Baker, Lockit and Rogers, how may I help you?" the receptionist answered the phone.

"Hi, this is Kyle Tredly. I was wondering if Walter is in?"

"One moment, I will see if he is available. You said your name is Tredly, correct?"

"Yes, Kyle Tredly. We are acquainted."

The phone clicked and began playing soothing easy-listening music. It did not last long. Walter picked up almost immediately.

"Kyle, how in the world are you? Are you still in Houston? I watched the media coverage. What a disaster. How did you fare?

"Hello, Walter. I am doing fine. I lost my job as a result of the storm. Now I am situated in Portland, Oregon working for a private company, Meisner Industries. It's a long story. I will give you the short version. Essentially, Softtek almost went bankrupt. Their business was flooded, and I got caught in the layoff. But I have a good-paying job now, in Portland."

"Good to hear. I would like to catch up on the details sometime. To what am I due the honor of your call today?"

"Walter, I am calling from a phone booth with limited time. I don't think I am in any personal danger, but I need help with a problem here in Portland. Do you think Lockit has time to do research for me?"

"Wow, phone booth? It sounds like more trouble than you are letting on. You are not concerned about being arrested, are you?"

"No, this is not at all the kind of problem I had in St. Andrews."

"You say you need Lockit? I think George can make time for you, buddy. I'll ask. Can you tell me what it is about?"

"Sure, but I have another idea. What if I correspond in email. I could provide the details, and you would not have to take notes over the phone."

"That would work fine. I would appreciate that. Do you have our email address here at the firm?"

"I do. I will be in touch in the next few days. If you don't hear from me within the next couple of weeks, I hope you will investigate. I am just kidding. I do not expect to be kidnapped again or even exposed to the same kind of shenanigans I experienced in St. Andrews. But it is vital this all be kept in the strictest confidence."

"That I can assure you, Kyle. I will be looking forward to hearing more about your needs."

"Great, I will be in contact in a day or two," Kyle concluded.

Kyle had a plan to communicate outside the surveillance of Mcisncr Industries. He would establish an alternative email address and utilize computers at the library to communicate with Walter and George. To be safe, he would turn off his cell phone in case security was also tracking his whereabouts. He would use a cryptic email name and a private virtual network application that kept the communications mostly encrypted.

Later in the week, he went to the library and outlined his needs to Walter and George.

Walter & George:

I work for Meisner Industries. Before my first interview, Richard Meisner, sole proprietor of the privately held company, met me in a secret meeting, letting me know that if I was hired, he had a special task for me. My former girlfriend from Houston, much to my surprise and delight, I might add, was in the same meeting. At a later meeting, Meisner and Laura McLaughlin asked me to help uncover a leak of company secrets, presumed to come from the team I was assigned to work with. Since then, he has left it to Laura and me to investigate. I must say this is not my strong suit. Laura offered to have a detective friend of hers do investigation for me, and that reminded me of the life-saving work you two did for me in St. Andrews.

I don't like having this secret task, but need to figure out how to proceed without getting fired. Do you think you could be of help so far from Portland? I am using a public library computer to ensure this conversation is not subject to my employer's supervision. Please don't call me. My phone and computer and emails are surveilled by virtue of my security contract with Meisner Industries. It could be a couple of days or more before I get another chance to check-in.

Kyle

Kyle was able to check back in on Saturday. (It occurred to him that someone at Meisner's could use the same library technique to leak confidential information which would be hard to track.) He got this response:

Kyle:

I hope you understand that George and I owe you a lot. If it weren't for the publicity your case drew here in St. Andrews, we would not be in such high demand at unreasonable fees. So, consider yourself at our disposal, pro bono, or more correctly at the expense of many well-paying clients. George did a preliminary look into Meisner Industries. He thinks your caution is well-founded. I won't go into the details here, but we can discuss it at your convenience. A couple of questions: Are you ever able to get away, take a trip, and possibly come to St. Andrews or some other site away from Portland? And, would you be okay with George coming to Portland for part of his investigation? Let me know, and we can get into more details later.

Walter

Kyle responded.

Walter:

I realize this method of communication has its limitations. However, I am not due any vacation time for at least six months, so coming to St. Andrews is out of the question. I am not sure about George coming to Portland. Not sure how necessary that would be, but I have no objections. I can get a day off here and there or a few hours every once and a while. Saturdays and Sundays are open. There is one complication. I have occasional meetings with Laura, usually on short notice, and I can call for a meeting with her anytime I have news or questions. If George does come up, please give me plenty of notice, so I can arrange my affairs to make it worth his time.

Kyle

Kyle and Walter continued to communicate this way and arranged for George to come to Portland in a month. Laura was back from Honolulu, but her rental posting notice had not changed; therefore, no meeting with Laura. Kyle decided to follow up on Laura's suggestion, and try to get the team together after work.

~ Kyle's Social Calendar ~

Kyle made arrangements for the team to get together again at the Red Robin on Grand after work on a Wednesday afternoon when everyone was available. Kyle was much more attentive to everybody's background and associations outside of work. The leaks could be coming from staff or their significant-others. Although he expected a typical social time, everyone was curious why he arranged it on Wednesday instead of their usual Friday. Awkwardly, Kyle shared that he was somewhat shy until he got to know people well, and he thought it was interfering with his work as a good team member. There were a couple of eye-rolling looks Kyle did not see, but everyone accepted his explanation. Here are facts he learned about the team members.

- Dennis Anderson was the most recent addition to the team other than Kyle. He was single living with his girlfriend in the Pearl District. Dennis claimed to be five foot eleven and three-quarters or six feet in shoes. Dennis had curly blond hair that he let grow to shoulder length. He was much more muscular than Kyle. Dennis lifted weights twice a week at a station in his basement on NE Mallory street. He liked to bike to work, weather permitting. It was early October, so the rains would be limiting his rides. He was adopted when he was five years old by a well to do family, an Asian couple in Westchester County, New York. His dad worked for IBM, and his mother worked at a travel agency specializing in trips to Taiwan and China. His mother had made numerous trips to China. Dennis graduated with a degree in electrical engineering, specializing in computers, from Polytechnic Institute of New York in Brooklin. He worked in New York City on Wall Street, a job his dad had arranged for him. Wall Street did not suit Dennis, so when his girlfriend moved to Portland for a job with Nike, he moved too and immediately got a job at Meisner Industries. They planned to get married. Her family wanted to help with the wedding arrangements. The problem was they were in Taiwan and wanted Jill to wait till they could arrange affairs to be in the states. Dennis was a lot of fun, liked to play practical jokes. One time, when Kyle tried to answer his phone, he couldn't because the phone handle had been taped with transparent tape to the base station. On another occasion, when he sat in his chair after he had gone to the restroom, Kyle realized he was sitting on a tack. Since the tack fortuitously matched the crack in his rear end, he could feel it but it did not puncture him. Kyle decided to ignore it and see who showed the most curiosity. Finally, Dennis came around and was outed. To get even, when Dennis stood up to talk over the partition to Jeneen, Kyle put water on the hollow form of Dennis's chair seat. He was a good sport when he sat in it.

- Josh Smythe was an Oregon native, lived in Portland all his life, and attended Oregon State University in Corvallis, Oregon. Although he said he liked to travel, he had, in effect, not done a lot until recently. Two years ago, he took a trip to London and Paris with his wife, Kaylin, whom he had met in Corvallis in a calculus class. Kaylin was studying environmental engineering. They were married when Josh was a senior, and Kaylin was a junior. They lived in off-campus housing. They both went on to earn graduate degrees, Josh in electrical engineering specializing in computer systems. Kaylin specialized in water quality issues and had a job with Intel on a team to ensure the water quality of their chip manufacturing processes. Their working hours did not match well. Kaylin worked an evening shift, Josh the day shift with his team at Meisner's. Josh was a contrast to Dennis, quite a bit shorter with a ruddy complexion and jet black thick hair that he kept cut collar length, long in the front, so he had to brush his hair to the sides continually. He was not bad looking, but not handsome, either. His eyebrows were thick and bushy, eyes deep-set, nose thin and small, very white straight teeth and thin lips. He had a generally pleasant no-nonsense disposition. Occasionally, he was arrogant, saying things like, "That's not the way I learned it in graduate school," implying with the tone of his voice that he was more educated than the rest of the team. Kyle could not discern any elements that put him in the bullseye for the person who leaked unless his arrogance might make him vulnerable to flattery and inadvertently telling secrets. Of course, what he and his wife shared in bed could theoretically make it to Intel.

- Jeneen Jenkins was the most difficult to get information on. She was quiet at work. It was a different story after a few drinks. Additionally, she had to leave early, she said, because of her ill mother. Jeneen was hired shortly before Dennis as a program tester. She said she was hired to break things, and chuckled. Her grandparents were from Vietnam. Her grandfather had been a prominent general in the South Vietnamese Army. Her grandfather and grandmother were expatriated and granted U.S. citizenship at the close of the war. Her mother was sequestered in the family compound in Saigon during the Vietnamese war. Her mother was eighteen when the family emigrated. Her mother met her husband, George Jenkins, in Lufkin, Texas. George died a few years later from a heart attack. Her mother currently has pancreatic cancer and is in hospice in Portland. The medical bills and other care for her mother have taken a financial and emotional toll on Jeneen. Kyle thought it could be possible that Jeneen had been compromised due to the financial and other stress taking care of her mother. He would have to explore this in more detail.

- Joe Walker was the designated lead for the team. Joe had graduated from Stanford University with degrees in mathematics and computer security specialties. He had graduated with honors, had been active in campus activities. His advanced degree was in Mathematics. His master's thesis was in topology. Kyle assumed Joe earned the most of anybody on the team, and judging by Kyle's salary, expected it to be a substantial sum. He also seemed to be invested in his family, especially the baby, Sara, and her mother, Tabi. He shared about his family on the slightest invitation, as little as a "So, Joe, how are things with you?" Jill, Dennis's girlfriend, left Nike to take a position with a local telecom company. Even as a supervisor, she could still work from home. So, even though Angela might have links to other competitors of Meisner Industries, it did not seem logical she and Joe would be the source of the leak. Joe was a handsome guy, a well-built six foot two, lean, square-jawed fellow. He had a pleasant disposition, leading the team. He was not like a boss of his fellow workers. He had a great sense of humor, seldom at the expense of others. He was collaborative, sought ideas from all the team, not withholding any specialized inside knowledge. He encouraged and inspired everyone on the team to do their best work, and was free with acknowledgments for work well done. He seemed quite satisfied, always with a positive outlook. Kyle judged him least likely to be the source of the leak. However, he did not feel he was in the best position to determine who was sneaking information to competitors.

Kyle made notes after he got home from the get-together so he would not forget any details when he consulted with Laura before Meisner requested an update.

Chapter 8

After Kyle's get-together at Red Robin, he began to ruminate over the fact that he had become embroiled in intrigue, secrets, and questions about who he could trust. Memories of his experience in St. Andrews, of being kidnapped, thrown in jail, and in general, not knowing what the hell was going on made him gun-shy about this new role. Laura had been someone he thought he might spend his life with. That is what he thought when they were together in Houston. He completely understood when she left to take care of her mother in Dallas. He thought that might be temporary. He was blindsided by her "Dear John" letter. She did not call. She did not give him a chance to ask questions, to understand what had happened, to know if it was something he said or did. Furthermore, now that she was all friendly again, her explanations did not seem satisfactory. Could he trust her? These thoughts kept coming up at unexpected times—often.

This was complicated because, despite how she had treated him in Texas, he still had feelings for her. There was something about her lively spirit. She had an attentive way of looking at him when he was talking that was disarming. She acted as though she liked him in a way that held out promise their relationship might rekindle. At the same time, there was a distance between them that he could not put his finger on. Hell, she had a spell over him, so he trudged on.

Kyle checked the newsstand to see if Laura had changed the rental tear-off they used to signal each other. Kyle put an arrow through the heart he drew, the sign for Laura that he wanted to meet. He did not know whether she was in town, so all he could do was check the newsstand each evening to see if they were supposed to meet that night. A day passed before he got the signal that they could meet that evening at 6:00 PM. He hoped she was planning on food. He stopped off and got a bottle of wine to take with him.

Kyle was prompt as usual. Laura buzzed him in. She was dressed casually, and he could smell the fragrance of an Italian meal. Kyle wasted no time checking out the stove. Eggplant parmigiana was nearly done, so he grabbed a couple of wine glasses from the cupboard and the corkscrew from the drawer beside the fridge. He poured generous glasses of Merlot for each of them, a good match for dinner.

After giving Kyle a peck on the cheek, she asked, "To what do I owe the pleasure of your company this evening? Work or play?"

Kyle was taken back by the peck and the suggestion he wanted to meet for "play." "Did I hear you correctly, ma'am? Did you say work or play? I was not aware I could request time to play?"

"Kyle, sometimes you are an old fuddy-duddy. As I recall it, you have lots of play in you. Are you getting all shy on me now? Don't answer that!" Kyle smiled at her comment. "We can do both. What's up?" she said.

"I need to debrief my meeting with the team. Your thoughts and suggestions on what I could do next would be helpful. If and when Richard wants an update from either one of us, we should be on the same page. I suspect it will likely be you since you have easy access. I am concerned my meetings with him can raise issues with my team. Although I am gathering more information, I doubt I know more than Richard. After all, he has a security team. What are they doing? What can I do that they can't? I need your advice."

Laura and Kyle took a break from their discussion long enough to dish up dinner and sit down to eat. Then Laura invited Kyle to tell her what he had learned, and they discussed each person on the team. Laura pointed out that Kyle had not learned anything definitive, but assured him that getting to know people better was useful. Laura's detective friend had not learned anything yet, either. Laura suggested they might create some fake information to give to one of the team members. She offered to meet with Richard and accumulate ideas so they could spring a credible trap.

After dinner and the table had been cleared, Laura suggested they relax. Kyle decided he needed to deal with trust issues. "Laura, I have concerns about what is going on?"

Laura bristled. "What do you mean? What do you think is going on?" Laura was caught in her web of deceit. She was compromised by her affection for Kyle and her duty as a competent undercover FBI agent, something she could not tell Kyle. She was concerned Kyle was wise to her multiple roles.

"I have thought this through and think it comes down to issues of trust and secrets." Kyle asserted.

Laura flinched, hoping Kyle did not notice. Yes, she did have secrets from Kyle, and she already felt guilty. *Does Kyle suspect my FBI role? Have I failed to keep that secret?*

Frustrating as it was, her only option now was to lie, to try to cover and distract. "Kyle, I have to be honest with you. I screwed up in Texas. When I moved to Dallas to take care of my mom, I fully expected to be tied down there for years, and you did not deserve a girlfriend with weights around her ankles about to jump off a pier into a lake. Shit, that was a terrible metaphor. I thought I was doing you a favor to write that letter, and by the time my mom had passed away, I figured you were on to some other wonderful woman that you fully deserved. I would understand if you hated me, and if you never spoke to me again. But you and I are involved in figuring out who is leaking information for Meisner Industries, and our current well-being depends on our figuring this out."

"Ugh, Laura, it was not for you to decide what was best for me. You hid. I could not find you. What was all that about?"

"What can I say. I made a stupid mistake; an apology is plain lame. I don't know what I was thinking? It was a confusing time with my mother. I am here now. That is the best apology I can make. Are we okay? Can you forgive me and help move past our history?"

Kyle did not say anything. Yes, it had been hard to take, but she was here now, working with him, being affectionate, or at least very nice. But the relationship seemed to be tangled up with Meisner Industries. He wondered what she was up to and if she liked him or just indulged him to please Richard. After a long pause, Kyle continued, "Trust is one thing, but all these secrets and intrigue. I don't know why I am the appointed one to find the leak. Why doesn't Richard make use of his security team? Doesn't he trust his people? I get that leaks can damage his competitive position, but why me?"

"Kyle, I guess you can blame me for that."

"Why?"

"When Richard believed he had leaks, at first he was beside himself. Based on what he pays for security, there should not be leaks at all. He was becoming distrustful of his staff. It was not more than a week later when your resume showed up, and he mentioned your name and relationship to Softtek. Kyle, I know you, I know you well. I know your history. You are a better person than I am. You are an honest person, solid with integrity. I suggested to Richard that you might be able to help, and since I knew you—sorry, I shared about our relationship in Houston—anyway, it was my idea you could be trusted and that between the two of us, we might be able to figure this out. Arg—more secrets, huh?

"Laura, I want to believe you, trust you. It's just that—I don't know how to explain it. I think it comes in part from my experience in St. Andrews. I may be damaged goods. Before that, and before you dumped me, I was a trusting person, but all these secrets, I have to keep facing my co-workers every day while trying to rat one of them out. That is not me. I think it makes me mistrust people when I might not otherwise." Kyle wondered, for example, who the detective friend was that Laura was consulting. But it would be disingenuous for him to ask, given he was secretly talking to George Lockit.

"I know, Kyle," as Laura put her hand on his. "I promise I won't desert you again. I need you. I want to get us back together. I want to be trusted, especially by you. You are the kind of person I want to have in my life."

Part of what she said was genuine. Kyle could feel it. He could not resist her charm despite his anxiety. He turned his hand over and held on to hers. He leaned over, and as he did, she leaned in too. Their minds may have told them one thing, but their lips had other ideas. He felt an involuntary sensation in his groin. His other brain had taken over as he put his arm around her, they embraced on the couch. She pressed herself against him, pleased to finally once again be experiencing his warm, loving embrace. *The hell with trust. The hell with secrets.*

This is the true experience of life, oneness with another human being. My work with the FBI is just a game I play.

They kissed a couple more times, but Kyle had the good sense not to let things get out of control, and it seemed to him that Laura had the same reservation and resolve. In this way, they could savor the experience, this memory, as a promise of a deeper future relationship.

~ Conversation with Jeneen ~

The events of the previous evening energized Kyle. He and Laura seemed to be back on track despite the nagging voice in the back of his mind. Trust was no longer a pressing issue, just a quiet whisper. Secrets could be dealt with as long as Laura was supporting him. Kyle needed to get back to the jobs at hand, testing and writing the code for the new read-head and seeing what he could learn about each of his team. He and Laura were working on two tracks. He would make more efforts to learn about each person on the team. Laura would see if Richard Meisner would agree to plant something that they could trace to one of the team when it was leaked. She would also follow up again with her unnamed detective friend. The way they planned on providing the information depended on each person's particular talents and interests. Kyle was to see if he could discover any unusual habits or likes his teammates had. He began with Jeneen, going over to her cubicle.

"Hi," Kyle said so as not to startle her. "Mind if we chat for a moment? I need a break from the code I am working on. Do you mind?"

Jeneen turned around and invited him to talk by pulling out the extra chair in her cubicle. "No problem. I need a break too, no pun intended."

"You must really like breaking the code we write. I can hear you yell 'Ya Hoo' every once and awhile."

"Kyle, if I was never able to find any bugs, what would be the point of my job? What would be the point of testing the code? If I find a few bugs, it is job security. By the way, do you ever put bugs in your code to test me?"

"Good idea, Jeneen. Here's the problem with that idea. You might get credit for finding the bugs, but I might get demerits for causing them. Anyway, I make enough mistakes as it is."

"You are not the worst by a long shot. I would not want to cite any initials, but Josh Smythe would get the award for most bugs per hundred lines of code on our team."

"Jeneen, the other night, I did not get to talk to you very much. The guys seemed to like to talk, and you had to leave early. I know you are dealing with your mother's cancer. How do you manage to keep up with work and your mom's needs? Oh, that was a poor way to put it. Try this; How are you dealing with your mother's cancer?"

"It seems that it is harder for other people to talk about it than for me. It is sad to see the life drain out of my mother and not be able to stop it. I get that we all have to die, but the reality is hard. My mom suffers a lot, but she never complains, at least not to me. There is a neighbor who looks in on her and spends time with her when I am at work. That is a huge relief to me. I know I can count on her to keep me posted. Mom feels free to complain about her pain to Nora."

"Do you ever get a day off from caregiving?"

"No, not really. Well, I do get out to do the shopping, and I have an occasional coffee when I am out and about."

"I thought you said you and Roja went to Hawaii last month."

"Yeah. Mom insisted I go. She was adamant. I can't deal with Mom when she gets something in her mind that I should do. She would not let it go no matter how much I insisted, so I gave in and worried about her the whole trip. Roja was sympathetic, but he could tell my mind was elsewhere. It turned out okay, though. Mom pumped me for details when I got back. I think it gave her a boost to hear about MY trip."

"Ever meet with anyone other than home and work folk?"

"I know what you are getting at. I don't have time for any dating if that is what you mean. I like Roja, but I don't have time for him either. He comes over, and we all watch a movie. Mom wants me to go out, but I can't deal with the guilt. She needs me."

"I wasn't trying to hit on you or see if you would go on a date. That is not what I was thinking," Kyle said.

Indeed, that is not what Kyle was thinking. He was trying to find out if Jeneen had any connections outside of work besides Roja that could be the source of company leaks.

Jeneen continued, "Sorry, that is not what I was thinking either. Roja is all I can deal with except for friends that I occasionally can have coffee or lunch with."

"Would I know them? Probably not since I have not been in town that long."

"One of them is strange. Her name is Phyllis. I am not sure if she wants to ask for a date or not. It seems like every time I do decide to have a cup of coffee, Phyllis is there at the Starbucks too and invites me over. Mostly, she wants to talk about work, has lots of complaints, and wants to know how I am getting along with my mom. Friendly, but strange. Sometimes I think Phyllis is following me to end up at the same coffee shop at the same time as me."

"That does seem odd. Is Phyllis hitting on you, suggesting things that make you uncomfortable? I could go with you and observe if you think that would help," Kyle suggested.

"I don't think that is necessary. She says she works for Intel, and wants to compare work environments. Phyllis asks questions about what it's like to work for Meisner Industries. I think she read that from my badge."

"Does she press with questions about your work at Meisner's?"

Jeneen unconsciously straightens her skirt and nervously looks at the clock. "I should get back to work. I have a bit of a backlog on my testing."

"Okay." Kyle answered, "I have more code and testing to do on the read-head." He flushed, realizing he needed to be careful not to divulge any secrets about his testing of the read-heads. Hard to work in a place where you could not trust your fellow workers. He could not afford to take any more time to chat with other team members today, or it would look suspicious. He was not used to navigating what now felt like undercover work. It occurred to Kyle that Jeneen got to see all the code his team wrote, and to debug it, she had to understand how it worked. However, she did not necessarily know what he was doing in Lab 3.

~ Library Visit ~

When Kyle got off work, he decided to go to the library to see if there was news from St. Andrews. As he was leaving, he checked the newsstand to see if there were signals from Laura. There were none. However, as he was looking on the bulletin board, the newsstand salesperson was watching him.

"You come around here almost every evening, but you never buy anything, just check the bulletin board. What are you looking for?" the salesperson asked Kyle.

"You talking to me?"

"You see anyone else around? Yes, man, you. What are you looking for on that board? I notice that you write on one of the postings every once in a while. Could you tell me what is going on? Are you a drug dealer or something?"

Kyle was taken off guard. He had to think of something fast. He also had to warn Laura that their scheme was in danger of exposing their ruse. "Ugh, I am checking to see if any new apartment listings are posted. To save time, I put a little heart in the corner of one to make sure I don't waste time looking it up again. And, if I were a drug dealer, you think I would tell you?"

"Maybe yes, maybe no. Maybe I am in the market."

"Well, you are out of luck. I don't deal or do drugs."

"Well, there is this good-looking woman that comes in and keeps putting up new postings—the one with the tear-off phone numbers on it. The one you keep looking at. Every once and awhile, someone comes back and complains that the phone number doesn't work. Like I can fix that. I told the lady once. She said she would correct it, but I don't think she wants any clients. The new number is phony too. Have you ever tried one of those?"

"No. Maybe I should take one now and see what I get. I will let you know." He had to think fast, "Do you have a copy of the Spokane Spokesman newspaper?" Kyle was pretty sure that was safe to ask for.

"No," the salesperson answered, "I don't get many, or I should say any requests for that here. You could check at Barnes and Noble. They carry lots of newspapers."

"Thanks, and thanks for the info on the postings. Maybe I am wasting my time checking in every day. I hope you don't mind."

"Hell, I don't mind. At least you are not one of the beggars that try to camp out in here. They try to hide out in the stacks like I did not notice them, or they try to pinch a candy bar."

"Yea, wish we could do something about the homeless situation. I will take a look at the library for the paper." The reference reminded Kyle of his interaction with the woman with the baby a few days ago. *Yes, we should be doing something about the homeless, but what? Maybe I should buy something for once.*

Kyle bought a candy bar and told the clerk to keep the change. He left and headed to the library wondering if the signal scheme he and Laura had devised would continue to work now that the salesperson had outed him and Laura. They might have to change the location, although that would not be as convenient to him.

~ Richard Meisner ~

Richard Meisner was the grandson of Phillip K. Meisner of Cantrell Inc., the distributor of medical equipment used throughout the world. Phillip had seen the potential of specialized medical equipment early in the twentieth century and gained exclusive contracts making him virtually a monopoly in the distribution. Richard's father had set up a hedge fund and made lots of money in the stock market. He died prematurely at the age of 58, leaving substantial funds to Richard. Richard was a senior at Stanford when his dad passed away. It was at Stanford that he met and became good friends with Li Tao. Both Richard and Li were studying mechanical engineering. Richard continued his studies, earning an MBA. Having inherited substantial wealth, he went to work on Wall Street like his father. Unfortunately, he lacked his father's intuitive skill about the markets, and after losing almost a third of his inheritance, left to start his own company on the West Coast.

Richard had the opportunity to purchase a small firm in Portland doing software development. He renamed it Meisner Industries. His talent in running a business was in contrast to his work on Wall Street. Under his creative leadership, Meisner Industries diversified into a general manufacturing company with several product lines, each with embedded software. It was not long before Richard was a well-known and regarded fixture on the Portland as well as Oregon scene. He had no ambition to run for office, but he supported many people for political positions earning him significant influence in Oregon's political circles. While he supported candidates from both parties, his leanings were more toward libertarians. The less regulation and tax on his business, the better he liked it. Richard failed to appreciate how the structure of the courts protected the integrity of well-negotiated contracts and corporate secrets. He was successful in helping support a friendly climate for businesses, especially his own.

Li Tao was from Taiwan and returned to the island after graduating. He, like Richard, was blessed with inherited wealth in the form of K & W Manufacturing. To resolve the debt that he inherited with the company, he sold partial minor partnership to a friend in Taiwan. Richard found it useful to utilize Li's company for the components needed for products manufactured by Meisner Industries. The arrangement proved beneficial for both companies. Contracts were easy to establish based on the personal trust between Richard and Li.

Richard's appearance was an asset to his influence and success. At six foot two, he towered over many. His blue eyes and blond hair contributed to a lean, sharp, and penetrating presence. At over two hundred pounds, clean-shaven, and devoid of significant body hair, he always appeared clean— almost shiny. In public, he wore a black or gray Brooks Brothers suit, white or blue shirt, red or yellow tie, and highly polished black shoes. He liked the appearance of success. Richard did not have to think every day what he was going to wear that day, unlike most of the women he surrounded himself with, particularly Laura McLaughlin. Having women friends helped him hide his gay leanings. Society circles considered him one of the most eligible bachelors in Portland, maybe even the state. While the title suited him, he tired of the constant attention single women gave him. Having Laura escort him to public events helped keep other women at arm's length.

His development of Meisner Industries was proof of his ambition. In a few years, he had grown the business from grossing a million to over fifty million annually. As a private company, he did not have to deal with an obstreperous board of directors. It gave him a great deal of freedom and the ability to hide his private ambitions. Although he did not seek political office, he did have the desire and ability to influence or control whatever he could in the area of regulations and laws that would hamper his business. He sought influence in politics. He liked having politicians owe him for their success. It was always a matter of a subtle war, taking control of all aspects of his success. Many people counted Richard as a friend. Richard only pretended to reciprocate. His relationships were more transactional.

Richard did not allow anyone to get close enough to see his dark side; his desire to influence local, state, and even national politics. He had shared this desire with no one except U.S. Senator Corning. He had no intimate friends or lovers who might discover his secret intentions other than Corning.

Richard considered a leak of information as a critical weak link for Meisner Industries, and by default, to him. For this reason, he was using Laura McLaughlin and Kyle Tredly to ferret out the source of a presumed leak. At least he made Laura and Kyle believe that was his true intention. His real concern was having his hidden intentions uncovered. He wanted to control the potential damage learning his true goal could cause him. He was paying Laura handsomely for her dual role of pseudo girlfriend, secret sleuth, and manipulator of Kyle. As long as he could keep Kyle searching for the leak, inside or outside Kyle's team, he felt he would be able to keep tabs on his true goal. Although successful, Richard was aware of the stakes of his ambition and sought to control everything. He slept well at night, unfazed by his naked ambition.

~ Communicating with Lockit ~

Kyle purchased a long-distance phone card to call St. Andrew's from a payphone and not be subject to Meisner Industries surveillance systems. He was unsure whether Meisner's security could listen to him even if his personal, registered cell phone was off. So, he developed a habit of leaving his cell phone on his desk at work, even when he went to lunch or out for an errand. That gave him cover to prevent tracking his trips during lunch. Concerned there was no easy way for George Lockit to communicate with him; he decided to purchase a "burner" phone to receive text messages hidden from Meisner security. His privacy was compromised. He was nervous about taking on more secret activities. He hoped the awkward feeling would diminish or go away with time. He did not like feeling queasy.

One day at lunch, instead of eating, he visited a small, out of the way, one clerk, hole-in-the-wall phone shop on the West side of the river.

"Can I help you?' the clerk asked.

"Yes, I need a, uh, what do you call it, a burner phone."

"Tell me more, and I am sure I can accommodate you."

"I am a bit paranoid about my boss, who tracks my cell phone. I need to make a call to an old friend, but I don't want anyone to track the call or listen in."

"I am required to ask you, is this—Is it for legitimate business or perhaps personal business?"

"Personal business. I could tell you more details about why I needed privacy, but I prefer not having to share my personal business."

"No sweat. I have to keep track of how many phones I sell, so the count of phones matches the money in the till. I have several varieties here. What kind do you want?"

"The cheapest."

"This is the cheapest," the clerk shows Kyle a flip-open model he pulled out of the case. "I can sell you this one, but I would not recommend it, and there are no guarantees, no money back."

"Why?"

"Do you mean why no money back, or why I don't recommend it?" the clerk asked.

Kyle said, "Why don't you recommend it?"

"You probably are thinking it is about money, huh? But it's not. This one has a cheap battery, and people have complained they can't even complete a thirty-minute conversation without plugging it in. It can't use the latest apps, so typing a text message is all but impossible. But if you think this is what you want, say so, and it's yours."

"Okay, that won't work. I need one that I can carry around, turned off, but available. I need to be able to send texts as well as receive them. I need to use it unplugged without it turning itself off in the middle of a conversation."

"Here is the most common one people buy, and I never, well rarely, have any complaints," the clerk showed Kyle a different slim, flat model. "This one is an android phone. It has a larger battery, will last longer on each full charge."

"How much longer will the battery last on a charge?"

"Well, that depends on how you use it. Generally, you can count on more than a couple of hours of continuous conversation. If you keep it off and use it for text only, the charge could last for a week, depending, of course, on the number of texts and how often you turn it on and off."

"That will do," Kyle said, and purchased the better phone with cash, no ID required. He did have to provide information on a form the clerk gave him. The clerk fixed Kyle up with a phone number and put the SIM card in the phone for him. He still had time to grab a bite at a Chinese food cart before heading back to work.

The next day at lunch Kyle used his long-distance phone card to give George a call at Baker, Lockit, and Rogers. The receptionist put him right through.

"Hello?" George answered.

"Hi, George. This is Kyle calling."

"The receptionist told me. Glad you called. Before I tell you my news, tell me how things are going?"

"Okay, at least I think so. But things are weird here."

"I figured with all the intrigue around these phone calls. You are not in trouble, are you?"

"No—No, that is not the issue I need help with," Kyle responded. "I wanted to tell you that I got a cell phone, you know, a burner type phone. I figured it would be easier to communicate than hunting down a working public phone where I could talk privately. There is a hitch, even with that."

"Good thinking, Kyle. What's the hitch?"

"I have to keep the phone turned off to avoid surveillance. Long story I had to register my own phone with work so they could track its use. I don't know the capability of their security. I don't want them aware we are communicating. Meisner seems obsessive about leaks."

"Keep it in a metal case if you want to be sure."

"I don't think that is necessary. I will keep the phone at home, turned off. When I need to use it, I can go to a coffee shop down the block from my apartment. Hey, here is my burner phone number. If it is convenient, we can exchange text messages tonight to make sure things are working."

"Good idea. I have news for you. It looks like I can get away to visit you next month around the 20th. I have a week off, and

Rachel can't get off because she has exams to grade. Will that work for you? Can you get any time off?" George inquired.

"How about I answer that this evening. I can double-check about the time off. Also, we can check out how my new phone works at the same time."

"Sounds like a plan. I will wait for your call. Remember, I am two hours behind you, so don't make it too late."

"Okay. I will call you about nine o'clock your time."

They hung up, and Kyle headed back to the office.

~ Paper Test ~

When Kyle got back to the office, there was a note on his desk from Joe. Kyle was supposed to calibrate the read-heads on a stack of paper delivered during lunch and left in the lab. Kyle shot Joe a note he would get right on it.

When he got to the lab, he found a stack of twenty packages of paper. Each package had about 50 sheets in it. The stacks were labeled with numbers beginning with 100149 ending with 100168. There was a typed form that he was to use to evaluate the paper providing information about each batch. He was supposed to run one batch at a time, record the stats, showing the average, maximum, minimum, and statistical deviation of the readings plus the software and hardware settings for the read-head. If the variance was too large, he was to adjust the settings for the read-head, rerun the batch, and record the new statistics. He was to make a note of the lowest deviation using a highlighter. Of course, if necessary, correct any problems in his code and start over, and rerun every batch.

Kyle did a mental calculation and estimated that the minimum time it would take to run all 20 batches would be a couple of hours. If many adjustments would be needed, it could take a few days. After twenty minutes of setting up all the parameters on the machine, Kyle began to run batch 100149 through the machine. It took a couple of minutes to sample all fifty pages in a batch, and then manually record the required data. After he ran the first batch, he looked at the detailed data that his code generated. The deviation was out of bounds. He explored his code for any calculation errors. He adjusted the read-head parameters and reran the test. Still problems. Finally, he took the read-head out of the machine, cleaned it, and replaced it. This time the batch ran as it should. Once he had recorded the data on the sheets as expected, he loaded 10050 and ran the test. The deviation measure was okay, but the average was significantly different than the first batch. To make sure, he removed the read-head, cleaned it. He reran batch 10050. It produced virtually identical results for each page, and the overall average remained precisely the same. The machine was detecting a difference in the batches. He pulled a sheet out of the first batch and compared it with paper from the second batch. There was no visible difference that he could detect, even under a bright light. There was an ultraviolet light across the room. He looked at the sheets under the UV light. There was no difference he could see. There was something different about the two sheets that only the hyperspectral read-head could detect. Kyle decided to pull one sheet out of every batch recording its code number in the lower-left corner. He could use these extra sheets later for calibration.

Kyle continued to run the batches. On batch 10063, the data was out of range again. He removed the read-head again and cleaned it. That did the trick, and he completed the remaining batches without a hitch. To make sure things were copacetic, he ran all the batches again, recording the results. He gathered all the paper records and wrote a cover memo of the process he had used. Then he scanned everything into a file on his computer. He sent the results to the team's shared file system.

Chapter 9

~ Phone Test ~

Kyle made it home a few minutes before seven PM. He grabbed his burner phone and headed to Caldera Public House; a nearby pub. Fortunately, there was a booth available for immediate seating. He ordered a pale ale and a cheeseburger. He called George.

"Hello?" George answered the phone.

"Hi! I guess the phone works. Curious, what did your display show?"

"Unavailable Number."

"Good. I have been stressed calling you from a phone booth. I never asked how you and Rachel are doing?"

"We are both doing fine. We seem to be too busy to have problems. I end up doing night work. When I do, Rachel takes the opportunity to work late at the school office and catch up on her work. It seems to me they overwork her, but she enjoys her work and students. The administration, on the other hand, challenges her patience. She dislikes the way first-year teachers are given the most difficult classes to teach. She says if medicine were organized like the education system, brain surgeons would be made hospital administrators, and interns would be doing the surgery. There is so much pressure, especially for men, to get out of the classroom and become administrators. So, no complaints, George said with considerable irony. But, more to the point of your phone calls, what is going on?"

"George, I hope nothing is going on, but I am involved in secret work-related tasks. I am uncomfortable and feel like I am dishonest every time I talk to my colleagues. I can give you a lot of detail when you come up, but here it is in brief.

My boss and my ex-girlfriend from Houston have asked me to secretly discover who in my work team is leaking information to our competitors. I am falling for my ex again, and am concerned because she seems so close to the boss. I sense that my work is not about a leak, but something I am not being told. I hope you can help me determine how to approach this without losing my job and my integrity. Of course, I can give you a lot more detail when we sit down together."

George was silent, thinking. "Hmm, please text me information about your boss and ex-girlfriend. I need whatever you can give me, name, address, phone number, approximate age. If they have lived someplace else, that could be helpful."

"Sure, I can do that. What are you going to do?"

"Well, a background check and research to see what I can learn about them. Okay?

"Sure. But please be careful. I don't want anybody to know you are involved. At least not yet. I don't know the reach of Meisner's security team," Kyle said with anxiety. "Meisner is wealthy, and I don't know what he could buy if you know what I mean."

"Don't worry. I have done this before. Have you forgotten my work here in St. Andrews?"

"No, well, maybe yes. That was a while ago. Listen, send me a text if you need anything more. I will check it every couple of days."

"Great. Until we chat again."

"Yes, bye," Kyle said and turned off the phone, finished his burger and beer, and headed back to his apartment. When he opened the door, his work cell phone was ringing. He answered it.

"Hello," Kyle said, frowning with concern. Who could be calling him from work?

"Kyle, hi. This is Laura. Just checking in. I tried to call you earlier, but there was no answer."

"I leave my work phone at home when I step out of the apartment," Kyle immediately was sorry he said that when he knew his phone was surveilled by Meisner security, "Why did you call?" Kyle was nervous because he knew Meisner Security could track this conversation. He hoped Laura did not try to arrange a meeting. He did not know if security was alarmed because Laura had contacted him or because the text was encrypted. He would be careful in this conversation. After all, he did not know who could be listening in.

"I was wondering how the test went today."

"What? What test?"

"Kyle, Kyle, Kyle. You should know I have eyes and ears everyplace."

"That's scary. Do you listen in to my phone calls too?" Kyle answered, a little irritated. He thought he had resolved the trust and secrets issue with Laura. Now she pulls this, what should he call it? Shit, that's what.

"Kyle, you didn't know that Meisner sends me daily updates on your team? I am supposed to be helping you. How am I going to help if I don't know what is going on daily?"

"Oh. You never told me you were also spying on me. What other secrets are you not telling me about?" Kyle could feel his face flush. He needed to control his attitude, especially on this phone. "Sorry, it was a hard day. What exactly did you want to know?"

"Well, all that I got was you were assigned a paper test. I was concerned that maybe Meisner was testing all of you with a psychological survey, or something like that. He is getting anxious. He wants me to report on our progress and texts me frequently.

"Frequently? How frequent is frequently?"

"Oh, I don't keep count. Maybe once or twice a week. Not every week, though."

"Hmm—so what was the question?"

"The test."

"It was not a written test; it was a test of samples of various batches of paper. I used the new hyperspectral read-head to measure its sensitivity to various papers. I was tied up most of the afternoon with it," Kyle explained.

"That's a relief. So, how did the tests go?"

"You're telling me you get briefs but not details? How does that help?" Kyle tried to divert Laura from her questioning. It did not work.

"Kyle, you can skip answering my questions if you want. I was concerned. I thought Richard was doing a strange testing thing and wanted to know more. Believe it or not, I was concerned when you did not answer your phone."

Kyle caved in and accepted that maybe her call was innocent after all. If she was concerned about him, that was interesting. He explained the test but not the details of the results. He did not tell her about the variation in the samples. He reasoned it was not important to share, at least not yet, since it was not detectable with ultraviolet, infrared, or the naked eye, only the reader. Laura either had no idea what was going on or was an excellent liar. He preferred to think she was honest. He still harbored the idea that they could resume their romantic relationship. Of course, he did not say that. They talked for most of a half-hour when Kyle finally gave in to his fatigue from the day's work and tension and excused himself amicably.

~ Team Meeting ~

Joe called a team meeting. Kyle suspected a message had come down from Richard Meisner. Everyone except Jeneen, the runner, settled in with coffee or soda and a pastry from the snack bar. Jeneen brought water and an energy bar. Instead of leading the meeting, Joe turned the meeting over to Jeneen.

"Glad you all could come. I am wondering if I can recruit any of you for Hood to Coast." Jeneen began. Everyone mumbled before she could continue. "One of our support team's wives is seriously ill, and he needs to attend to matters at home."

"Who was that? Do we know him?" Josh asked.

"I don't think you know him. He works in Wilsonville."

Josh persisted with a grin on his face, "Oh, so his name is secret?"

Jeneen's face expressed chagrin as she answered, "Jordy McCallister. Do you know him?"

Josh visually shrunk down in his chair, "No," but not to be deterred, asked anyway, "and what, pray tell, does the team in Wilsonville do?"

Jeneen took a deep breath and sighed. This was not the point of the meeting. Joe and Dennis rolled their eyes, almost in unison. Josh did not even notice. "The Wilsonville team manufactures and sells ballot paper. You know, the special paper used to record people's votes that will run through

Meisner ballot-counting machines. I think Jordy told me once there were twenty people on their team. Now Josh, can I continue?"

Josh nodded, sheepishly satisfied with her answer. Jeneen restated her question. Could she recruit anyone? After the exchange with Josh, Kyle, hesitating to enter the conversation, tentatively held up his hand. He liked to run, had run marathons. He might not be in the best shape at the moment, but he could get in shape quickly. He needed more information.

"Great, looks like we have a volunteer!"

"Wait, Wait!" Kyle exclaimed, "I had a question, I was not volunteering. I can't say I am in all that great of shape at the moment. I need more information before I can commit."

"He glanced over to see if Joe was rolling his eyes. He wasn't."

"Alright, what's your question?" Jeneen asked.

"I know about Hood to Coast Relay, but I don't think I am in good enough shape to run, at least not this year."

"Ah, what is needed is not a runner, but a driver for the van."

"Van?" Kyle asked.

"Oh, I forgot. You don't know how the race works, do you?"

'Well, I know you start at Mount Hood and run in relays."

Janeen continued, "It's a two-hundred-mile course to Seaside on the Coast. Twelve people constitute a team, and each member runs three of the thirty-six legs that vary in distance from three and a half to eight miles. They limit the number of teams to around one thousand, so you have well over 12,000 participants plus the support groups. We use two vans, and one of our drivers is now out of commission." Jeneen was one of the runners. "My team is called MI TEAM, you know, MY Team.' We are all Meisner Industries employees from various work units. We would love to have you join the support group."

"Drive a van? I think I can manage that," Kyle responded. It would be an excellent way to get to know more people working for Meisner. He might also learn more about other Meisner Industries teams.

"You do know how to drive, don't you?" Josh jocularly interjected. He thought it was a reasonable question since everybody knew Kyle did not have a car. Kyle gave Josh a look that said, in effect, *Silly question, Josh. I would not volunteer to drive if I did not know how!* Everyone else ignored Josh or gave him a classic eye roll.

"Great," Jeneen answered. "We can meet later, and I can fill you in on all the details."

"Joe, Josh, and Dennis peeled off to their chores. Kyle stayed around, and Jeneen filled him in on the duties of a driver. Kyle knew he would have to study the route in more detail, maybe even rent a car and trace out the course. Laura owned a car. Perhaps Laura would help him get better oriented to the Oregon Coast. He would also need to learn the specifics of how a runner's relay made use of the vans. Fortunately, he was attentive enough to have already obtained an Oregon driver's license. That had not been trivial given he did not own a car. Laura had loaned him her car.

Kyle looked up Hood to Coast on the internet, but it did not give him the details he would need as a brand-new van driver. The next day, Kyle asked Jeneen if she could get him a list of the team runners and other support people for the relay. In particular, he wanted to talk to the other van driver. The list included the name and contact information of the other van driver, Big Bill Butler. Butler worked for the MI Wilsonville Team. He looked forward to the chance to talk to someone who worked on a different team than his own. It was always possible the alleged leak of Meisner secrets came from a different team.

Kyle did not waste any time getting hold of Bill Butler. He called him as soon as he got back to his desk. Since he wanted two kinds of information, he tried to schedule a time to meet. As it turned out, Bill was relieved to know they had a replacement van driver for Jordy. Bill knew it was a bit complicated the first time he drove to manage the van, so he was happy to schedule a meeting and get to know Kyle. They arranged to meet at a Starbucks at Gladstone and I-205 in two days. That Starbucks was about half-way between Portland's office and the Wilsonville Meisner location.

~ Kyle Meets with Bill Butler ~

Kyle took a taxi to get to Starbucks to meet Bill. They were supposed to meet at 10:00 AM. Kyle managed to arrive ten minutes early. Bill was already there. He told Kyle the traffic from Wilsonville, where he lived, was unpredictable. They spent over thirty minutes learning about each other's backgrounds. The next hour-and-a-half was spent going over the details in the eighty-plus page Hood to Coast manual, which detailed the legs and routes for the runners and vans. There were so many details, it made Kyle nervous, but Bill assured him all the runners were experienced with the relay and could guide him with any questions he had in route. Bill suggested they walk over to a Mexican Restaurant for an early lunch.

Kyle held up his hand as if to say, "One moment." He used his pen to write a note on a napkin. The note said, "I have MI questions. Could we leave our cell phones in your car?" Bill nodded. Bill realized Kyle was concerned about Meisner security. As they walked over to the restaurant, they each dropped their cell phones off in Bill's car.

When they got to the restaurant and had ordered, Bill initiated the conversation with a quizzical look, "What's on your mind, Kyle?"

"Bill, as a relatively new employee, I don't understand why security is so tight at the main office. I never know if the security team is listening to my conversations. I also know very little about Meisner Industries other than the team I am working with and what is on the web. I am curious about a few things. For example, on the Hood to Coast relay, do the runners ever talk about work? Or is security tight as a drum for every team?"

"Somewhat tight, I would say. During the relay, we don't share a whole lot about our work. But most of us don't take our work phones with us. We all feel the security is much more extreme than any place we have worked before."

"Do people from other teams even know what various teams are working on?" Kyle asked.

"Not so much. You willing to share what your team is working on?"

"Good point," Kyle noted. "I am willing to make a trade. Can we share with each other safely, or are you also part of the security system group?"

"No way, Kyle. We work on manufacturing processes for paper that will be used for election ballots. Internally, we call ourselves the Election Team, ET, for short. That gets me razzed during the Hood to Coast relay, by the way," Bill shared, hoping that would demonstrate he was trustworthy. He was also curious about the various Meisner enterprises."

Kyle did not hesitate to take up the challenge. "I don't know the details of what all my team members do. I know Jeneen does the code testing. You know Jeneen, right?"

"Of course," Bill answered immediately. "She has been running Hood to Coast before I got involved. She is an awesome member of the team. How many are on your MI work team?"

"Five, counting me. Joe Walker, Josh Smythe, Dennis Anderson, Jeneen, and me. Joe is the team leader. I work on code to utilize the features of a special hyperspectral read-head. I think it is to be used somehow in machines related to paper ballots. Maybe the ones you are working on?"

Bill had a thoughtful look on his face and did not respond immediately. Kyle allowed the silence to prompt Bill to say more. "Kyle, this seems to relate the work your team is doing and the work of my team. We are working on the chemistry of special invisible coatings that is put on the ballot paper. I assume it is to guard against voter fraud. Although that makes sense to my team, it seems extreme. To protect against counterfeit ballots getting counted, we use different kinds of coatings."

Kyle had a visceral reaction to Bill's information. Perhaps he could get a better idea of what Meisner Industries' intentions were with the hyperspectral read-heads. He queried, "Last week, I ran hyperspectral tests on 20 packages of paper. I believe they were labeled 100149 through 168 or something close to that."

Before Kyle could continue, Bill jumped in, "Hyperspectral? I was wondering how the various coatings could be detected. Those came from us. We have been working on the chemistry of the coatings for over a year. Out of curiosity, can you share what you found?" Bill clearly understood what hyperspectral tests meant.

"Sure. Every packet was distinctive. The range of values for each packet was within one standard deviation, and there was no overlap between all twenty sets. I will confess I was puzzled about what was making the difference, so I cheated and kept a sample sheet from each packet. I saved them to use for reference sheets and keep the read-head at the same calibration level. They will also be helpful if I am sent more packets to test."

"Wow! Meisner hasn't sent us the results yet."

Kyle had a sudden concern. "You won't share this with your team, will you? I can't afford to be the source of a leak. Speaking of leaks," Kyle paused with worry wrinkles furrowing his forehead. "Bill, forget my reference to leaks, okay?"

"Of course. Did you say something about needing to take a leak?" Bill smiled with a wry conspiratorial grin and continued after a brief pause, "I can't remember what you said, but I can see we could benefit from further discussion about ballot paper."

Lunch arrived. Kyle dug in, anxious to compare food here in Portland with the TexMex food he had enjoyed in Houston. The conversation turned to Hood to Coast. After lunch, Kyle retrieved his phone from Bill's car and ordered a taxi back to the office. On the way back, Kyle pondered the conversation with Bill. His thoughts switched back and forth between anxiety about Hood to Coast Relay and what he had learned about ballot paper coatings. He chastised himself for mentioning leaks. He hoped Bill would honor his commitment, not to mention that to anyone. What exactly did Meisner have in mind with the invisible paper coatings? Would his job as van driver enable him to get any more information about Meisner Industries? Furthermore, was there a leak in his team, and what were they leaking that made Meisner so concerned? He needed to talk to Laura.

~ Laura in Taipei ~

Kyle tried to signal Laura for a meeting, but there was no response. Laura was on an unannounced trip. Kyle assumed she was in Hawaii, but she was in Taipei, Taiwan, to meet with Tao Li. She was there to pick up samples from the batch Li was shipping to Meisner.

Laura checked in to the hotel and took a shower before going down to the bar. She had expected to hear from Huang, her CIA contact, but there was no note or message for her. Laura went down to the bar, and the booth she and Huang sat in last time she visited Taipei. No Huang. After a few minutes, a handsome Asian gentleman approached the booth.

"Good Afternoon," he said. He was tall and dressed in dark slacks and a gray-blue sports coat and a white shirt with no tie. His shirt was open, so you could see his hairless chest and gold chain that hung around his neck. "Do you mind if I join you?"

Laura decided to use a polite rejection, "I am sorry," she said. "I am waiting for someone."

"Perhaps I could join you until your guest arrives?"

It was time for a more forthright rejection. "I think not. I did not come here to meet new people. I am expecting an acquaintance to arrive at any moment." That was not a lie. She was expecting to meet Huang. But given he was not already there; she was not sure she should expect him. "I do not need a chaperon in the meantime. Am I making myself clear?"

"I do not think Huang would mind," he said, dropping Huang's name in her lap. That raised lots of questions for her. How did he know who she was waiting for? Was he also CIA? She doubted a CIA agent would be so mysterious. He would have introduced himself at first if he was Huang's substitute. Laura kept a calm and collected look. She did not even flinch at this disclosure. Internally, however, she shuddered. If Huang had sent someone in his place, he would not have played this game. *Who is this guy? What does he want? Where was Huang? How to respond?*

"Who are you talking about? Who is this Hang?" she said, deliberately mispronouncing the name pretending she did not know anyone named Hang.

"I was told you were tough. I request you not make a scene. I am going to sit down now. I am no threat to you. My interests are in Tao Li." He sat down across from her, waved at a waiter, and ordered a Coke. "Would you like another drink? What are you having?" he said to Laura as the waiter did what waiters do, he waited.

"Make mine a Coke too, with ice and a straw," Laura said to the waiter. Her curiosity had been piqued when this stranger mentioned Tao. Her FBI training kicked in. Get all the information from an unknown interruption you can when plans do not develop as expected. The waiter left to retrieve their order.

"Laura, you can call me Sam. I work for Tao Li. After your last visit, Tao discovered that the CIA was investigating him and his son Chao. Before he could reach out, he heard that Huang had been murdered. Aware you had met with Huang; he is naturally interested in your relationship to Huang. Tao is concerned that he might, somehow, be implicated in the murder, so the need to contact you this way. Could you answer a few questions for me?"

Careful Laura, she thought to herself. *You don't know who this guy is and who he represents. He could be from the mainland. He could be Taiwan secret police. You need to get verification that he represents Tao Li.*

"Sammy, you say?" Laura played for time to think.

"Just Sam, Laura," he patiently answered even though he was getting impatient.

Laura noted the fact she had not given "Sam" her name. "Okay, Sam. Here is how it is going to go. I am not talking to you until I can verify your credentials, and only Tao himself can do that. So, this conversation is going to be over before it starts. If Tao authorizes me to talk to you, then we can continue. So, for now, goodbye," Laura said forcefully then stood up to leave. Sam stood up too and grabbed hold of Laura's arm. Startled, Laura said, "So, you don't want to cause a scene?" She jerked her arm away from Sam. Her adrenaline was flowing now. She was ready to take this guy down if it came to that. He did not attempt to touch her again as she strode out, leaving Sam standing there perplexed by his inability to get any information from Laura. She was a tough cookie, alright. His preparation for the meeting was accurate, although unsuccessful.

The next morning Laura was rested. She ordered breakfast in her room, hoping to avoid running into Sam again. When the food was delivered, she did not answer the door. Instead, she asked that they leave the cart by the door. She watched through the peephole until the server retired before she opened the door.

To exercise additional care, she called Tao's plant and talked to the receptionist. She asked that the driver be given the password, ARIZONA. She also asked for the cell phone number of the driver. That would help identify him when he called. However, she did not know if her phone was being tapped by whomever Sam represented and knew phone numbers could be spoofed. She was sure Tao had not sent Sam. Finally, to apply an additional assurance, she texted the driver's number and instructed him that he should not use the password the receptionist had given him and instead use KITE. Laura felt confident she had placed enough roadblocks in the way, that whoever wanted information from her would not react quickly enough to arrange a different driver with the correct phone number and password. Around ten, Tao's driver called her cell phone that he was waiting at the front door. She asked the driver for the password. He responded with the correct one, KITE. Ready, she went down immediately, taking her carry-on bag with her. She did not bother to check out. She could do that online. There was no sign of Sam. On the ride to the factory, Laura checked out of the hotel using her cell phone. She wanted to avoid any additional encounters with Sam. She wondered how to bring up her encounter with Sam. If he was not Tao's man, she did not want to alarm Tao.

Tao warmly greeted Laura. They discussed arrangements for shipment to the U.S. There were two hundred thousand read-heads in the shipment. The ship would leave Taipei in two weeks and arrive in San Francisco in another two and a half weeks. That made arrival at Meisner Industries in Portland within the month. Tao gave Laura a small case with a few samples from the lot. The samples were encased in lead toothpaste tubes like last time. She planned to carry them in her carry-on rather than allowing them to go through checked luggage.

Laura asked Tao if he knew anyone by the name of Sam. She said there was a guy in the bar last night who tried to pick her up. She did not reveal his assertion that he worked for Tao. Tao said he did not know anyone with that name, so Laura dropped the issue. She would have to report this to her FBI boss when she returned to the States. Being a well-trained agent herself, she had managed to surreptitiously get a picture of Sam while he talked to the waiter. Laura was careful not to leave any identifying or compromising items in her carry-on. On the way back, she directed the driver to a different hotel and checked in with false identification. She wanted to avoid Sam at all costs. She flew out early the next morning on her leg to Hawaii. She could check in with the FBI office there and utilize a secure link to post her incident to the office in Portland. She double-checked to make sure the Honolulu FBI office did not recognize Sam's picture. Sam was a mystery man.

The FBI office in Portland passed along the picture of Sam and report of the incident to the CIA. A week later, a CIA contact communicated directly with Laura. They asked Laura to delete the photo from her phone. Under persistent pressure from the FBI, the CIA confirmed that Huang had been murdered under mysterious circumstances. Furthermore, Sam was identified as an agent of the MSS, Ministry of State Security office in Shenzhen, China. They were unaware of why the MSS would be interested in Tao. From Laura's perspective, the number of secrets was getting almost out of hand; Meisner, Tao, and her own lies. She wondered if Kyle also had secrets that he was not sharing with her. That had not occurred to her before this latest incident. She was aware that Kyle was seeking a meeting, so she changed the signal at the newsstand and planned a sumptuous dinner at her apartment.

~ George Lockit Request ~

Kyle needed to check his messages to see if George had tried to contact him, so after work, he took his secret cell phone and went to the pub. George had indeed left a message to call him. It was already 7:00 locally, so 9:00 for George. He called as soon as he had placed his order.

"Hey, Kyle. You got my message. Thanks for calling."

"What's Up?" Kyle was anxious to get to the heart of it.

"What do you know about Tao Li?" George asked.

"Caught me up short, George. Who is that?"

"When I was tracking down information on Meisner, I ran into references to Tao Li. It seems they were good friends in school at Stanford. Tao has a factory in Taipei, Taiwan, manufacturing electronic components. You know anything about that?"

"No. Never heard of him or his factory. However, I know Meisner is getting the hyperspectral read-heads from Taiwan. When I was running tests on the read-head the other day, I had to take one out and clean it. I noticed a small imprint on the board that was marked "K & W Mfg. Taiwan."

Does that mean anything to you?"

George replied, "Ah-Ha! Yes. I think Tao is the CEO of K & W Manufacturing. I wanted to check on this before I wasted a lot of time. I will look into Tao to see if this has anything to do with Meisner and your search for the leak. How are things going for you?"

"Fine, I guess. Well, fine if you ignore a couple of things."

George pressed, "So what things?"

"Well, I volunteered to be a van driver for a relay race here. In the process, I met with another Meisner employee who works in a different office. He too finds the security a bit much."

"Van driver for a relay race? What kind of relay race needs a van driver?"

Kyle spent the next ten minutes, giving George a Hood to Coast relay summery. "In addition, George, I get to meet more than twelve other Meisner employees, many working in other buildings around the area. I think there are even a couple coming up from California to run."

"When is this race?"

"In a couple of weeks. So, I should have a broader view of Meisner Industries before you get here, at least I hope so," Kyle answered.

"You said two things?"

"Yeah. I got to meet Bill Butler. He works with a team located in Wilsonville, a town about twenty miles south of downtown Portland. It was a cool meeting. We left our cell phones in his car at my suggestion and had lunch so I could ask him questions."

"Okay?" George said in a way that encouraged Kyle to continue.

"Glad we can talk. This would be a lot for a text message or email. It seems that his team is the one responsible for the coatings on the ballot paper."

"Hey! Slow down. What do you mean, ballot paper and coatings?"

Kyle realized he had not told George about the paper. He filled George in on the conversation with Bill Butler and the fact that he had been testing paper produced by Bill's team. "George, I find this invisible coating only detectable by a hyperspectral read-head very curious. I have no idea what Meisner has in mind. He leaves us all in the dark about the future use of our work. I guess it's his privilege given he is the sole owner. He certainly seems paranoid about the details leaking out."

"Kyle, I would not put it that way. Because he is the sole owner does not mean he can do anything he wants. Eventually, he has to be accountable if he is up to something illegal. Well, that is if he is caught."

"Illegal? I don't know that is the problem here. He could be super concerned about losing proprietary information to a competitor. That is what he claims concerns him. By the way, are you still planning on coming up next month?"

"Yes, by all means. In the meantime, I will keep digging. I am going to ask our FBI friend if he can shed any light on Tao and Laura for that matter."

"Whoa! Laura? You think I should be concerned about her? Are you trying to break my heart?"

"Slow down, Kyle. If you want my help, I need to check out all angles. You need to know the truth, where ever it leads. Is that understood? No point in my coming, if not."

"Yeah, obviously—the truth. You are right. Wherever the truth leads."

"Good! If I find out anything, before I come up, I will let you know." As it turned out, George found it difficult to get information from the FBI on Tao. But he did get other significant details. He thought it wise to wait until he went to Portland to tell Kyle what he discovered. He mulled over how that was going to work out.

~ Kyle Tests New Version of the Read-Head ~

Joe, team captain, let Kyle know that three read-heads that needed to be tested were in Lab 3. Meisner wanted them tested as soon as possible. Kyle conducted the tests on the same twenty sets of paper products and got virtually identical results. Fortunately, his experiments did not indicate how many sheets were tested in each run, reflecting the fact that he had removed one sheet from each packet. As an extra test, he took the twenty sheets he had taken from each packet last time he tested and ran them through the machine three times with each of the three read-heads installed. He was satisfied that there were minimal non-significant variations between each of the three new heads versus the tests he ran on the original read-head sample. He would continue to keep this set of twenty sheets in case there were further tests to be made. As a final test, he created a twenty-first packet of standard ballot weight copy paper. This would serve as his control of paper with no specialized coatings.

His curiosity was haunting him. After meeting with Bill Butler and learning that the paper was coming from his team's work in Wilsonville, he wanted more information. He began to ask Joe more questions. What were the read-heads to be used for? Why was he testing them on paper? What was to be the product of his team? Joe was circumspect in his answers. He cautioned Kyle about asking too many questions. Kyle found this very disturbing. The secrecy at Meisner now seemed more than a security issue about competitors getting Meisner proprietary information. It appeared to Kyle that something was going on, but what?

Chapter 10

~ Kyle Visits Laura Again ~

Kyle was prompt, reaching Laura's apartment at precisely 6:30. Laura buzzed him in, and he proceeded to her third-floor apartment. Her door was ajar, and he could smell the distinct odor of garlic and curry. His mouth watered involuntarily. Whatever she wanted; it was likely to be merged with a delicious meal. Laura, he had learned, was an excellent cook, something he did not remember from living together in Houston. He also suspected her of using food to loosen up people when she wanted information.

"Where did you learn to cook?" Kyle asked.

"From my mother and a culinary school in Dallas. I always wanted to cook but never had the time until I had to cook for my mom when she was ill. Food had been one of the things that made her illness more tolerable. Once she passed, I decided to take classes."

"I learn something about you every day. What's the occasion today?"

"Kyle, Richard happened to mention he had you testing hyperspectral read-heads. Before I could ask more questions, Richard changed the subject. I thought I could ask you."

Hesitant, Kyle thought of the security restrictions. He had left his phone at work, but he did not know if Laura's house was wired by security or not. "Just a routine test, that's all there is to it."

"So, can you tell me how you do the tests? What do you test them on?" Laura inquired.

"Laura, I wish you wouldn't press me on what I do at work. Even though I know you work with Richard, I am still concerned about the security of the work I do. I know that Richard expects it. The contract I signed expects it. Maybe I should ask Richard if I can share the details with you. I don't know."

"I am sure he would not mind."

"I would prefer to know he would not. Please let me ask him to spell it out."

"No point to that. I should have known you were a strict by-the-rules person. I will talk to Richard myself," Laura responded, and changed the subject. "Sorry, I did not see your request to meet. I had to go to Hawaii unexpectedly."

"What for?" Kyle did not realize he put Laura in a position to lie to him again.

"We had a timeshare unit that got trashed by one of the groups I scheduled. The owners were furious, and they needed someone to harass. I am a good person to yell at, lots of experience." She meant to imply that she deserved to be yelled at by Kyle, but he missed the point. She added more detail to her explanation than was necessary. Although one ought to be suspicious of lots of detail when not required, Kyle did not pick up on her blatant lies.

As they ate, Kyle brought up the problems he was having getting any useful information from his team members. He reviewed what he had learned so far, which was interesting, but not that helpful in discovering the source of the leak. Laura suggested they try something new.

"I was wondering if we could place false information with your highest suspect and see if that gets leaked to a competitor?" Laura suggested.

"Like what?"

"Well, let me think. What rumor could we introduce that someone would need to share? I got it, how about the rumor that Meisner Industries was in negotiation to sell the company to an overseas group?"

"Might work, but wouldn't a rumor like that pass pretty quickly to all the team members. If it were leaked, we would not know which one leaked it, would we? Furthermore, if the press got hold of it, I doubt Richard would be pleased."

"Okay, yes. Do you have any ideas?"

"My team is sharp, but they don't know squat about hyperspectral read-hcads. I could pass along fake capabilities to the team, different ones to different people. Then maybe it would track. What do you think?"

"That sounds great. Like what?"

"Well, I could tell Jeneen that the read-heads could capture data from cell phones that came within three meters of the heads. I could say I was testing them for department store devices to identify shoppers and handle transactions without people having to check out when they left a store. That's one idea.

"I like that. How soon could you do that?"

"I am working the Hood to Coast Relay next week. I could do it on the trip."

"Let's give it a try."

"I don't know. If I can swear Jeneen to secrecy, and she keeps the secret from the other members of the relay group, it might work. But what if she shares it with the whole Hood to Coast team, then where would we be? Of course, if she learns the real facts, I will be toast with her."

"True, but hopefully by then, you can explain why you played this trick on her."

"I suppose." Kyle and Laura discussed possibilities for other team members. None of their ideas held up to scrutiny. It would have taken a month or more to work through the other four team members if that became necessary. As the evening wore on, they had come up with nothing workable. Stymied, Kyle and Laura reminisced about their time in Houston. The spark was still present for both of them, but they knew the importance of keeping the relationship platonic, at least for the present.

"Laura?" Kyle addressed her by name when he was about to ask for something. "Do you think you could drive me along the Hood to Coast route this weekend, or maybe loan me your car? I will be more comfortable if I preview the route once before driving the van

"Of course, Kyle. That sounds like a good idea. I have a suggestion. How about we drive over early Saturday, spend the night and drive back Sunday afternoon?"

Is she suggesting what I hope? "I think that is a good plan? Should I come to your place Saturday?"

"Remember, Kyle; I know where you live. I will come by for you, say 8:00 AM?"

"It's a date!" Kyle said before he had time to think about it. He relaxed when he realized "date" could be taken more than one way.

~ Hood to Coast Practice Run ~

Laura was a prompt person. One minute before 8:00 AM, Laura was outside Kyle's apartment and about to phone when he came out to the car. He would have liked to leave his cell phone at home, but he wanted to track the route on his phone to look at later. He had not told Laura he had a burner phone, so he left that at the apartment. First, they headed to Government Camp at Mount Hood, where the race would begin. When he heard how many people would be running, he wondered how the race managed 12,000 runners and 2,000 vans racing across Northern Oregon. However, he learned they had a decent plan. They let the fastest runners leave first and released a group every fifteen minutes. That way, slower teams seldom overtook the more rapid teams, and the vans spread out too.

Kyle had thought this might be an excellent chance to talk to Laura more about his concerns about finding the leak in his team. Instead, following the directions for the thirty-six legs of the racecourse required their attention. It was not until they finally reached Seaside on the Oregon Coast that Kyle could relax. It looked like this van driver task was not as easy as he assumed when he had eagerly volunteered, and wondered how much information he could learn on the trip. At least, he thought he would get contact information that he might be able to follow up on later.

When they reached Seaside, they looked for The Gilbert Inn Bed and Breakfast. Before they got out of the car, Kyle signaled Laura as he put his cell phone in the glove compartment. Laura got the hint and put her cell in the glove compartment too. Laura had made the arrangements at the inn. They were to share a room. Kyle wondered if that meant what he hoped. After they were checked in and settled in the room, Laura asked, "So Kyle, what was that with the cell phones?"

"I wanted to talk to you privately."

"You can't do that with our cell phones around? I thought you did not want any interruptions during our evening."

Kyle blushed and quickly changed the subject to answer her question. "Laura, surely you are aware of Meisner Security Protocols. They have my cell phone bugged."

Laura frowned, "I guess that is one way of looking at it."

"How else is there to look at it. I can't use my cell phone at work unless it is registered and unblocked from use at work. You don't think security can intercept my calls?"

"Well, yes, at work. They are concerned about leaks."

"You do know that no cell phone will work in the building unless it is unblocked, right?"

Still frowning, Laura paused. Then she responded. "Mine always works in the building. At least I think it does," She tried to remember if she ever used it when she was in the building, "I was not aware if it was ever blocked. I did not register it with security."

"Did Richard have your cell number?"

"Yes, I gave him my number when Richard and I met in Texas."

Kyle was surprised that Laura did not get it. "So, you were unaware of the cell phone security feature in the building? Maybe Richard registered your phone for you."

"I don't know. I am trying to think if I ever used my phone when I was in the office. I don't think I ever did. Maybe it was blocked, and I never knew that. Of course, Richard could have registered it without my knowledge." Confused, Laura asked, "So, what was with storing the phones in the car?"

"Laura, I know my phone had to be registered. I know they have installed equipment in my apartment to monitor my PC, and I assumed that included my phone. I don't know whether they can intercept communications when I am away from the office or home, or possibly at your apartment. Did they install equipment at your place?"

"If so, they never told me about it," Laura answered. This conversation was getting awkward because she knew the FBI was surveilling Richard, and they had not told her if Richard had installed any equipment. She did know the FBI could trace her phone calls but did not think they listened to her phone conversations. She wondered. That was not out of the question, however. As an agent, she had signed away her right to privacy. She hated lying to Kyle, so she changed the direction of the conversation.

"Okay, I get it. You wanted to talk privately. What is on your mind?" she said.

"Let's go find someplace to eat first. Then we can come back here and see what develops," Kyle said with a sly grin. Laura smiled, walked over to him, pecked him on the cheek, and put her arm in his. She guided him to the door, and they were off to dinner.

They had dinner at Nonni's Italian Bistro. There was a thirty-five-minute wait, but the food was worth it, and the atmosphere was great. Kyle was a bit schizophrenic about trusting Laura; tonight, it did not matter. Without cell phones to raise Kyle's suspicions, they spent the evening talking about Meisner Industries. Kyle explained the tests he had been running, and his conversation when he spoke to Bill Butler. Kyle talked about his curiosity related to what Meisner was up to. Why were read-heads so important? Laura could not provide answers and tried to show sympathy for Kyle's frustration without disclosing her concerns and relationship with the FBI. However, she did encourage him to get information from any source he could, including other work units. Laura was unaware that Kyle was harboring a secret, too, the fact that George Lockit was coming to Portland to help him locate the leak.

After dinner, they returned to the Bed and Breakfast with a bottle of wine. There was a comfortable small couch in the room, so Laura snuggled up to Kyle as they reminisced about their time in Houston. Laura asked Kyle if he forgave her. It put him on the spot. Although he had forgiven her, he was unsure he could trust her current interest in him. It could still be working for Meisner. Laura, on the other hand, was feeling guilty about being constrained by her secret work as an FBI agent. However, her concern did not prevent her from wanting Kyle. For Kyle's part, his affection for Laura was getting intense, and this romantic get-away fueled his fire. He had no idea how George's visit was about to put Laura on the spot.

Kyle put his arm around Laura, and she responded similarly and reached up to kiss a willing guy. As they embraced and kissed, Kyle could feel the warmth of Laura's small firm breasts pressing against his chest and the chain reaction in his groin. They were so tightly pressed together; Laura could feel his erection. She stood up, unbuttoned her blouse, and dropped her skirt. Kyle took the hint and removed his shirt and pants leaving only his skivvies. They both laughed when they each, in turn, reached for protection, demonstrating their mutual forethought about the weekend. Laura led him to the bed, pulled down the covers, and invited him to join her. They caressed each other lovingly as they removed what remained of their clothing so that their bodies melded together in the ecstasy of lovemaking. It was like old times in Houston again. Kyle dozed off quickly, escaping the stress of his work and secret task and relishing lying next to Laura as she draped her leg over his torso. Before Laura went to sleep, she mused about her muddled emotions as they lay entwined with each other. When they awoke, the sun was still below the Eastern mountain range but casting light in the room. Laura prompted Kyle, and they made love again, after which they were hungry. They showered together, dressed, and went down for breakfast with silly grins on their faces. The host was gracious, smiled knowingly, and did not ask a lot of questions. They were not the first couple who found romance at the Gilbert satisfying. Both of them looked forward to a fun day at the beach, all while anticipating another romp in the sack soon. Maybe even at her apartment? Both came true.

The ride back was faster than the detailed map reading trip on the way over —no need to trace out the Hood to Coast Relay course again. The conversations turned to finding the leak in his team. He decided he would try the hyperspectral cell phone scheme they came up with on Jeneen to see if it produced any results, any results at all were better than what they had now. He would have to call George and consult with him to make sure it was a sound plan. When he called George and went over the idea, George assured him it couldn't hurt, even if she inadvertently spread the information to other team members. After all, Jeneen might not even believe him.

The next few weeks went by quickly. Feeding false information to Jeneen did not produce any evidence that she was the source of the leaks. Kyle survived the Hood to Coast Relay. He only made one wrong turn, which was corrected quickly by one of his awake van passengers. He parked in the wrong spot once, but before it threatened his team with a violation, he corrected it. He did get to meet several other MI employees and got contact information. He also asked about security at the relay party in Seaside. Not all the work units were as secretive as in the headquarters building where he worked. That meant he could follow up with some of them to find out what else Meisner Industries was working on in their shops. He did meet a woman runner that worked on ballot-counting machines. She observed that there were many public questions about accuracy. Their companies would not disclose how the machines worked, claiming it was proprietary information. The ones of most concern were the ones that produced no paper records. She indicated that with the national concern about these voting machines, many states and jurisdictions were replacing these voting machines with paper ballots, and Meisner Industries was in a position to be one of the major suppliers of ballot-counting machines. Oregon was an active market even though they already had paper ballots and existing ballot-counting equipment. He also found out from her that they were waiting on a new-type read-head to install in the machines as well as software from another team. She did not know which team it was. Kyle pressed her on why they needed special read-heads, but she did not know. "I just do what I am told," she said.

George was scheduled to be in town next week. Kyle was looking forward to that, but he was concerned about what Laura would think when he disclosed his secret. He would deal with that later.

~ George Lockit Arrives ~

George flew into Portland, PDX, on Southwest Airlines, arriving at 8:30 PM. In preparation, Kyle had bought a used Toyota Prius so he could pick up George, and they could get around town as needed. Kyle had arranged to take the following week off using earned vacation time. When he picked George up, he left his work cell phone at home. No need for security to see him go to the airport. They had arranged to meet at baggage claim. When they met, Kyle invited George to stay with him, but George would not hear of it. Besides, as

George pointed out, neither he nor Kyle could be sure they could have private conversations in Kyle's apartment. George had booked a hotel room in the Hilton DoubleTree near the Lloyd Center and hence also near Kyle's office.

After the perfunctory greetings, Kyle asked, "Did you know the hotel was virtually next to my office?" They took George's two suitcases to Kyle's car as they continued the conversation.

"Yes. when you are at work, it would make having lunch together more convenient."

"I thought I told you. I managed to get the week off. I had vacation time coming."

"That's good, but we won't necessarily be working together this week. I have research I need to do. By the way, I may need to borrow your car or go back to the airport and rent one."

"You can borrow mine. I have managed without a car so far."

Kyle had a lot of questions about Walter, and George's wife, Rachel. He also wanted to know how the partnership was working out back in St. Andrews. On the trip to the hotel, George caught Kyle up on everything going on at Baker, Lockit, and Rogers. Business, George pointed out, was more than they could handle, specifically due to the publicity they got from Kyle's case a few years back. They had hired additional staff, including another detective that George supervised. Since then, they had many excellent clients and mostly successes. Kyle asked George questions, and George happily supplied stories about B L & R's work. Kyle dropped George off and parked the car. He left his cell phone in his car and walked over to the hotel. He met George in the lobby. They went up to George's room on the fifth floor.

They did not waste time with trivia. "So, what do you know so far?" Kyle queried.

"Well, finding out about Meisner Industries has not been easy. I must say, Richard Meisner plays his game close to the chest."

Kyle responded, "Tell me about it. Security and secrecy drive me crazy. In your experience, is business espionage that popular these days."

George added, "You would not believe how much money is involved in stealing information. It takes a lot of money to steal information, and a lot of money is made in utilizing the information gained. Meisner is not the only paranoid owner in the world. However, his is particularly strange."

"Should I be concerned?" Kyle mused.

George hemmed and hawed. "Frankly, I don't know. At least not yet. What can you tell me about his relationship with this Laura McLaughlin?"

"I am pretty sure Meisner keeps her around to hide his sexual preferences. He asks her to accompany him to public gatherings to create the appearance he is heterosexual. At least that is what Laura tells me. Do you know something I don't know?"

"Not exactly. I think you are probably right, but I was wondering, didn't you and Laura used to be together when you were in Houston?"

"Yes, what are you getting at?" Kyle was curious and concerned with where this was leading.

"Does she have any other source of income besides Meisner Industries?"

"Sure. She works for a real estate outfit that manages timeshares on the Islands in Hawaii. Didn't you check her out? I sent you her name along with the others." Kyle was getting peeved with this conversation. It seemed like George was accusing Laura of a dastardly agenda.

"Yes, I did. I don't know if you know everyone she is working for. Maybe you should sit down."

Now he had Kyle's full attention. The way George was talking concerned him. Was Laura holding out on him? He responded, "Okay, but I don't think I like where this is going. What don't I know about Laura?"

"Maybe what I know, you don't know, Kyle, but if you do, you never mentioned it to me."

"What, damn it! Spell it out already."

"Kyle, Laura is an FBI agent," George said and let it sink in. It was apparent from the shock on Kyle's face that he did not know.

Then, Kyle reacted, "No way. And how would you know anyway? I have not seen any evidence whatsoever that she is an FBI agent. Hell, George, we have been having sex for God's sake. No way I tell you. Where did you come up with that?"

Do you remember how the FBI broke the case when you were accused of murder back in St. Andrews? I developed a close relationship with the St. Andrew FBI office. They occasionally help me out with particularly complicated cases, and I share information with them too. I was checking on the names you gave me, and they got excited when they saw Laura McLaughlin was on my list. After a dance around the reason, they finally told me she was an FBI agent, and she has been one ever since she got out of college. You didn't know that?"

"Hell no. That means she was an agent when we were in Houston?"

"Well, yes. It was the FBI that set you up with your job, and they assigned Laura to look after you for a while."

"Look after me? What the hell! I thought she genuinely liked me. Was she sleeping with me to look after me? What am I, a basket case that she has to keep in her sights? In case you have not noticed, George, I am pissed!"

Kyle could not get over being stunned. Every encounter with Laura was going through his mind, from the time they met in the coffee shop, to the Dear John letter she sent to him after she moved to Dallas. Now he questioned their relationship. Was it all fake? Did she ever like him? Was she faking it now? He was angry and hurt. There was nothing he could say. He brooded.

George let everything sink in. Finally, George snapped his fingers in front of Kyle, "Kyle, come back. Surely this is not all bad. First of all, the FBI seems to have your back once again. In addition, it gives us important information. The FBI is concerned about Meisner Industries. They have an undercover agent watching his actions. You know, you could be grateful."

"I think grateful is going to be an uphill battle. Wait till I get hold of Laura. I bet our lovemaking was all fake. God, this hurts, George. I don't know whether to be happy I asked you for help or sad to have my bubble burst. My chest hurts."

"Don't jump to conclusions. I think Laura deserves a chance to have a say, don't you?"

"I don't know if I care what she has to say. I will have to think about it. I think I better take off, and see if I can sleep off my—I don't know what to call it."

George patted Kyle on the shoulder, "Get a grip Kyle, I know you will get through this. You are an ultimate survivor. And who is to say she is not and has not always been in love with you? She could not have told you herself, or she might lose her career with the FBI."

Kyle grunted, "We'll see. Right now, I feel betrayed by a person I thought I loved, a person who might even love me. Am I a fool?

Kyle had the same feelings when his mom passed away, and his dad could not be reconciled to the fact. Kyle was like a kid again, abandoned by his mother, left to deal with his verbally abusive dad. George's bombshell was all he could take tonight.

"See you tomorrow at 10:00 AM?" was all Kyle could say.

"Sure," George responded, concerned about whether Kyle would get a grip or lash out. From what Kyle had told him so far, and the research he had done, there were issues and secrets to uncover. He was here because he cared about Kyle. This was not a job to George.

Kyle headed back to his apartment to stew on what he had learned. He did not sleep it off because he could not sleep.

~ The Confrontation ~

Kyle got up at 5:30 AM. He was not sleeping, and when he did doze, the dreams were disturbing, although he could not remember them. With nothing to do until he met George, he decided to take a long hot shower. Nothing like a long shower when you are upset. By the time he had shaved and showered, the sun was coming up. He turned on the radio to hear the news, partially as a distraction. Strangely, he did not hear the news as his mind turned over the revelation that Laura had been lying to him for years. He had never actually believed she was lying, but he had questioned it. He had been puzzled by the Dear John letter. As he thought about what had transpired over the years, things came into focus. If she genuinely did like him, maybe he was looking at this the wrong way. If she did not love him, then what was her attention about? Was sleeping with him part of her job? Did she like him or what? Which was it? He was frequently confused by her behavior, something he had passed off as not understanding women. He harbored a deep hurt at being used. It made him mad, and he was looking forward to telling her how angry he was with her. He decided to be early to see George, so he left his apartment at 9:15.

He went to the bank of phones in the Hilton and rang George's room. It did not take George long to answer. George was still on St. Andrew's time. He, too, had been up since 5:00, 7:00 St. Andrew's time. George suggested he come up so they could talk about the day's plans. Kyle took the elevator and knocked on the door to George's suite. George had ordered a pancake breakfast for the two of them. Kyle was ready for another cup of coffee, and the breakfast was inviting. They sat to discuss plans for the day.

George began, "Kyle, I am sorry I disturbed you last night. I was not aware you still liked Laura."

"Used to like? I think past tense fits. At the moment, I am so angry I don't know what to do with the information. I want to give her a piece of my mind. What a mess she has made teasing me, leading me on when all she wanted was information about Meisner Industries. She couldn't trust me?"

George interrupted, "You are too hard on her. She had a job to do. I don't believe she has put you in harm's way. I think she likes you and wants to be with you."

"Still, she messed up with that Dear John letter. What the hell was that all about? She has been using me since we met in Houston. It is a load of crap! And then, she just happens to show up in Portland, in a car, at the bus stop?"

"So, Kyle, what do you want to do? You said you wanted help with a work-related problem. What are you going to do about that? It seems to me that Laura is an ally, even if not a lover."

"It's the lying I am having problems with, George. How can you work with someone who lies to you, seduces you, fucks you over? How can that work?"

George suggested, "Kyle, I think we should meet with Laura as soon as possible, and review the situation. I believe that she will work with us to help unravel these mysteries and answer for what she has done to you. You remember Buck Rogers, don't you, the FBI agent that worked with us in St. Andrews?"

Kyle answered, "Sure. If he had not believed me, I think I would be dead now or at least in prison. What about him?"

"Buck is the one that researched Laura for me when you told me she met you again in Portland. He is the one who told me she was an agent. He did not have to tell me that. We both took it as a good sign. If we had not worked together on several cases, I don't think we would know that now. I think you need to hear Laura's side."

"I know. I know. I realize I have to face this sooner or later. Let's go see her right now."

"You might be too angry to do that now."

"No, we need to get it over with. I need to give her a piece of my mind."

George hesitated, "Look, Kyle, you had me come up here to help you. Pay attention! Listen to me! Take my advice. You should NOT give her the what-for! If we are going to see her now, let me do the talking. Just introduce me as a friend from St. Andrews, and let me carry the conversation. I will let you know when you can have your say. Are you willing to do that? If not, we have other work to do, and should postpone seeing Laura."

Kyle would not be dissuaded from seeing Laura. Finally, after George insisted, Kyle said he would let George do the talking. "I can do that. But when I get my turn to talk, you know where I stand. Let's go."

They finished breakfast and headed downstairs to Kyle's car. Kyle drove to Laura's apartment. Kyle wanted to appear unannounced. Kyle was hoping to catch her at home and surprise her. George encouraged Kyle to relax, assuring him things would work out. Kyle rang Laura, announced he was at the lobby door and wanted to come up. Laura seemed flustered but buzzed him in. When they got to her floor and knocked, she immediately opened the door. She was dressed in a tee-shirt and house slacks. She did not have makeup on. Her hair was brushed, but not for going out in public.

"Kyle," She said. She was both surprised to see him and to see he was accompanied by someone she did not know. She was initially alarmed. She could see the stress on Kyle's face but not on the man who was with him. She wondered who this person was and why Kyle had brought him to her apartment unannounced. Was she in danger? Was Kyle in danger? Had this stranger forced him to come. She did not know, and not knowing was when she knew she should be very cautious.

"Hi, Laura. I want to introduce you to a good friend of mine from St. Andrews." Laura breathed a sigh of relief. A friend, not a foe. "He has come up to Portland for a few days. Hope you don't mind us showing up like this."

"Of course not," She did mind but decided to play it cool till she knew what was going on, "Any friend of yours will be a friend of mine too," she said. "Could I get you two a cup of coffee?

Kyle responded, "Sure." As she left, Kyle and George walked down the hall behind Laura. George gave Kyle a warning glare and put his finger to his lips with the gesture that said, "You agreed to let me do the talking!" Kyle pointed to a chair in Laura's living room where George could sit. Laura went into the kitchen to get the coffee. Her apartment had two bedrooms and a generous living area. The kitchen was partially hidden behind a bar. All the décor in the apartment was modern and chic. George once again signaled to Kyle putting a finger to his lips. Kyle got the message to remain cool and let George do the talking as they had agreed. Laura helped by asking from the kitchen, "So George, what brings you to Portland?"

"Just business," George answered, being intentionally vague.

"Mind if I ask what kind of business?"

"Not at all. I am a private investigator. I am a partner in Baker, Lockit, and Rogers. I have a situation I am investigating here in Portland."

"Oh," Laura responded with a wary tone of voice. Laura knew better than to ask him directly what case he might be working on. Finally, she asked, "And how is it going?" Laura returned with cream, sugar, and three cups of coffee. She wore an awkward smile, but it successfully hid her curiosity and alarm.

"I flew into town last night, so it is too early to know. I might need some contacts here. Who do you know in Portland?"

That was a question Laura needed to avoid. She waved her hand without actually answering George. Both George and Kyle noticed her evasion.

As they augmented their coffee and began to drink it, George began, "Laura, do you know Buck Rogers in St. Andrews?"

"No. That name does not ring a bell," she said. That was honest. That connection was a while ago, and lots had happened in the meantime.

"Well, he knows a lot about you."

Laura visually squirmed in her chair. *Where was this going?*

"He does?" she said, "I don't recall anyone by that name. You said he is in St. Andrews?" She racked her brain for the connection. George persisted.

"Are you sure, Laura? I believe you have talked to him before," George continued, intending and succeeding in making Laura very uncomfortable. It suddenly dawned on Laura. She was being interrogated. She realized she was on the wrong end of this inquiry, and she was trying to figure out what was going on. Why did Kyle bring this person, this private investigator, to her apartment, early in the day, without warning? It made her nervous being interrogated in front of Kyle. Why was Kyle putting up with this verbal assault? Why was he so quiet? She had been trained and tested. She had demonstrated composure under challenging circumstances. Yet, here in front of the person she loved, she was nervous. Was it all the lies she had told? Was it the secret way it had been arranged for her to meet Kyle in Houston? Was it the mistake an agent makes to fall in love with a client? It was quiet in the room, and George let it sit there. Laura, for her part, knew to keep quiet until she knew what was going on. She had been well trained, but she did not recognize the name.

"Buck Rogers is the one that saved Kyle's life in St. Andrews. He is an FBI agent," George introduced the name. With the mention of FBI agent, little droplets appeared on Laura's forehead. She remembered. This had never happened to her during her training. She had been in tense situations before, but never so nervous. "Laura, I know it is against FBI protocol, but Buck and I do a lot of work together, so he did me the honor of disclosing he had talked to you when you were in Houston." It suddenly dawned on her who Buck Rogers was. Not a joke, but a fellow agent. She felt her secret was safe. Then, as she relaxed a bit, George continued. "He told me you are an FBI agent too." Laura flushed. *Buck had violated standard protocol. Why would he do that? He should have known better than to put her undercover work at risk. Why?* Laura was backed into a corner with no place to go. She could not get up and leave. It was her apartment. Here she was being outed as a liar in front of Kyle. He was staring at her. It was humiliating. The droplets turned into rivulets. Why didn't Kyle say anything? Had he known all along? Had he also been lying to her? The conflict of being in love with Kyle and keeping it a secret from him about her other agenda finally got to her. Her heart ached; her pulse increased. She could feel her heart pounding. Her head spun. A flood of emotion welled up in a way she could not control. Tears flooded her eyes. This is what they warned you about, *don't get involved with subjects in an investigation!* She thought to herself. She put her hands up to her face as though she could hide when she began to sob uncontrollably.

This is not what Kyle expected. His throat tightened. He realized at that moment that he loved Laura, and this exposure of her secret was painful for him too. A moment ago, he was ready to wring her neck. Now, witnessing her humiliation, her flood of emotion, his anger evaporated, and tears ran down his cheeks too. He got up and went over to Laura. Kyle grabbed her hand that was wiping away tears and pulled her up out of the chair. He kissed her tears and embraced her tightly. Both of them were sobbing now. George let them be. Even George was touched by the scene of humiliation and forgiveness of compassion and love.

It took several minutes for Kyle and Laura to settle down as Laura tried to tell Kyle how sorry she was that she had lied to him. Kyle apologized for bringing George to Portland without letting her know what he was doing. Both of them promised each other there would be no more secrets. Their promises to each other were sealed with a fabulous long kiss, which lasted until George finally cleared his throat, "You guys know I am still here, right?"

Chapter 11

~ Revisiting Dear John ~

As they recovered their composure, Laura and Kyle began to revisit events of their history. In particular, Laura was now in a position to explain the Dear John Letter. She needed to clarify several things. Now that her status as an FBI agent was out, she could do that.

"Kyle, one of the most painful things since Houston was writing the Dear John letter to you. Agents can lose their status as an agent if they become emotionally involved with people they are working with. Yes, agents are allowed to fake it, but be disciplined enough not to get emotionally involved. Yet, I fell in love with you when we first met."

When Laura said, "I fell in love," a tear rolled down Kyle's cheek. He felt the impact of her statement in his chest. His heart skipped a beat. A wish secretly left unrevealed was now disclosed, and he was not in control of the wash of emotion that swept over him as she continued.

"It made my job both easy and hard. It was easy making sure you were safe. It was hard not to tell you our meeting was arranged by the FBI in St. Andrews. Everyone was concerned. What you had been through could expose you to a kind of Post Traumatic Stress Disorder. The people who caused you trouble in St. Andrews may have eventually been arrested. However, no one knew how large the organization was and if they would seek revenge and arrange to make sure you were out of the picture. It was a relief when you wanted to move out of St. Andrews, but no one knew for sure if you were still in harm's way."

A flush of anger rose: *They were managing me, without my knowing it? Give me a break.*

"They were concerned that there might be additional parties that could hunt you down. They needed you to remain safe in case you were needed to testify in a trial. They were concerned that if you knew you were under protection, you would refuse it."

Damn right! But it occurred to him as his mind reacted that he would never have met Laura, would not have fallen in love with her, had their meeting not been arranged.

Laura continued without so much as taking a breath or letting Kyle react. "So, it was all because they cared about you and your potential testimony. As it turned out, the parties were convicted and sentenced to long jail time just as my mom got sick. So, when I had to go to Dallas, they terminated the oversight. I wanted to be able to maintain contact, but it was denied."

So, actually, her job was more important to her than I was. What if I had not come to Portland? Would Laura and I have met again? Can I trust her work won't take her away again?

Laura continued, afraid to give Kyle a chance to object. "The FBI said I had to sever all contact, hence the Dear John letter. I can't tell you how many drafts of that letter I wrote. I wanted—I needed to tell you I—was falling in love with you. I had to break it off cleanly, and they helped me hide my location from you. I can't tell you how much I grieved over that. I was heartbroken. Kyle, there has never been anyone but you, but I knew I would hold you back having to keep my secret."

Finally, Kyle could not contain himself any longer, and he jumped in as Laura paused to take a breath, "Laura, there has not been anyone besides you in my life either. It was like a dream when I ran into you here in Portland." Reflecting briefly on the coincidence of meeting Laura again in Portland, *was that set up by the FBI too? Was A.J. Stenz somehow also involved in the deception? How could he be? Didn't I initiate the call to A.J.? I did, didn't I,* he questioned.

Laura interrupted his thoughts, "About meeting me again in Portland; I guess you have figured out that was arranged too. My job here relates to Richard, not you. When you moved to Portland, I was notified and hatched the plan to meet you. I talked you up and encouraged Richard to interview you. If you had not applied, I would not have been able to arrange things like I did. Richard has no idea the FBI is involved, and he can't. Although he may have suspicions, I don't think he knows how much I care for you. And, just because you know now, it does not make our relationship any easier in relation to Meisner Industries."

George had been observing this gush of words and emotion as he sipped his coffee. "Could I possibly get a refill?"

"What?" Laura had been so intense in repairing her relationship with Kyle that she became unconscious that George was in the room. "Oh, sure," Laura smiled. She went to get George a refill.

"George, you are a master. When I came here today, I could have committed murder—well maybe not murder. Thanks for the way you handled things. I can't tell you how frustrated I was."

"Kyle, buddy, that was obvious. I don't think those feelings will disappear, however. You and Laura will still have to work things out. Keeping secrets from one another is not the best way to develop a relationship, so don't think things are fully resolved."

"Maybe not, but now, just maybe, Laura and I can be more open with each other, unless the FBI manages to get between us again. But I appreciate your help. Thanks!"

"You don't have to thank me, Kyle. The scene I just witnessed said it all."

Laura returned with the coffee. George spoke up, "Kyle, Laura, I suspect you two will have lots of time to address your mutual histories in the weeks and maybe years to come. For now, could we address the reason I am here?"

Laura was so consumed with explaining things to Kyle that she forgot she did not know why George was here. She did need an explanation. George and Kyle explained their relationship regarding their experiences in St. Andrews. Kyle and George reviewed how Kyle, concerned about all the secrets and strange things going on, asked George for help. Kyle explained that he knew he could trust George because he had nothing to do with Meisner. And, when he first contacted him, he did not know Laura was FBI. That caught Laura up to date.

The three of them began to review what Kyle and Laura had been doing since Kyle began at Meisner Industries. After they had exhausted that review, George spoke up again, "I think we need to visit the FBI office as soon as we can. Could we do that today, maybe now?"

Laura blinked and mentally left the room. She wondered how this would play when she told her local boss that she had been outed by a detective from St. Andrews. First, she would have to call the office.

"Let me think," Laura said as she closed her eyes, cocked her head, and thought. Then she picked up the phone and dialed her contact. George and Kyle could only hear Laura's end of the conversation. They would have preferred Laura to put the call on speaker, but she dialed before George could make that suggestion.

"Yes, this is Laura McLaughlin calling for Kameron Wilson." There was a long pause as she waited for Kameron to come to the phone. She smiled and gestured with her arm extended, palm up to Kyle and George. Before they could suggest she put them on speaker, Kameron answered. "Hi, Kam, I have a situation I need help with." —pause— "Sorry, I know you are busy, but this can't wait" —pause— "No, you can't call me back" —pause— "You know I am working with Kyle Tredley. He just introduced me to a friend from St. Andrews. —pause— "George" Laura put her hand over the phone and mouthed "Last name?" to George. George answered her. Back on the phone, Laura quickly continued, "George Lockit. He is a private detective. —pause— "Yes, he is here, right now." —pause— "Yes, he is standing here right now. He is friends with our agent Buck Rogers in St. Andrews." There was a reaction to that news as Kyle looked at George. They both could hear Kam without the speaker being on, as Laura held the phone away from her ear. He was having a conniption with the news. Although he was loud, they could not make out what he was saying. Meanwhile, Laura sheepishly gritted her teeth, lips slightly ajar. Then Laura continued, "I know, I know. There are just things you can't control, Kam." —pause— "Do you think I could bring them by the office and maybe read them into the Meisner operation," —long pause— "If we don't, it could complicate things. I don't think Kyle would work with me anymore," she said winking at Kyle and George. —long pause— "Okay. I will be here right by the phone. Don't make it too long, Okay?" After a couple more acknowledgments, Laura hung up, "They are going to call me back. Hopefully, it will only be a few minutes. More coffee?"

George nodded, "But first, could I use your facilities."

Kyle said, "Ditto."

"Kyle, you know where it is, show George."

~ Richard in Washington ~

Richard Meisner owns a four thousand square foot house on the lake in Lake Oswego, a suburb south of Portland. He has a full-time housekeeper-cook who lives on the property and is available at his beck-and-call. Unmarried, Richard has the whole place to himself and elects not to entertain there. He does have an occasional male friend over for the weekend when his housekeeper has days off. Richard spends a lot of time there working on projects that few people know about. The only people who have been to his house are the housekeeper, his male friends, and the MI security team when they originally installed his security system. He has a computer network with backup and central server. The primary system has no external connections to the Internet. In addition, he has one computer he uses for a private virtual network for communications. It also provides access to entertainment. It is connected to the Internet via a high-speed connection. He can use a secure encrypted video link over the Internet to converse confidentially with Senator Corning about their mutual interests. Today, he needs to go to Washington for a private meeting. He does not trust his secure link to the conversation he needs to have with Corning. Richard also owns a house that backs up to a golf course in Glendale, Maryland, Northeast of Washington, D.C. It is also protected by advanced security and privacy. This house is not staffed continuously, but he can call for service when needed.

Richard is an accomplished pilot and owns a Learjet-24 that he keeps in a hangar at the Hillsboro airport 20 miles west of Portland. When he wants to visit Washington, D.C., he sometimes personally pilots his private jet to the College Park Airport in Maryland. A pilot, employee of Meisner Industries, also flies Richard to College Park. The pilot usually goes up to New York City and takes in a play or two until Richard signals him to meet back at the airport.

Richard arranged to meet his friend and co-conspirator Senator Rolfe Corning at his private residence in Glendale Friday evening. Richard piloted the Learjet alone out of Hillsboro on a Thursday morning. After landing his plane in College Park, he drove to his house in Glendale using the car he kept at the airport. He had called his hospitality service in Glendale before he left Portland, so the house was clean and prepared for Rolfe's visit. He did not have the hospitality staff stay for this visit. Rolfe drove alone to Richard's house arriving just after 7:00 PM. He parked his car in the open garage. After Richard closed the garage door and both were securely inside, Richard greeted Rolfe with a kiss and warm embrace. Their relationship was a well-kept secret. Both of them looked forward to a weekend of business and pleasure. Corning was five-years Meisner's senior.

They began the weekend with pleasure. In the morning, Richard cooked the two of them a hearty brunch. By late morning, they got down to business. Richard and Rolfe had a plan to take advantage of public mistrust of voting machines as jurisdiction after jurisdiction studied and planned significant changes in voting. California and Washington states had passed legislation that would transition their voting systems to mirror Oregon's paper ballots, administered through the U.S. Postal service and drop-off boxes. Other states were following suit before the next major federal election. Everyone was expecting bid announcements within the next six months. Richard and Rolfe had a plan to make money selling all the machines and consumable ballots required to meet what they expected to become a national movement. Richard sold Corning shares at a discount in Meisner Industries to make sure Corning stayed committed to the endeavor's success. Although there would be competition as jurisdictions transitioned to paper ballots, Rolfe was in the process of getting support for legislation that would give Meisner Industries an inside track to win the bids.

By controlling the machinery to produce tamper-proof ballot-paper and ballot-counting machines, they both would become unfathomably rich. With the money they made selling machines and ballot paper, Senator Corning told Richard they could fund (buy) loyal legislators of the various jurisdictions they wanted to control. Making money was only one of the goals. Corning and Richard aspired to influence the outcome of certain elections. They both sought political control in states as well as the nation.

Richard filled Rolfe in on the progress made, the production of coated ballot paper, and success of the specialized hyperspectral read-heads used in ballot handling. Richard assured Rolfe that he had segregated the work in the company so effectively that only a hand full of his staff knew more than their small part of the intrigue. Rolfe assured Richard that the legislation that would make Meisner a shoo-in to win bids was close to passing. He had the help of bipartisan groups in both the House and Senate that would mandate electoral standards in ways that would not inflame States Rights advocates. Only Meisner's machines would be prepared to match Requests for Proposals to purchase voting systems when initially issued throughout the country. They celebrated progress looking forward to the many rewards they expected to be theirs.

Corning let Richard know that he could not avoid a hearing on the legislation that he and his colleagues had written. Of course, it was with the senator's secret help. The hearings were scheduled for next month. He was confident he had greased enough palms to keep the hearings from causing any delays to a Senate vote. He was also optimistic that the House would approve the legislation without amendments or hearings. Richard had spent a lot of money on lobbyist and well-disguised campaign contributions through a well-known and trusted PAC to ensure smooth sailing.

Early Monday morning, Richard flew back to Portland and was in the office by noon. He called Joe, the team leader of Kyle's team, to his office for a meeting.

~ Joe's Assignment ~

Joe received the message to come at 1:30 PM to Richard Meisner's office. Joe assumed Richard would want a progress report on the software his team was working on, so he quickly put together a short power-point presentation. At 1:30 sharp, he went up to Richard's office.

Richard greeted Joe cordially, "Thanks for coming up. I wanted to get an update on your team's progress."

"I figured as much. I brought my laptop with me so I could show you where we were."

"Good. Let me open up the wall display. It will be easier to see the details." Richard gave a verbal command, and two wall panels slid to the side, revealing a giant video screen. Joe connected the laptop and gave Richard an update. Joe's team was working on a module with several interfaces, one for input and one for output. Data was to come from another team to flow through the user interface. Kyle was working on data from the hyperspectral read-heads. Joe's team worked on controls that would allow a master user to manage all the interface functions. The interface also had multiple output parameters to manage the various machines that ran the complete system. Richard had different teams working on both ends. The interface could control parameters related to paper-ballot production. Another managed ballot printing. Another to control mailing of ballots. And finally, one that controlled ballot counting. The fact that Joe's team held such an essential part of the process explained Richard's apparent obsession with potential leaks from Joe's team. Richard was not 100% convinced there was a leak, at least not on this particular project, but having Kyle search for one helped reduce his anxiety, especially as they neared completion of the whole scheme. Additionally, Kyle's work with other teams positioned him for other plans Richard had not disclosed.

Joe ran through the various parts of the interface. Richard wanted to know if they had integrated the work of the team members yet. "Joe, I want to do the integration of your team's components within a month. Let your team know they need to finish up last-minute coding and testing so we can run a test soon."

"We can do that. Everything is well developed. Just a few things to mop up," Joe responded. He closed up his computer and left Richard's office. Richard had recorded the entire session, including the conversations.

~ Kyle, George, and Laura meet with the FBI ~

Kyle, Laura, and George made their way over to the FBI office near the Airport. Kam arranged for them to bypass the security checkpoint. Kam was not anxious for the whole office to know about George and Kyle. Laura led them to Kam's office. All three waited in a waiting room with a window to the Northeast. They could see planes coming in for landings. Before long, a gentleman entered the room. He invited Laura to report to Kam's office. When the man turned his back to

George and Kyle to open the door for Laura, George put his finger up to his lips, indicating Kyle should remain silent. George was not sure of their status and did not want Kyle to complicate their visit. The man stayed in the room with Kyle and George. When he turned around, he spoke.

"Greetings. My name is Agent Richard Mercer, but you can call me Dick," he said with a grin on his face. "Unfortunately, my last name is not Tracy," he added and waited for a reaction. This frequently opened up the conversation with suspects he interviewed. In this case, he received silence. The silence was uncomfortable for Kyle, but George knew the ropes. He had used silence many times to get people to open up. Kyle fidgeted, which Dick noticed.

"What's your name?" He directed toward Kyle. Kyle glanced at George, who was seated against the opposite wall. George nodded, so Kyle answered.

"Kyle Tredly."

"What brings you to the FBI headquarters today?"

Kyle wanted to glance at George again but thought better of it. He decided to be parsimonious in his responses. "Laura," he answered.

"Laura?" he repeated as a question. Kyle decided not to respond. "Are you deaf? I asked you a question." Mercer was acting like a prosecutor in a courtroom interrogating a hostile witness.

George spoke up, authoritatively, "Sir, what is your name?"

"I just told you, Richard. And who are you?"

"I'm George. To you, I am Mr. Lockit."

"I can see you two are a pair of wise guys. What are you doing here?"

"Dick," George addressed him, using the diminutive name to refer to Mercer's small stature, "it might be above your pay grade. How about you just leave us alone until someone with real authority to ask us questions invites us to their office, like Kameron Wilson, for example."

Dick flinched at the name of his boss, "Okay, have it your way," he said in a sing-song. Kam had not told him why this threesome was here, and maybe this rube, George, who knew Kam's name, realized it. He looked at his watch as if that was somehow related to their situation. Then, he continued. "I will leave you two. Sorry, but I have to lock the door, so you don't wander around. Protocol, you know." As if it was standard protocol. He rechecked his watch as if making an excuse, turned, left, and Kyle and George could hear the door lock behind him."

"What the hell was that all about?" Kyle ventured.

"Standard intimidation protocol," George said and once again put his fingers to his lips, indicating they should not carry on a conversation. George was a cautious detective. In St. Andrews, he had a great relationship with the local FBI office, but each one had its peculiarities. George was not sure what to expect here in Portland. Before they had entered the building, George turned off his cell phone and had Kyle do the same.

They did not have to wait long. A woman entered the room and told them Mr. Kameron was ready to see them. George inquired whether Laura McLaughlin would also be present. The woman assured them she would be, so they followed her down the hall to Kameron's office. George mentally compared what he could see with his experiences in Buck Roger's office in St. Andrews. This office was larger.

Kameron, in contrast to the encounter with Mercer, greeted them warmly. Laura was already seated, and they took chairs beside her. Kam, as he preferred to be called, let them know he had already received a recommendation from Agent Rogers in St. Andrews. They could be trusted with confidential information, and that George, in particular, could be trusted to work closely with the FBI. As for Kyle, Agent Rogers testified to his valor and trustworthiness. Laura had explained the situation to Kam too.

Kam began, "George, Kyle, it is good to meet you both, although I must say the circumstances are a bit unusual. Rogers spoke highly on behalf of both of you. I have also consulted with the assistant to the FBI director, and they have given us the green light to utilize your services. As a result, and Laura has agreed, I will need to give you a brief outline of our interest and swear you in as unpaid lay agents. You will have to take your directions from Laura. George, in your case specifically, you need to coordinate with Laura on any investigations you undertake in Portland, regardless of whether or not they seem to be related to this case. Of course, without FBI training, your roles will be limited. I will read-you-in to our concerns with Meisner Industries, but before I do, I will need you to sign papers that obligate you to participate and agree to confidentially in all matters as Laura or I require. In no case whatsoever are you to identify that you have any relationship to the FBI generally or to this office specifically. George, you are prohibited from making any references to the FBI working in Portland or St. Andrews. In any event, because of how Laura is now exposed, you are bound by law and FBI policy to confidentiality on the risk of severe penalty for violating Laura's cover. Can we proceed? How about you, Kyle?"

"Not a problem at all. I am willing to do as you and Laura dictate. Well, so long as what I have to do is legal."

"Of course. What about you, George?"

"You already know the answer. Yes, of course."

Kam continued, "I will brief you today, but both of you will have to sit through one orientation and read and sign rules and regulations that you will be bound by. I will let Laura make the arrangements with the two of you. Laura, that needs to be done within a week. Are you two okay with this process?"

Both Kyle and George nodded their heads and said, "Yes."

Kam went over the documents they would be signing today. They signed with Laura acting as a witness in addition to Kam.

Once they finished, Kam gave them a brief outline of the case that Laura was working. It related primarily to the financial affairs of Meisner Industries. He explained that Laura could answer their questions within strict guidelines. Kyle mentally noted that Laura would still be privy to information she might not be able to share, might have to lie about. He decided to live with that. It was the unknown secret process that had upset him. The paperwork they had signed put Laura in charge of what they were allowed to do. The FBI wanted to avoid compromising the FBI surveillance operation. She would be the gatekeeper of the information. They would be reporting to her, and she would communicate with the FBI office as needed. From this point on, only Laura would be communicating with them on behalf of the FBI."

George had a question, "I need to be clear. I am not working for Laura. I was hired by Kyle. I will be doing work for Kyle. However, in that work, I can generally coordinate with Laura to make sure I don't adversely impact FBI work. So, although I don't work for Laura, I will be sensitive to her advice regarding anything that is of mutual interest. Is that clear?"

Kam thought about how to answer George. "George, by the fact you are here, you are bound by certain administrative laws. Those will be spelled out in your training, so until you have been through that, I strongly suggest you use special caution on anything related to the FBI case. Is that clear?"

"Okay. I can wait. Laura, please schedule the training as soon as possible." George realized he would most likely need to stay in Portland longer than the one week he had initially planned. "I will need to contact my office and arrange to be in Portland longer than I had expected. Any other things I need to be aware of?"

Kam responded, "Can you do this without explaining how the FBI is involved?"

"Of course. That will not be a problem. If necessary, I could make that call with Laura or other FBI source listening in."

"Work with Laura. She can cover this for the FBI," Kam responded.

Having finished the briefing, Kam asked Kyle and George again if they understood and agreed. They both did understand and agree. After the brief outline of the case, the signing agreements identifying Laura as their sole contact, and follow-up questions, they left together and headed back to Laura's apartment. When they got there, George did a sweep of her apartment to make sure Meisner Industries had no bugs in her place. Before she reactivated the FBI listening devices, she let Kyle and George know that the FBI bugged her home, and they should be aware their conversations might be recorded. Laura reactivated the FBI bugs, so George quietly did another sweep to test his equipment. His equipment did discover the FBI equipment.

~ Tiananmen Square, 14 Dongchangan Avenue ~

In a conference room of the Chinese Ministry of State Security, 14 Dongchangan Avenue, a small group of men met to discuss what they called in English, "The Influencer." Through assets in Washington, D.C., they had learned of Corning's desire to influence the outcome of elections and some of the details of his work with Richard Meisner. They knew Corning planned to manipulate election outcomes through specialized vote-counting equipment. The MSS had a spy among Corning's staff who could, when the time came, coordinate with Corning. They were aware of Corning's relationship with Meisner Industries and his relationship with Richard Meisner. They had also been able to establish a source of information within Meisner's headquarters software development team. The info provided led them to believe they had an excellent opportunity to influence the United States favorable to Chinese interests. Spies in both the Senate and House of Representatives were working on compromising legislators.

It was fortuitous to the MSS that Tao Li had decided to outsource production of a critical component of the Meisner vote management system: the hyperspectral read-heads that were integrated into every part of the Meisner Industries vote management system. The Shenzhen Xiazhen Manufacturing Plant was easily coerced to accept modifications to the read-heads that Tao Li had ordered in a manner neither Tao nor Meisner Industries were likely to detect. The modification would allow the Ministry of State Security to monitor the use of these read-heads and affect their operation to meet MSS objectives. Tao Li was utterly unaware of the involvement of the MSS. Meisner Industries was not aware the read-heads were produced on the mainland. Richard had trusted Li and believed his plant in Taipei was manufacturing the read-heads according to Richard's specifications.

The men in the room reported that everything had developed as planned and that they had been successful in monitoring the tests Meisner Industries, Kyle, had been doing with the read-heads. Everything seemed to be working as intended and on schedule. One of the things they had not been able to learn was the precise plans and time frame for deployment. Their sources in Washington let them know that Corning had scheduled the hearings, and expected no particular issues. That meant that the specifications would be finalized within a couple of months, and various state agencies would issue Request for Proposals within six to twelve months. Everything seemed to be on track.

The team's responsibility included political analysis of potential candidates and the prospect of close races that might be influenced. The MSS maintained an extensive database of current and potential elected officials at the national, state, city, and county offices throughout the entire United States. As any new candidate appeared on the scene, another division made a database entry, and sources in the U.S. began their research and data gathering. Their data was extensive, including family relationships, voting records, funding sources, and other influences, including social media information. They had managed to collect data without being detected.

The MSS was able to send a report to Beijing Officials that "The Influencer" was on track to do China's bidding.

~ Looking for Leaks ~

Kyle and Laura had been unsuccessful in finding a leak in Kyle's team at Meisner Industries. There were plenty of potential candidates, but none of them appeared to be the source. Laura and Kyle had doubts they would be successful in uncovering any leaks. Although Richard was not certain about the leaks, he did not want to take any chances. He continued to press Laura to put pressure on Kyle to come up with answers. Kyle was hesitant to express concerns about a person when he had no proof. If Richard was suspicious that someone had leaked, he might fire them as a warning to others. Laura thought Kyle should begin to reach out to a few of the people he met on the Hood to Coast run. She suggested to Richard that he give Kyle a pseudo-assignment that would allow Kyle to be out of the office without suspicion of the other workers. They hit upon the idea that Kyle needed to help implement the hyperspectral read-heads into various machines. That allowed him to be out of the office to meet other workers and evaluate them as possible co-conspirators of a leak. This suited Kyle and Laura because it would allow Kyle to do research for the FBI with excellent cover for his questions and research.

Kyle began his research with Bill Butler, the other Hood to Coast van driver, the head of Wilsonville's team. Kyle made an appointment and drove out to the plant where Bill worked. The receptionist at the front desk notified Bill when Kyle arrived, and Bill came to get Kyle. He gave Kyle a Meisner Industries Visitor ID badge for the Wilsonville Team office.

"So, Kyle, good to see you again. Now that it has been a few weeks since Hood to Coast, what is your reaction?" Bill asked as he escorted Kyle to his office.

"Very impressive race. I was scared to death that I would miss a turn or transfer point, but all the runners kept me on track. The guys and gals on the team are great. How many years have you been driving the van?"

"Four years. I was a bit concerned about you. Before I drove the van the first time, I had been to the coast many times for weekend getaways. I was impressed you made it without screwing up. It helped us out in a pinch."

"Just luck. Laura McLaughlin took me on a tour of the route the weekend before. That helped me a lot. I did make one wrong turn, but one of the guys straightened me out quickly," Kyle bantered.

"Laura McLaughlin? Who is that?" Bill asked.

Kyle was caught off guard. He had incorrectly assumed that Laura, being so close to Richard Meisner, was known by most people. Kyle had to think quickly. "My girlfriend," he answered, avoiding any complicated explanation. That seemed to satisfy Bill.

"Just the same, I was impressed," Then Bill changed the subject to the day's agenda. "So, the message I got from Mr. Meisner was that I should show you around, and introduce you to the team, and explain what we do. The note suggested that you were the hyperspectral read-head expert. Oh, I should have asked you, would you like coffee or something else to drink before we head out?"

"I'm good. I stopped at a Starbucks on the way down and got a latte.

Bill showed Kyle where the restroom was and told Kyle to come back to the office when he was through. Kyle took that opportunity to look around and read a bulletin board in the hall. When Kyle returned, Bill took Kyle on a tour of their facility, introducing Kyle to team members as they went. These people were not all programmers like at headquarters. There were mechanical engineers, chemists, mathematicians, as well as programmers. They also had technical types that ran the machinery that produced the various paper coatings. Bill explained how the hyperspectral read-heads made a real contribution to their work. Kyle wanted to know what the paper was for, so he asked Bill.

"Odd that you ask that," Bill said.

"Odd? Why do you say that? Haven't they told you what the coatings are to be used for?"

Bill frowned and hesitated, "I think," he started to say, hesitated again, and then continued. "I signed a non-disclosure agreement as a part of my contract. I need to think about whether or not I am allowed to answer your question."

"I understand. Meisner is a stickler for security and privacy but consider that he sent me here to review things. He wants me to understand more about the workings of various divisions of Meisner Industries."

"I know; I got the memo from him. Do you mind if we wait on your question until we return to my office? I want to make sure there is no conflict with the NDA," Bill said, putting off answering Kyle.

"No problem. My question can wait."

Bill finished showing Kyle the production equipment and introducing Kyle to the rest of the team members. Kyle was trying to remember everybody's name but finally had to give up in confusion. When they returned to Bill's office, Bill hunted through a locked file cabinet for a copy of his non-disclosure agreement as Kyle waited patiently. When he found it, he took a minute to look up a section and read it. Satisfied, he asked Kyle to repeat his question.

"Before I forget, I have a hard time remembering lots of names all at once. Could I get a list of the people working here?"

"Sure," Bill answered. He called a clerk to his office and asked him to make a copy for Kyle.

"So, the question I asked, Bill, is what are the coatings used for?"

"As I understand it, they deal with voter fraud. The coatings are to be used for ballots to ensure that forged ballots are not counted. It is to avoid influence by people who want to tamper with the paper ballots."

"So how does that work. Like the chords placed in paper money?" Kyle asked.

"Yes, but our coatings are invisible, as you know, so as long as we can maintain the secret, forgers won't know the ballots are even marked. And, if, and I say when, the forgers learn about the coatings, we have so many variations, they won't have sufficient time to forge counterfeit ballots. Besides that, the process is secret, so they would have to develop significant facilities to get away with forging ballots. The theory is, it will be so much trouble, it will be easier to buy candidates likely to win."

"Interesting. So, the hyperspectral read-heads embedded in the machines that create the paper and the ones that read the ballots are essential to maintaining voting integrity. Is that what you are saying?" Kyle asked.

"Well," Bill responded, "you are telling me something that I did not know. I was not aware that Meisner Industries was also going to make ballot-counting machines. I thought they would be selling the read-heads for others to use." Bill got a very quizzical look on his face. He did not say anything for what seemed like a couple of minutes, but it was probably only a few seconds. "I guess there is no harm in providing both ends of the voting process, maybe advantages. I will have to think about this more."

"What are you thinking?" Kyle asked. Kyle's alarms were telling him there was more to this paper coating thing than he had realized.

"Oh, I don't know. Just an interesting question," Bill responded. Changing the subject as the list of team members was delivered back to the office, Bill continued, "Anything else?"

Kyle sensed he had received all the information he was going to get today. "That should do it. Thanks for showing me around. It was beneficial. You seem to have things well under control." With that, Kyle got up, and Bill showed him out.

"See you next year at Hood to Coast?" Bill asked.

"I don't know. Don't you have a regular driver? Thought he was ill."

"Well, he made it known he wanted out, so if you will, you are the new driver."

Kyle swallowed, "Well, I guess I can. At least I shouldn't be so nervous next year," and chuckled. Bill chuckled too, and they parted.

Chapter 12

~ The Hearing ~

As Chair of the Senate Commerce, Science, and Transportation Committee, Senator Corning scheduled a hearing on SB 1076, Federal Rules for Voting in Federal Elections. Samantha Scorcy, chairwoman of the United States Election Assistance Commission (EAC), provided written testimony.

U. S. Senate Commerce, Science, and Transportation Committee
"Over-site of the U.S. Election Assistance Commission"
June 18, 2018
Samantha Scorcy, Chairwoman
Karl Jorden, Vice Chair
Phillip Thompson, Commissioner
Palmer Ingersol, Commissioner
United States Election Assistance Commission (EAC)

Good morning Chairman Corning, Ranking Member Colburn, and members of the committee. Thank you for the opportunity to testify this afternoon to detail the work of the Election Assistance Commission, better known as the EAC. Chairman Corning and Ranking Member Colburn, you both understand the importance of the EAC's work to protect the voting systems' integrity throughout the nation and its territories. As you are aware, there is significant interest in many states and U.S. Territories in moving away from electoral systems that are difficult to audit and toward the use of paper ballots. The EAC "has proven to be a significant resource in preparing specifications for technology that will address the full range of issues related to elections. We have developed specifications for systems that manage voting rolls to ensure their integrity. We have developed technical specs for equipment that can manufacture and print secure ballots, address ballot envelopes to ensure the correct ballot is delivered to each voter, validate signatures on cover envelopes, and record votes. Local jurisdictions can use these specifications to prepare Requests for Proposals (RFP's) to industry manufacturers to purchase the necessary equipment. With the funding of the Help America Vote Act (HAVA), Congress has provided funds to help states implement upgrading their voting systems utilizing the specifications of the EAC. Forty-eight of the 55 states/territories have expressed interest in moving to the mail-in paper ballot methodology that has proven its integrity and usefulness in the state of Oregon. If the states and territories make use of the standards and specifications to acquire the necessary technology to move to the new mail-in ballot systems and equipment in accordance with the specs we have drafted, we can be confident that not only will it ensure the integrity of elections to federal offices, but also to all levels of the various jurisdictions. We wanted to provide you an update. The detail is provided in our written attachments to our testimony today.

The update includes the 420 pages of specifications that our commission has prepared with the assistance of vendors and other government officials.

Samantha Scorcy's presentation continued with expressions of appreciation to the committee and additional details related to the development of the specifications. Senator Corning thanked Scorcy and continued with presentations from vendors and interested parties. Corning was pleased that there was no conflict over the work or direction of the EAC. They could continue their excellent work. The hearing was closed. Corning had arranged a closed-circuit video of the session which Richard Meisner had watched with interest. After all, Meisner had been instrumental in drafting many of the specifications and was prepared to bid and deliver equipment to as many jurisdictions as generated RFP's. Utilizing the EAC specifications, companies would have short reply times that would prevent significant credible competition. Meisner Industries was prepared to win a substantial number of the bids, having been instrumental in designing the specifications. Not only would they make a significant profit, but be in a position to influence the outcome of close elections across all jurisdictions utilizing Meisner Voting System equipment.

Meisner was not the only one monitoring the hearing and following the development of the specifications. **America Votes**, a registered lobbying organization, was closely following the development and supporting specifications that would provide considerable advantage to Meisner Industries. **America Votes** had a representative present at the hearing. Meisner Industries was aware of their interest. At least, they did not seem a threat since they fully supported the specifications in the bill. Richard was curious, however, because it might represent competition.

Contrary to the law, **America Votes** was funded through laundered money from the MSS, the China Ministry of State Security. They had a particular interest in having Meisner Industries win bids for voting equipment. For all Meisner machines, MMS would be able to secretly use Meisner's technically modified hyperspectral read-heads. Their modifications of the hyperspectral read-heads would allow them to influence election outcomes. Beijing had shown interest in using Meisner machines in Chinese elections—a nod to a supposed increase in democratic reform.

~ The Stuffers ~

Richard Meisner gave Laura a list of places that he wanted Kyle to check out. Fortunately for Kyle, he knew someone from each of the sites listed, but not necessarily the team leader. The next place he visited was a group that called themselves "The Stuffers." This team was responsible for machines that printed ballots. The ballots, privacy envelopes, and return envelops are stuffed into slightly larger envelopes. The package sealed, and machine addressed, based on voter rolls. Then they are mailed to registered voters via the U.S. mail.

(**How Mail Ballots Work**: Voters are mailed a ballot, privacy envelope, and self-addressed envelope. The voter *marks the ballot and seals it in the **privacy envelope**. That unmarked privacy envelope is then placed in a larger postage-paid envelope. The voter signs the postage-paid envelope with a legible signature that can be compared electronically with one on file. Once signed, the voter mails the signed envelope or places it in a designated drop-box. With this signed external envelope, the voter can be validated and prevented from voting more than once. When received at the local jurisdiction that counts ballots, the signature is electronically verified. Once verified, the inner envelope can be separated and sent to a different group for the ballot to be removed and counted. The system successfully prevents voter fraud while ensuring the vote remains secret. Using Meisner's special invisible coatings for the ballots, illegal ballots can be detected and not counted. The only place open to voter fraud is with the group counting the ballots. It had occurred in the past that one of the staff was able to mark ballots to either add votes or disfigure votes so the ballot is voided.)*

It was a sensitive process since there were various ballots based on the particular precinct in which the voter resided. In closed primaries, the ballots had to be coded by party affiliation and include only the candidates for that particular party and voter precinct.

The Meisner Industries Stuffers had two groups; one group manufactured the equipment and was staffed to provide maintenance. The other group wrote the software that ran the stuffing equipment machines. These two groups called themselves strange names, the Hards and the Softs referencing whether they worked on the hardware or software. Each sub-group had a designated liaison person that coordinated work between the two teams. Kyle was scheduled to meet with Cal Monfort, liaison from the Soft Team of the Stuffers. Kyle traveled to Troutdale east of Portland to the office of the Soft Stuffers. The machines themselves were manufactured in Troutdale, but in a different facility staffed by the Hard Team.

Cal greeted Kyle, "Mr. Tredly, so glad to see you again. Are you going to drive a van next year?" Cal met Kyle when Kyle drove for Hood to Coast.

"Yes, in fact, I will. I see you are wearing jeans and a sweatshirt. Is that normal attire? I wish we were that informal."

"Yes, of course. We are very informal here," laughing, Cal added, "sometimes too informal."

"Oh. How is that," Kyle responded before he thought. He realized that was a bit confrontational, so he added, "I suppose you guys are good friends with each other."

"Men and women," Cal added.

"Oh, yeah. One of my bad habits of referring to everybody as a guy. I blame it on Southern Influence," Kyle responded, trying to excuse his faux pas.

"No problem. As I said, we are very informal. How can I help you? I got a note from Mr. Meisner—alarmed me at first. Not sure I have seen him more than once, and that, at a Christmas Party. I deal mostly with Joe Walker."

"Joe's my team leader," Kyle responded.

"Oh, so what is your role?"

"Since my specialty is in the hyperspectral read-heads used in almost every machine, he wanted me to be informed about the use of all the machines. Mr. Meisner has me visiting relevant sites. I think he needs information that he can't get if he visits since he is the boss. And being relatively new to Meisner Industries, I naturally ask questions because I don't have any preconceived ideas about the various segments of the company. At least that is my theory."

"So, do you write him reports of your visit?"

"Yes, why do you ask?"

"Will I get to see the report?"

"I don't know. That is up to Mr. Meisner. He does not tell me what he does with the reports. I don't even know if he reads them, although he must since he asks for them. Do you have any concerns?" Kyle wondered if there were things Cal wanted to tell him but could not if they might show up in a report to Mr. Meisner.

"No, just curious," Cal said. "Do you have any particular questions for me?"

"I don't have a list of questions in mind. I want to see your operation. That will generate my questions."

"Sure, okay. We have designated liaisons for the two groups. I know our names are a bit weird. My group is called the "Softs." The other group is the "Hards." Frankly, our friends tease us about the names."

"How is that?"

"I don't know why I am telling you this. It is a bit embarrassing. It's a sexual reference. I think we need to change the subject."

"Okay, now I get it. That is pretty funny. So, do you tease each other?"

"You would not believe all the ways this comes up. Practically every day—we can be talking about something unrelated—somebody makes a wisecrack."

Amused, Kyle persisted in spite of himself, "What about the women in your group. Don't they get offended by the jokes?"

"Hell no! They are the worst. "There is a woman from my Soft Team that keeps accusing her teammates of being "Wimps' or suggests they need to join the Hard Team. Or she asks members of the other team if their machine parts are erect. Things like that."

Kyle could not help himself and chuckled, but needed to move on, "Cal, could you tell me about the software you are developing?"

Cal spent the next half hour describing the software that would control the machines that stuffed ballots into envelopes. When he finished, Kyle asked, "What about the coated paper. Does your software care about the special coatings on the paper?"

"Sure," Cal said. "The software makes sure the paper is coated and records the kind of coating and creates a database that pairs the coating with the voter name printed on the front of the envelope. We use a module that I think you wrote, Kyle. Am I correct?"

"Probably," Kyle said. "But Cal, that seems like it could be a problem. Doesn't that mean that when the votes are tabulated, the counting machines can tell how a voter voted? Wouldn't that be a violation of the secret ballot?"

"It might seem that way. However, other than collecting summary data, the only function would be to reject a ballot. When a run is declared complete, the data is summarized to reflect how many different coatings and what type were seen by precinct and voter registration only the summary information is preserved. The person's data is never recorded. Besides, after the ballot is removed from the security envelope, we no longer know to whom the ballot belongs. The data accumulated data is this summary information used to manage the machines and integrity of the process."

Kyle wondered if this process might warrant further inquiry, but he decided to wait until he talked to members of the Hard Team. "How far along are you in completing your part of the software?"

"We are waiting on a final version of the user interface, version 1.0—from your team. We are still working with beta version 0.9b. Do you know how much longer until we get V1.0?" Cal asked.

"Not sure, but I think it should be less than a couple of weeks. I think Joe and Jeneen are very close. You know Jeneen?"

"Of course. She is one of our best runners on Hood to Coast. She does the testing, right?"

"Yup! She sure gives me fits. Nothing ever seems to get by her. High energy gal," Kyle said, agreeing with Cal.

Cal responded, "She sure has lots of energy on the run. Tell her I said hi, will you"?

"Sure. Cal, I would love to talk more, but I need to get back to the office before too long. Could you introduce me to the liaison for the Hard Team? Also, could I get a list of all the people on the Soft Team?"

Cal called his aide, and he came immediately with a team roster for Kyle. Cal offered to lead Kyle to the Hard Team manufacturing plant a few blocks away. Cal introduced Kyle to Whipping Bull, a tall, 275-pound Native American fellow. Cal did not hang around as Kyle assured him, he could find his way back to I-84 to get back to his office. Whipping Bull had a deep, commanding voice.

Curious, Kyle asked, "I know you must get asked this question a lot, but if you don't mind, how did you get the name, Whipping Bull?"

"That's not my name. They call me that because they say I try to whip them in line all the time with my bullshit—real name is Hank Norton. I did not grow up on the reservation, but they kid me all the time, anyway. And I don't mind. I have names for all of them too. It's a friendly game we play to confuse the security systems that we all hate."

Sympathetically, Kyle rejoined, "Tell me about it. Meisner Security even bugged my apartment. Could you show me around? I have never seen an actual manufacturing plant. How many machines can you produce in a day?"

Hank hesitated, "Well, that is hard to say. It can take three days to put a machine together if we have all the parts and another day to shake it down. We usually have about five machines in process, so our output right now is a slow two or three a day. The plant has a much larger capacity if we get lots of orders. They estimate we could produce as many as thirty a day in full-out production. Right now, we do not have the finished software, so we can't sell any machines. There are about a hundred in inventory. It will take a day or two to update each machine when the Soft Team has finished the software. Sorry if that is a wishy-washy answer."

Hank took Kyle all over the plant, answering questions and introducing Kyle to most of the staff. It struck Kyle that these did not look like the factory workers he imagined in his mind, but a bunch of professionals dressed in jeans and white shirts. Kyle asked Hank for a list of workers in the plant. The tour took over two hours, including a brief break for lunch in the employee lunchroom. Kyle snacked on a sandwich from a vending machine. What was most impressive was seeing one of the prototype machines in operation, folding and stuffing ballots, return envelopes, and secrecy envelopes in mailing envelopes. For this demonstration run, the machine did not print on the envelopes.

~ Roadway Reflections ~

Kyle reflected on everything he had seen on the way back to headquarters and what he would report to Mr. Meisner. He also wondered what he would report to Laura, and therefore to the FBI. On the one hand, he saw many places that information could leak out of Meisner Industries. Having operations spread over so many physical locations made it difficult to determine where to look. He surmised that is why Meisner had sent him on these errands. He doubted Meisner would have entrusted this to him had it not been "arranged" by Laura. At least that was his theory. If it was the case, he wondered how she happened to have so much influence. How much were her actions suggested or directed by the FBI? It was complicated working on two fronts at once, one for Meisner's leak concern, and the other fishing expedition for the FBI.

The work he had done on the hyperspectral read-heads looked like a critical component of the whole voting machines operation. However, he was still unclear why they needed a read-head in every machine and why this was such an essential element of concern to Meisner. It seemed to Kyle that securing the ballots' integrity could be accomplished much more easily than bothering with expensive specialized secret and invisible coatings of the ballot paper. As he thought about it, it seemed to him there was more to the coatings than anyone was telling him about, that is, if they knew themselves. Surely, someone could explain why the coatings were necessary to manage election ballots. It seemed like a lot of trouble to prevent an unlikely and probably rare voting fraud event. Maybe that was a marketing point, and the development of the coatings was for another purpose. He needed to talk to Laura and George. Maybe George had come up with something. George had arranged to stay longer now that he was working with the FBI too. A lot to think about and discuss with George and Laura.

~ Leaks that Cause a Stir ~

Not long after Kyle returned to the office, he got a message that he was wanted in Meisner's office immediately. The urgency of the meeting concerned Kyle—as it should have—his concern was merited. Kyle let Joe know that he had to report to Meisner about his visits to other facilities. Joe tried to get more information from Kyle, but Kyle put him off since he was urgently requested to report. He went up to Meisner's office and was ushered in immediately. Meisner was alone. He seemed agitated, something Kyle had not observed before.

"Kyle, thanks for coming up. I have a problem. You are supposed to be helping uncover leaks from someplace in the organization. They seem to be initiated from information that only your team knows about. Now, there has been a new leak, one that could be damaging to the company. I was under the impression by asking you to visit other teams that you might find a link to how proprietary information was being leaked. I don't have a lot of time before these leaks can damage the company, and possibly people's jobs. What's the problem, Kyle?"

"Mr. Meisner, I do not know exactly why you are counting on me to resolve this issue. It always seemed to me that your security team should be the ones to answer the question. They have access to information and professionals experienced in protecting information assets. Nevertheless, I have been working hard with Laura's assistance and advice to uncover the source of the leaks. Frankly, the possibilities are huge considering not only the employees, but their spouses, significant others, and friends. Of course, the source of a leak has to originate with an employee. A leak could have been an innocent comment or carelessness, under the influence of alcohol or something else. It could even occur by careless disposal of working drafts. I have only had occasion to look at a couple of sites so far. I still have to make sure my code works properly on the read-heads."

Meisner interrupted, "Kyle, I don't want excuses, just results. My reasons for picking you to address this problem are mine alone. I need you to step up to the task and get results. I know that Laura has a keen mind and is capable of assisting. She can't do the actual grunt work because she is not on the inside. You are the inside man. I need results."

"I get it; you want results! I am doing the best I can."

"Kyle, let me make myself clear. Best is not enough! I need more than what you think is your best. I need results. So, get out of here and get me results."

"I do have a question. Could you tell me the nature of this additional leak? Given that it appears to be recent, I could focus on it."

Meisner hesitated before he answered, considering whether or not it was important for Kyle to know. He decided it was, "The leak is related to the coatings on the paper ballots we are manufacturing. That should be enough information," and Meisner turned his back on Kyle to return to his desk. Kyle waited a moment to see if he was going to add anything else. He did not. Instead, he signaled for Charla to come in.

Kyle had nothing more to add. He gave a pathetic salute-like motion, turned around, and left the office, passing Charla, who was headed in. He said hi to her as they passed.

Now he was frustrated. He had never been good at standing his ground with a boss. He would have to find a way to do better than best if he was to satisfy Meisner, and, by implication, save his job.

~ George's Discovery ~

George asked Kyle if they could meet. George wanted to meet privately before they talked to Laura. George was concerned that if Laura knew what he had found out, it might go directly to the FBI, and then George and Kyle would suddenly be out of the loop. Kyle arranged to meet with George that evening at The Sudra, a local Indian food restaurant on Glisan in North East Portland. Indoor seating was minimal, but the weather was decent, so sitting outside was an acceptable option.

Kyle quizzed George, "What is so private that we needed to meet without Laura?" Kyle felt a certain kind of betrayal now that he and Laura were on such good terms.

"Kyle, do you think you can keep a secret from Laura, at least for a while until you hear me out, and we see where my information leads?"

"You are putting me in an awkward position, George. The best I can do is promise to listen to what you have to say. If you convince me to keep it a secret, I can do that, at least for a while."

George hesitated then continued, "Let's say we put a time frame on it. Say, two weeks. If you could hold off for two weeks, then we both would know how to involve Laura. Can you live with that?

"That is asking a lot, George. How about you tell me, and then I can judge for myself?"

George realized that Kyle was hopelessly in love with Laura and would not put their relationship at risk. He would have to take a chance. If Kyle blew it, then so be it. So, he decided to go ahead. "Okay. Promise me you will hear me out."

Kyle nodded agreement.

"Remember, you introduced me to Jeneen, one of your co-workers?"

"Yes. We ran into her when we were having dinner the other night."

"Do you remember how you introduced me?"

"Yes. I was caught off guard. I introduced you as a private eye I met in Texas."

"Right, and I said I was up here on a case and looked you up. Remember?"

"Okay. So, what does your secret have to do with Jeneen?"

"I ran into Jeneen again, and she asked for my number. She said she needed to ask me a question. She has a niece who is attending Stanford. Jeneen and Maddy are very close since Jeneen babysat for Maddy. Maddy is five years younger. Maddy is majoring in Political Science. At a party about four months ago, Maddy ran into Chao Li. They got to be friends and have been dating. Her niece says they are pretty serious. They started rooming together two months ago. Last month she was looking for papers she had misplaced and found a note addressed to Chao that concerned her."

"George, get to the point," Kyle said impatiently.

George ignored Kyle and continued, "The note was a threat to Chao to keep quiet about his father's relationship with Meisner Industries. Do you know anything about this?"

Kyle frowned, "No. Who is his father?"

"Be patient. I tracked down the source of the hyperspectral read-heads you told me about. They are manufactured by K & W Manufacturing in Taipei, Taiwan. The owner of the factory is Chao's father, one Tao Li. Tao Li also attended Stanford at the same time as Richard Meisner, and they became good friends."

"So why would Chao be threatened to keep quiet? It seems like anybody could discover what you have uncovered," Kyle asked with curiosity. Kyle was wondering why this should be kept from Laura. He suspected she already knew about Tao Li being the source of the read-heads.

"Kyle, I think the question is not why, but what he is supposed to keep quiet about? Who is concerned?"

"Go On," Kyle's frown now displayed dark furrows on his forehead.

"Okay, here's the thing. I discovered that K & W Manufacturing does not make the read-heads. Li has been outsourcing the work to a factory on the mainland."

"So what? A lot of electronic equipment is manufactured in China. Why keep this secret? Why threaten Chao? Kyle retorted.

"That's the interesting part. Why threaten Chao? I have a theory, but I need to do more investigation. I also need to see if Jeneen, because of this tie with her niece and Chao and the read-heads, is inadvertently a source of the leaks from Meisner Industries."

Kyle was puzzled. "You think she is sharing information with her niece, and her niece is somehow sharing that information? If she is, I will bet Jeneen does not realize Maddy is leaking information."

"Jeneen might not realize it. And, her niece might not be sharing with anyone but Chao. What I am concerned about is getting the FBI into this before I can do more research. That is what I am asking time for, Kyle. What do you think? Can you give me a little time?"

"George, why tell me these things now. Why not wait until you had more? You put me in an awkward position, you know."

"Because you asked me to help, and I want you to know what I am doing. Don't you want to know what I am doing?

"Yes, of course, I want to know. Keep me posted. I can keep it a secret for a little while."

"Thanks. I will keep you posted. Be sure to let me know if you can't keep the secret before I get myself in trouble. And, I might add, keep an eye on Jeneen, see if you pick up anything.

Maybe you can get her talking about her relatives, who they are, where they are, so forth. Maybe she will tell you about Maddy. Don't be too obvious, though. Be your normal curious self."

After their meeting, Kyle realized he did not ask George how he got the information about Chao and his father's plant in Taiwan. Maybe that was a secret too.

~ Chao and Tao ~

Chao Li made it home once each semester, mainly because his mother insisted. She liked to hear what he had been up to, how school was going, and especially if there were any girls in his life. She also arranged for him to meet some of the hometown girls of marriageable age, hoping he would find a nice Taiwanese girl to marry. On this most recent trip, he confessed to his mother he had a girlfriend in Palo Alto, California, who had moved into his apartment. His mother wanted all the details and insisted on seeing all the pictures he had saved on his phone. Chao tried unsuccessfully to explain to her why Maddy did not come with him on this trip home.

Chao could not explain that he did not want Maddy here this trip; he needed to talk to his father about the threats he had received. Chao did not know Maddy had seen the threatening note. He arranged to meet at a local bar after his father got off work.

"Chao, why did you want to meet here?" his father asked.

"I did not want to worry Mother. I have concerns I need to talk to you about alone."

"Concerns? Is there a problem with school? Are you keeping up with your classes?"

"Father, I am not having any school problems. Classes are going well. I like my professors. And I like my girlfriend Maddy. My concern is about something else."

"Girlfriend? You came to me about your girlfriend? Is she pregnant? I can help you with that.

"No, no, father! It is not about my girlfriend.

"Surely you don't have money problems. You know you can count on me if you run short."

"No money problems. Listen and stop trying to guess. I received a threat. The threat said I should keep quiet about your relationship with Meisner Industries. Is there something I should know? Why would that be of anyone's concern? I thought everyone knew that you and Meisner were good friends. Do you have any idea why I need to be cautious?"

Tao was quiet. He sipped his drink, racking his brain why his son would receive a threat. Tao wondered if his sexual preferences were known to his son. He decided discretion was the best option. "Chao, I don't have a clue why anyone would be concerned about my relationship with Meisner."

"Do you still communicate with him?"

"Yes, yes. He buys electronic equipment from my factory. We communicate regularly. I recently shipped him a large order."

Chao pushed ahead, "What was in the order?"

"Hyperspectral read-heads, for a project he has going." I don't know for sure what he is using them for."

"How big an order?"

"Two hundred thousand read-heads."

"Wow. That many?" Chao thought for a moment, then asked, "Did your group design them?"

"No, the specifications came directly from Richard. He has a courier who hand-delivers them."

"Hand-delivers them? That seems excessive. I would have thought he could have air expressed them to you." Chao wondered if there was some secret that Meisner needed to protect that led him to hand-deliver specifications.

"Richard can be a bit paranoid," Tao said, "He was always dreaming of projects and concerned someone would steal his ideas. I assumed he was still being paranoid. He won't even tell me exactly what he needs the read-heads for," Tao reflected.

"I get that. From what I hear from my professors, industrial espionage is quite prevalent these days. But I am not sure why they would want to warn me to keep quiet. I would think somebody would want information, not the other way around."

Chao wondered if Meisner could be behind the threat, concerned that Chao would compromise his secret project. "What can you tell me about the read-heads? Anything unusual about them?"

Tao had a sheepish look on his face. He flushed too. "Chao, I have to tell you something that you should keep secret. K & M Manufacturing has been having cash flow problems recently. We have several clients that are significantly in arrears in their payments. Not Richard, mind you."

"How much in arrears?"

Tao visibly made a little shake before he answered. "Two hundred and ten days. They were big orders. As a result, I had to furlough several people in the factory. When Richard's order came through, I knew I would not be able to deliver. So, I subcontracted with Xiazhen Manufacturing in Shenzhen because they could do the work for considerably less and would give me one hundred eighty days to pay. I knew Richard was a prompt payer, so I could deliver two hundred thousand units on time even though I was cash poor and short on staff."

"And did you deliver the read-heads on time?"

"Yes."

"And did Richard pay promptly?

"Yes."

"And, are you still having cash flow problems?"

"Yes. I have good people working on it. They assure me it can be resolved, so I don't think I will need to borrow or worse yet declare bankruptcy."

Chao scratched his head unconsciously. "So, this does not seem to be about money. Does Richard know you outsource the job to China?"

Tao was embarrassed to confess these things in front of his son. "No, Richard does not know. I don't think the read-heads had any markings that would identify them from Xiazhen or the mainland."

"So, back to the warning. Why would anyone want me to be quiet? Could it be from Meisner's security folks?"

"Son, I don't think so. I am pretty sure he would communicate with me. He knows that you and I get along, that you would do anything for me. I can't imagine Richard would send goons to threaten you."

"So, are you sure you don't owe someone that has it in for you? Any rivals that want your business?" Chao asked.

Tao wondered out loud, "We get all the work we can do here in Taiwan. Cash flow can be a problem, though. But how can my cash flow cause anyone to threaten you? Why would they warn you not to talk about Meisner placing orders from me? The only thing I can figure out is the Xiazhen secret. Who, besides me, would want that to be secret?"

"Father, who owns Xiazhen? Chao asked.

"I don't know? The only connection I have there was recommended to me by a friend. Why do you ask?

"What if MSS owns them? That might be a secret MSS would want to keep quiet."

"Oh, god! If that were true and Richard found out, I would be ruined, and so might Richard." Tao began to think about how he could find out more about Xiazhen without raising suspicions. Tao added, "Chao, I would take that threat seriously and not tell anyone what we talked about. Can I count on you?"

"Of Course, Father."

Tao and Chao were not aware that they were being watched. There was a secret about the read-heads that needed to be kept secret at all costs. Those watching could not hear the conversation, but by the intensity of the conversation, they had concerns that would be reported.

Tao and Chao went over things again, but without any new results. Both were puzzled, but it was getting late, and they were expected back at the house. Chao's mother assumed Chao and Tao were spending "man time" together as they used to do when Chao was growing up and went to the factory with his father. She asked no work-related questions, but she had a lot of questions about Maddy. She expressed her preferences for Chao to marry a Taiwanese girl. Chao tried, unsuccessfully, to convince his mother not to worry. After all, Maddy was a

Taiwanese girl. She was born in Taipei, but her family moved to America when she was only four years old.

Chapter 13

~ Kyle and Vote Counting ~

Once again, Kyle elected to visit one of the Meisner Industries sites. He met Roger Worthington on the Hood to Coast relay event. Roger was not the boss or team leader, but he worked on the Counting Team. Kyle did not have an opportunity to talk to Roger much. Roger seemed like an articulate fellow at the beach party at the close of the relay. Kyle went to Beaverton west of Portland to visit the Counting Team facility. The Counting Team was the group that manufactured ballot tabulation machines.

When he arrived, Roger Worthington was the first person he ran into. Roger was asking the receptionist something when he walked in. Roger warmly greeted Kyle and graciously briefed Kyle on the work of the team. As in other cases, there were two groups, one that worked on software and another that manufactured the actual ballot/vote-counting machines. Once again, there was a general separation of duties between the software and hardware groups. After showing Kyle the manufacturing plant operation, Roger took Kyle to Hal's office. Hal was the team leader. Roger introduced Kyle.

"Hal, I have someone here that would like to have a word with you. Kyle Tredly."

Hal turned around, got up, and extended his hand to Kyle. "Kyle, so good to meet you. I had a note from Meisner you would be visiting. I don't get many notes directly from Mr. Meisner."

Roger, hearing the reference to Richard Meisner, assumed they had private things to talk about, gave his excuses, and left Kyle and Hal to talk.

"Good to meet you too, Hal. Roger showed me around the plant. You are the "big dog" here?

"I guess you could call it that. I lead the software team for the voting counting machines and oversee the hardware too. We have three programmers that work on software and a dozen that work on the machines. Hey, it is almost time for lunch. You interested in going someplace to get a bite?"

Kyle looked at his watch. It was only 11:30 AM, but he took the suggestion as an invitation to get away from the office, away from listening ears. "Sure, I have plenty of time. Are there any good places to eat around here?"

"I have a cozy place I like to eat. You like Vietnamese?"

"Sounds good. I have only had good Vietnamese food once since I have been in Portland."

"Great, there is this place, Pho Tango Bistro, that I like. I can drive us there."

Kyle and Hal headed out to the parking lot. Kyle was surprised to see that Hal drove a Tesla. Kyle knew they were expensive. He assumed Hal must have saved his pennies to buy such a nice car."

"Wow, I have never ridden in a Tesla before. How long have you had this?"

Hal answered with electric-car pride, "Just a few months. I am in love, I must confess."

Once in the car, Hal quizzed Kyle about his work. Kyle shared a few details and about his visits to several Meisner sites. Kyle realized that Hal had not received the information about any other visits from Richard. Kyle explained that he was in charge of the software module for the hyperspectral read-heads that Meisner Industries seemed to put in every machine they produced. Meisner wanted him to be familiar with all the machines. He did not tell Hal he was also looking for leaks of proprietary Meisner Industries information. "So, your team is working on software for the vote-counting machines? What modules are you working on?"

Hal suggested they wait for details until they reached the Bistro. As they got out of the car, with lots of background traffic noise, Hal leaned over, took out his cell phone, turned it off, and threw it into the car seat. Kyle took the hint and turned his off too. Kyle was not certain that protected their privacy, so he decided to be cautious and threw his on the car seat too. After they were seated and served, Hal began, "Kyle, we work on the ballot handling software. There are twenty-two different motors and levers that have to be activated depending on the ballots' contents. We write a controller for each of them."

"Do you also have a degree in engineering?" Kyle asked.

"Yes, I graduated with a mechanical engineering degree and then got a master's in software engineering."

"Wow. Meisner hires only the best. What about the other members of your software team? You work closely with them, I assume."

Hal did not immediately respond as if mulling over how much he could trust Kyle. Hal knew things, but he did not know whether what he knew came from Mr. Meisner directly or was an unintentional subversion of the voting machines. "I do work closely with most of my team, Kyle. The reason I wanted to go to lunch to talk is about a concern I have."

"Well, that is one of the reasons I visit places to hear concerns. Meisner likes things to run smoothly."

"That is one of my concerns, Kyle. I am aware of a project that is so secretly guarded I don't know if it is something expected or sabotage."

"Interesting. Tell me more."

"Okay, there is one member of our team who is working on a module that none of the rest of us can view. Normally, there is a team review of all software to eliminate obvious bugs before they're merged into the complete system. This guy's work is never submitted, and no one is telling him to do so."

"Do you know where the module is supposed to be inserted into the final control system?"

"That's all I do know," Hal said with frustration.

"Go on," Kyle prompted Hal.

"It goes in between H-read and F-count."

"You lost me."

"Oh. H-read is the module that reads data from the hyperspectral read-heads. I think you wrote one of the modules that is a part of our H-read. F-count is the module that tabulates the various marks on the paper. It depends on data from the C-Mask module that tells the machine where the marks could be on the ballot and what they are associated with. We run a special ballot mask through the machine to interpret the marks on the ballot. Did that answer your question?"

"Yes, I think I follow you," Kyle said. "So, this mysterious module fits between the time the read-heads read the ballot and the time the tallies are added to the counters. Do I have that right?"

"Exactly. What worries me is that none of us know if that module will work properly when installed. And our merging process does not merge source code but machine language code, which will make it more difficult to analyze. Difficult, but not impossible, given enough time."

Kyle realized that Hal probably did not know that all the ballots would contain an invisible coating only detectable by the hyperspectral read-heads. Of course, the read-heads could also read the marks on the ballot. If the secret module's purpose was solely to reject fake ballots, why keep that purpose secret. Kyle realized he would have to think about this and discuss it with George and Laura.

"Hal, I appreciate your sharing this. I think I can do research and make sure things are on the up and up. I suspect they are. Probably they want to make sure no one has a chance to think of a way to mess with the ballot counting."

Kyle and Hal continued their conversation, mostly general things about their lives, loves, and dreams while they enjoyed a delicious Vietnamese lunch. Hal drove Kyle back to the office, and Kyle slummed it driving his Prius back to headquarters.

~ Palo Alto ~

George decided he needed to talk to Maddy, Chao's roommate. He decided to drive down from Portland to Palo Alto, just south of San Francisco. If he left by 6:00 AM, he figured he could be there easily by 6:00 PM. He was using an Enterprise rented car he had for an indefinite period. He stopped for lunch at the Caldera Brewery & Restaurant off Interstate 5 in Ashland, Oregon. The view of the mountains was inspiring to a guy who lived most of his life in the rather flat plains of Texas. As he ate, he reminisced about a visit he made as a child to the Colorado Rockies with his father, who loved to fly fish. He remembered one trip in particular when he was playing upstream from his father. He slipped on moss-covered rocks and cascaded down a small waterfall into the pool where his dad was fishing. His dad laughed, but it scared George to death, and he could still feel the cold water of the stream as he shivered involuntarily at lunch. On another trip, he recalled his older brother using a fly swatter to hit a porcupine hiding under a cabin where they were camping. It pulled out quills that his brother showed him. He remembered a bear coming up to their car on one of their trips. He had nightmares about that for several years. Deer and bears are cute at a distance, but a bear up close, not so much. After lunch and reverie, he paid the bill and headed on to Palo Alto and the Stanford campus.

George arrived before 6:00 PM and checked in at The Cardinal Hotel, a quaint hotel built in 1924 a few minutes from the Stanford University complex. He was stiff from the long ride, so he decided to take a walk after settling in his room. After about an hour, he returned to get a bite to eat and see if he could contact Maddy Hilburn, Chao's roommate. Jeneen had given him Maddy's cell phone number. He called, but she did not answer. He left a message for her to call him when she returned, whatever the hour.

The phone rang at 1:00 AM. George had not expected the call to be so late. Groggily he answered the phone, "Hello?"

"I was calling for Mr. Lockit," Maddy answered.

More alert, George sat up on the edge of the bed, "This is Lockit, George Lockit. Is this Maddy?"

"Yes. Jeneen said you might get in contact. You are in Palo Alto?"

"Yes, I was hoping we might get together to discuss the concerns you expressed to Jeneen. I'd like to get more information. When could we meet?"

"Let me think. I have classes tomorrow morning, but I have the afternoon free. We could meet for lunch if that would work for you."

"Maddy, that works fine." George and Maddy discussed places they could meet and settled on Tootsies at the Stanford Barn, an Italian restaurant on Welch Road. They agreed to meet at 12:30 the next day.

The next morning, George went to the campus and walked around for a while to sample the atmosphere. It was energizing to be around so many young people, many eager to get a superior education or at least a degree from a superior university. Most of them looked eager. He ignored the ones lying around the campus doing things George believed they probably should not be doing. He remembered his college days at the University of Texas in Austin, years earlier. He had not been as serious about his studies as he should have been. Still, he did graduate with a degree in Political Science. He located Tootsies, and he decided he should drive in case Maddy wanted to go someplace more private. He would like to see

Chao's warning note if possible, but that seemed like a long shot. He returned to the hotel around ten, took a shower, and made notes for his conversation with Maddy. He went to Tootsies early to be sure he was there when Maddy arrived. She was a few minutes late. George recognized Maddy from the description Jeneen had given. Hard to miss a petite, fair-skinned, naturally bright, Asian redhead. He approached her when she came in the door.

"Hi, Maddy. I am George Lockit," he extended his hand to shake hers, and she reciprocated.

"Good to meet you, Mr. Lockit," She said politely.

"Let's get a table where we can talk. I asked the hostess for a booth near the back where we can talk privately." George waved at the hostess, and she motioned them to follow her to the back of the restaurant. It was not long before a waitress came by.

"Could I get you two anything to drink besides water?" the waitress asked, filling their glasses.

George and Maddy looked at each other. Maddy answered, "I would like a Coke, please."

George added, "Make it two." The waitress returned with their drinks and took their orders. George turned to Maddy, "Maddy, so good to meet you. Thanks for making time for me. Have you been friends with Jeneen long?"

"Since she was my babysitter in Medford," she said, hesitating when George's forehead wrinkled. Then she added,

"Medford, Oregon. Jeneen was older, and I missed her when she graduated from High School and went to college. But we keep in contact. When we can, we schedule our visits home at the same time to catch up. My aunt still lives in Medford, but my parents moved back to Taipei."

"Those are the kind of friends we all cherish. I can see why Jeneen wanted me to talk to you. I hope you don't mind me asking lots of questions."

"Not at all. Jeneen says that you are a detective. What are you working on?"

"Sorry, Maddy, that is one of the problems of this profession. I can't always share what I'm doing and why I'm doing it. All I can tell you is that I hope we can help each other. I am interested in the note you told Jeneen about. She is concerned and wants me to assess the situation. I hope you can trust that I will do what I can to help you."

"If Jeneen trusts you, then so do I."

Their conversation was interrupted when their food arrived. After the waitress left, George continued, "You told Jeneen you found a note written to Chao that he had not shared with you."

"Yes, I made a copy for you if that helps." Maddy reached into her purse and pulled out a folded piece of paper. She handed it to George. George opened it and inspected it.

Chao Li, you are hereby advised that you are not to share any information you may become privy to related to your father's work in Taipei or his relationship with Richard

Meisner. You should be aware that your actions are being observed, and you and your friend's wellbeing is dependent on your compliance. We know where you live as well as your class schedule. You are a bright guy, do not be stupid.

George inspected the page carefully. "Maddy, I see why this concerns you. I assume the "friend" reference, is you?"

"That was my assumption too. But I am mostly concerned about Chao. He is not one to lay down for this. I think that is why he left mid-term to make a visit home."

"Look here. See this Chinese character at the bottom of the note. Do you know what that means?"

"No. I have no idea. It looks like a Chinese character, but not one I have ever seen," Maddy answered.

"Have you discussed this note with Chao?"

"No, Maddy answered. I feel a bit awkward about that. Generally, we seem to get along great, to share the most intimate times. Yet, he never mentioned the note. And since I found it going through his things, I did not want to confess to getting into his stuff. Do you know what the character means?"

George did not know either, but it was of concern. He did not want to alarm Maddy any more than she was already. He hedged, "I don't know Chinese. I am sure it is not important."

"No. I don't know exactly when the note came, but he began acting weird about a week ago, then he suddenly needed to take a trip home to Taipei in the middle of the semester, in the middle of his classes. That is very unlike him."

George asked Maddy if he could take the note with him. She agreed.

"Maddy, are there any other things of concern to you?"

"I am probably getting a bit paranoid. I think I saw the same two guys several times when I was out with Chao. I would probably not have thought anything about it had I not found the note."

"Can you describe the fellows?"

"Well, the reason I noticed was the fact they were older than most of the students we see around the campus. They both looked like they were Chinese or maybe from Taiwan. I am pretty sure they were not from Japan or Korea. They had stocky builds, almost six feet tall, wearing black suits with purple shirts."

George frowned, "Purple shirts? Every time? How many times did you see them?"

"Maybe three altogether. I don't know. I am just on edge. Should I be concerned?"

George did not want to alarm her, so he tried to be reassuring. "I don't think you should be too concerned. However, if it would ease your mind, why not try to secretly take a picture of them if you see them again and text me the picture. Here, let me give you my number," which he did. "I was wondering if it would be possible to take a look at your apartment? It might help me get a sense of things if I could look around."

"I suppose that would be okay. It is a bit of a mess right now. Well, it is usually a mess, but if you don't mind that, sure. You want to do that now?"

George and Maddy finished their meals and headed over to the apartment she and Chao shared. George spent an hour checking out the apartment, shuffling through papers. He did not find anything of particular interest other than the original note. It matched the copy Maddy had given him. He said his goodbyes, checked out of his hotel, and was about to head back to Portland. However, he had two flat tires. Given they were on opposite sides of the car, it looked intentional. He had AAA insurance, so gave them a call, and they sent a guy out to repair them. The holes were in the sidewalls of the tires. The mechanic said he could not repair sidewalls. It appeared to him this damage was intentional. George called AAA, and they told him who to call at the rental agency to get two new tires. It held him up for three hours.

~ Meisner Marketing ~

Richard Meisner followed the progress of SB 1076, Federal Rules for Voting in Federal Elections. His sources informed him that the post-hearing had gone well, and the bill had been scheduled for a vote two weeks later. Corning was a very influential senator, especially when it came to legislation that he sponsored. Richard realized that once the bill passed and the President signed it, it would only take a month before the specifications would come out. Any number of jurisdictions would use the federal specifications to put out Requests for Proposal (RFPs) for new voting equipment. His marketing department had been in touch with several of them, promising Meisner Industries would be able to respond in a very short time frame to RFPs based on Federal Rules. Marketing had also alerted potential buyers that MI's voting systems would be state of the art, hack-proof, and establish a new standard in voting integrity. Marketing had let Richard know that clients were eagerly waiting on the chips to fall so they could get new equipment on-site to be ready for the next major election coming up in eighteen months.

Richard was getting anxious about being ready. He stood to make a lot of money selling Meisner Voting Systems and to lose a lot if not. He wanted to check on the progress of all his teams. He hoped to get useful information from Kyle. He had not told Kyle all the reasons he had sent him to various teams. He had led Kyle to believe he was looking for information leaks. In fact, he thought his security team should be able to handle most issues around leaks. Kyle was extra insurance Laura had convinced him to take. He would want a report from Kyle to get his take on the readiness of the various components. Kyle also arranged to visit the Voting Systems Integration Team to ensure all the pieces were working together. The integration team worked in Vancouver, Washington, just across the Columbia River.

A week before Kyle arranged a visit, Richard made arrangements with his driver to visit the Integration Team office site. He was scheduled to meet with the Team Leader, Bret Lambert, at 10:30 AM. Bret was waiting for him.

"Mr. Meisner, so good of you to come to our office. Could I get you coffee or tea? I arranged for lunch to be catered for the two of us at noon."

"Bret, good to see you again. I would like coffee if it is not too much trouble," Richard answered. "There are a lot of details I want to cover today, so lunch sounds like a good plan."

Richard asked Bret about his family and patiently listened to Bret's stories about his two daughters and one son. Bret's oldest daughter was attending MIT. The younger daughter was still in High School, a private boarding school in Boston. The daughter at MIT was able to check in on her little sister from time to time. Both of them were expected to be home in a week for a few days. His son was turning thirteen, interested in computers, music, science, and math. Bret had no idea where all these interests would lead. Right now, all his kids were doing well in school. Once the coffee arrived, Bret closed the doors to his office, and they got down to business.

Bret was able to assure Richard that everything was on schedule. The various pieces of the voting systems were on target. He had already tested Alpha and Beta versions of the software pieces and the various prototype machines that made up the Meisner Voting System. Each unit worked as expected. The paper ballot coatings were being applied correctly and properly detected by the vote-counting machines. They had run through several thousand test ballots. After a few errors in the early runs, all the bugs appeared to have been worked out. It appeared they were almost ready to give their stamp of approval to the entire system. The only remaining activity was the final integration of the various components to create version 1.0 of the software systems that operated the machines of the entire system from ballot prep, to stuffing, mailing and vote counting.

Bret felt sure Richard liked the progress. Although you never knew how a last-minute glitch could create a delay. Progress seemed to be on target. He had one last request to ask of Bret. Richard asked Bret if he was aware of the hook in the vote-counting machines. The so-called hook would allow a last-minute addition to the software.

Bret answered, "Sure, I am aware of the hook, the place we can insert a diversion to an adjustment module if there was a last-minute addition or correction. We could make a last-minute correction without having to reassemble the whole system. Is that what you are referring to?"

"Yes. Keep in mind that when we ship the units, we may need to add last-minute adjustments at the point of the hook."

"Okay. Although I don't think you will need one. Everything looks pretty solid to me."

"Bret, I might need to have another of my teams that oversee all software marketed to customers do an independent verification of the system. If it appears necessary, the hook will be installed at that point. Your team won't have an opportunity to be involved. I am sure you understand. The voting systems can make or break Meisner Industries, and I have organized lots of redundancy in this project. I am sure you are aware that I have several teams working on various aspects of the voting system. The hook on the counting machines is a small but essential part.

Bret did not particularly like it that his contribution was considered small and needed to be reviewed. Still, Meisner had a reputation with most of his employees of being paranoid about security. Richard expected the best, and when a team had assured him, they had done their best, Richard would ask them to do better and then have someone else check out the result. Bret knew this, although he did not like being double-checked. He was concerned about a module added at the last minute and not getting to test it himself. If the addition introduced a problem, would his team be held accountable? Wouldn't it complicate debugging any error that showed up? However, knowing his place, he answered Richard, "Of course, Mr. Meisner. Let me know how I can help."

"I will keep you posted. Everything is in good shape, and it should not be long before we are shipping Meisner Voting

Systems. Your team's work will turn into supporting our customers. Do you like to travel?"

"Sure," Bret answered. If something went wrong, who would get the blame? Would his team get the blame? How would he work in the field if a problem came up, and there were parts of the system he knew nothing about? Before he could add anything to express reservations about traveling too much, Richard continued.

"Good. We will need competent oversight in any number of places around the country if things go as planned. I will expect some of your staff to travel as well. You might as well begin to figure out who you would recommend for the support phase."

"Looking forward to it," Bret said obediently.

Richard and Bret continued their review regarding the role of the counting machines in the overall system. There were individual machines for production of ballot paper, coatings, stuffing, mail sorting, signature recognition, opening, separation, and finally counting. It was a complete system with checks and double-checks built in to ensure the system's integrity. It was the integration of all the pieces that made the system so tight and hack-proof.

At least, that was how it would be marketed and appear to operate. Only a tiny handful knew the module's secrets that would be installed at the hook at the last moment. Meisner went back to his office after lunch, confident all was well. Bret was not as confident. The "secret" last-minute module bugged him. Meisner told him that the person most involved with the read-heads, Kyle Tredly, would be scheduling a visit soon. He explained that Kyle was charged with helping ensure all the systems that used the read-heads understood their operation. Bret acknowledged Kyle would be welcome.

~ Kyle Visits Vancouver, WA ~

The Voting Systems Integration Team was on Kyle's list to visit. He figured it would help him understand their operation better if he had visited the other components of the system first. Besides that, Bret, the team leader, had been especially cordial to Kyle when he drove the van for Hood to Coast Relay. Bret had been the one that prevented him from taking a wrong turn as well as avoiding a relay parking violation. Of all the people he met on the relay, he liked Bret the most.

Additionally, they seemed to have a similar background in application development. Bret had the same kind of pride in generating error-free computer code. Kyle expected this visit to be both the most interesting and warm.

After Kyle called, Bret was looking forward to his visit. Coming on the heal of a stressful meeting with THE Meisner of Meisner Industries, he felt more relaxed meeting with Kyle. He liked Kyle, his easy-going style, yet seriousness about something so simple as driving a van. Kyle had shared with him the experience he had in St. Andrews, being kidnapped, incarcerated, almost being convicted of murder, and confusing sadness when the two women were murdered. Kyle trusted

Bret not to share all the details with others. Bret did not share, and he felt close because Kyle had shared those private stories with him. Kyle had trusted him. He thought he could trust Kyle as well.

Kyle made the trip over to Vancouver after lunch on a Friday evening. He had no plans to see Laura, and George had left town to check on Jeneen's friend, so he had no plans for the weekend. Kyle was looking forward to a do-nothing weekend. When he arrived as scheduled, the receptionist at the Voting Systems Integration Team office gave Kyle a visitor's badge and directed him to Bret's office. Bret was hunkered over a computer screen when Kyle walked into his office.

"Kyle!" Bret jumped up and extended his hand. "It is so good to see you. Let me show you around." Bret introduced Kyle to many of the staff. Some of them were working in a cubicle pool while others were running tests on various machines of the Voting System. After an hour of touring, meeting staff, and asking lots of questions, they retired to Bret's office. Bret and Kyle spent another hour talking about the Voting Systems, Kyle's visits to other sites, and his work coding for the hyperspectral read-heads. Around 3:00 PM, Bret asked Kyle if he had time for a drink. Kyle did not easily socialize, but Bret was an exception. He eagerly agreed. They took Bret's car to a local bar and restaurant for drinks. Following the protocol they had used before, both left their cell phones in the car. Bret ordered a pitcher of one of the many local beers in the Portland-Vancouver area.

Kyle began, "Bret, how are the kids getting along?" Bret filled him in on all three of his children. He also bragged about his wife's job as a designer at Nike. Kyle brought Bret up to date on his relationship with Laura. He did not share her relationship with the FBI. As the trust level increased, Kyle told Bret more about the strange way he was hired. He did not share about meeting with Meisner before he had interviewed. Kyle did not feel comfortable sharing the unique role he had secretly looking for leaks. He had to be careful.

Despite Kyle being so open, and sharing confidential information, Kyle sensed Bret's discomfort. However, Kyle's openness made it easy for Bret to share HIS concerns.

"Kyle, one of the reasons I wanted to have a beer was to get away from the office so I could speak freely and confidentially."

"Okay," Kyle said in a way to encourage Bret to feel free to talk.

Bret began, "Just two days ago, Mr. Meisner--- ," Bret noticed the frown on Kyle's face. "I know you call him Richard. But I never, never call him that. Certainly not to his face, and seldom behind his back. Okay, Richard visited the office to check on our progress. That was a bit unusual. Normally, I send weekly updates on our work."

"Is everything going alright?" Kyle asked.

"Oh, yeah. Things are in excellent shape. I was able to let Mr. --- Richard know that, but he asked me about something that has me very curious, and frankly concerned."

"Good to hear things are going okay. What has you concerned? Is Richard putting pressure on you? He sure expects a lot out of his employees."

"Nothing like that. Here's the thing. In the integration code, the specifications required us to place a hook in the final stages of the vote-counting machine software."

"Hook?"

"Well, Richard calls it a hook. It is a place in the code where a module could be installed to analyze all system's data up to that point, and if adjustments were necessary, make them. Richard calls them a safety hook. It is a good place for patches if we discovered at the last moment that an adjustment was necessary."

"Why is that a concern. It is not uncommon. I suspect there are multiple so-called hooks in various modules. Have you found any others?"

"My team has not told me about any, but they might not, as you say, hooks are not totally unusual. The existence of the hook is not what concerned me. It is what he said about it."

Kyle's attention was focused now, "Why, what did he say that concerns you?"

Bret hesitated, "Kyle, maybe I am overthinking this. I am not sure it is worth sharing."

"Bret, you did not bring me here to tease me. Out with it, buddy!"

"Okay, okay. Mr. Meisner, Richard that is, said he has another team working on the module that would be installed at the hook before the systems would ship.

Kyle noted, "I don't think that is too surprising. Meisner Industries partitions the work among lots of different teams, and, for the most part, these teams don't share details of their work, only their interfaces and work product." "But, when it comes to integrating them," Bret said, "my team, the Integration Team, sees them and makes sure they all work together. Richard said we won't get to verify the module that goes in at the hook. Richard said that would occur later by work from another team."

Was Bret harboring a hurt or slight? Did he feel insulted by Richard? Did he feel that Richard did not trust his team to do the final integration? So, Kyle asked, "I am not sure what your concerns are. Do you feel slighted by Richard, like he does not trust you?"

"No! No. That is not it. I know this is going to sound crazy. I have thought about it, but it is hard to say out loud. A module placed at the last stage of the Voting System could tinker with the output, and in a way that no one would know the changes had been made." There he said it. He felt a certain kind of relief, but he was anxious about what Kyle would say.

"So, you are saying this last-minute code could subvert results coming from all the other modules? Ah. I see what you are alluding to. I see why you are concerned. I will have to think about it, Bret," and he was already thinking about it. Kyle was beginning to be even more certain that several strange things were going on at Meisner Industries. *Was the smoking gun that the FBI was after?* What to say to Bret? "That is an interesting point. I wonder what team is working on that? *Meisner gave me a list of teams to visit, which I have been doing. Bret's is the last one on my list. The one Bret is referring to, one that writes code for hooks is not on the list.* To Bret, he said, "I can't think of any team that I know about that could be doing that as a side project. You're sure you don't have someone on your team working on code for the hook?"

"No, I know what every group in the Integration Team is doing. Hell, as the integration team, we know about every other team. We have to ensure the integration actually works. No one on my team has time to work on a secret module to be installed at the hook."

Very interesting." Kyle mused.

Bret asked, "Can you look into it? Please leave my name out of it if you can."

"I am not positive that I have the latitude to look into it. But, if something else comes up, I will certainly find a way to pursue it. I am interested and can probably find a way to look into it. Bret, if I figure out it is not anything to be concerned about, I will let you know."

Bret was relieved that Kyle seemed concerned enough to take him seriously. Kyle seemed interested despite his casual assurances. Bret felt he had done the right thing sharing with Kyle.

It was hard for either one of them to focus on business after talking about the hook, so they changed the subject. Kyle and Bret began to share reflections about Hood to Coast and local sports events before going back to Bret's office to get Kyle's car.

On the way back to his apartment, Kyle mentally reviewed the conversations with Bret. Typically, he might have talked to himself, but he had turned his phone back on when he left Vancouver. Kyle suspected the day was not wholly satisfying to Bret. Bret probably felt he had done what he could to raise the issue. Right or wrong, Bret had gotten the monkey off his back and onto Kyle's, although that is not how Bret probably thought of it. Kyle, on the other hand, felt the monkey jump squarely on his back. He would have to discuss this with George when he got back, and perhaps Laura too. It was complicated with Laura. He was definitely in love, but her job as an FBI agent made discussing things honestly and openly awkward. On the one hand, he could tell her things and trust she would not pass them on to her FBI boss if he asked her not to. He felt confident about that. However, that put her in a very awkward position, maybe even a job threatening situation. If he had not known she was working for the FBI, he would not have been concerned about what he shared.

~ Kyle Probes Laura for Information ~

After getting back to his apartment, Kyle decided to press Laura for information without telling her what Bret had shared. After all, he did not get hard data about any illegal or questionable motivations on Richard's part. George had concerns based on his trip to Palo Alto, and now Kyle was concerned too. Kyle began to think about all the meetings he had been having, puzzling how his work with the read-heads fit into the picture. He checked with Laura to see if she was available to meet him. She was available the next evening. She said she had scheduled a call to a college friend this evening, and she did not want to cancel. The next day after working on reports he had to send Richard, he headed over to Laura's. She had prepared them a salmon dinner with all the trimmings. A bottle of Chardonnay topped it off. After cleaning up the dishes, they sat together on the couch. Laura nuzzled Kyle, which flummoxed him because he wanted to talk, not nuzzle.

"Laura, I was wondering. You never told me why the FBI was interested in Meisner Industries. You told me you arranged to connect with Richard back in Dallas. That was a long time ago. What is so concerning to the FBI that they would keep this up for so long?"

Laura was surprised by Kyle's question. She assumed he had figured it out. She could not share the details with him even though he had been read into the case. It compromised both work and love to have secrets. What could she tell him? "That is a difficult question to answer, Kyle. As long as I work for the FBI, I have to keep certain things confidential. Our protocols prevent me from sharing things with you even though I trust you completely. Loving you makes that painful for me. Now that I have said that I can't answer your question, I have to ask you one. Why do you need an answer all of a sudden?"

"Laura, I love you even if you have to keep secrets. It does not feel balanced; however," Kyle was feeling a bit paranoid, "Can we make it? Can our relationship survive secrets? If we have secrets from each other, how will that impact the two of us? I don't know. All I know is I love you, and if I want to be with you, I have to take the good with the—should I call it the bad? Don't look at me that way; that is unfair." Laura sent a loving gaze directly at his eyes. If there were a magic power, she had it with her look. With an invisible laser, her love of Kyle could cut through any resistance he had. So, he continued, "Okay, here is what is on my mind," as he shared his concerns about the Voting System that Meisner was developing. He told her about the secret development team, and the prospects of adding a last-minute module to the vote-counting machines."

Laura's gaze evaporated in a flash as she thought about what he was saying. It fit into FBI suspicions that Richard Meisner was up to no good. This might be the inside information they had been looking for. Kyle noticed her attention go someplace else and then come back.

"Kyle, is there anything else that concerns you?" Laura began to act like an FBI investigator and made Kyle uncomfortable. Kyle had obviously touched on something important to Laura, and most likely, the FBI. He needed to dissipate the tension, so he leaned over and gave Laura a peck on the cheek. She reacted by turning to Kyle, putting her arm around his neck, and drawing him closer for a real kiss. One thing led to another, and she led Kyle to her bedroom, where nature took its course. She had successfully deflected Kyle's curiosity, or so she thought.

After a passionate session of lovemaking, they lay intertwined, skin to skin. Laura whispered into Kyle's ear, "I don't want you to be concerned. Just tell me what is on your mind. Spend the night. We can make love all night."

That was the wrong thing to say to Kyle. He suddenly felt used. Had she bedded him to get information out of him? All his misgivings from a few months ago flooded back in. Was her claim to love him a way for the FBI to get information? *What the heck. I can deal with this later.* He rolled over, facing Laura, and embraced her, fully prepared to make love again. He never did answer her questions. When he woke up, he could smell the sharp scent of bacon and maybe pancakes. When he finally made it to the kitchen with only his skivvies on, he saw Laura had prepared breakfast. He poured a cup of coffee and sat on a bar stool as Laura served him two pancakes topped with an egg, sunny-side-up, and a couple slices of bacon. Having expended a fair amount of energy the evening previously, he was hungry. Laura said nothing about the unanswered question, so neither did Kyle. After he ate, he took a quick shower, dressed, and headed to work, giving Laura a kiss at the door. He tried to hide the fact he was still a bit aggravated that she would not or could not share more about why the FBI was interested in Meisner Industries, but the consolation lovemaking was a great distraction if there had to be one.

Chapter 14

~ Senate Bill Passes Senate ~

Everything was on course. Senate Bill 1076, HAVA, Help America Vote Act, passed the Senate with a substantial bipartisan majority. The House was scheduled to take it up in a couple of weeks. Corning had already discussed it with the President, and he agreed to sign it as a routine matter. Meisner's lobbyist worked with various jurisdictions helping them write Requests for Proposal that would make them eligible for federal grants. These RFPs would be ready soon after the President signed the legislation. Meisner was confident his company would respond to the RFPs, especially since they not only knew what the RFP's would contain but had his crew writing up the principal elements of RFP responses before any other company would be prepared to respond. Certainly, his research indicated only one other firm was capable of providing early competition, Systems Tech, in Virginia. Systems Tech's advantage was being close to Washington. Meisner was someone who did not leave things to chance, so he had a spy working for Systems Tech that kept him well informed of their intentions and preparation. They were not as prepared as he was, and his spy was prepared to do technical sabotage if necessary. He also had a disreputable PR group ready to post disinformation about Systems Tech on social media to discredit them if it was necessary. Richard was leaving nothing to chance.

Richard had a team to make sure his secret advantage produced the desired outcome, and as a result, would allow Corning and him to influence elections. Then there was the secret team, composed of three people. They also stood to benefit substantially from their work on this project. They were designing and coding the module that would be applied at the "hook" for the vote-counting machines. This application would be installed in a particular way that would be hidden throughout the system in encrypted form. Even if discovered, it would be virtually impossible to figure out what it was doing. In essence, the module utilized the unique Meisner Voting Systems coated paper to fix outcomes in selected close elections. The team understood what they were doing and its purpose. They knew the risk if they were exposed. They even had added code to support agendas they were secretly contracted for, unbeknownst to Meisner, on such things as abortion and LGBTQA rights.

Richard had his driver take him to his home in Lake Oswego at noon. He had the driver stop on the way so he could grab a lunch. He told the driver to take the rest of the day off. After lunch, he got his own car out and drove to a house on NW Glencoe Road Northwest of the Hillsboro airport. Meisner Industries owned the farm in the name of the woman who lived there. His secret team worked on the property. He got there around 2:00 PM. Meisner Industries' security group did not know about this location. Therefore, security had not wired it like they had other Meisner employees and Meisner locations. Even their salaries did not appear on any Meisner books. Richard had arranged payment through a Delaware corporation he had set up. Funds to this corporation were provided via private sources outside the country. The paper trail would be difficult to follow.

Richard drove up to the site and rang the doorbell. When there was no answer, he rang again just as someone came to the door. It was the woman who lived in the house and managed the farm. She recognized Richard from a picture she had seen in the newspaper. She showed him to a small metal barn on the back of the property that served as the secret team's offices. There were three cars parked beside the barn. The team had no name. The three guys who worked there referred to themselves as The Gurus. The Gurus were a bit surprised to see Richard. They had been in frequent encrypted communications, but it was rare to see him in person. They all stopped what they were doing and turned their attention to Richard.

"Mr. Meisner," Dan, the designated leader of the Gurus, greeted Richard. "I did not expect you today. What brings you out here?"

"Hi Dan," Richard responded, nodding to the other two. "I need an update on your progress. I wanted to hear it in person. The Voting System project is moving along very quickly now, and I want to be sure you are on schedule. How are you guys doing?"

Dan pulled over a metal folding chair with a cushioned seat and back and motioned for Richard to have a seat. The other two members of the group stopped what they were working on and turned their chairs, forming a circle with Richard. Dan continued, "We are putting the finishing touches on things, right guys?" Dan directed his attention to the other two. They simultaneously nodded.

Richard began, "I am confident essential legislation has passed the Senate, and will be passed by the House, and signed into law within a couple of weeks. I have technical support people working on responses to expected RFPs following almost immediately. That means we are close to moving the product out to customers soon. I don't want to do that without your module integrated into the system."

Dan answered for the team, "We will be ready. Initially, the only thing we will add is a loader that will allow us to provide updates as needed."

"What about the process of integration? I don't want the integration team involved. How will you accomplish the integration?"

"Richard, we have that covered. We have written the vote manipulation—excuse me, the vote verification code, so it is encrypted, and it will be dispersed throughout the system on the initial load done by each site. The initial integration will reserve space, so as we add code, the overall size will remain static, hiding the fact additions have been made. We have written a loader to do the integration. You get us the completed code from the integration team, and we will run our loader that will integrate our code. It will be well hidden."

"Sounds good. The customers won't be able to detect anything going wrong, will they?"

"Nope. It is all done remotely. Each customer is required to periodically hook up their system to an internet link that allows software updates. The customer turns it on when they are notified of an update coming. The internet link is on only long enough to do the update, so they can be confident no one else can hack their systems. Controlling our module will be done surreptitiously through that connection."

"Good. I have set up an offshore account so I can send your rewards to the offshore accounts you each have set up. No one will be able to trace this work back to you. Once we are operational and things are working as expected, you guys can take a well-earned vacation with your families. But I need you to be on call when we get one of the close elections."

Dan responded, and the others smiled, "We have been working our tails off. We are looking forward to a break. Our families will appreciate the chance to see us for a change," and he chuckled.

After discussing other details for over two hours, Richard bid the team good wishes and left, satisfied, heading back to his house in Lake Oswego.

~ George Returns from Palo Alto ~

When George returned from Palo Alto, he called Kyle to see when they could meet. George suggested they meet away from Kyle's apartment and without Laura. George suggested a diner Kyle had never visited. When Kyle walked in, he found George was already seated in an isolated booth, separated from other booths by an emergency exit door. They were unlikely to be disturbed. George had already ordered for the two of them.

Kyle greeted George, "Hey, thanks for ordering for me. Good guess on the cheeseburger and onion rings?"

"Kyle, you are predictable, and I aim to please. How have you been doing?"

"I am good. How about you. How was your trip to Palo Alto?"

"Very Interesting and not uneventful. Someone or something punctured two of my tires. Fortunately, I have AAA insurance. However, I ended up needing two new tires."

"Two?" Kyle asked, "That seems unusual."

"You think? The repair guy said it did not look accidental, especially since I had not driven the car for a day. Judging from the hole's size, the service guy said the tires would have gone flat in less than five minutes. He said it looked something like an ice pick in the sidewall that did the damage. I quizzed the guy, and he said he had seen several of these kinds of punctures. They were distinctive. I ended up having to work with the rental company to get two new tires."

"Wow! Do you think it was random, or were you targeted?"

"Of course, I don't know for sure, but I asked the guy if there had been any other instances of this kind of sabotage recently in the area. He told me they kept records at AAA. He pulled out his cell phone and called the AAA office. He said AAA had not seen any in the last six months. He reported my instance while he was on the phone. He said that AAA kept track as it cost them money. If this occurred often enough, they alerted the police."

"Well, I am glad you had AAA insurance." Kyle said, "What a hassle it would be if you hadn't. Out of curiosity, do you think this had anything to do with your visit with Jeneen's friend? What was her name?" Kyle asked.

"Maddy, her name was Maddy Hilburn. I don't know about the tire thing; it could have been random. But it sure got my attention."

"So, what did you learn from Maddy?" Kyle continued.

George filled Kyle in about the trip. He told Kyle about the note to Chao and Chao's unusual trip to Taiwan in the middle of a semester. He explained that Maddy was concerned. George got to look around Chao's apartment, but nothing, other than the note, caused concern. George turned the conversation to

Kyle. "Kyle, what have you been doing lately. Any new information?"

"I have continued to visit Meisner sites. The most recent one is a cause for concern."

"Oh?" George asked, quizzically. He was about to take a bite but put it down to give Kyle his full attention.

"I visited the Integration Team a couple of days ago," Kyle paused to formulate his description of the meeting.

In the pause, George asked, "Integration Team?"

"Give me a second," Kyle was still formulating how to present his experience. "Okay, yes, the Integration Team is the one that integrates all the software for all the machines in the Meisner Voting System. Meisner is preparing to market comprehensive systems to manage all parts of the election processes. I mean the whole thing."

"Explain," George interrupted.

Kyle had not previously given George a complete rundown of the Meisner Voting System, only parts of it. He explained about the hook and Bret's concerns.

George listened and then had questions, "Interesting. Who is that team leader? Do you think he is concerned or aggravated he is being bypassed?"

"I know him about as well as I know any Meisner employee outside of my team. I met him doing the Hood to Coast relay. We enjoyed each other's company. I think he trusts me, and I trust what he tells me is true. He strikes me as a level-headed guy."

George asked again, "His name?"

"Oh yeah. Bret Lambert. The team is located in Vancouver, Washington, just across the river."

George pulled out a small booklet from his pocket and wrote Bret's name in it, "Do you think he would be willing to talk to me?"

"I don't know. I could introduce you, but he might not be comfortable if he knew you were a private investigator We could certainly try. You want me to contact him again and see?"

George thought about it for a moment then answered, "I would like to talk to him, but it might be good to get more information first. Maybe if you went with me, it would ease his mind. Do you think you can find out what this team is concerned about?"

"I don't know. Meisner gave me a list of teams to visit. I have completed the list, and the team Bret referred to is not on my list. I can ask around?"

"Let's hold off on asking for now. We probably need to talk to Laura and get her take on this."

"I already told her about my visit with Bret. She acted as if it was important information."

"Okay, then let's get the three of us together," George suggested.

Kyle agreed to contact Laura for a meeting with the three of them.

~ Retest of the Hyperspectral Read-Heads ~

Kyle decided he needed to look at the read-heads again. He went into Lab 3 and found the latest version of the read-head, and began his test. Once again, he noticed a strange electronic noise on the oscilloscope screen. Last time, he had ignored the radio frequency (RF) noise. The read-heads were not certified like most electronic equipment because they were supposed to be read-only devices. He picked up a hand-held BugHunter BH-03 RF Signal Detector to see the range of the RF noise. He noticed that it was a signal he could pick up across the room. He left the lab and went to his desk, where he could still pick up the RF noise. He decided to test the signal out of doors. To do that, he would have to call security and arrange to take the hand-held device out of the building. Security asked a lot of questions that Kyle was able to satisfy. Security called the security desk at the entrance to Meisner Industries and gave the front desk security staff directions to allow Kyle to leave the building with a Meisner hand-held device.

Dennis Andersen was watching Kyle when he went into Lab 3. Curious, when Kyle came out of the lab with a BugHunter, he asked Kyle what he was doing. Kyle tried to put him off, suggesting he was double-checking the read-heads. Dennis persisted with questions about the BugHunter Kyle was holding. Kyle decided to let him know what was going on and told him about the RF noise the read-heads were making. He was going to see if he could still hear the signal outside the building. Dennis jumped up to go with him. Kyle gave him a puzzled look and then left with Dennis tagging along.

Kyle kept the device on as he descended the elevator, and sure enough, he could still detect the RF signal. The noise was still evident when he left the building, but he had to hold it up to his ear to hear it. He took earbuds out of his pocket and plugged it into the device. He could hear the noise outside on the sidewalk. A passerby assumed he was listening to a radio. Dennis tried to ask Kyle what he heard, but Kyle waved him off.

The fact that it sounded like noise to Kyle presented a problem. Noise might be detected for various reasons in the RF rich environment that cell phone towers produced. He was not confident he was listening to the read-heads. He would have to conduct a better test. He explained what he was thinking to Dennis and headed back to the building. Kyle returned to Lab 3 and checked to see if the read-heads were still in operational mode. Dennis tagged along this time even into Lab 3 with Kyle. It was a distraction for Kyle, but he did not want Dennis to think he shouldn't ask questions. He got out a Tektronix RSA5000 spectrum analyzer to look at the signal he was getting from the read-heads. He found that the noise was coming from a combination of frequencies. Dennis suggested putting time constraints on the signal. When he did put time constraints on the analyzer, he observed that it was a bunch of frequencies whose signal bounced around from one frequency to another in what looked like a random fashion. He tested to make sure the read-heads were causing the noise by systematically turning them on and off to see what happened to the signal. This confirmed to him the noise was coming from the read-heads. He had several read-heads in the lab, so he took the time to install each one and tested to see if each produced the signal noise. It took twenty minutes each time to uninstall one and install the next one. They all gave the same readings. Dennis helped him.

"What do you think? Is it a problem?" Dennis asked.

"Could be, but not necessarily. It could be an artifact of the way the read-heads do their scanning. The scans are in the infrared and ultraviolet spectrum but not in the RF range I was detecting. The electronic circuits controlling the scanning might be causing it unintentionally. Maybe these are nothing more than harmonic frequencies caused by the scanning process," Kyle elaborated.

"So, what next?" Dennis pushed the explanation further.

"I don't know, Dennis," Kyle answered in a slightly exasperated tone. "I have to think about it. Anyway, do you know much about RF signals?

"My undergrad degree was in electronics. Originally, I planned to be an electrical engineer, but software development looked a lot more lucrative. I still have a small electronics shop at the house," Dennis disclosed.

"I didn't know that," Kyle said, a bit surprised. He did not know Dennis knew anything about electronics. It occurred to him that Dennis might have been capable of doing what Kyle was doing with the hyperspectral read-heads. Kyle wondered why Richard didn't have Dennis do this? *Does Richard suspect Dennis is the source of the leaks?* "Tell you what, Dennis. Let me ponder this problem a bit more, and I may be able to use your help. I know a lot about the specifics of hyperspectral techniques. Still, I might need more electronics expertise to figure out this noise problem. I have other tasks I need to take care of, so how about we discuss things in a couple of days. Will that work for you."

"Sure. If you don't call on me, I will BUG you!" Dennis responded. Kyle did not catch his pun about the BugHunter detector, so Dennis turned and went to his cubicle next to Kyle.

As soon as Dennis got to his computer, he began looking up information on RF noise and ways to analyze it for a meaningful signal. He also looked up frequency hopping since Kyle had mentioned the noise seemed to skip around. That evening, Dennis stopped by to pick up beer, wine and a pizza. He wanted to celebrate his one-year living arrangement with Jill. Jill was still hesitant to get married since her last marriage did not work out all that well.

Jill Huang, Dennis's girlfriend, was from Taiwan. Jill was her American name. American friends made fun of her Chinese name, BoonHuey, so she told people her name was Jill. She came to the United States to school when she was in High School. She lived with a relative. When she finished college, she applied for a green card and decided to stay. Jill was attractive, petite, and outgoing. She complemented Dennis's shy side. She was a good listener, and Dennis was a good talker when just the two of them were together. What attracted Dennis to Jill was that she seemed to love everything about Dennis, listened to his stories, and was good in bed, willing to engage in any kinky thing Dennis suggested. When Dennis shared about his work with Kyle and the noisy read-heads, Jill perked up and pumped Dennis with questions. It surprised Dennis a bit because Jill did not usually ask so many questions about his work. She asked technical questions, something Dennis had not noticed about Jill in the past. She was usually satisfied to hear his stories without many questions.

Jill had a good Facebook friend with whom she kept in constant contact. Dennis asked Jill few questions about her former life and was uninformed about her friends. Whenever she visited home, Jill and her friend, Chen Chin, spent lots of time together. The next time Jill talked to Chen Chin, Jill told her about the conversation with Dennis. Chen was very interested and asked Jill to see if she could get more information. Jill and Chen exchanged several emails and texts trying to determine what the MSS was after. Jill and Chen shared their mutual respect for the MSS and its power. Jill did not know Chen sometimes shared information with her MSS contact. Chen cautiously asked Jill to see if she could get any more information from Dennis about the voting system.

The next time Dennis came over to her place, Jill tried nonchalantly to ask him about Meisner Industries Voting Systems. Dennis knew a lot about what went on in his team, but not much else. He said that Kyle had not mentioned the problem with the read-head noise since that one time he had already shared with Jill. Dennis did share about his particular part of the Graphical User Interface that his team was developing. Only Kyle, he said, was working on the read-heads.

~ MSS Report ~

Wen-je Shieu turned in his report to his boss at the Ministry of State Security in Bejing. Translation Follows:

Potential issues on two fronts. (1) Chen Chin has received new information in a conversation with Jill Huang, a close friend of hers. Jill is in a relationship with Dennis Andersen, who works for Meisner Industries. Kyle Tredly, as previously noted, is working on testing an implementation of the hyperspectral read-heads manufactured by Xiazhen Manufacturing for K and W Manufacturing in Taipei. Dennis told his friend Jill that he and Tredly had been investigating noise coming from the read-heads. Jill reported that Tredly told Andersen he was concerned that there was something wrong with the read-heads. Dennis told Jill he was suspicious that the so-called noise was, in fact, a signal, a feature, not an anomaly. Tredly has been doing additional tests but has not shared the results with Andersen. Dennis is planning on taking test equipment he owns to work to record the signal and possibly decode it. Chen Chin has encouraged Jill to get more information, but Jill is reluctant and may have become suspicious of Chen Chin. Chen Chin was instructed to ease off further pressure. (2) Tao Li's son Chao made an unexpected trip to Taiwan. While he was gone, a private detective named George Lockit visited his girlfriend. Mr. Lockit likely knows about the threatening note sent to Chao. Mr. Lockit, from Texas, is a friend of Mr. Tredly. Our agent in Palo Alto, without authority, punctured two tires of Mr. Lockit's rental car. This was unfortunate as it will likely result in inquiries, not to our advantage. We will continue our surveillance work.

Wen-je Shieu

The MSS contact forwarded his communique with the following note attached, translated:

What action, if any, do you want my office to pursue regarding this information?

There is no record of the response available. However, Fuj-Sheng Wong, co-owner of K and W manufacturing, subsequently disappeared after these memos were exchanged. There was one additional message to MSS headquarters.

As ordered, regarding the report from source Chen Chin, the prescribed target has been neutralized.

Fuj-Sheng Wong, co-owner of K and W Manufacturing in Taipei, left his home, but neither he nor his driver arrived at the factory. There were no leads to his whereabouts. There was no indication of foul play and no indication that he had left the country. His disappearance remained an open case. The NSB, Taiwan's National Security Bureau, is involved in the investigation. Tao Li was questioned extensively by the NSB, considering the possibility that Tao sought sole ownership of K and W Manufacturing. But in Taiwan, such mysteries were always also suspected activities of the MSS. Concerned about the fate of K & W Manufacturing and its impact on his son's future, Tao felt obligated to let Chao know about the disappearance and investigation. Chao offered to return to Taiwan, but his father insisted he stay and apply himself to his school work.

~ George, Kyle, Laura Meet ~

Kyle contacted Laura as he had promised George and arranged a meeting at Laura's apartment. As he usually did, George scanned Laura's apartment for bugs. When he found one, he was initially alarmed, but Laura told him she had not deactivated the FBI listening equipment in her apartment. To satisfy George, she called the FBI office and turned off the devices long enough for George to run another scan. When all clear, Laura let the FBI office know. It was against protocol for Laura to meet without the listening devices turned on.

George filled Laura in on his trip to Palo Alto and Chao's mysterious trip to Taiwan in the middle of the semester. Laura let George know that Chao's father's partner at K and W manufacturing had been missing for several days.

George asked, "Is that the reason he went to Taiwan?"

"No," Laura answered. "The disappearance has happened since Chao returned to school. The only thing I know is that Fuj-Sheng Wong, Tao's partner, visited the NSB in Taiwan."

"NSB," interrupted George and Kyle in unison.

"The National Security Bureau of Taiwan. They are roughly equivalent to our FBI and CIA combined. The NSB and the MSS are constantly trying to co-opt the other one," Laura answered. "Anyway, the MSS tries to keep track of people who visit the NSB. They may have bugs or spies in the NSB for all I know. Anyway, shortly after Wong's visit, he disappeared. Of course, it could be the NSB or the MSS, or coincidence, no way to tell. The NSB does not always share their secrets with the CIA or the FBI. All I know is that he disappeared. It could have nothing to do with K and W manufacturing. There is always the possibility he is escaping family responsibilities, or it's an insurance scam, or something like that."

The room was quiet as all three of them were lost in considering all the possibilities. You could hear the clock on the wall tick, tick, tick. The calm lasted for what seemed like five minutes when, in fact, it was only about thirty seconds. Laura suddenly broke out in a big smile, and pulled out a piece of paper and wrote on it. She handed it to Kyle and George. It said, "I bet the local FBI office is having a fit since everything went quiet." That broke the tension, and they all three broke out in laughter. As they thought about the guy listening in, they laughed harder.

Once they settled down, Laura asked Kyle what he had been working on. He glanced at George, who nodded for him to answer. Laura took note of the nod. She wondered if George and Kyle had secrets she should be concerned about. There were too many balls in the air for Laura's comfort.

Kyle told Laura the details of his curious findings regarding the read-heads. He also shared his visits to various Meisner offices, including the concern of Mr. Bret Lambert, Integration Team Leader.

"Bret Lambert? I don't think I have heard about him before. He told you there is another team developing software that is included at the last minute?" Laura inquired.

"Yes," Kyle answered. "Bret has no idea what this team actually does and why it needs to be secret. I think he is a bit put off because his team is supposed to deal with the integration of the whole system. Yet, there is another team Bret has never heard of that gets the chance to possibly change and add things. He is concerned that if something goes wrong in the field, his team will be held responsible. It will be his team that has to go to the customers to try to make things right, and there will potentially be code his team knows nothing about."

"Is he put out, or is he suspicious of what is going on? I know I am suspicious," Laura barked as though she was the one being set up.

George chimed in, "Easy, Laura. We don't have enough information. We need to get more to find out what is going on. There could be legitimate reasons Meisner has another team looking at this product. Meisner Industries has a lot at stake. At some point, we might need to confront Meisner himself."

That got a sarcastic response from Laura, "Yeah, Richard would love that! He can seem very charming, but I have seen another side of him too. I agree that we need to tread lightly. My hands are tied by my FBI role," Laura said. Her facial expression conveyed that George's and Kyle's hands were not bound as tightly by the same constraints. Their careers would not be on the line if they messed up the same way Laura's would with the FBI. George and Kyle did acknowledge they would have to be careful not to violate the agreement they signed.

The discussion turned to the next steps. Laura had to write up a report based on their analysis. Kyle indicated he needed to do more research on the read-heads. He told them about Dennis's interest in the anomaly. Dennis had a piece of electronic equipment he had promised to bring to the office so they could take a closer look at the anomaly. George was going to find out what he could about the *secret* team. The three of them knew the Voting System was close to being deployed. Kyle would also find out what he could about the deployment plans. He did not expect to get that information from Richard Meisner himself, but that is what happened.

~ Richard Calls Kyle To His Office ~

Kyle got a message that Richard Meisner wanted to see him. Kyle was not sure it was a coincidence that he had wanted to talk to Richard too. Kyle responded, and it was scheduled for the next morning. Kyle went up to his office and had to wait for twenty-five minutes. Finally, he was ushered into Meisner's office. Kyle looked around. It had been several weeks since he was last here. Nothing had changed. Richard was seated behind his desk and motioned to Kyle to sit in a chair opposite the desk. This felt less cordial than previous meetings. The window shade that was usually down when he visited the office was up, making it challenging to look at Richard. It happened to be a relatively bright day, and the light from the floor to ceiling window made Kyle uncomfortable.

"Kyle, so glad to see you. Are you enjoying your work here at Meisner Industries?"

Kyle found that both a strange and disturbing question. *Was there an implication his job might be in jeopardy?* Kyle answered, "Yes. This is one of the most interesting jobs I have had. I particularly appreciate having the chance to visit various teams and understand their work."

"Ah, yes. But you have only seen a small part of the Meisner enterprise. We have several product lines, and you have only visited teams developing one line, the Voting System line. I have appreciated your reports. I want to follow up with more detail. First, I want to know if you have made any progress on the leaks."

"Richard, there have been so many possibilities I have not had time to investigate them all. I am not a trained investigator, so there are limitations on approaching employee family members, much less the employees themselves. I have not been able to make any useful progress in that area. One thing, I told you earlier I had a chance to participate in the Hood to Coast relay," Kyle said.

Richard interjected a question, "You did? You ran in the relay? I did not see that in the report."

"No, I drove one of the vans. One of the van drivers dropped out at the last minute, and I got a chance to be a driver. Janeen recruited me. She runs in the race. It was beneficial in several ways. First, I got to meet several people from other Meisner teams. Secondly, it gave me a chance to get a feel for the quality of the staff. I did not discover anyone that I thought would even consider leaking information. Your staff is tight-lipped."

"What about your team. I was suspicious the leak might have come from someone on your team," Richard said.

"As you know, Laura and I have been working on that for a while. So far, I can't see any suspect worthy evidence. If the leaks are of substantive value, I can't imagine any of my team doing that."

Richard nodded. He had not told Kyle that his security staff has also reached the same conclusion. Richard changed the subject, "I also wanted to follow up on your visits to various teams."

"Of course," Kyle responded. He had expected that he would have the opportunity to answer Richard's questions. Written reports only go so far. "What would you like to know?"

"I am interested in your assessments of the team leaders you met."

"Not sure exactly what you are looking for. I found them all to be competent. Well, more than competent. You have hired exceptionally talented people, sir."

"Let's not use the *sir* bit. Just call me Richard. I am most interested in the kinds of questions they asked you as much as what they told you about their operations," Richard said.

"Well, for the most part, they wondered what I was doing. I think they thought I was a spy. You run a very private and segregated operation, so most team leaders do not get the full picture of how things are going. One or two of them may have seen you only once or twice and wanted to know more about you as a person."

"Interesting. How did you maneuver those questions?" Richard asked.

"It was easy. I don't know you that well myself, other than the private thing I am working on about the leaks. There was not much I could tell them they did not already know. I told them you were a great boss to work for, that you pushed hard but rewarded well. They already knew that."

Richard ignored the compliment and inquired, "Did you run into any dissatisfaction or concern about their work?"

This made Kyle a bit uncomfortable since Bret Lambert in Vancouver had expressed concerns. Without hesitating that might give Richard any hint about that, Kyle answered, "Not really. I guess the only curiosity people had was about seeing the whole picture. You know, how their particular jobs played in the scheme of things. I think everyone wants to be important, not a cog in a machine." Kyle hoped he was not displeasing Richard with that comment.

"I get that. Meisner Industries is a big operation. At times I am not sure I see the details that make MI one of the most competitive operations in the country, hell, the whole world. I am proud of our work. I probably don't tell people how important their particular work is and how it fits into making the company successful."

Kyle, without thinking, said, "I know! Money is not everything. You can't always buy loyalty. A person needs to feel important, a contributor, someone who is making a difference. Some people don't get that through work and have to find outlets elsewhere."

"Were you speaking for yourself, Kyle? Are you not satisfied with your role here?"

"No. No, I was being philosophical. I am very satisfied, and I appreciate the trust and responsibility you have given me. If I am not doing my job, I know you would be the first to let me know."

Richard did not say anything. He had a quizzical look on his face. Kyle felt the awkward silence. Then Richard spoke, "Kyle, there is something I want to ask you. I got a briefing from the security department that you needed to take an RF reader out of the building, something about noise. Could you tell me what that was about?"

Ah, now we get to the real reason Richard wanted to see me. Kyle did not know if he might be in trouble. He felt a bit uncomfortable, guilty of something. He said, "Yes, I did. I was trying to see if an RF signal I detected in Lab 3 could be detected out of doors. I was getting a noisy read on the read-heads in Lab 3 and then in the office. I was trying to determine how far I could still detect it. I was concerned we might run into problems with the Federal Communications Commission if the RF signal interfered with radios or cell phones."

"Noise, RF signal?"

"Yes, I would call it noise. I checked out several read-heads, and they all produced the noise."

"Kyle, are you saying they are defective?" Richard was surprised and alarmed by this news. It would be a significant setback if the read-heads were defective. Hell, he did not want trouble with the FCC.

"Yes and no. I don't think they should be giving off RF noise, but I retested their accuracy, and they seem to be operating fine. I don't see anything to worry about."

Richard was quiet again, and Kyle waited for him to ask another question. Finally, he responded, "Interesting. We should test a few more read-heads to make sure these particular ones are not defective or something. I will have inventory pick out a dozen or so random samples and send them to Lab 3. How long would it take you to test them?"

"I could test a dozen in less than three days. That is if you want me to verify that they perform to specifications. If you want to know if they are noisy, I can do that in one day."

"Here's the problem, Kyle. If these are defective, if they do not do the job they are supposed to do, it could cause a significant delay, and I can't afford to delay this project. Pressures make it important to have the Voting System ready for the next election cycle. Also, if the FCC gets involved, that could hold us up for months."

Kyle added, "If they perform to specifications, I don't see why the noise should be a show stopper. We can always find ways to reduce the distance the noise is detectable with minor shielding. Unless there is an aspect of the systems that I don't know about that the RF noise could compromise I can't see a problem. Anyway, I can begin tests as soon as I get the read-heads. How long do you think it will take to get me the samples?"

"By the first of next week for sure, maybe sooner. Stay close to the office. I want the test results as soon as possible." With that, Richard got up, indicating the meeting was over. He came around his desk, shook Kyle's hand, and ushered him toward the office door. Before he opened it, he patted Kyle on the back. Kyle chose to take the pat as a friendly gesture. Then he asked, "Kyle, when the Voting Systems go live, we will need people with specific knowledge about them to meet with existing and potential clients. I have set it up, so you know a lot about the whole set of products in the Voting Systems. I am counting on you to do some fieldwork. Do you like to travel?"

That caught Kyle completely off guard, but he recovered in record time, "Yes, I love to travel. That sounds like it would be fascinating."

"Good. Go get ready to test read-heads, and we will talk again soon." Richard opened the door, and Kyle left.

Kyle went back to his office. He decided to make a few notes about the conversation. Having done that, he went to Lab 3 and developed a plan that would allow him to quickly test the read-heads that Meisner would send him. He felt he could accomplish that within the three-day estimate he had given Richard, assuming no new problems or issues arose.

Chapter 15

~ Read-heads Testing ~

It took three days for the read-heads to be delivered to Lab 3. While he was waiting for them to arrive, he reported to George and Laura about his visit with Richard. Laura reflected on his meeting and wondered if Richard would contact her or if he had finished with her assistance. It was not one day before she got an answer. Richard's secretary called and wanted Laura to accompany Richard to the Opera the following week. Her role as companion to cover his proclivity for men was still operative. She looked forward to the chance to get an update on Richard's view of Kyle's work. She could feed Richard a story of how she was grooming Kyle to get inside information for Richard. So far, so good.

Kyle methodically tested the read-heads that Richard had sent over. He was a bit surprised at how consistent the results were. The read-heads detected the various samples within 0.1% of each other. This implied they were prepared with a quality that would please Richard. It also produced this curious RF signal. It was apparent that the RF signal did not compromise the quality of the read-heads. Kyle fabricated several small shields to reduce the RF noise. While they worked to reduce the signal, it did not eliminate it. However, the shields did reduce the consistency of the read-heads' operation. It would take someone with more engineering skill than he had to address this problem if, indeed, it was determined to be an issue.

After Kyle prepared his report and sent it to Meisner, he decided to do more investigation into the RF noise. He asked Dennis if he would help. Dennis brought in some test equipment from home. When they ran the tests, Dennis noticed that the noise was, in fact, a rapidly rotating sequence of frequencies. While they appeared to be random, they were, in fact, a repeating collection of specific frequencies that produced what looked like noise. Dennis became intrigued and waved Kyle away so he could think and play with his equipment. Finally, he decoded the intricate pattern and called Kyle to come see what he had found. The signal was not noise but a complex carrier wave that could carry information. Kyle set up a run, and Dennis set up a recording device so they could look at the signal. Sure enough, when they ran through a stack of sample ballots, the carrier wave matched the read-heads' signals. That meant that someone could remotely read the information from the read-heads as they were in operation.

Was this an artifact of the read-heads? If you tried to read hyperspectral signals, was it inherent that RF signals would be produced? Dennis thought that was highly unlikely. To Dennis, this looked more like an intentional feature of the read-heads. If the RF signals were intended, what were they for? It was Kyle's, not Dennis's, responsibility to communicate with Meisner so Dennis had no intention of doing so. He did not ask Kyle what he planned to do. But that night, he did share his concerns with his girlfriend, Jill Haung. Dennis left Jill's place early that morning. He wanted to go by his place and calibrate a piece of test equipment. His equipment might help Kyle resolve the curious anomaly. Right after he left, Jill got a call from her friend Chen Chin. Chen carried on a general conversation, finally getting around to Dennis, and how he liked his work, etc. Chen was quite adept at maneuvering a conversation and managed to get Jill to tell her about Dennis's testing of the read-heads. Jill was proud of Dennis. She thought he was so smart, and she was lucky to have him as her boyfriend. She was hoping he would eventually propose. She bragged about Dennis. She told Chen that Dennis had an additional test device that would give him a more detailed analysis. After hearing this, Chen made an excuse to hang up. It did not take Chen long after she hung up to report to her Ministry of State Security contact in Beijing.

The very next day, Dennis did not show up for work. That was unusual. Joe Walker, Dennis' team leader, put out a call to his apartment. There was no answer. Joe also called Jill Huang to see if she knew where he was. Jill reported that Dennis had spent the night at her place and had left for work very early because he needed to drop by his place first. That raised red flags for Joe, and he talked to all the members of the team. No one had heard from Dennis. Kyle had worked with him the day before. They all expressed concern as it was unlike Dennis to be absent without making arrangements, much less to be late. He was always one of the first to arrive each day. Kyle was the most surprised since Dennis was so enthused about the testing they did yesterday. He fully expected to see Dennis arrive with additional equipment today to run more tests. Joe called HR to see if Dennis had a next-of-kin contact or emergency contact listed on his HR record. The only contact he listed was Jill, and his parents, who lived in Detroit. Joe got the number and gave Dennis' parents a call. It was afternoon before he heard back from them. They were in good health, and they had not heard from Dennis for a couple of weeks. They had no clue where he might be.

Joe called the team together, concerned Dennis might have been in an accident. He gave each team member a hospital to contact. Joe would contact the police. After all the searching, there was no clue where Dennis was. The police were no help. They did not want to consider him missing until all other efforts had been exhausted. Little work took place that day as everyone tried to think of an explanation for Dennis' absence. Joe called Jill again, and asked her to have Dennis call him when he arrived at her place. Jill called back around 10:00 PM to let Joe know Dennis had not shown up at her place or contacted her. Joe did not sleep well that night. The next day, Joe put in an official missing person report.

~ George's Research ~

George was busy digging for information on the secret software group Kyle had told him about. He discovered the team working in a nondescript house out on NW Glencoe Road in Hillsboro. By visiting various bars in the area, he found out their names, Dan Wilcox, Stan Carpenter, and Stewart McNally. Dan was the team leader and notoriously private. When the three of them visited the Horse Shoe Bar and Grill in Hillsboro, Dan seldom said a word. Stan was more talkative. Stewart was the one that seemed to do the most talking. George staked out the bar and noticed that Stewart sometimes came alone. On one of those visits, George was able to make Stewart's acquaintance. Stewart was a bit of a braggart, which, fortunately for Stewart, Richard Meisner did not know. After running into Stewart a few times, George pieced together what his secret team was doing. They were writing code that would allow the manipulation of election outcomes in close elections. George was hesitant to go for too much detail, so he could continue to get information from Stewart. On George's most recent visit, he learned that the team was essentially through with their work. There were only a few details to work out, and they would be ready to integrate their code into the Voting System. Stewart indicated it could be within a week or two at most.

As soon as he discovered the team was almost finished, he called Kyle and asked Kyle to set up a meeting with him and Laura. The meeting took place two days later at a bar in East Portland, where none of them had visited before. Traffic in the bar was light, and they got a private booth. George was anxious to fill them in on what he had discovered, so they could decide what they should do next.

After they ordered drinks and hamburgers, Laura began the conversation, "Why did you call this meeting, George?"

"I think I understand why everything is so secret. Meisner has to know what is going on. He is surely behind it, otherwise why a secret team?"

"Go on," Laura urged.

George took a breath and continued, "Meisner Industries is planning on influencing elections."

Laura made a face as if to say, "Duh." Then she added, "Of course he is.

That surprised George. Did she already know what the secret team was up to? If so, why had she kept that secret?

But then she went on, "That is what all wealthy people do, influence elections with their mega-bucks."

"Not that way," George said. "I think Meisner is planning on altering the vote counts with his Voting System machines."

That was shocking news. Both Laura and Kyle felt Richard had not been telling them everything, but this? Kyle was listening carefully, trying to think how the Voting Systems might accomplish that. Kyle asked, "George, exactly how do you think that would work?"

"Hell, Kyle, I don't know. All I know, at this point, is that Stewart is bragging about it. He bragged that his secret team— he did not call it secret—was writing the code to accomplish it. Not in so many words, but I am sure that is what he was implying. Of course, he would not come out and say so. I had to be careful about how I asked him things to avoid suspicion. I told him I worked for an out of town company looking for a place to open a branch near Portland."

Kyle continued to puzzle over how they could do that. *Of course, the machines could be made to miscount, but how could that be done over and over. The machines were not directly connected to the Internet, at least not the counting machine. Well, it was not connected while in operation, only for updates.* Lost in his thought-world, he missed out hearing part of the conversation between George and Laura. He heard the end of a statement by Laura, "... the FBI."

"Wait—what?" Kyle said abruptly.

"I said I could not keep this a secret. I have to let the FBI know about this possibility. This is why they assigned me to Meisner Industries. They were suspicious of Meisner but did not have a credible lead as to what he was up to," Laura repeated for Kyle.

"Okay, I get that. But when do you have to report? Shouldn't we do more research first?" Kyle said.

"I can't wait long. One of the first questions they will ask me is, when did you learn this? How did you learn it? Why did you wait to report it? They will ask me an endless string of questions that will put me on the hot seat. Also, George is not the only one with investigative talent. The FBI has lots of experience and resources. No, I need to tell them right away."

George wedged his way into the conversation between Kyle and Laura, "Laura, how about I report it to the FBI. My report would not be so credible, and that might give us extra time. You could always say you did not believe me when you first learned about it; told me to report it if I thought it was important. Could that work? You know your team better than Kyle and I do."

"Let me think. So, you would report this when? Laura asked.

"Oh, in a couple of days, maybe a week," George answered.

"Okay, but you need to let me know when you plan to do it. Then, I can make my report, too, as if I learned it from you. I can make that work."

After covering other life events since they last met, they split up. One of the things that Kyle regretted was not getting to see Laura as much. They had decided not to be too cozy to confuse things. Laura was concerned about her FBI job and managing her relationship with Richard.

Kyle could not get this out of his mind. How could secret code installed at the last minute be used in machines all over the country to influence election outcomes? What was the strategy?

~ Meisner Gets Good and Bad News ~

Meisner Industries Marketing delivered Richard Meisner good news. The orders were coming in for Meisner Voting Systems. Every order included the full range of equipment and processes. The systems for mail-in ballots included the following:

Registered Voter Management System

Ballot Preparation and Printing System

Envelope Printing and Stuffing System

Envelope Receipt and Processing System

Ballot Vote Counting System

The whole indivisible set of systems was expensive. Still, the new federal law, the HAVA (Help America Vote Act), providing financial assistance to states to upgrade their systems. It was a no-brainer decision for many jurisdictions around the country. The orders were beginning to pile in.

Various teams working on the project were advised that one or two of their team might be needed to help install, set up, and train personnel at the various sites. There was excitement and energy in every team, except Kyle's. His team was still mourning Dennis. Everyone assumed the worst had happened since it was totally out of character for Dennis not to show up for work or be with his girlfriend.

The bad news came about a week after Dennis had disappeared. His car was discovered in the Willamette River not far from the falls. It looked like it was driven off a boat ramp in West Linn and dragged about a half a mile down the river. Dennis's body was found inside, still in his seat belt. Of course, everyone was speculating, not only how this could happen but why. It did not make sense. There was no indication of foul play, so the assumptions were that either he made a wrong turn or intentionally drove into the river. Dennis was not a heavy drinker, although there was an almost empty bottle of vodka in the car. The postmortem indicated Dennis had not been drinking and died from drowning. The bruise on his forehead was consistent with crashing into the steering wheel. It seemed like an open and shut case of accidental death. Neither Kyle nor any member of his team believed it could be intentional. It was so uncharacteristic of Dennis. There were absolutely no hints he was depressed or likely to harm himself. Jill, his girlfriend, was devastated. George looked her up to see if they could do anything for her. Richard agreed to make all the arrangements for Dennis's funeral and burial plot. He hosted a reception after the memorial at a downtown hotel.

The first Voting Systems were installed in Multnomah County, home of Portland. Richard asked Kyle to visit the installation and see if the county officials were satisfied with the installation. The first chance to use the system would come in about four months, so they had to work quickly to make sure everything was working correctly. The factory near Salem was producing the special paper used for the ballots. The ballot printing machines would apply the special coatings that prevented anyone from submitting fake ballots. The supply of select chemicals used for the coating materials were produced by a plant in Federal Way, Washington. The ballot printing machines were essentially laser printers. They were different in the sense they required five toner cartridges. One of the "toners" contained the magnetically readable black ink for the synchronization marks. Another contained regular black ink. The other three were used to create the invisible coatings. The five toner cartridges had to be replaced every one hundred thousand ballots printed. Since the coatings were invisible, the read-heads that Kyle had worked on were required to verify the coatings and alert operators if any cartridge needed to be replaced.

Another team from Meisner Industries was responsible for helping with the one-time mass loading of registered voters into the Voter Management System. It took specific formatting of existing data and running a program that loaded the data into the new system. When Kyle visited the installation site, the team loading the data was almost finished. They were running verification comparisons. From everything Kyle could see, the installation was going smoothly and on schedule. Everyone he talked to seem to have heard about Dennis and expressed their condolences to Kyle.

~ Jeneen and Maddy—George and Chao ~

When Jeneen and Maddy exchanged an email, Maddy commented on how Chao was depressed. Jeneen called Maddy to get more information. Maddy said that Chao seemed fine when he first got back from Taiwan, but in the last week, he had been so depressed he skipped classes and just sat around the apartment. Jeneen wanted to know if he had received more threatening notes. Not any that Maddy knew about. However, she did get in an argument with Chao about the one he had received before he went to Taiwan. Maddy was doing fine otherwise.

Jeneen debated with herself whether or not to share her conversation with Kyle. The team was depressed with the death of Dennis. If Kyle had not asked Jeneen how she was doing and mentioned Maddy, she might not have said anything. Kyle listened and then asked if it would be okay for George to contact Maddy again. Jeneen shrugged and gave Kyle an ambivalent okay. That evening, he called George and shared what Jeneen had told him. After discussing the pros and cons of contacting Maddy again, they decided it could do no harm.

George called Maddy. Chao answered the phone. Chao said that Maddy was in class and offered to take a message. George had no reasonable option but to leave a message. Tell her that George in Portland, Oregon called.

Chao responded, "George, the Private Investigator?" Maddy had obviously talked to Chao about his visit when he was in Taiwan.

"Yes, one and the same," George responded, trying not to add anything that might cause Chao to be upset.

"I'll tell her. Does she have your number?"

"I don't know," George answered. "Let me give it to you just in case." George made a snap judgment based on the tone of

Chao's voice even though he had never met him personally. He took a chance. "Chao, if you don't mind, I called about you."

"Huh? You are checking up on me again? Why?"

"It's a long story, but I heard you were a bit down, and I wondered if I could be of assistance. I planned on having this conversation with Maddy, but since I have you on the phone, maybe this would be more appropriate."

"You looked at that note when you were down here, didn't you?"

"Yes. I thought it was threatening. If you have received another, I would not ignore it."

"No, no more notes. I am down because of something back home," Chao reflected.

"Care to elaborate?" George asked.

Chao hesitated. He hesitated so long that George spoke up, "You still there?"

"Oh, yeah. I was trying to decide whether or not to tell you what was on my mind. Let me ask you a question. Do you have any contacts in Taiwan?"

George answered, "Why, in fact, I do. I have a Taiwanese friend who lives in Taipei. He works there as a private investigator too. Why do you ask?"

Chao, still hesitating, said, "I have a question about something in Taipei."

"Chao, what about if I come down, and we can visit. It is hard to discuss things over the phone. And, given the note you received, it might be a good idea to make sure we are discussing things privately. Could I do that?"

"How much would it cost me?"

"Chao, my expenses are covered, so it would not cost you."

"I don't know. What did you say your name was again?"

"George Lockit. I would like to talk to you."

After a pause, Chao responded, "Okay, when can you come?"

"Would tomorrow be too early?"

"No, that sounds good," Chao responded, and started to give George his address, but George already knew it and cut him off.

"Good, I will get a flight out first thing in the morning and will call you when I get in. See if you can find a place you know we can talk in private. You will have to decide whether or not you want Maddy involved."

"I think I know the place. See you tomorrow then."

George and Chao said their goodbyes, and George made arrangements to fly to Palo Alto on the first flight in the morning. That evening, he called Kyle and let him know he was going to Palo Alto again.

~ Test Run of Ballot Printing ~

The installation of the Voting System was going well in Clackamas County too. They decided to do a test run of the Ballot Printing System. They pulled out a representative sample of voters from the registration system to make sure the system properly prepared ballots for the various towns on their list, Canby, Milwaukee, West Linn, and Estacada. They printed a thousand ballots. Everything worked fine. They had a protocol for marking the ballots so they could test the results against the vote-counting system. When they ran the results, everything was perfect. They gave the ballots to Meisner Industries so they could validate the findings on their own machines. Kyle got the first shot at looking at them using the read-heads in Lab 3. The results matched the vote counts from Clackamas County. Because of the noise, Kyle had discovered earlier; he wrote a module that would do other tests. He wanted to match votes with other readings he could get out of the hyperspectral read-heads.

When he ran his special tests, he discovered that the invisible coatings correctly identified the town associated with the ballot. However, Kyle was able to fine-tune the read-heads to measure the deviation in the coatings for each city. This process showed that the variations in the coatings stayed within parameters. However, there also appeared to be several sub-ranges within each town. At first, he did not see any reason for those sub-ranges to exist in specific bands. There did not seem to be a consistent relationship with how the pseudo voter marked each ballot. Kyle, being good at computer puzzles, kept working on the problem. He could not find any explanation for the anomaly. He wrote his notes for Meisner but did not include the anomaly. He would report that later when he had more time to figure out the cause.

Based on the suspicions of Bret Lambert of the Integration Team and the strange events of the past few weeks, Kyle decided to keep his investigations quiet, sharing only with George and Laura. Clackamas had also sent over a data sheet that identified individual pseudo voters. When he got more time, he was able to get the data from the sample of the voters that were part of the test. There was no way to associate one ballot with a particular voter. However, every ballot could be identified—not by the voter, but by their party preference. Why? What was the point of that? Was that a check and balance issue? Kyle needed to think about this before he shared his findings. Perhaps it was a way of ensuring voters in primaries were voting in the correct party primary. Kyle wrote a report for Richard but did not include his party-related-coatings to Richard. That could wait.

A few days after Kyle had submitted his report to Richard Meisner, he got a thank you note from Richard. Richard sent his appreciation for all the work Kyle had been doing for the company. Richard had received positive feedback from several divisions that Kyle had visited. Richard expressed his expectation that Kyle should look for a promotion before long to take advantage of his particular talent. Kyle was both pleased and cautious, knowing that the FBI was interested and following the work of Meisner Industries, especially as it applied to the Voting Systems. He was not sure he wanted to increase his level of accountability if Richard was, in fact, engaged in something illegal.

~ Voting Systems ~

Meisner Industries Voting Systems were a hit. Within a month, orders were skyrocketing. The federal dollars provided to jurisdictions to improve the integrity of elections made it easy for authorities to move to mail-in ballot elections using MI Voting Systems technology. Because of Richard Meisner's secret work with Senator Corning in writing the specifications, Meisner Industries had an inside track and was the first and lead provider of the systems. In the next month, orders came in for over four hundred fifty Voting Systems, which Meisner Industries had already manufactured and were in inventory. At $575,000 per system, Meisner Industries was doing quite well. There were other manufacturers currently developing or improving systems, but were not fully prepared to meet the demand nor provide complete systems. A few complaints were sent to Corning, and one press report that claimed the rush to mail-in ballots could lead to serious problems with the public acceptance of election results. While the tradition was well accepted in places that had been using mail-in ballots for many years, it was new in many jurisdictions, and anything new generated a set of objections.

As the systems were implemented and after the first election in which they were successfully employed, the objections gradually declined. Only a small segment of radical elements persevered in their complaints. The loudness of the objections was fodder for the press, and hungry reporters scoured the field for a good story. One reporter in Portland nosed around Meisner Industries and found Kyle Tredly. They began to track his movements and to interview people working for Meisner Industries. They also traveled to jurisdictions new to mail-in ballots and interviewed skeptical citizens. When their article was published in *The Oregonian*, a local newspaper, it was picked up by national press and republished in many towns and cities that had acquired one of Meisner's Voting Systems.

Meisner was not at all amused by this negative publicity, and hired a local public relations firm to counter criticism generated by the publicity. In general, it worked, and in no time at all, things had calmed down as orders for the Voting Systems continued to pour in.

~ Confabulation ~

George, Laura, and Kyle met to compare notes on progress. George reported on the death of Dennis. The official cause of death was drowning. George had been able to interview one of the people who had helped with the autopsy. George did not disclose the name of his contact but agreed that he would if it was necessary. This person told George that there were suspicions at the autopsy because they could not verify that

Dennis had been drinking at the time of the accident as the police had assumed. However, when the police reported the cause, they claimed Dennis had been drinking based solely on the almost empty bottle of Vodka in the car. George had tried to interview one of the detectives, but none of them would talk to him. George felt there was more to this story than he had been able to discover, at least up to this point.

Laura had a conversation with a friend who also worked for the local FBI office. Her friend was not an agent but one who helped manage internal communications. She called herself a glorified file clerk. Her friend reported that she had seen communications for the FBI headquarters, indicating they were investigating possible illegal manipulation of the bill that provided the funds for the new mail-in ballot initiatives around the country. She said she saw the name of Senator Corning. Still, she did not have time to read the entire communication of several pages. Laura asked her boss, Kam, for directions and was told to keep her relationship with Richard Meisner and take note of all the people he talked to when they went out together. Kam wanted Laura to ask Kyle for any names of people he saw visit Meisner Industries.

Kyle was quick to note that he worked on a different floor and seldom saw anyone who came to visit Richard. Kyle then shared with George and Laura the results he had seen when testing the ballots from Clackamas County. Kyle asserted that the invisible coatings on the ballot paper were not there solely to ensure the ballots were valid. The hyperspectral read-heads also identified the particular city of the ballot and the party affiliation of the person voting. Before he could add anything else, Laura spoke up.

"What? Say that again."

"I said that every ballot's invisible coating identified the city and party to which the voter of the ballot belonged."

George jumped in, "Wait a minute. How could you know that?"

Kyle explained how Clackamas County had run a test set of 1000 ballots. "They used the system to pull a sample set of voters from various cities. They printed ballots for this selection and then had their staff hand-mark, that is: vote, each ballot. Then, they ran the ballots through the counter and compared the votes with the marked ballots. There was a perfect match, so they were satisfied that the system was working as it should."

George asked, "So how do you know the ballots were marked with city and voter party affiliation?"

"I wasn't finished, George. Be patient. I thought it would be useful to understand the tolerances required to keep the machines in good working order, so I asked if I could have the ballots for internal validation. They gave me an electronic list of the one thousand voters, the city, and party affiliation used in their test. They gave me a copy of their results from their machines, which they had verified, and the stack of one thousand ballots."

"Go on," George said.

"George, don't get so excited. I am going to explain. So, I ran the ballots through our in-house system several times, adjusting the read-heads' tolerance levels. Set at the normal level, my results corresponded exactly with the county's results. But I noticed an anomaly with the actual read-heads' readings. At first, I could not see any reason for it when I stumbled on the relationship of the minor differences in the readings with the voter's party affiliation. At first, a curious artifact. But when I analyzed it, there was a perfect correlation. The implication was the ballot PRINTING machines were marking the ballots with party affiliations as well as the city of the voter. However, the county officials were not looking for that. They were interested in whether or not the marked vote count was correct. They were unlikely to discover that unless they adjusted the sensitivity of the reader-heads looking for the artifact. Even then, there are no options in the standard software to discover this fact. Perhaps this is a feature only related to primaries."

Laura and George said simultaneously, "Wow!"

Laura spoke next, "Do you know why the system marked the ballots that way? How could that be related to election integrity?"

"I don't know," said Kyle, "I have been pondering that. Is that a mistake, or was it designed that way on purpose? You could not tell who the voter was, just his or her party affiliation. I suppose you could write code that would report this information. Maybe the local parties would want to know how their party members performed. Maybe it was used to make sure all votes cast in primaries were from voters registered for the correct party. Maybe it could be used in the post-election analysis in some way that would be useful. I don't see how it could hurt."

Laura continued, "Kyle, you are so honest. I doubt it is there for a good purpose, given it has never been discussed in any of the marketing materials. Has anyone talked to you about marking ballots this way?

"No," Kyle said, "But I am not sure why anyone would have told me."

"You know the FBI keeps track of all the materials and manuals produced for these voting systems. They want to ensure the integrity of elections too. I will check to see if these markings are described in any of the technical specifications of the system."

"I would be surprised if you did find anything, but please let me know if you do. I am curious if this was planned. I'll think about it. I will put on my devious hat and see if I can come up with an evil purpose."

George commented, "I will think about it too. I wonder if I should see if I can meet up with Stewart again. He was part of that team doing the so-called secret code. Maybe he knows something."

After discussing things at length with no new ideas, George left. Laura and Kyle spent the rest of the evening talking about nothing in particular, which eventually led to more intimate investigations. Kyle spent the night. Fortunately, Laura had given him a drawer and closet space so he could change clothes before work the next morning. It was a pleasant and mutually rewarding evening.

Chapter 16

~ The Search for Stewart McNally ~

When George met Stewart McNally at the bar he frequented, George found Stewart refreshingly forthright. It was almost uncomfortable. On the one hand, George did want information about Stewart's work. On the other hand, he felt Stewart should have been more circumspect. However, Stewart did not reveal the purpose of the work of the *secret team*. George learned that the team would insert their code at the last moment. He learned that their code could be updated via the internet connection that was used to update the Voting Systems to the latest software versions. Stewart was less clear on the purpose of his team's work. All he would say was something about keeping track of the voters' intentions. Intentions? What did that mean? George felt like he could get detailed information out of Stewart if they met a few more times, so he went out to the bar to see if he could catch Stewart.

When he got to the bar, Stewart was not there. He waited for an hour and a half chatting with the bartender. He did not ask about Stewart. George was not successful on his first visit nor his second nor his third. On his third visit, George inquired about Stewart with the bartender on duty.

"Hey, I have been here several times trying to catch Stewart McNally. Have you seen him around recently?" George inquired.

"Oh, you didn't hear?" the bartender said.

"Hear what?"

"There was a drive-by shooting near here a couple of weeks ago. The cops think it was gang-related.

George interrupted, "Was Stewart hurt?"

"Killed him. It set the car on fire. "burned the guy up in his car."

"Were there any witnesses?" George asked.

"Naw. It was after the bar closed. Stewart was not in the best shape when he left. I was concerned he might not be able to drive," the bartender reported.

"Were you a witness?"

"Naw. But the cops that showed up are the ones that come by here frequently. One of them is sitting right over there," he said as he pointed toward three guys sitting at a table.

"Thanks," George meandered over to the table where they were sitting. "Mind if I join you?"

"Sure, are you buying?" asked one of the guys at the table.

"Huh—sure." George waved for the waiter, and ordered rounds for the table. At first, George did not know which one was the cop, so he waited for introductions. Since no one identified as a police officer, he stated his reason for coming over, "The bartender said one of you was a cop."

"So, what's it to you?" one of the guys responded.

"I was a friend of Stewart McNally, and wondered why I had not seen him recently. The bartender said he had been shot. Anything you could share with me?"

"Shot and incinerated," said the one that George took to be the cop. George waited to see if the cop would add anything. He didn't.

George pretended to be in remorse and said, "Oh—no. How terrible. How did this happen?"

One of the other guys at the table felt the need to add his two cents, "I know, Stew was one of a kind, a good guy. We all met Stew here at the bar. He was a gregarious kind of guy. Whoever did this, they shot him, and set the car on fire; burned the guy up."

Knowing the typical police procedure, George asked, "Positive ID?"

The cop responded, "Not yet. But we are pretty sure. It was his car; it was shot up. It happened right after he left the bar. We won't know for sure it was Stewart till the autopsy. However, I am confident the autopsy will confirm it. Who else could it be driving his car at two in the morning? It happened three blocks from here. Right now, we think it was a drive-by shooting mistake. There is a lot of gang activity in the area, a couple at war for the past six months. We think one of the bullets set the car on fire. The car had eight bullet holes and one that penetrated the gas tank. We have no witnesses, but I suppose that is not unusual for two in the morning. One of the bullets caught the driver in the head, so no chance to escape the fire."

"Hard to think about it; being burned up like that," said one of the guys. "I don't like to think about being burned up in my car. I have watched that on TV and had to change the channel."

George asked the cop, "When do you think the autopsy will be done?"

"I don't know. It's in the detective's hands, and they don't always tell us the results. I guess his car looked like one of the gangs, but even that is hard to figure. He drove a Prius, and that is not the normal car for a gang member. I don't know what to think. But I don't have to. The detectives will take care of it now."

George made small talk about Stewart with the guys to see if they had any information about his work. They told him they never talked about work, just football, and basketball.

George left the bar and headed back downtown. When he got to his place, he called Kyle and reported what he had found.

"Damn," Kyle said. "That's two people associated with the Voting Systems dead within the month. Do you think there is any relationship between these two guys?"

"I don't know, Kyle. I have not put the pieces together yet. Have you come up with anything new?"

"No. Not yet anyway," Kyle answered. "I have this queasy feeling that it has something to do with the read-heads. Or maybe that is me thinking everything is about me." Kyle chuckled to himself. "One thing that worries me is Richard. He seems down, which is curious since the machines are selling like hotcakes. My hire was unusual—to say the least. Am I being used in some way I can't follow? Are things going on that I should be able to see but am not? This whole experience with Richard and Laura and the FBI is strange. I think people know things, and they are not telling me."

George said, "I get how you feel, Kyle. Welcome to the detective's life. Rarely do things in an investigation turn out like you initially think. I live in a fog with most investigations until things start to fall in place. I must admit this whole thing is quite curious." As he talked, he got a text on his phone from Jeneen. "Gotta go, Kyle. I will check in with you soon." The text from Jeneen asked him to give her a call.

~ FBI Alert for Laura ~

Laura got a call from the local FBI office asking her to drop by for a briefing related to her work with Meisner Industries. Laura knew these could be important meetings, and she was concerned about the implications for the effort she, Kyle, and George were working on. She responded immediately.

The briefing was scheduled in two days. She decided not to inform Kyle or George before she heard the contents of the briefing. When she arrived, she went to visit Kameron Wilson. Kameron's secretary buzzed him to let him know Laura had arrived. Laura had to wait three minutes before the secretary let Laura know she should enter Kameron's office.

Kameron greeted Laura, "Good morning, Laura. I appreciate your dropping by for a briefing. Dick is on his way down to meet with us." Richard Mercer is the FBI agent assigned to investigations related to voter fraud.

"Hi, Kam. What's going on?" Laura inquired.

"Let's wait for Dick. How are things with you? You still keeping an eye on Kyle?" Kam asked with a sly grin on his face. He was well aware Laura was sleeping with Kyle even though that was frowned on.

"Of course, I am keeping an eye on him," she said as she blushed. "You know well and good that Kyle and I get along just fine."

"And how about that detective? What's his name? Lockit?" Kam asked

"Yeah, George Lockit. He is doing well. I assume you have read the reports I have been submitting."

"About that, can you tell me anything more about his trip to Palo Alto?" Kam asked.

"It's all in the reports I have sent you. He did not uncover any evidence except to see the threatening note sent to Chao. Do you know something I don't know?"

At that moment, Richard Mercer entered the office and closed the door, preventing Kam from answering Laura.

"Hi, Laura. Thanks for coming in. I wanted to make sure the information I am going to share was not intercepted."

"Got it," was all Laura needed to say.

Dick began, "Laura, this thing with Meisner has gotten more complex. As you know, our initial investigation of Meisner Industries was about his business practices. We have learned that Richard has been meeting privately with Senator Corning. We are aware they were friends. There may be a gay relationship between them, but we are not sure about that. They have had several meetings. While we don't know what the meetings were about, we are suspicious they are related to the Help America Vote Act that recently passed and enacted into law. It seems readily apparent that Meisner has had an inside track providing voting systems under HAVA."

Laura asked, "Is that the one that awarded federal dollars to states that moved to enhance the integrity of their voting systems?"

"Yes, the HAVA. We believe that Richard and Corning conspired to create specifications to support Meisner Voting Systems specifically. Meisner Industries has been the successful bidder on almost all requests for proposals put out by voter jurisdictions. The HAVA was very specific on the specifications for voting systems, and Meisner Industries is the only one able to provide a solution immediately. Other vendors will either have to make modifications to their systems or develop new ones. By the time they are ready to compete, Meisner will have the lion's part of the market share. We think Meisner had inside information and was working with Corning to eliminate that competition, at least at the outset of the awarding process."

"Any evidence?"

"Mostly circumstantial at this point: Richard's secret flights to College Park Airport in Maryland and a house he owns in Glendale. At the same time, we know that Corning was not home or at his Senate office during the same time. We suspect they occasionally met at Richard's place. We don't know if they met for business or pleasure."

"Okay, not proof, but a powerful coincidence," Laura responded.

"But that is not the reason we called you in. We got a heads-up from the CIA that they have been tracking Chinese MSS interests in U.S. elections. We don't know if there is any connection, but you need to be on the lookout. The MSS has been known to be rather ruthless, and is very skilled in covering their tracks."

"You think Richard is working for the MSS?"

"We don't think so. We have been watching for this carefully but no sign of it so far. But it is not out of the realm of possibility. If he is, and Corning knows about it or is in on whatever scheme they might have going, we are dealing with some dangerous guys. We want you to keep your eyes open and your back protected. We can't rule out Kyle or Lockit having something to do with this either."

"You've got to be kidding me. Kyle and George working for the MSS? C*ould I have been fooled?* "They are about as straight as I can imagine. Does this mean I have to keep this a secret from them?"

"Sorry, kid. That is how the cookie crumbles. Yes, this is for your eyes and ears only. We don't want this spoken of outside FBI headquarters."

"But what if they come up with this possibility independently?" Laura asked.

"Alert us immediately. Then we can assess the situation together." Dick quickly responded.

The three of them finished up some details of the situation, and Laura left the office burdened with yet again having to keep secrets from Kyle. She wondered if their relationship could survive another round of secret-keeping. At any rate, she now needed to use extra caution in conversations and activities in case the MSS also had her in their surveillance activities.

~ Torture ~

Stewart awoke from a stupor slowly. His head was killing him. Everything was blurry. He wanted to rub his eyes, but he was too weak to raise his arms. He did not realize, yet, that he was bound. It was the worst hangover headache he had ever had. He slowly awoke enough to raise his head. He was bound to a chair. He could not move his legs or arms. The room was out of focus, and the world seemed to be slowly rotating. His nose itched terribly. He was dizzy, so he closed his eyes. The sensation of the room tilting did not go away. He felt sick, about to throw up. Then he heard someone behind him say his name, Stewart McNally. Possibly they would help him, explain what was going on. Instead, a muscular man, about thirty years old, walked around in front of him. Although blurry, Stewart could almost make out the guy's face. Was he Japanese, or Korean, or maybe Chinese? He could not be sure. He needed to close his eyes again.

The man was talking to him, asking if his name was Stewart McNally. Stewart knew he was in trouble, but he did not know why. He wanted to resist. He wanted to shake his head to answer negatively, but when he started to shake his head, the world swirled around him, and he had to close his eyes and try to remain still. Why was he dizzy? Had he had too much to drink? It did not feel like being drunk. It was more like being ill, seriously ill, much like the flu. But his mind was beginning to clear. Why was he tied up? How did this happen? Where was he? How did he get here? It was too hard to think.

Again, the man asked him if he was Steward McNally. The last thing Stewart could remember was having a drink at the bar. A fellow struck up a conversation with him about football, soccer. He remembered now that the fellow seemed to know a lot about soccer and spouted off about his favorite team in Great Britain. He remembered thinking the guy was not British; he had no British accent. It was not American. He could not place it. In the course of this guy's monologue, the guy ordered up drinks for the two of them. He could not remember what he ordered; it was a name he was not familiar with. It was strong, and the guy suggested they go to a different bar. He remembered leaving, but that was all he could remember. Had he been drugged?

The man facing him was becoming insistent now asking him if his name was Stewart McNally. He realized he needed to play along, so he nodded, yes. It set the room spinning again. The man complimented him for his cooperation and began to ask all sorts of questions about his life, living arrangements, relationships, his work. Stewart realized he was being interrogated, but he could not tell by whom. Clearly, it was not the police or any legal group. He was tied up! Lots of questions. He tried to answer them, but the ones about work were the most disconcerting. He realized that under normal circumstances, he would gladly brag about his work. It was his livelihood. He also realized his job depended on maintaining the confidentiality of the details of what he did or what it was supposed to accomplish. He resisted answering those questions. The man was becoming more agitated and insistent on getting the answers he wanted.

Again, the man asked about Stewart's work. Stewart resisted answering, shaking his head. His head was beginning to clear up a bit. The man slapped him. Stewart was shocked. He knew he should not have been surprised given that his arms were duck taped to the arms of the chair, and his feet were tied or taped to the chair legs. He began to realize how vulnerable he was to the wishes and actions of the man interrogating him. He tried to think of a way to escape, if not from the room, at least from violence. He hoped in vain. The man asked specific details about the code Stewart wrote for Meisner Industries. His interrogator seemed to know the nature of what he knew, what he did and wanted to know the details. It was alarming. Stewart knew what he had written was contributing to an illegal intervention in the Voting Systems of Meisner Industries. Could this possibly be a test of his willingness to break his Non-Disclosure Agreement? He knew that Richard Meisner was a demanding boss, but would he go to this extreme to test him? That was crazy talk. He needed to resist.

The man insisted on getting answers to his questions. Stewart was a bright guy. His head was not as clear as it usually was at work. Could he spin a false scenario? He began to lie about his work for Meisner Industries, what code he had written. He described code that could provide more detail about how people were voting and how the operators could get that data. This time the slap came suddenly, stronger, and with an abruptness that knocked him and the chair over. He hit his shoulder and head on the floor, and the pain in his head shot through his spine so sharply that he did not notice the pain from his elbow when it instinctively tried to extend when he was knocked to the floor. Someone behind him, someone that he did not know was in the room, picked him up like a rag doll, and set him upright again. Stewart hurt all over, but it made him madder and more determined not to allow the intimidation to work. Now, it was not so much about the NDA as pure obstinance.

Little by little, they got the gist of what Stewart and his team had done, create software to manipulate voter counts, but not the detail of how it worked. Stewart refused to answer any more questions. He endured a fist to his face, an electric shock, a torch against his feet. He passed out a couple of times and revived with a bucket of ice-cold water in the face. Stewart resolved to resist. The interrogators became even more aggressive. After the extreme abuse, they could not revive Stewart. In his stubbornness, he sacrificed his life. The team proceeded to dismember the body and place the parts in several extra heavy plastic bags. They cleaned the site of blood and tissue and took the bags to a remote site and buried Steward's remains.

~ George at Stanford ~

While all the other things were going on, George made another trip to Palo Alto. Jeneen passed along Maddy's concerns. Chao was willing to talk to George. In Chao's mind, he might need the support of a private investigator. When George arrived, he contacted Chao, and they arranged to meet. Based on his experience of having his tires punctured on the last visit, George was cautious. George made use of a burner phone to call a similar burner phone that Chao had purchased to arrange a time and place to meet. George gave Chao instructions on how to check to make sure he was not followed. George did the same. They met in a small bar off-campus at 2:00 AM. The early hour simplified observing any followers. Neither were followed as far as they could tell.

George was sitting at the bar when Chao arrived. The bar closed at 2:00 AM. George had arranged to meet at a time no one else would be in the bar. Chao looked around and realized they would be alone. Given his concerns, he had apprehensions about whether he could trust George. However, he did not know any other PI, and Maddy had spoken highly about how he had worked with her when she had concerns about him. He certainly had reason to be concerned, and based on experience in Taiwan, he had reasons not to go to the police.

"Chao! Over here," George called to him. George stood to shake Chao's hand and noted Chao had a firm, confident handshake. George motioned Chao to the comfort of a booth with an overhead light. "Have a seat. Glad we can finally meet." Chao surveyed the room. Indeed, they were the only ones left in the bar except the bartender. As they sat, the bartender left the room as George had paid him to do.

"Mr. Lockit, I am pleased to meet you."

"It's George to you, Chao."

"Thanks. I don't know if my concerns are valid, and I need help figuring that out. I hope you will be able and willing to help."

"Let's start from the beginning. I like to put people's concerns in context. When did you first have any concerns or inklings that things were not right?"

Chao described his history. He told how his father had come to the U.S., Stanford, to study engineering. That is where he met Richard Meisner. Richard was also studying engineering and business administration. They had become very close friends. According to his father, he and Richard hung out together a lot.

Chao made no indication that he knew Richard was gay, and George did not know whether that was evident at the time he met Tao, so made no comments about that.

Chao said he grew up around his father's manufacturing business and knew K & W Manufacturing frequently produced components for Richard Meisner's business interests. He aspired to be successful like his father and expected to join the business after he graduated. So, it was with some alarm a month or so ago that he received the threatening note that resulted in George's first visit to Palo Alto. He described how he was first upset that Maddy, his girlfriend, had told her friend Jeneen about the note, and then agreed to meet George while Chao was visiting his father in Taiwan.

George asked, "If you don't mind, I hope you are not upset at Maddy. She was truly concerned, first when she found the note, and then the fact you headed home in the middle of the semester. Could I ask, was it the note that prompted your visit or something else?"

"Partially the note, and partially the fact I was being followed. At least I thought I was. I could have been paranoid, but I kept seeing this Chinese guy in a lot of different places. Whenever I looked his way, he would act like he was interested in something else. I needed to talk to my dad to see if something was going on at his end. I did not get any particularly concerning information from my dad that caused me alarm, so I returned after only one week's absence. I have been trying to catch up ever since. But frankly, I am distracted and concerned. I still think I am being followed."

"Did you, by any chance, get a picture of the guy?"

"Crap. I never thought of that," Chao replied. "If I see him again, I will try to get a picture, but as I said, whenever I look his way, he turns."

"Maybe Maddy could help you, you know, so between the two of you could get a picture."

"No. I am not doing that!" Chao said sharply, "Maddy does not need to be involved if I can help it."

"Okay," George said. "Continue your story."

Chao continued, he had received another threatening note, and this has him concerned not only for himself but for Maddy too. The note suggests that he needs to keep quiet about his father's use of Xiazhen Manufacturing in Shenzhen. Chao told about the conversation he had with his dad about Xiazhen when he visited him. That made the threat more alarming. That conversation was supposedly confidential.

"Wait, so K & W Manufacturing contracts with a mainland plant for its products?" George asked.

"Yes. Specifically, some of the parts sold to Meisner Industries. Dad said Richard Meisner did not know, and it was essential to keep that secret. I don't trust the mainland Chinese. I know the MSS has their hands in all sorts of international shenanigans. That is why this threat is so alarming. I believe that the MSS has agent operatives here in the states. Most of them are businessmen. Who knows which have been compromised by the MSS? Some of the people they hire," Chao paused, thinking of how to finish the statement, "Who knows what they are capable of?"

"I see. You are right to be concerned. What does the guy who has been following you look like? How old would you say he is? What is his height, weight, etcetera?

Chao closed his eyes and answered, "I would guess he is in his thirties. He is taller than I am, so I would say five foot eleven, and weight, rough guess, ninety kilos. He had the usual Chinese complexion and crew cut."

George observed, "I think I might have seen the same guy on my last visit here. Do what you can to get a photo. Maybe you could find someone he would not suspect to help you. Just be careful. So again, what can I do to help you?"

"Well, the reason I called you is the second note." Chao pulled out the note and handed it to George.

George read the note. Held it up to the weak light in the bar, inspecting the paper. He asked Chao if he could take a photo of the note.

"You can have the damn thing if you want. It makes me nervous."

George folded the note and put it in his pocket. "I can see why you are concerned. The fact they mentioned Maddy suggests they are upping the stakes. I can get on this right away. Meantime, keep as low a profile as you can. And, on second thought, forget the picture. That might cause you more trouble than it is worth. Well, if you can get one without any risk, it might be helpful."

Chao and George continued to discuss options and concerns. George gave Chao practical advice about keeping a low profile, mainly trying to ignore the note, and, above all, not calling his father until he and George talked again. George suggested they continue to communicate via text on their throwaway cell phones, powering them on randomly during the day to check for communications. George left the bar first to scout the surroundings. It seemed safe enough, so he texted Chao the all-clear.

~ Comparing Notes ~

Laura, Kyle, and George met again at a new diner in Gresham. It had been over a week since they met. Laura wanted to know how long George was able to stay in Portland. When she initially learned about George, she had thought his visit was going to be short. George indicated he had arranged to be in Portland indefinitely. That eased Laura's mind since George had been doing research that no one else could easily do.

George planned to share about his trip to Palo Alto to meet with Chao. He had also learned about Stewart McNally's demise. Laura had met with the FBI about possible MSS involvement. Kyle had been working on the read-heads mystery. They needed to compare notes, but Laura had to live with her secret about the MSS. They all started to talk at once when the bug sweep was completed. Laura quickly deferred to Kyle and Kyle to George.

George reported on his visits with McNally, followed by his disappearance and death in the drive-by shooting.

Laura asked, "So, Dennis Andersen dies in a car accident, and Stewart McNally dies in a drive-by shooting. Doesn't that seem strange to you?"

"Of course, it does," George answered. "You know we are waiting on the autopsy to confirm Stewart's identity, right?"

"You have your doubts about it being McNally? What are you thinking?" Laura asked.

"I don't know. It is a gut feeling. His murder feels suspicious. Of course, it could be a case of mistaken identity, but his Prius makes me doubt a gang mistook it for another gang member's car. The fact there were eight bullet holes says this was very intentional. It is not that I expect any particular thing from the autopsy. I simply want to know what they find."

Kyle spoke up, "I can't imagine how they can even do an autopsy on a burned-up corpse. Gives me the creeps, the whole thing."

"Yes, it creeps me out too," George said, and Laura nodded agreement.

Laura felt it was important to warn George and Kyle, but she was prohibited from telling them what she learned at the FBI. She said, "I think we all need to be careful. We don't know what is going on, at least not yet. You two will be careful, won't you?"

George and Kyle made a resigned kind of acknowledgment.

"The other thing I wanted to report is about my visit with Chao. We are keeping things confidential between us, are we not?" And he looked at Kyle and Laura. Both nodded.

"Well, Chao has received another warning note. When he visited his father, he learned that the read-heads that Kyle has been testing were not manufactured in his father's plant. His father had outsourced the work to a factory in China and claims that Richard does not know he did that. He was in a cash flow bind and took a shortcut. Chao is concerned because he fears his father has unwittingly made himself vulnerable to blackmail from the Chinese. He thinks the warning notes he has received are possibly authorized by the Ministry of State Security, the MSS in China. Chao says every electronic component manufactured in China carries the risk of sabotage or espionage. He has been followed around by a Chinese looking guy, so he was scared, wanted my help."

Kyle said, "Now you have me scared shitless. Excuse my French. The Chinese could be behind what's going on?"

Laura got a big frown on her face. This was something she needed to report to Kam at once. She wondered now if the CIA was involved somehow too?

"Don't get too nervous, Kyle; it is all speculation at this point," George said.

Thinking about the implications, Kyle asked, "Do you think the Chinese have an interest in Meisner? Could they possibly be involved in Dennis and Stewart's deaths? Could we be in danger too?"

"Kyle, hang on. Don't jump to conclusions so fast. Just watch your back. If there is a relationship between Dennis's death and Stewart's death, we have to look for it. I should say I will look for it. That is not your job. If someone is in danger, it will be me, not you."

Kyle continued to ruminate over everything, trying to make sense of the Chinese being involved.

Laura spoke up, "George, you know I need to report this to the FBI. They might be working on parallel tracks, so we need to compare notes."

"Compare notes? I have not noticed your friends in the FBI being all that willing to share," George noted. Laura, despite herself, blushed. That did not pass George's notice. He surmised she knew more than she was sharing. He had worked with the FBI before, so he realized that was probably the case and would not change.

Meanwhile, Kyle had been off on one of his mental ventures and blurted out, "I never thought about the possibility the read-heads could be used to send signals. "Oh, my god. I bet those mysterious RF emissions from the read-heads could be used to spy on the elections. I better run more tests."

"Careful, Kyle. If the MSS is involved, we need to be more careful about what we do that other people know about. Could you run the tests secretly?"

"Not sure. I will have to think about that. Do you think the MSS is involved? Do you think they know I have been running these tests?"

Laura had been very quiet during this part of the conversation. She knew the MSS was active but was not allowed to share it, at least not now. George and Kyle noticed Laura's silence and turned to her. Kyle asked her, "You are unusually quiet; what are you thinking?"

"What am I thinking?" Laura said, searching for an answer. "I think that if the MSS might be involved, we need to be extremely discrete. It makes our work on things much more dangerous. Do either of you think Richard might be in cahoots with the MSS?"

George spoke first, "It's possible. What do you think, Kyle?"

"Sure, anything is possible. But what would be the point? He has a successful business; he is financially well off. We know he does not seek out the limelight, so I don't see what he would gain by working with the MSS."

"Unless they have something on him. Who knows he is gay? Does he need to protect that?" George asked.

Laura answered, "I could be wrong, but I think it is general knowledge he is gay. He seems okay about it, just does not want to call attention to it. If they do have something on him, I don't think that is it."

Meanwhile, Laura began to wonder about everything she had been involved with. Did the FBI have these suspicions way back when they asked her to con Richard again in Dallas? If they did, then they had set her up without telling her of the dangers. She began to think about all the ways she had been used by Richard to see if anything jumped out for her. She could not make any connections that led her to believe Richard was working with the MSS. One of the few times he had ditched her when they were out was the time in D.C. when he met with Corning and sent her to her hotel. If he was doing the MSS's bidding, he was hiding it very well."

Kyle broke her reverie, "Laura, are you listening?"

"Oh, yes. This is disturbing information. What if I have been helping Richard and did not know he was working with the MSS?"

George answered, "Laura, don't jump to conclusions. We need to be on alert for anything that might help us get to the bottom of things. Okay?"

"Okay," she said. She was anxious to get the meeting over so she could report to Kameron at the FBI what she had learned from George. She had to wait because Kyle had not reported yet. "Kyle, what have you been up to?"

Chapter 17

~ George Lockit and Dennis Andersen ~

George was both curious and concerned about the disappearance of Stewart and the death of Dennis. He needed to know more details about both instances. He called the Clackamas County Medical Examiner to see if he could get additional information about Dennis. When he met with the Medical Examiner and identified himself as a private detective looking into the death of Dennis Andersen, the ME was at first hesitant to provide any information and referred him to the Sheriff's office. The Sheriff's office referred him to the District Attorney, who agreed to meet him. The DA made note of George's credentials, including an ID provided by the FBI office in St. Andrews. He had agreed not to reveal his work with the FBI in Portland, but they had said nothing about St. Andrews. After asking George lots of questions, he finally agreed to share some of the case information. George managed to learn that Dennis had not died from drowning but from asphyxiation. George asked about the alcohol in his car. There was an open bottle in the car, but the ME said there was no indication Dennis had been drinking. This left the case open as a possible homicide. George told the DA he was inquiring for a friend of Dennis's who worked alongside him. The DA insisted on knowing the friend's name, and George had no choice but to provide Kyle's name. Given the circumstances, George decided he needed to talk to Jill Huang, Dennis's girlfriend.

George decided not to call but just show up at Jill's place that evening on the chance he would catch her at home. She was at home. He rang her doorbell. He could see when she looked through the spyhole, and thought she might not open the door, but she did open it a crack. She had a chain on the door.

"Yes, may I help you?" Jill asked through the partially open door.

"Hi, Jill. My name is George Lockit. I am a friend of Kyle Tredly, who used to work with Dennis. I want to ask you a few questions about Dennis to fill in a piece we are writing about him. Do you have a few minutes?"

"Who did you say you were again?"

"George. George Lockit. I work with Kyle Tredly."

"I don't want to talk about it," Jill responded, hoping he would go away.

Jill, I talked recently with the Clackamas County District Attorney. I learned Dennis's death was not an accident nor a suicide. They said his death is suspicious. I could fill you in if you like."

That got her attention. Jill closed the door, and for a moment, George thought she had closed the door on him. She opened it again after removing the chain.

"My place is a mess. If you don't mind that, come on in," Jill said. George entered into a living area open to an efficiency kitchen separated from the living area by a bar counter. Jill quickly picked up some clothes on the couch and motioned for George to have a seat. She left with the clothes, returned empty-handed, and took a seat on the other side of the room in front of a credenza that had a flat panel TV sitting on it. There was a coffee table between them with a half-full glass of what could have been liquor, tea, or soda; George could not tell which.

"You knew Dennis?" Jill asked.

"Unfortunately, no," George answered. "I work on another project with Kyle, and he asked me to look into Dennis's death. Something about it did not seem like Dennis."

"You got that right. One day he is as happy as a lark. We had the best sex ever the night before,"—she hesitated—"you know." she commented unashamedly.

"I know what you mean, Jill," George said, moving on to the point of his visit. "Kyle tells me he and Dennis were working on a problem at work and that Dennis seemed interested, his background is in electrical engineering, wasn't it?"

"Yeah. Well, anyway, I am just a clerk, so I don't know what he was working on. He has a shop in the spare bedroom at his place and a bunch of equipment in there. His place is a lot nicer than mine, I mean, look at it. Anyway, he came home the night before— He came to my place all excited about, I think he said something about noise. I can't remember for sure. Yeah, it was about noise. Ever heard someone excited about noise? Anyway, Dennis thought he could help Kyle figure out a problem they were having at work. Dennis thought he had figured it out. He wanted to take some test equipment he owns to prove it. He left early to go by his place to get a piece of equipment to take to work. He seemed happy as a lark."

This piqued George's interest. "Did he tell you the nature of the problem he and Kyle were working on?"

"Well, he tried. He was always trying to, you know, educate me, but I did not follow much. But I did get that something was radiating information from equipment that should not have been. He thought he could read the information with the equipment he had. He seemed excited like he had discovered something important, and he told me he was concerned it could be a problem for the company.

"Interesting. Jill, did he tell anyone else about his discovery?"

"Not that I know of," Jill answered.

George noticed that she had started to fidget and developed deep creases in her forehead. He asked, "By any chance, did you happen to mention this to anyone?"

Defensive now, Jill continued to fidget and frown. She said, "I don't know anything about what Dennis did at work. Everything was top secret."

That did not answer George's question, so he tried it a different way, "When you realized that Dennis had disappeared, did you talk to anyone about it? Do you have any friends who shared your concerns?"

"I have friends at work. I told some of them."

"You told them about the noise and Dennis's interest?"

"No. Just that Dennis seemed more interested in his damn machines than me."

"What about people outside of work. Do you have other friends?"

"Some," Jill answered, being somewhat coy. She was feeling George's pressure, his push for information. She did not want to get in any trouble.

"Jill, please don't misunderstand my questions. I am trying to find out, for Kyle, who else knew about the noise issue. I am trying to figure out if that had anything to do with his disappearance. So, anyone you might have talked to might also have information that would help figure this out. Please tell me if you can think of anyone else you talked to during this time."

Jill had been in love with Dennis. She would have done anything for him. As she pondered George's questions, she still wanted to find out what happened. She decided to tell about her conversations with Chin Chen.

"Well, I do have a friend that does not live here that I talked to. But they would not know anyone around here to talk to besides me," Jill finally said.

"Who was that?"

"My best friend back in Taiwan, Chin Chen"

"Say that again?"

"Chin Chen."

"Could you spell that for me?"

Jill spelled it for George and gave George her phone number. She realized she would have to warn Chin Chen that George might call.

"When did you talk to her, before or after Dennis disappeared?"

Jill thought about it. "She called me late, after Dennis had left to go play with his equipment, the night before he disappeared. At the time, I thought it was odd."

"Why odd?"

"Well," Jill answered, "We usually only talk on Saturdays."

"Saturdays? You had a regular time to talk?"

"Yes. You know, time zone differences. I would talk to her around ten in the morning when it was night time in Taipei."

"So, she called you that last night that Dennis was home?"

"Yeah, but what does that have to do with anything. She is halfway around the world."

"Maybe nothing." But George made a request anyway, "Jill, I have a favor to ask. I promise you that I will not call Chin Chen and bother her. I request you not tell her about me. I don't want to get too many people concerned about my inquiries. Is that something you can do?"

"No problem," She said, but she lied. She did not keep things from Chin Chen. It did concern her, however, at how interested George was in her good friend Chin Chen.

George followed up with a few innocuous questions to wind down the conversation. Then he asked, "Jill, if I have more questions, would you mind if I follow up with you?"

Hesitant to seem unhelpful, she answered, "I guess not. Whatever."

George left Jill's, and pondered the possible relationship of Dennis's disappearance and this Chin Chen person halfway around the world. Why did Chin Chen call Jill at the precise time she did? Was she connected in some way to Dennis's death? He had an uneasy feeling about it.

~ The Success of Meisner Voting Systems ~

Meisner and Corning were delighted at the success of Meisner Voting Systems (MVS). In three months, Meisner Industries had orders for over two hundred MVS units at $575,000 a pop from jurisdictions in twenty-five states. Corning was pleased that the systems were being placed in political jurisdictions dominated by both parties, but especially in states that were typically closely contested. Corning was pushing MVS wherever he had opportunities to speak, which, as it turned out, were numerous. Meisner had built up an inventory before the Help America Vote Act passage, so he was able to get systems out the door quickly. The machines were utilized in several local elections with virtually no problems. Based on the purchase contracts of the MVS, Meisner Industries had the opportunity to inspect data from the machines on a few days' notice. The contract stipulated that customers would install upgrades within 30 days of release and conduct elections with only the latest updates installed. Meisner employees conducted the initial installations and staff training for customers. On the few occasions where technical assistance was needed, Meisner provided it without additional charge prior to the first use. So far, there had been no problems or issues with the machines. Meisner (and Corning) had decided not to impact any elections until after everyone had been through a successful election. That meant the secret code would not be invoked for at least one year, and maybe four. Manipulating elections was a long-term strategy, not an immediate one. Where particular jurisdictions were cautious, test runs were made to verify the machines' accuracy.

Kyle had the opportunity to visit several sites. He presented himself, per Richard's rather forceful suggestion, as a quality control officer. It offered Kyle the opportunity to take along with him noise detection equipment. From these experiences, Kyle was able to verify the "noise" issue was consistent over all the sites he visited. Without Dennis's interventions, he did not presume to investigate the noise in detail so long as it had no apparent impact on the operation of the machines. At one location, he ran into an inquisitive employee who asked lots of questions about the machines, some of which Kyle could not answer. The employee pressed Kyle on his use of the spectrum analysis he was doing. Kyle avoided a detailed answer with a partial truth. He told the employee he was monitoring the RF noise the MVS made during its operation and when idle to make sure it stayed within parameters. Of course, there were no parameters. The noise was probably above the FCC regulated values, but no one had complained so far. The signals were mostly within an unregulated band, yet to be auctioned by the FCC. It did not occur to Kyle that Senator Corning's committee could keep that band open as long as he wanted.

~ George and Stewart McNally ~

As much as George wanted to stay in Portland and work with Kyle, there was business back in St. Andrews that needed his attention. He was not able to return to Portland for forty-five days. In the meantime, Kyle had been taking trips to MVS installations, and Laura had been dealing with her timeshare business and data analysis for the FBI. Kyle's workgroup was now working on another project for which Kyle was not essential. The project gave him time for his fieldwork while his team engaged in coding sessions. Kyle was not sure which he enjoyed most, field visits or successfully coding a project module.

As soon as George returned, he checked in with Kyle and Laura. George had not told them about his inquiry into Dennis's death. He did not plan on sharing his investigation into Stewart's death until he had more information. George looked up the DA for Washington County to see if there was additional information on the disappeared Stewart McNally.

Washington County DA, "So you are a PI?"

"Yes. I work mainly in St. Andrew's, Texas. I do a lot of work with the FBI there as well."

"Oh Yeah? I know a few guys there. I lived in Tucker a few years. I was the DA there. I knew some of the guys in the FBI. Who in the FBI did you work with?"

"I worked with Buck Rogers."

"Good ole Buck. Yes, I knew him. We mostly saw eye to eye, but on occasions, not so much."

George continued, "The first case Buck and I worked was very interesting."

"What was that?"

"I don't know when you were in Texas, but it was a case that caught the Governor in a conspiracy to commit murder."

"Oh, yeah, I remember that one. I was not in Texas then, but it made the national press. I read all the press reports that crossed my desk. You worked on that?"

"Yeah. I was working with the falsely accused guy. The Governor and his cronies set him up for two murders. It looked a lot like they had successfully framed the guy for the murders to cover up their dealings with organized crime in the state."

"I forgot, who did they try to frame?"

"A guy by the name of Kyle Tredly. I was his PI. A local lawyer and I managed to catch the Governor in the process. Buck Rogers in the FBI and I worked hand in hand. It was an interesting case, one that made my career."

"So, what brings you to Washington County and the Portland area?"

"Believe it or not, Kyle Tredly."

"You don't say. The same guy you helped in St. Andrews? What has he gotten himself into this time?"

"Well, to tell the truth, probably nothing. He works for Meisner Industries. You know about them?"

"Sure, everybody knows about Mr. Meisner, one of Portland's most eligible bachelors."

"Kyle works closely with Mr. Meisner. That is not a problem, is it?"

"Naw. Meisner has a decent reputation. You know he's gay, don't you?"

To make it appear he knew less, George responded, "Gay? I thought you said he was Portland's most eligible bachelor?"

"Well, yes, I did. That is the way the press here plays it. I think that is what Meisner wants people to think. I can't prove it, but I think he buys good press. I think his being gay is fairly common knowledge. He does, however, seem to go to extremes not to advertise it. He has a good friend, woman friend, who accompanies him to most public events to keep up appearances."

George decided to see if the DA had any more interesting things to say about Meisner. He kept quiet, and the DA filled in the awkward silence.

"That's the word on the street," the DA said. "So, what can I help you with?"

"There was a supposed gang shoot-out a couple of months ago in Hillsboro. Guy got incinerated in his car in the process. Did that come across your desk?"

"Yes, everything comes across my desk. Way too much." the DA said without additional comment waiting for another question. He could play the silent game too.

George took the hint and continued. "Well, the guy in that car supposedly worked for Meisner Industries. Is that correct?"

"Hmmn. That is still an open case."

"How so?" George asked, somewhat surprised. He assumed the gang members had already been rounded up.

"Well, we thought it was gang-related at first. The car belonged to McNally, so we presumed it was him in the car. We did round up some gang members, but they were insistent it was not gang-related. All the gangs in the area insisted it was not related to their turf wars, that they had no interest in McNally. We tended to believe them because of the car, a Prius. Hardly any gang member would be caught dead in a Prius. No pun intended there."

"And ..." George prompted for more information.

"Well, we never got a missing person report on this McNally. He was sort of a non-person, little history. I had the Medical Examiner see if he could get DNA so we could use one of those new databases to see if we could find any relatives."

"Interesting, did that work?" George was fascinated by the development of this new fact.

"Not how we had planned. It turns out the guy in the car was not McNally. It was another guy who had an entry in our felon's database. It was a guy who just got out of prison. When we looked up his records, we found his only relative was dead, so no one was looking for him, no missing person's reports here or any place. We interrogated some of his prison buddies but came up with nothing."

"So, you are saying the guy in the car was not McNally? What happened to him?"

"Your guess is as good as mine. We are holding the case open. Now McNally is a person of interest. We have registered it on the national database in hopes of finding a connection someplace. So, I should have asked you, what is your interest in this guy?"

"You do know that McNally worked for Meisner Industries, don't you?"

"And how do you know this?"

"I met with Stewart several times at a Hillsboro bar he visited often. I managed to learn some things about his work. Turns out he was part of a small team working in Hillsboro on some secret project. But most of Meisner's projects are secret until they are not."

"When did all these meetings take place?" The DA was getting very interested in getting a new lead in this open case.

"I met with him a few weeks before the event. I went to the bar expecting to meet him again when I learned of the shoot-out. Everyone I know assumes he was killed in that car."

"I know. I would like to keep it that way for a while if you don't mind."

"That's fine with me. But where is the real Stewart McNally?"

"That is the sixty-four-thousand-dollar question, isn't it? We are wondering if he set up the car shooting."

Both George and the DA were quiet for a moment. Then George answered, "That is an interesting possibility. If I run across anything that might have a bearing on this, I will let you know. Would you do the same for me?"

The DA nodded and then lied, "Sure. Looks like we both could use some help."

George and the DA exchanged phone numbers in case additional information came up. It was one week later when the DA called George to report a development in the case of the missing Stewart McNally. The DA told George that in an unrelated case, Stewart's remains were found in an unmarked grave in the forest.

George asked if the medical examiner had issued a report yet, and if so, could he get a copy. The DA said he would send an electronic copy. When George got the report, he was surprised to read that the remains had been cut up into many parts. The DNA confirmed it was the remains of Stewart. This news was very concerning. Whoever did this, whatever was going on, the stakes were very high. He needed to meet with Kyle immediately.

~ George, Kyle and Laura ~

The threesome met in a place they had never met before in Lake Oswego, South of Portland's downtown. George wanted to make sure no one was listening in on their conversation. Kyle and Laura were instructed to leave their phones in their apartments, so no one could track their location. Something serious was going on, and George did not want to put any of them in danger. They met at 9:00 PM. The bar did not close until 2:00 AM, so they had plenty of time to talk. They stuck to beer and burgers for nourishment.

George began, "Since we last met, I have been looking into Dennis and Stewart's disappearance. I found out that Dennis did not drown; he died from asphyxiation. You don't smother yourself, and you can't kill yourself by holding your breath."

"So, you are saying he was murdered?" Kyle asked.

"And where did you find this out?" asked Laura.

"Be patient guys; I will fill you in," George answered. He then began to fill them in on his visits to the Clackamas County DA's, where he got his information."

"That puts an interesting spin on things," Kyle interjected. "Did you find out any more? Did the DA have a suspect? Did he have theories about motive?"

"No suspect, yet. And no motive yet either. But I am aware of another interesting fact that could have a bearing on both. It seems that his girlfriend, Jill Huang—"

Laura jumped in, "Huang, did you say?"

"Yes, Jill Huang. Why? Does that mean something to you?"

This placed Laura in the position of having to confess something she was not sure she had shared with Kyle or George, her multiple trips to Taiwan. She hesitated then began, "Sorry, it never came up, but I knew a guy who worked for the CIA whose name is Huang. I met him on one of my trips to Taiwan for Richard."

"What? When did you go to Taiwan? And why? What does Richard have to do with these trips" Kyle asked, a bit miffed because this was the first time it came up.

"Sorry, Kyle. I have too many secrets to keep, and I don't know which ones I already shared. You know my timeshare work is both real and partially a cover for my work with the FBI."

"I figured as much. I never found a good time to question you about that." Kyle said.

"Well, it was also a cover for trips I made to Taiwan for Richard. Remember when you got the first beta version of the read-heads? I went to Taiwan, to Tao Li's factory to get them for Richard. He did not trust Fed Ex or the mail. You know how he is. Anyway, I told you I was going to Hawaii for my timeshare job. I did go to Hawaii, but then to Taiwan to get the prototypes, and deliver new specifications to Li."

George jumped in, "Tao Li, you knew him, you knew him personally?"

"Yes."

"You knew him, and you did not say anything when we discussed the threatening note to his son Chao?"

"Sorry."

George grunted his disapproval. He wondered how this motley team of three ever made any progress on the mysteries around this case. Kyle was shaking his head."

Kyle responded before George had a chance, "SHIT, Laura, you are so full of secrets and frankly lies, it is hard to feel your heart is in this effort."

"I resent that, Kyle. I was involved before you came to town. It is not only my job; it is my passion. That's why I work for the FBI. I want to be a part of making this country better. And, frankly, I think I have been making a difference."

"Sorry," Kyle said, backing down. "One of the things I love about you is your passion for justice. I get frustrated that you keep secrets. I know, I know, it goes with the job. It is hard to accept. My idea of a good relationship is one without secrets. I guess that is my problem."

"I'm sorry too. I want it both ways. But as long as I work for the FBI, there will be secrets I can't share. I can't do anything about that. But hear this, Kyle, if I have to choose between the FBI and you, I will choose you. I want you to know that!

Before Kyle could stop himself, he said, "So, you are saying that if push comes to shove, this time you would choose me over the FBI?"

Laura wanted to say yes, but she knew that would be a lie. "Sorry about that letter Kyle."

"No, I am selfish. I want it both ways too, but I know better. Sorry I lashed out."

George took the opportunity to bring things back to the topics at hand. "You guys got things settled now? Can we get back on the subject of this meeting?"

Kyle and Laura nodded, only slightly ashamed of their outburst.

"Laura, I think you were about to tell us about someone also named Huang," George prompted.

"Oh, yeah. Huang was a CIA agent that met me whenever I went to Taiwan to meet Li."

"How many times did you go?" asked Kyle.

"I don't know. A bunch of times, but most of them were before you came to Portland. Let me think. I think there were only a couple of times since you have been here."

George asked, "And Huang met you every time?"

"Every time but the last one. He did not show up the last time. I never followed up. Oh, I forgot, the last time some guy tried to strong-arm me in the bar where Huang and I normally met. I reported it to Kam. The picture I secretly took matched one the bureau had of a Chinese MSS agent. I had forgotten that."

"You were strong-armed?" Kyle asked, alarmed he had not known. "and you forgot to mention it?" Kyle was frustrated again.

"Kyle, no big deal. I know how to handle myself. He got nothing, although he did bruise my arm."

George jumped back in to deflect these two lovers from another argument, "Do you think there could be a relationship between Jill Huang and the one that met you in Taiwan, Laura?"

"Possible. On the other hand, that is a relatively common name. But talking about Jill, you never finished what you were saying about her."

"Well, I found out Jill had a Taiwanese girlfriend by the name of Chen Chin," George spelled her name for them. "There is an odd coincidence of the timing of a conversation Jill had with Chen and Dennis's disappearance. It is possible Chin has connections with the MSS. Any thoughts on this, Kyle? You worked with Dennis. What was he working on at the time?"

"Oh, dear. He was working with me on the anomaly I discovered in the read-heads. Dennis was like a puppy dog following me around. He was very interested. The day he went missing, he was supposed to bring in equipment to help me look at the anomaly. He thought there might be information in the signal we were seeing."

"That is curious. For the moment, let's put this on hold. I have more information that is as shocking," George said.

"What!" Kyle and Laura said simultaneously.

"Okay, I also met with the DA in Washington county about Stewart McNally, the guy on Meisner's secret team. Remember, the guy that told me about Meisner's interest in manipulating elections? I wanted to see if the DA had any information on

Stewart's demise. He told me the guy in the car was not Stewart after all."

"Not Stewart? Well, who was he? Where's Stewart gone?" Kyle asked.

"The guy was a recently released felon. The DA says it was not a gang shoot out either. Then a couple of days later, he called me to say they found Stewart in a shallow grave in the forest when they were looking for something else. The DNA confirmed it."

"How did he die?" Laura asked.

"They don't know that, but for a good reason. Stewart had been hacked into pieces, like someone trying to cover up something."

Laura summarized, "So it looks like two murders trying to cover up what Meisner was up to. I never thought he was capable of murder, but I know you can't always tell about someone backed into a corner."

George suggested, "Laura, you might be jumping to conclusions. Meisner's overall behavior suggests he takes care of his employees, not kills them. Of course, being exposed could be a motive. But I have a sense there is still more to this than we know yet. We need to check out this Chin Chen too, remember?"

"Maybe so, but I can't keep this from the FBI. It is explosive, and I have no idea what they know or what they have been tracking. Chin Chen could be news to them, or it is one more thing they are not sharing with me. I will get hold of them right away."

George held up his hand to signal a stop, "Wait. Consider another possibility. What if we met with Richard and disclosed what we know and see his reaction? Then, we can decide what to do next?"

"We can do that, but first, I need to clear it with the bureau. I can't be a lone ranger on this."

Chapter 18

Two weeks passed before George, Kyle, and Laura met again. This time, they met briefly at a private location. George brought everyone up to date on the investigations. In neither case had any real progress been made on identifying the murderers. Based on the few body parts they could analyze; Stewart had been tortured. In Dennis's case, an interesting fact was a missing spectrum analyzer. He had left home with the analyzer that morning when he headed to work, but it was not in the car when the car was recovered from the Willamette River. Since the windows of the car were closed, it could not have floated away. They also determined that the car was not running when it went into the river. It appeared it had been pushed violently by another vehicle based on marks on the rear of the car. They had confirmed those dents had not been there when he left for work based on video footage from a Starbucks drive-through security camera.

Kyle confirmed that he had successfully downloaded the software from the Olathe, Kansas Meisner Voting System installation. Kyle's team had installed a back door in the system interface specifically to be able to download the system software in case issues developed in the future. The system fit comfortably on a 256 GB thumb drive.

Laura indicated that the FBI had been researching Meisner Industries for a couple of years. They were highly suspicious of trips Richard had made to Washington D.C. and secret meetings he had with Senator Corning. They suspected collusion preparing the specifications for voting machines in the HAVA legislation but had not been able to establish any hard evidence to date. Laura insisted they go to the FBI offices to discuss options with the FBI. George was hesitant while Kyle was very quiet, not knowing whether to follow George or Laura's lead. Laura finally prevailed, and they left to go to the FBI office where they met with Kameron and a couple of agents neither George nor Kyle had met.

Unlike the previous visit, when George told Kyle that Laura was an FBI agent, they were promptly ushered into Kameron's office. An aide offered to get them coffee, but they declined and were seated at the conference table in Kam's spacious office.

Kameron greeted them, "Well, here we are again. I understand you have updated information to share."

Before Laura could say anything, George spoke up, "First, I need to know if this is to be a one-way share, or will you bring us up to date too?"

Kameron responded, "I will share as much as I can, considering this is an ongoing investigation, and two of you are not FBI employees. I will share information with Laura. She can't share that with you, but she can provide guidance based on what she knows. Laura, what have the three of you been up to in the past few weeks? What did you want to discuss today?"

"Kam, George has been talking to the DA's in Clackamas and Washington counties and has learned something we thought we should share. That is, in case you don't already know these things."

Kameron nodded and turned to face George. He asked George to share what he had learned.

George made his comments brief and to the point, "In the case of Dennis Andersen, the Clackamas corner's evidence indicates he was murdered. In the case of Stewart McNally, Washington county Corner's evidence confirms he was murdered. In fact, tortured before he died."

Kameron waited, expecting more from George, but George said nothing. Finally, Kameron said, "Okay, you have been talking to county medical examiners. I think it would be useful for me to call in another agent working on this case if you all don't mind." Everyone nodded an okay. Kameron walked over to his desk and punched in a number. All he said was, "Yes, you should come," and hung up the phone, and came back to the conference table.

"George, how do you like Portland?"

"You mean other than dealing with such intrigue? I like it. Your traffic is terrible, but the weather suits me."

"This is my fourth post. I have worked in New York state, Rochester, Minnesota, Kansas City, Missouri, and here. The operations are similar, but the weather is substantially different. This has been the most interesting place to work."

About this time, another person knocked on the door and then entered. Everyone stood up to be introduced. Uri Stokov greeted each one of them warmly. Uri was a tall and slender man with a bush cut. He wore a poorly fitting suit with a light blue shirt, open, no tie, showing the top of a profusely hairy chest. Uri spoke in an accent that George recognized as Russian. Uri sat down at the end of the table beside Kameron.

"Uri, this is the team I have been telling you about. You know Laura, of course. Kyle works for Meisner. George is a private investigator who is working for Kyle. Both Kyle and George have been vetted and have been providing us additional information about Meisner Industries," Kameron said, and then turned to Laura, "Have I left anything out, Laura?"

"Well, sorta. Kyle and George know that I pass along critical information to you, Uri. To date, I have not told them the names of any of the agents besides Kameron and me that are assigned to the Meisner Industries investigation. We came here today because of what George discovered and wanted to make sure the investigation was aware. We also need guidance on what to do next; I should have said, from the FBI's point of view. George works for Kyle, not the FBI, but he is more than willing to work with us. He is friends with FBI agent Buck Rogers in St. Andrews, Texas, and has worked with him on cases in St. Andrews. That said, George is no stranger to FBI protocols. I think that is enough to start with."

Uri asked, "So, Kameron, what did you call me in for?"

"George followed up on a couple of cases we had not pursued. The relatively recent disappearance of Dennis Andersen and Stewart McNally, both employees of Meisner Industries. George, you want to tell Uri why these should be of interest to the FBI?

"Sure," George said. "Where to begin? I am going to start with Stewart since I have more first-hand knowledge there. Kyle asked me to come up to Portland a few months ago based on a secret Mr. Meisner asked him to keep. Since Laura also knew the secret, and Kyle could not figure out her role, he asked for my help. Kyle gave me the names of his co-workers, Meisner, and Laura, here. When I looked into them, I discovered that Laura was an FBI agent, which Kyle did not know. I bet you have heard about this."

Uri nodded, "Yes, continue."

Noticing that Laura was looking a bit uncomfortable, George continued, "Anyway, skipping to what brings us here today. When Dennis Andersen disappeared and was then found in the Willamette river, everyone assumed it was an accident, or worse, suicide. I followed up with the Clackamas Medical Inspector and discovered that he died of asphyxiation, not drowning. Given all the other circumstances, it was clear he was murdered. But why? I think it was because of what he was about to discover. He had been dogging Kyle, who was investigating an anomaly in components of Meisner's Voting

System he could not explain, and Dennis had taken an interest. Dennis had technical skills in electronics, and the day he disappeared, he was on his way to work, bringing a spectrum analyzer. That analyzer might, not saying it would have, might have uncovered an inconvenient fact. I think this might have been related because the spectrum analyzer disappeared out of Dennis's closed car. The only conclusion I can make is that someone took it out of his car after killing Dennis and before shoving his car into the river.

Uri, who had been sitting back in his seat, was now leaning forward with his elbows on the table listening intently to George. Uri said, "Okay, that is interesting. I assume you don't mind if we double-check your facts, do you?"

"Of course not, but that is not all that I think leads to a mystery that involves Meisner in some way."

"Continue," Uri said, intently engaged.

"Consider the case of Stewart McNally. He was a strange guy. I was looking into a supposedly secret team working on the voting systems that Kyle told me he thought existed. No one seemed to know who they were or what they were doing except one guy, Mr. Bret Lambert, head of the Integration Team for Meisner Voting Systems. He told Kyle that a different Meisner team would insert code into the Voting System after the Integration Team finished and the Integration Team would not be able to review it. That was a red flag for Lambert, who shared it with Kyle, who then told me. I did research and found out where they were stationed. I went there, and a lady that answered the door was kind enough to tell me where they hung out after work, a local bar in Hillsboro. I spent several weeks going to the bar and watching the group. Stewart was the most talkative of the three, so I waited till I could catch him alone. He was so proud of their work; he told me some details, including their plan to influence close elections with the code they wrote. The next time I was to meet Stewart McNally to get more details, I was told he had been killed in a gang shoot out late one night after he left the bar. That struck me as ironic, so after a trip I made back to St. Andrews to take care of local business, I checked up on the police reports in Washington County DA's office. There I found out he had not been killed in the shoot-out, only his car burnt up containing a recently released felon. So, where was Stewart? I followed up later and discovered his dismembered body had been found in a grave in a forest near Hillsboro. The medical investigator said Stewart had been tortured before he was killed or killed in the process."

Uri had a blank stare on his face. His thoughts were racing. *Why would Meisner do that? Or was it somebody else? If somebody else, who?* Finally, after everyone was quiet for what seemed like a minute or two, Uri spoke, "Okay, I hear you. Have you drawn any conclusions? Have any idea what is going on?" Uri knew the Chinese were interested in U.S. Elections, so he was curious if George had run into that.

George responded, "Understand, my suspicions are just that, suspicions. I don't have any proof yet."

"Of course," Uri answered.

"I think Kyle should tell you about the anomaly first. Kyle?"

Kyle perked up, "Yeah—I was assigned the job at Meisner's to write code and verify the operation of hyperspectral read-heads that were in all of the Meisner Voting System equipment."

"Hyperspectral read-heads?" Uri asked. He knew the vote counters could 'read' data on the ballots, but not that they had specialized capabilities. He needed more information.

Interrupted, Kyle explained, "Normal read-heads usually detect the difference in light and dark spots on a ballot. Some read-heads might also be able to identify the difference in shades of gray or even colors. But the electromagnetic spectrum is much broader than what our eyes can see. Hyperspectral read-heads can see things invisible to the naked eye, both infrared and ultraviolet, which are beyond the range of the human eye. As I understand it, to ensure that fake ballots don't make it into the voting system, Meisner equipment uses specialized ballot paper coated with a material that is only visible with hyperspectral read-heads.

Kam's curiosity was piqued, "You are saying Meisner is coating ballots with invisible marks?"

"Yes and no. I don't know for sure about any specialized marks. I have been testing sample ballots whose entire surface is coated with a single, call it a color. I have run tests on ballots on several different machines. What first drew my curiosity was the fact that Meisner used a variety of different "shades" of invisible coatings. I assumed that it was to keep someone from forging the coatings. He could use different shades for different elections or sites. It is his proprietary formulations that made it almost impossible to sneak in a forged ballot."

Uri commented, "So, this makes sense. I think I read a part of the federal rules that asked vendors to provide a way fake ballots could be recognized and discarded during the reading process. Sounds like Meisner found a clever way to do it."

"I agree," Kyle said. "But when I had a chance to test actual ballots from an election, I discovered something else. Not all the ballots had the same coating. Not random shades, but limited to three or four shades. I stumbled on to a correlation of the shades reflecting information about the voter of the ballot."

Kam almost jumped out of his seat, "What? Are you saying you could tell who the voter was? Damn, we knew Meisner was up to something, but this could be explosive information."

"Wait, there were only three or four different shades, so no, he could not tell who the voter was. The voter's secret ballot was protected, well, mostly protected. After puzzling over this, I realized the colors corresponded to, or I should say it seemed to correspond to a voter's registration. The colors identified the voter's party. I would not have figured that out if I had not also had both the voter registration information as well as the actual physical ballots."

Kam asked, to clarify, "So you are saying that the ballots sent to the voters were coated to reflect the party registration of the voter?"

"Yes. But that did not seem wrong to me at first. If you were counting ballots from a primary election, coding the ballots as a voter properly registered for that party made sense."

George jumped in, "Kyle is an optimistic guy. I thought of a more sinister possibility. If in a general election where the vote was likely to be close, knowing who was voting offered the opportunity to manipulate counting in a way no one would question. Every run through the machines would produce the same result."

"True." Kyle said, "but you could always do a hand count."

Kam observed, "Maybe, but if a mark was added to disqualify a ballot, it would not be used to do the hand count either."

Kyle continued, "Okay, but I don't know if the ballot-counting machines could somehow make a ballot disqualify. Nevertheless, it seems like Meisner Machines are going to exceptional lengths to uncover fake ballots. It seems to me the whole process of producing ballots and mailing them to the right people might offer more opportunity for nefarious action."

Kam commented, "I get what you are saying, Kyle. This fits nicely with the investigation and suspicions we have about

Meisner. However, you said something about an anomaly. Is this, what did you call it, 'spectral' reading thing, what you meant by anomaly?

"Actually, no. I have not gotten to the anomaly yet. When I was testing, as Meisner had requested me to test, the prototype and finally the production hyperspectral read-heads, I was plagued by what initially was a radio-frequency noise. At least I thought it was a noise. This is where Dennis enters the picture. When I wanted to test the RF noise range, I had to leave the building, and Dennis followed me. He seemed to have technical knowledge I did not have about RF signals. He was scheduled to come to work with a specialized spectrum analyzer that would help us breakdown the noise to see if it contained data. But that was the day he did not show up."

George interjected, "It is possible that a party or parties did not want that noise studied with a spectrum analyzer of the sophistication of the one Stewart owned. That was the piece of equipment that disappeared out of his car when it was shoved into the river."

Kam interrupted the discussion and suggested they take a break. Uri offered to show Kyle and George the restroom and break room. Laura stayed behind with Kam. George did not like the idea of being separated. He wanted to know what Kam and Laura were talking about. Once Uri showed Kyle and George the facilities, he disappeared. George suspected Uri headed back to the private meeting Kam and Laura were having. George wondered if, and how much, they knew about the potential Chinese involvement.

When they all returned, Kam began, "Laura has informed me that you have other information to share, George. Would you like to elaborate?"

"Sure. I will get to my conclusion first. I think the Chinese have an interest in Meisner machines. I believe something is going on that they are willing to murder people over. Here is how I got to that conclusion."

When he said Chinese, George observed Kam's eyebrows twitch. He turned to look at Uri. His pupils had enlarged. George realized they knew something about Chinese involvement. He continued.

"My first hint came from Palo Alto. Chao Li, the son of Tao Li of Taiwan, received a threatening note. His girlfriend Maddy Hilburn, Jeneen Jenkins' friend, who works with Kyle, found the note, told Jeneen, she told Kyle, and Kyle alerted me. I went to Palo Alto and looked at the note. Maddy reported that recently Chao had left school for an unscheduled trip to Taiwan to visit his family. I later learned that Tao Li's company, K & W Manufacturing, provided the read-heads for Meisner. They were old friends from their days together at Stanford. Much later, I learned that K & W did not make the read-heads; Xaizhen Manufacturing produced them in Shenzhen, China. As far as I know, Meisner was never told the read-heads were outsourced to a Chinese company. Laura has probably already reported to you about the disappearance of Huang of the CIA and Tao Li's business partner. This made me suspicious, but even more so when I discovered that Stewart McNally had been murdered too, and tortured. I assume you got that information also. But you probably did not know why it had been set up to make it look like he disappeared, and why it was done. Stewart was doing too much talking about the secret team's work. I am guessing here, but I think the Chinese are involved somehow in these read-heads, their manufacturing, and operation. I think they don't want the read-heads investigated. Personally, if they know about me, I suspect I am on their list to neutralize too, but carefully, so as not to raise too much suspicion. I think the anomaly Kyle discovered has something to do with it. For me, it all fits together."

Kam commented, "George, I am impressed with your work. Frankly, and I hate to admit it, you have gotten more information than our team has. Sometimes, when people are talking to the FBI, they clam up. I think there are things we need to do, and it is going to be touchy. First, we need to see what those signals are coming off the read-heads. Second, we need to figure out how to handle Meisner. George, Kyle, I think you deserve to know more, so Uri will fill you in. Then Uri and Laura will meet with others on this team to decide where to go from here. I would appreciate it if you, Kyle, and George could lay low for a few days while we get our ducks in a row. By all means, don't shake any trees or raise any issues. I don't want either of you to become the next victim. Do you think you can do that?"

George and Kyle both agreed. The meeting adjourned, Kyle and George left, while Laura stayed behind to strategize the next steps.

~ Strategy Meeting ~

Kameron, Uri, and Laura, and two other agents working on the Meisner investigation, joined the meeting to discuss what they had heard and what the next steps should be. The team had been tracking several suspected Chinese MSS undercover agents but had not determined what they were working on. They had suspected it was related to Meisner, but they had not come up with any evidence. George and Kyle's revelations were a surprise in the sense that George, as a lone PI, had uncovered it. However, the MSS agents were part of a more extensive investigation that involved key figures in the Senate, including Senator Corning. As a result of George and Kyle's sleuthing, they had a clue to how Corning and Meisner planned to influence elections. They discussed the need to get ahead of the situation before Corning managed to successfully influence an election. They were not certain he had not already done so. They had heard rumors Corning had ambitions to be elected President, so if he could skew the votes, he might be able to reward his friends and punish his enemies. They did not know how much influence Corning might have, but they did not want to discover it after he had swayed a key election.

They all agreed that Corning had to be stopped as soon as possible. It had to be done in a way that did not compromise the other investigation into MSS influence in American politics. The office in Washington, D.C. was in charge of the MSS investigation. They were working closely with the CIA with their overseas part of the investigation.

Considering all the possible scenarios for how things could develop, they decided their best bet would be to turn Meisner against Corning. That might mean letting Meisner escape prosecution for what he had done. He would have to pay a price, but maybe he could avoid prosecution and loss of his business if he fully cooperated. Laura, the one who knew Meisner personally fairly well, suggested that the only possibility of that was convincing Meisner that they knew about his plans and his alliance with Corning and let him know that Corning would put Meisner Industries at risk. Meisner would convince Corning to cooperate.

Laura knew Richard Meisner better than she thought Richard knew himself. Richard managed to avoid bad publicity through tight employment contracts, segregated working groups, and strict control of public relations. The FBI felt they were close to confronting Meisner, but they still lacked the detail that only Kyle was in a position to obtain. Laura was able to keep pretty good tabs on Kyle, but for his protection, they thought they needed to assign a team to tail him and protect him. Kameron agreed to appoint two agents to keep watch twenty-four-seven.

Laura was also to keep tabs on Kyle and what he was working on. They agreed she could tell him generally what they had in mind without details or specifics. Laura also needed to tell Kyle and George to see if they could get any more information about the anomaly but to be very circumspect in the process. As soon as Laura was ferried back to her place, she contacted Kyle and conveyed the FBI's intentions as instructed.

~ George & Kyle Keep Low ~

Since George had driven out to the FBI office, he gave Kyle a lift back downtown. Laura would have to find a way back on her own. George stopped on the way so he and Kyle could debrief on their meeting with Kameron and Uri. They stopped at a Sheri's to have a bite to eat.

"Kyle, were you surprised at the meeting?"

Kyle answered George, "In fact, I was. I thought the FBI would be way ahead of us, given all the resources at their disposal."

George agreed, "So was I. I don't think they realized the possibility the Chinese were in the middle of whatever is going on. Do You?

"I don't know," Kyle said, "They did not seem surprised when you mentioned the Chinese connection, but they are pretty good at masking their reactions. I learned that the hard way with Laura. She certainly kept me in the dark for a long, long time." Kyle said, wistfully.

George observed, "I think we may need to be more cautious ourselves, not only in what we say to Laura but what research we do."

"Got that! But I need to figure out what is going on with that anomaly. I have been thinking about that."

"Okay, let's hear your idea."

Kyle waited until their food was delivered, "I was thinking, I could take you with me to one of the new sites I am supposed to visit. You could nose around. You could help me with testing. I could get a download of the particular version they were running and then see if I could find anything of interest in the code. We would need to take the best spectrum analyzer we can find so I can take a good look at the anomaly, assuming it presented, but I think it always does."

I would have to act like your assistant. Maybe present me as a quality control investigator for Meisner Industries. Think that would work?" George interjected.

"Perfect cover. With the title 'assistant investigator,' you would be expected to ask a lot of questions without suspicion. I think it would help me do my tests without someone looking over my shoulder, asking me a lot of awkward questions. I wonder if you would mind seeing if you could find the spectrum analyzer. I don't want someone in Portland asking me as a Meisner Industries employee too many questions, and the news possibly getting back to Richard or my team leader, Joe?"

"Get me the specs or name of the particular one you want, and I will get it for you," George answered.

"I did not mean for you to buy it. I think you could find someplace in Portland to rent it. I will pay for it."

"Kyle, don't worry about the money. I think you are going to end up paying for it one way or the other in my expense report."

"Oh, yeah. That. When do I get to see the expenses? Sometimes I forget this is an expensive adventure I am having."

"And potentially a dangerous one too. Good thing you are practiced in experiencing danger," George said, without realizing they both were in for even more surprises.

Kyle and George finished lunch and continued to make plans to investigate the anomaly in greater detail in the next week or so. George dropped Kyle off at the office and headed out to search for a spectrum analyzer as specified by Kyle.

Chapter 19

~ Hennepin County, Minnesota ~

The new Meisner Voting System in Hennepin County, Minnesota, was installed at 300 South 6th St. in Minneapolis. It was part of the Hennepin County Government Center. Kyle let Joe, his team leader, know, as a courtesy, he was headed to Minnesota. Joe's team was well aware that Kyle was assigned a system support role once his code to manage the hyperspectral read-heads was completed and tested. They were a bit jealous of Kyle since Meisner obviously favored him. The Hennepin County system had only been installed two weeks before Kyle and George visited to check things out. They were warmly greeted and shown around the Government Center and the excellent voting processing facilities. It involved a complex of several rooms. Hennepin County had wisely separated the ballot processing equipment from the ballot counting portion of the system. Each one had its own manager and staff. When vote counting was not active, that group worked on validating the registration role, sometimes with visits and sometimes with phone calls. It was a large county, so this was a constant process, cleaning up the voter rolls that were fed into the ballot processing equipment.

George had managed to locate a spectrum analyzer, but not the one Kyle had requested. The model George found was more advanced. It was also a spectrum signal generator across a broad range that included the ranges Kyle was investigating. Initially, Kyle was frustrated by George's choice because he was unfamiliar with the machine, and had to read parts of the manual to ensure he could operate it correctly. Another feature Kyle had not requested was a paper readout feature. If Kyle wanted to record results, he could send it to a USB stick and print key data on a strip of paper like an adding machine. The machine came with a full roll of the strip paper.

Before they visited, Kyle had communicated with the person who was managing the Voting System, asking for a random sample of one hundred voters they could run through the system. He asked the manager to have ballots produced and marked to verify the counting machines met specs.

When they arrived, Kyle and George split up so George could ask questions while Kyle ran his tests. The idea was to engage the person who otherwise might interfere with the tests Kyle wanted to run. That was trickier than either one of them imagined. The manager and tech in charge of vote counting seemed to be concerned that Kyle might adversely impact their system by running unsupervised tests. Nevertheless, George was skilled at manipulating people to answer his questions and managed to distract the two men. This gave Kyle a small window in which to test the system with the one hundred ballots.

True to expectations, the ballots showed differentiation based on the registration of the voter. The counts were true each time he ran them. However, the anomaly was persistent, and interestingly, showed identical results for each run of one hundred ballots. Although he had not planned it systematically, he decided to run the spectrum signal generator during one of the runs. He adjusted the settings on the analyzer. He was surprised when three of the ballots were identified as damaged ballots. He reran the test run without the signal generator, and the run was clean. He repeated the run with the signal generator running, and the same three ballots were rejected. Puzzled, he tried another run and changed the settings on the signal in the generator. On this run, two ballots, not the same ones, were rejected. The whole thing was very curious.

Kyle was shocked when he discovered that the cable connecting the signal generator to the vote-counting machine was plugged into the wrong voting machine input/output slot. The input/output slot was, in fact, inactive. No data was passing to or from the vote-counting machine, which meant that the signal generator had affected the vote-counting machine without even being properly attached. He decided to run another test. This time, he disconnected the entire spectrum analyzer signal generator from the vote-counting machine. He ran the vote counter with the signal generator running at the previous setting, and the same two ballots were rejected. He had a notebook in which he recorded his findings, printed reports, and data on the USB stick.

Kyle recalled the experiment that he and Dennis had tried when they took the test equipment out of Meisner

Headquarters and still detected the anomalous signal. He wondered if the signal generator could have that effect if it was running in a different room. He called George over and explained in cryptic descriptions what he wanted to do. George understood and took the spectrum analyzer signal generator to another place that was about 100 feet away. He plugged it in and turned the signal generator on. He entered the spectrum frequency Kyle had given him. Once it was running, he took out his phone and sent a text to Kyle. The text said, "running." Kyle ran the 100 ballots, and the same two ballots were rejected. Fortunately, the mechanism that normally put distinguishing marks on disqualified ballots was not turned on. Otherwise, the ballots would have been marked as invalid and would not run through the machine again. Had the Disqualified Ballot Marker been on, Kyle might not have made his discovery. Initially, this did not register with Kyle.

Kyle and George concluded their visit in Minneapolis and headed back to Portland by air. They did not have a chance to discuss the trial on the plane because they were not seated together. Before boarding, they arranged to meet after returning to Portland.

On the way back from the airport, they stopped in the Hollywood District at Chin's Kitchen, off I-84 on NE Broadway, to get a bite to eat and discuss what Kyle had discovered. After they ordered, George began, "That was an interesting trip."

"You can say that again. The implications are staggering," Kyle responded.

"What do you make of it? Do you agree the tests definitively prove you can affect the counting of the ballots remotely?" added George.

"True, but I did not dare take more time to figure out the exact pattern that would do what. I know I gave you a hard time about the equipment, but if you had not picked up an analyzer that could generate signals too, I would have never known about this."

George had a pensive look on his face. Then he said, "Kyle, do you think this was part of Meisner's design or what?"

"I think it is an 'or what,'" Kyle responded. "Meisner's crew drew up the specifications; we know that much. We also learned that Laura hand-delivered them to Tao Li, so there was no interception of the specs on the way to Li."

"Yeah, but we know, and I don't think Meisner knows, those specs were sent to Xiazhen Manufacturing to be produced. They could have been modified in China," George said in an almost whisper, looking around, seeing several Chinese people seat themselves in the adjacent booth. "That is an interesting possibility." George put a finger to his lips. He realized Kyle had his back to the booth next to them.

"Possibility? Are you thinking what I am thinking?" Kyle said in a lowered voice.

"Probably. What if somebody over there," George said quietly, "over there," so as not to mention China out loud. He started the sentence again, "What if there is a scheme afoot for someone other than Meisner to influence the thing." He said "thing" rather than elections. George was suddenly nervous. He began to look around at the other patrons to see if they were looking at Kyle and him. *I need to check to see if we are followed when we leave here.* George was not prone to paranoia. He had been in tricky spots before, but this had the potential of being more dangerous. Then, George held up his hand when Kyle started to talk and said, "Kyle, let's take this conversation offline, for now, okay?"

Kyle nodded. He was able to guess what George was implying. He was nervous too. It was one thing to imagine Meisner planned to manipulate the voting machines, and quite another if the Chinese had similar plans. He assumed Meisner did not know, but he could not be sure. *Why would Meisner encourage him to study the anomaly if he wanted it to be kept a secret?* Kyle ignored the food when it arrived. *What if Meisner knew and wanted to find how easy it would be to discover, so he asked Kyle to test and report what he found?* This was hard to figure out. George broke his gaze by waving his hand in front of Kyle.

"Kyle, eat up. We can't stay here too long. We have things to discuss," George said.

They ate their food, each of them hoping nourishment would enable clear thinking. They avoided alcohol taking tea instead. When they left Chin's, they headed toward George's hotel room. George took a circuitous route to be sure they were not followed. Instead of going to his hotel, George headed to a motel and checked in for one night. When he moved his car, he told Kyle the room number and suggested he wait and see if anyone followed him. If not, Kyle was to come on up to the room. George was unaware that a tracking device had been attached to his rental car. In fact, there were two. One had been placed there by the always suspicious FBI. Usually, he would have been more alert. George thought he was taking no chances. When Kyle joined him, they continued their conversation.

Kyle started, "It seems clear to me that someone would be able to use a remote signal generator to alter the operation of the read-heads. I don't think it is Richard. Based on what we know so far, he could have done that with the code from his secret team, Stewart's team."

"I agree," answered George. "I think Stewart was talking too much, and whoever wanted to control those machines with remote signals needed him to shut up. They did not want any inquiry into Richard's scheme. I don't think it was Richard who shut him up because the guy was tortured. Somebody needed to know what his code did and tortured him to find out. No need for Richard to do that. My working theory is that the Chinese, the Ministry of State Security, is behind this."

Kyle looked quizzically, "You think the Chinese want to influence American elections?"

"Hell, yes! They are anxious to be the new world powerhouse. America is the biggest obstacle to achieving that goal. They take a long view, so a few elections here and a few there, and they can get America to back away from the East. At the same time, China consolidates its influence there."

Kyle added, "Kameron and Uri said there were MSS agents in the area. Maybe this is one of the things they are working on. How can we find out who is behind this?"

"Kyle, I am not sure that is our problem. This is much bigger than what you and I can do. This is a job for the FBI and other agencies to handle. We need to carefully document what we know. For all we know, Dennis's involvement got him killed. We don't want to look too eager to blow the whistle on this. Let's work through the FBI. They have a lot more guns, so to speak."

"Okay, so what's next?" Kyle asked.

"Document what you discovered in Minnesota. I suggest you take a few days off work and try to get off the grid a bit. You can pick up a laptop to document things away from work and your bugged apartment. Get a motel room. Use an assumed name. I can help you put a plan in place."

"I will make the arrangements tomorrow. Do you think our burner phones are safe?"

"To be sure, I will get two new ones so we can communicate safely. Also, I suggest you encrypt the documentation. Then we can review it and deliver it to the FBI. Do you think you can do this without contacting Laura?"

"That is tricky. Maybe you and Laura could arrange to have coffee, and you could explain what is going on to her? She would ask me too many questions, and I don't want to lie to her. You, on the other hand—" Kyle said, implying George could get away with lying to Laura.

"Fine. I will take care of Laura. Now let me drop you off at your place so you can get your car." George and Kyle discussed a few more details and concluded their discussion. George took Kyle to his car, and Kyle headed off to a motel for the next few days, careful to be sure he was not followed. While at the motel, he ordered his meals delivered and paid with cash. When he had finished his report, he called George on the new cell phone. George arranged to meet Laura again. Laura called Kameron and arranged a visit where the three could meet at the FBI office. All were nervously careful to note that they were not followed, unaware that George's car was being tracked.

~ The FBI Involvement ~

Kyle delivered his report to Kameron. George and Laura had joined him. The report was only a few pages, carefully precise on what Kyle had tested and how the tests came out. Kameron asked Uri to come and handed him the report to read. When Uri finished, he turned to Kyle, "Kyle, this is one of the best analyses I have read. I think you have answered the mystery of how and why the Chinese are interested in Meisner Industries. The potential is alarming." Uri turned to Kameron. Kameron knew what Uri was doing. The next steps were up to Kameron, Uri's boss, to direct.

"Kyle, George, Laura, the next steps are a bit above my pay grade to determine," Kameron said. Kam was being honest. The implications were significant and involved complex issues. Kam would have to run this new data up the chain of command to know what to do next and who would be a party to it. "You three have done an amazing job. I think we have shared enough with you, so you know this is a complex investigation. I will get back to you as soon as I possibly can. In the meantime, please be careful. Do I need to assign another agent to give you cover?"

Laura spoke up, "Another agent? You think that is necessary? I am fully qualified to keep tabs on Kyle and George as long as they don't run in opposite directions."

"I know you are Laura, but I think you should stick with one of them. I will get another agent to shadow George till we get a handle on things. You object to shadowing Kyle?"

"Of course not. It would be my pleasure. You are suggesting we stay close to each other, right?"

Kameron burst out in a big smile and chuckle. "I am not saying how close. That will be up to the two of you. Okay?"

Laura, who rarely blushed, blushed as she thought of how close she would like to be to Kyle. She responded. I think he ought to stay at my place. You guys have the place wired, and I have my "tools" handy." After she said that, she blushed again. Then she added, "What do we do about work?"

"Give me a day or two to answer that. In the meantime, Kyle, can you avoid going to work?" Kameron asked.

"I can arrange that," Kyle answered. He liked the idea of being close to Laura for a few days if that was necessary.

Kameron consulted his boss in Washington, D.C. For direction. His boss suggested he fly an agent working on the Corning investigation out to Portland. He also wanted to send an agent working on the Chinese angle too. It would take a couple of days to make the arrangements. Meanwhile, he agreed with Kameron that Kyle and George ought to be protected.

Kameron assigned agent August Bomgarten, nicknamed Boomer, to shadow George. They suggested that George change motels to one they could protect better. Boomer was able to arrange for George and him to share adjacent rooms. The motel also had a food service, so they could stay put easily for the next few days. George said he would need to retrieve his things from the current motel but could be at the new place within a couple of hours. Kyle's situation was comfortable. He would room with Laura at her place. She had a couple of bedrooms. That would satisfy FBI protocol, but she did not expect the two of them to use both bedrooms. Neither did Kyle. Kyle felt he might as well enjoy himself under the circumstances.

When George got to his present motel to pack up his things, he failed to notice a car close by with two people in it. Had he noticed; he would have seen two people parked near the entrance to the motel parking lot. When he left, he did not notice that they made a U-turn and followed him at a distance. When the FBI put a tracker on George's car, they didn't realize it already had one placed there by someone else. The two men following George did not have to follow closely since they could track him on a laptop they had in their car. This prevented George from noticing he was being followed. Even if he had, he might have concluded the FBI was following as there was no way, in his mind, that anyone knew his whereabouts. He wasn't in his original digs at the Hilton. Tonight, he wouldn't even be at his second place. He would be safely ensconced in a safe house with protection by the FBI.

The two guys following George were using a tracking device cleverly designed to disguise its function. It had a listen-only mode. In this mode, it was not transmitting any signal, only receiving a specific signal. In the listen-only mode, it could turn its broadcast mode on and off. When off, it emitted no signal so that a bug detector could not detect its presence. Secondly, in transmit mode, it utilized a frequency skipping technology so that even when transmitting, there was no single carrier wave detected. It would look like noise, and in a public environment, where there was already lots of electromagnetic noise, it would be practically indistinguishable. The technology was similar to that used on the Meisner Voting System read-heads designed to disguise their existence. When George arrived at the new, supposedly secret location, he parked his car and carried his few things up to the motel room arranged for him. His FBI shadow arrived twenty minutes before and had opened the door between the suites. Boomer greeted George with a warm smile and handshake. George noticed he was armed. Boomer asked George if he had been followed. Unaware of the tracker, George assured him he had not. George had taken extra precautions, circling a full two blocks to make sure. Boomer made him feel safe, and he could relax a bit. In St. Andrews, he had a few tense cases, but not anything like this one. He had never felt danger so close. He had not noticed how tense he had become. Now, perhaps, he could relax a bit.

Boomer asked Kyle what he wanted for supper. George opted for a cheeseburger and onion rings, which Boomer ordered for himself as well. It was delivered in half an hour, and Boomer and George ate and shared stories of their work experiences. They avoided alcohol. Boomer stayed till around 9:00 PM. Finally, he bid George a good night's sleep and went into his motel room using the door between their rooms. It could be locked from either side. Boomer closed the door for the night, but he did not lock it in case one of them needed to access the other. George felt exhausted and, after watching a show and the news, he retired.

Boomer did not go to sleep immediately. He checked in with headquarters to tell them George had retired. They let him know the surveillance equipment was online and working. At 1:59 AM, there was a brief power outage, which Boomer did not observe since he had fallen asleep, fully dressed, lying on the bed with the TV on, and the volume turned down low. He was not aware the power outage had disabled the listening equipment in the adjacent room. If he had left the door to that room open, he might have been awakened by the steady beeping of the equipment alarm. Unfortunately, it was during a shift change at FBI headquarters, and the new agent silenced all the alarms at headquarters by mistake. He thought he was rebooting equipment.

At precisely 2:10 AM, George, sleeping fitfully, awoke with a loud thump followed by a muffled sound in the adjacent room. The loud thump was Boomer's room being forced open. But George, being asleep, could not make out the source of the sound. Nevertheless, it alarmed him, and his heart raced as his body filled with adrenaline. He got out of bed and pulled on his trousers over his pajama shorts. He was shirtless. His heart was racing. This whole thing with the Chinese had him on edge. Was he in danger? He got his revolver out of his catchall and went to the door between the rooms. Now he heard nothing. Suddenly there was a knock at his motel door. Quietly, he opened the door between his room and Boomer's room. The bedside lamp was knocked over but still on, and Boomer appeared to be asleep, so George stepped into the room. He was about to wake Boomer when he noticed blood on the pillow. There was a bullet hole in the back of Boomer's head. George had not heard the shot. He noticed that Boomer's gun was lying on the bed beside him. Boomer lie on his side with his arm outreached toward the gun, blood staining the pillow below his head.

The knocking continued on the door to his room. Quickly, he retraced his steps and closed the door to the adjoining rooms, and turned the lock. It made a noticeable click. He looked around the room and saw a door on the opposite side of the room. He tiptoed to it and gently tried the handle. It turned but did not open. Then, he heard the door to his motel room burst open, and two men speaking in Chinese talking excitedly. He tried the door again and found the lock nob. He turned it, and the door opened. As he did, he heard a gunshot that shattered the door between his bedroom and Boomer's, where he was now standing. Quickly, he turned the lock, went through the door, and locked it from the other side. This room was filled with equipment that looked like a listening station with a constant beeping noise. He opened the door to the hallway and carefully checked. No one was present, so he cautiously entered the hall, rushing down the hall toward the exit. As he turned the corner, he heard two men yelling at him. There were stairs, but he decided to go down the outside hall. Before the men had time to get to the corner, George banged on the railing to the stairs sounding like someone running down the stairs that led to a courtyard. He quickly dashed into the open door of the soda room close to the stairs and aimed his gun at the opening. He heard the two men round the corner and go down the stairs. That was only a temporary win. Now he retraced his steps down the hall back toward his room to the stairs on the other side that emptied into the parking lot. He raced down the stairs and arrived beside his car. Fortunately, he had his keys in his trousers, so he started the car and began to exit the lot. By then, the two pursuers had spotted him. One bullet shattered his rear window as he was leaving the motel—racing, tires squealing. He pulled out of the lot and toward the local police station he had seen on the way to the motel. As he approached the station, he saw a car racing down the street toward him. He jumped out of his car and raced up the steps toward the police station. As he reached the door of the police station, the car passed, and someone in the vehicle sent a volley of shots from an automatic gun his way. They missed him, but a bullet hit the side of the brick framed doorway he was about to enter, chipping a brick and throwing a chunk at him, grazing his forehead. He literally fell into the station, falling on the floor in front of the officer's desk. It alarmed the officer on duty who drew his gun in self-defense. George laid his handgun on the floor beside him, and awkwardly held up both hands as he lie there on the floor, forehead bleeding. The officer yelled for assistance, ran around the desk, and kicked George's gun to the side out of George's reach.

~ Navigating the Portland Police ~

George was treated for the cut on his forehead. It only took a band-aid. He was ushered into an interview room and cuffed to the table. He was familiar with police procedure, and he was now having the experience of Portland's particular version. His situation was complicated by the fact that he did not have any ID on him. He had put his beltless pants on over his pajama bottom shorts and wore no shirt. The only items he had were his gun and the keys to his rental car. If they bothered to check the gun registration, they might discover it was registered in Texas. There, they would note the name to whom it was registered. That would match the one he gave them. Of course, they could reason he stole the gun. If they contacted the car rental agency, they would discover the vehicle was rented to a non-existent firm in Texas. The firm was usually a useful cover. In this case, it was a complication. He knew better than to say too much. He counted on them not bothering to check either the gun or car until they got more information from him. They could hold him for twenty-four hours before he was allowed to make a call. Still, he needed to contact the FBI as soon as possible.

George answered their question. They asked his name. He answered truthfully. They wanted to know who was shooting at him? He said he did not know. Why were they shooting at him? He tried to avoid the real reason. He thought about telling them about Boomer and the motel, but finding a dead guy might complicate his position, so he held back that information. Right now, they had him, and it was the middle of the night. They did not intend to investigate anything until George gave them more information. Finally, George decided he needed them to move faster, so he told them about the motel and a dead guy there who had been shot. Finally, after a couple of hours, they dispatched someone to the motel. They found Boomer's body and called crime scene investigators.

After the call, one of the officers said, "George, there was no dead person at the motel." They lied to see if they could get more information out of George. George refused to comment. It was possible, but unlikely the team that attacked Boomer and him had enough time to go back to the motel and clean up the place. He knew there was not enough time to fix the busted doors. He figured they were lying. He guessed they found the body, thought his head injury was a bullet graze that the dead guy in the bed had fired at him. For all they knew, George had been the one that killed Boomer. Finally, after two hours of fruitless questioning, a detective arrived. It was now past 5:30 AM. The detective had been awakened and called in to interview George. It started all over again with "What is your name?" Finally, George felt he was talking to someone who understood investigation procedure. He told the detective that they should call the FBI number George gave them. He explained that he was limited in what he could disclose until he had heard from Agent Kameron of the FBI. This did not sit well with the detective. He knew that once he called the FBI, the case would be taken over, and he would not hear any more about it. Something was going on in his precinct, and he felt he should know what it was. He acknowledged George's request but insisted on knowing more before notifying the FBI.

George knew that time was probably of the essence. Still, he also knew he had been sworn into an investigation that prohibited him from sharing information unless specifically authorized by the FBI. He refused to provide any information except the number and name of his FBI contact. The dance continued for another hour until the detective finally gave up and directed an officer to put George in a holding cell until they could find more information. He got the report from the officers who had investigated at the motel. There had been shots fired, doors broken, and a ton of special listening equipment in one of the motel rooms. There was one dead body, shot in the head, at the motel as George had indicated, which gave credence to George's insistence that it was somehow related to the FBI. Had the police been instructed not to tamper with anything at the location until the crime scene investigators were finished, they would have discovered that the deceased was an FBI agent. The FBI would rake them over the coals for the sloppy work.

At 9:00 AM, another detective arrived at the station, dispatched from downtown. They brought George back into the interview room. The new detective began again with many of the same questions, a technique designed to catch a criminal in a lie or contradictory story. It did not work with George. He knew the technique. He had kept his answers brief, consistent, and entirely truthful, without elaboration. Once again, the question of the FBI came up. George repeated the name and number, and stated that he should be allowed to make a phone call. He reminded the detective that he would be required by law to do that soon. He suggested they might save everybody time and energy by either allowing him to make the call or by doing it themselves. The detective did not take kindly to being told what he could and could not do and let George know it. Finally, George decided to break protocol and told the detective that the dead man was an FBI agent. That got his attention. He left the interview room with George chained to the table. In ten minutes, he returned and apologized to George. He did not need to say so, but George knew he had been dressed down by Kameron when he called, primarily because of the long delay.

George was unchained and ushered into the bullpen with other detectives who had arrived for work. They offered him coffee, a breakfast bar, and a doughnut. George thanked them. They still had questions for him, but George had one for them instead. When would he be released? He was told that a representative from the FBI would pick him up in a few minutes. Realizing he was being rescued, George suddenly broke out in shivers, which he tried to conceal. The tension was released. Now he would have to go through another session of questions, to be debriefed by an FBI agent.

~ FBI Follow Up ~

Kameron personally came to pick up George. He already had investigators at the motel. Boomer had indeed been executed with one shot to the head. The damage to his door, and bullet holes were evident. It was clear they were recent. George recounted the horrific scene, the execution-style murder, the chase. He suggested they look for a bullet in his car. His rear window had been shattered, but no evidence it had exited the vehicle. Kameron put in a call to the crew to get his car to the impound lot for investigation. Kameron seemed both professional and rattled that their safe house had been compromised. George explained to Kameron how he had recently moved to a new motel without checking out of his hotel to escape surveillance. He did not notice anyone following him, but they must have since they knew where he was staying at the safe house location. George apologized to Kameron, knowing how hard it is to set up safe houses. Now, the current one was compromised, and a new location would have to be found. The impound lot where George's car was taken called Kameron to report they had found the bullet that shattered George's window. In addition, they said they found two tracking beacons on his car. One was an FBI tracker. The other appeared to be of Taiwanese or Korean origin, although they could have come from China. Kameron cursed. His team had failed to check George's car. Boomer should have done that, but they did not know George went to his former motel before going to the safe house.

Kameron could not bring George his clothes and things until the site investigation was complete, so he took George to a shop used by the FBI to get new clothes, and then to the FBI offices, where he met Kyle and Laura. They were both shaken. They had realized their work could be dangerous, but neither of them had so far felt it personally, even though they knew Dennis and McNally had been murdered. Everyone was blaming themselves for being so negligent.

George recounted the experience from the time he woke up until Kameron finally arrived to bail him out of the situation. He suggested they consider their safety seriously and have the FBI ensure there were no trackers on their cars. Kyle asked Laura if she was armed. "Of course," she said. Laura assured Kyle she would protect him, although, given the story George relayed to them, she was not so sure she could do it single-handed.

Now that George had encountered what they assumed were foreign agents directly, their guesses about Chinese involvement in the hyperspectral read-heads seemed more like accurate insights. Kameron and Uri suggested they re-assess their plans. It seemed to them that the timeline needed to be moved up. Kameron shared that the Washington Office was very interested in moving forward and was sending a team to Portland by the first of next week.

With what happened, that might even be moved up to the end of the current week. Washington agreed that a confrontation or intervention with Meisner seemed like the most promising avenue forward. Given the green light and reinforcements from Washington, they all began to think about how this might be structured. The possibility that Meisner took a hard position denying everything was the worst-case outcome. They needed as sure a result as they could engineer, and they needed to do it quickly.

Kameron reminded them that although the Chinese liked to take the long view, they seemed to have made a significant investment in this strategy to impact U.S. Elections. They would not give them up easily.

George asked, "Do you think they would sacrifice Meisner himself if they thought their scheme was about to be exposed?"

Kameron was silently awed by George's insight. He would make a great agent. He said, "George, I had not considered that possibility. If they did, what do you imagine their reasoning would be? Have you thought about that?"

"Yes. they must also know that Corning is involved. At least it seems reasonable to me. They seem to know more about this than we do at the moment. So, if they can keep Corning supporting the HAVA act and Meisner Voting Systems successful, with or without Meisner, they can continue to play their secret vote counting manipulation plan."

"So, not only do we need to confront Meisner, we need to warn him and protect him?" Kameron said.

"Yes, as much as it hurts to support him at all," George answered.

Kameron continued, "Then, let's get started. We can share our thoughts with the Washington team when they arrive. Better to have a plan than to feel like we are starting all over again. It will take time to bring Washington up to date with what we know and what we suspect. I know they will have their ideas, but we can share ours too. What about it? Are you up for lots of work in the next few days?"

Everyone nodded and answered, "Yes!"

~ Making the Plan ~

Everyone was agreeable to placing themselves in quarantine at the FBI office until the Washington team arrived and to engage in planning for the Meisner Intervention, which they humorously referred to as *the* MI, the same as the initials of Meisner Industries.

The group discussed any number of options to get Meisner to confess his plans to influence elections and to turn on Corning. It was essential to get Meisner into a place he would not have support and could not easily escape. They settled on a cocktail party with an invitation from a woman who solicits donations from public figures for the Portland Opera. People did not turn down her invitations. It so happened that she was the wife of one of the FBI agents. No one knew that, so Meisner would not suspect the setup. The invitation would expect a second, Richard would be expected to be accompanied, so Laura would be the most obvious person he would choose on his own. When he arrived, he would discover it was a small intimate gathering. Initially, he would not realize all the men and women were FBI agents posing as couples. They would include George and arrange a female FBI agent for a companion, and confuse Richard by having Kyle appear in the middle of the reception. They asked Kyle how he would feel about describing his work in front of Richard? Although it technically would be a breach of his Meisner Industries contract, he thought he could do it. He would describe the details of his findings in Minnesota. They would then divulge that everyone present, except for Kyle, George, and the host were FBI agents and that they needed Meisner's help. They would fill him in on the China involvement and their suspected goal of election interference. Ask him how he felt about that. Disclose that the read-heads were manufactured in China and most likely using modified specifications. Reveal that his friend Tao Li had not divulged the fact he had lied to him. They would then introduce George as a private investigator investigating these facts, which the FBI can validate. That George had been attacked and almost killed because he suspected Chinese involvement, and that an FBI agent had been killed. They would disclose the events around Dennis Andersen and Stewart McNally. They would continue to unwrap the facts and ask Meisner what his intentions were in using hyperspectral read-heads in his machines, why he was using invisibly coated ballots, and why one could tell which party a voter belonged to at the time the ballots were being counted.

In their plan, they would slowly wear down Meisner's resistance and denials until they got to the point of his connection to Corning. They would make it clear they had enough evidence to arrest Meisner now and most likely enough to put him away for many years. In fact, to put Meisner Industries out of business if necessary. At the very least, to provide enough publicity to stop all further purchases of voting systems and the disuse of those already sold.

They felt they could get Meisner to fold. That was the theory, anyway. When the Washington team arrived, they laid out their plan, and with a few tweaks, it was approved, and the party was scheduled for two weeks. That would give them time to set it all up.

Chapter 20

~ Kyle's Problem ~

Kyle could not stay sequestered at the FBI office since he was expected to be at work. The FBI arranged a ride to work. It was not long after he arrived at work before Charla called Kyle up to Meisner's office. Kyle was busy with details on improvements to the read-heads code, and the request did not specify a time, so he took a few minutes to finish up a few lines of code, saved his work, and headed up to Richard's office. Kyle was a bit nervous, knowing that the process to trap Richard was about to happen. He hoped his nervousness did not show or his anxiety about his planned role in the cocktail party.

It was around 4 PM when he arrived, and Charla told him Richard was ready to see him and to go right in. When he entered, Tom Bosworth was already in Richard's office. That struck Kyle as strange, and he was expecting Tom to excuse himself, but he did not.

"Have a seat, Kyle," Richard said, pointing to the empty seat. The chairs were in a U shape with Tom and Richard sitting in the other two with a coffee table in the center. "Thanks for coming up. I have a few questions for you about your work here at Meisner Industries. I hope you don't mind."

"Of course not," Kyle said warily. What can I answer for you?"

"I understand you went out to Minnesota recently, is that correct?"

Kyle squirmed internally. He hoped it did not show, "Yes. I have been periodically checking in with customers who have purchased Voting Systems to see how things were going and head off any complications as you asked me to do. Were there problems I did not detect?"

"No, that is not it. I understand you had someone with you in Minnesota. Was that a Meisner Industries employee?"

"No, is that a problem? They did not have access to any of our proprietary information."

Meisner asked, "Kyle, what are the rules about bringing a non-employee onto the premises?"

"Of a customer site?" Kyle asked?

"A Meisner site," Richard responded.

"I was not aware that a customer site was considered a Meisner site."

"It is in your contract."

"In that case, I guess I should have obtained permission first."

"You guess? I think you know. If you read your contract carefully, it also applies to customer sites. Did you seek permission first?"

"No. I told Joe where I was going, but no, I did not get permission to have a friend go with me."

"Then you violated company rules. You were in breach of your contract. Is that correct?"

Kyle began to see where this was leading. He was trying to think of a way to address this, "I suppose that is technically correct, but I can assure you no harm came to the customer."

"Harm is not the issue here, Kyle. The issue is company policy, the policy you agreed to abide by. Who was this person you brought with you?"

"A friend from Texas. He was visiting, and I thought it would be okay for him to see Meisner Voting Systems in operation. I was bragging on your successful product. Don't we want to sell systems in Texas? I did not think there was any harm in promoting Meisner Industries."

"In general, I want Meisner Industries promoted. We have organized ways that it is done. It is not your job to do the promotion. It is clearly stated in your contract that all promotion should be done by our marketing group. You are prohibited from that action. We don't take random friends and strangers to customer sites without proper notification and preparation. You should know that. You should know better. You have committed a serious breach of your contract."

"This is an oversight on my part. I will never do that again. I am truly sorry.

"By the way, did you meet a fellow by the name of Leo Yung there?"

"I don't recall that name." Kyle was now, inwardly, very nervous. What was Richard fishing for? And, the Chinese name was alarming."

"Seems your friend had a lot of questions for Mr. Yung. He felt they were out of line, intrusive, uncalled for. He called me personally to complain."

"Oh, I am very sorry, that was not my intention. I was busy validating their vote-counting machine and did not know my friend was causing any difficulty. Anything I can do to fix this?"

"Kyle, so you admit you allowed a non-Meisner employee to be in a customer voting system installation without your direct supervision."

"Richard, when you put it that way, yes, I suppose I did. I stand corrected and will never do that again. I will re-read my contract to make sure I comply.

"Kyle, what you have done is a serious violation of company policy. First, you should know better. Second, you upset a customer, an excellent customer. I understand you asked for a set of ballots to run through the machine."

"Yes, I asked for one hundred sample ballots I could use to test the vote-counting machine. I understood that when I visited a site, that was an acceptable protocol to assure the customer everything was working properly. I have done that at several sites. Is there a problem with that procedure too?"

"No, I would expect you to do test runs, but Mr. Yung told me that when he looked at the machine counts, you had run the ballots multiple times. Did you find any issues you have not told Minneapolis or me about?"

This put Kyle on the spot. He could not tell him the truth about the multiple runs. He came up with a cover story quickly. "You know how I told you about the anomaly I had found in the read-heads? I was testing to see if that was still happening at the customer sites I visited. I ran multiple runs to make sure it was consistently present and yet produced consistent results in the counting. It worked as expected." That was not completely true. The spectrum analyzer had produced unexpected outcomes.

"Yung says you brought test equipment. However, I did not see that you had checked out any equipment. How do you explain that?"

"I rented equipment. I wanted to make sure any equipment I took from the office was not somehow faulty. I was validating work we did here."

"But," Richard said, "you did not ask for approval to use non-Meisner equipment. Neither did you fill out the proper forms. And you did not ask for any reimbursement either. How do you explain that?"

The conversation was turning ugly. Kyle had the feeling that Richard had an agenda, and he did not know what it was. He had a hint, however, with Bosworth present. Richard was about to discipline him, put something in his official record. He answered, "I have no explanation. I am sorry. I will be more careful next time."

Richard looked over at Tom Bosworth. Kyle looked there too as Tom nodded to Richard. Richard turned back to Kyle, "Kyle, Tom agrees with my assessment. Your actions, actions that you have acknowledged and verified, have been a clear violation of your contract. I am sorry, but as of this day, your position with Meisner Industries is terminated. By the terms of your contract, you need to surrender your badge to Tom now."

Bosworth held out his hand, expecting Kyle to surrender his badge. This meant that any information on his work PC would no longer be available. He could not believe, after all he had done for Meisner, that his position could so quickly come to an end. He took off his badge but did not immediately hand it to Tom.

"Is there no negotiation on this, Richard? I have given the better part of two years to perfect the operation of your hyperspectral read-heads. I don't think the process is finished yet. Is there no appeal to this decision?"

Tom continued to hold out his hand. Richard said, "Kyle, I will admit that you have done some good work. However, you knew I was an exacting boss, and you have violated the contract that you signed and agreed to respect. I am not sorry; it is just business."

"Does this also mean you will blackball me from any other position in the programming field?"

"I don't have that power, Kyle. You did agree to limitations on leaving Meisner, and your termination does not make those null and void. You can review your contract, but you will see that termination does not invalidate your commitment to its terms as it applies to future work in the field. I am afraid that your violation means you will need to find a new field of work. Do you have a hard copy of your contract?"

"No. It is only available to me on the company server. However, if you intend to terminate my employment, I would like a copy."

"Sorry, that will not be possible. You signed away that option when you signed your contract and non-disclosure agreement."

"That's a bit harsh."

"That, my dear boy, is business. Better get used to it. This is the way the world works. Please give your badge to Tom. There is nothing you can say or do to alter our decision. I do not tolerate violations of the employment contract." Richard said, standing, making it final. He continued, "There will be a member of Security outside to escort you out."

"So, this termination was already a done deal before I entered the room?"

Richard did not answer that question but continued, "Security will escort you back at your desk. They will provide you with a box to collect your things, only those things that belong to you. They will check each item to ensure it does not belong to Meisner Industries. Then they will escort you out of the building. Tom will secure and invalidate your badge and all access to Meisner systems." Richard turned to Tom and simply said, "Tom?"

"Wait, I still have a question. What about my personal phone? What about the security installed in my apartment? When will that be removed?"

"Kyle, you should have read your contract more carefully. You seem to have forgotten a lot that it includes."

With reference to Kyle's name, Richard pointed toward the door, indicating Kyle should leave. Tom again asked for Kyle's badge. Sure enough, there was a security person outside the office door, and Kyle was ceremoniously escorted to his office desk. He did not have much there that was personal. Tom added, "Kyle, you will also need to surrender your phone. It will be returned to you at your apartment tomorrow. According to your contract, the security system in your apartment will remain active for thirty days, after which it will be turned off. If you try to deactivate it or destroy it, you will be sued." Joe noticed the commotion and came out to see what was going on. Joe asked, "What is going on?"

Kyle started to talk, but the security officer shushed him and spoke himself. "Joe, this is none of your business. Kyle will be leaving Meisner Industries and is collecting a few of his things. Please go back to your office."

Joe did not take well to the security officer's directions. By this time, Jeneen and Josh had both come around the end of the cubicles and stood by Joe. Kyle spoke up, "Don't get involved, guys. None of this involves you. I can explain it later offline. I will try to make one of the weekly gatherings and explain things after I reread my contract and determine what I can tell you. Thanks for the great time we have had working together."

Tom Bosworth spoke up, "Kyle, you will have no access to your contract. I have a document I will give you that reminds you of the restrictions you have on communications about Meisner Industries. I will give it to you as you leave."

The security officer was not sympathetic to Kyle's attempt to talk to his former co-workers. He told Kyle it was time to go and beckoned for him to follow, which Kyle did, having finished getting the few things he had at his desk. The officer escorted Kyle out of the office to the outside entrance and left him standing there without a word, handing him the document Bosworth had promised.

Well, this throws a monkey wrench into things. I have to call George and Laura immediately.

Kyle headed home to get his burner phone. He then made the call to Laura and explained what happened. She was shocked and wanted all the details. He suggested it would be better to share them with her and George at the same time. He left his phone at the apartment, caught the bus to the closest Max station, caught the green line, and transferred to the red line till he got out to the airport. From there, he used a payphone to call the FBI office and arranged to be picked up. Kyle, Laura, and George, now all at the FBI office, heard Kyle's account of what happened.

~ Reinforcements ~

The reinforcements arrived from Washington about the same time Kyle was being fired. Kameron brought a car with a driver to the airport to pick them up. On the way back to the office, Kameron tried to fill them in on the developments to date. He had not yet heard that Kyle had been fired, so the Washington team was brought up to date about Kyle's and George's exploits.

Don Swartz, Ron Ableson, and Lark Bryle were the three agents from Washington. Don was the team leader. Most of the conversation was between Don and Kameron.

Don asked, "Kam, have you been thinking about how this case might break open?"

"Yes. you know agent Laura McLaughlin, right?"

"Sure," Don answered.

"Well, Laura, Kyle Tredly, and George Lockit, have been tripping over this case for the last few months. Frankly, they have made more progress than our office was able to make. Having Tredly on the inside was key to the whole thing. He is a competent programmer and has specialized knowledge of hyperspectral thingies."

"Yeah, I read about that technology on the way out here. How does that play in this investigation?" Don asked.

"I am going to let Tredly fill you in on that. For a technical guru, he can make it pretty simple to understand. Tredly was suspicious of things and called an old friend, Lockit, the PI from Texas, for advice. One thing led to another, and Lockit came up to visit. Lockit is good friends with Buck Rogers, FBI agent in St. Andrews, Texas."

"Yeah, I know, Buck. We worked on a case together about ten years ago," Don interjected.

"Anyway, Lockit outed McLaughlin's status as an undercover FBI agent, and we had to read Tredly and Lockit into our investigation. That has worked out extremely well, one guy on the inside and a top-quality PI working with us on the outside. I will fill you in with details when we all get together to make our plans. I wanted to add that the Chinese are implicated in this case. One of my agents was murdered, and Lockit barely escaped being killed in the same incident." Since the FBI office is close to the Airport, there was no more time to talk in the car. Kameron gave the driver instructions on where to take the agents for local accommodations, and they left to check-in for the duration of the case.

Kyle needed reinforcements too. After he dropped the box of things from work at his house and headed out to the FBI office, he met with George and Laura. George and Laura were having coffee. George poured a cup for Kyle. Kyle told them he had been fired.

"What happened? What caused you to get fired?"

"Minneapolis," was all he said. He was hoping George would pick that up and tell about going to Minneapolis with Kyle. He didn't. Kyle continued, "Seems that somebody in Minneapolis complained about George and my visit there.

"Complained? What about?" George asked, although he had an idea he knew.

"Sorry, George, this is not your fault. They complained about you asking too many questions, for one thing."

"Oh my god. Shit. I am so sorry, Kyle. I did not think the guy was being bothered. He was very willing to answer my questions, which were mostly about how the operation ran. I did not think any question I asked could have been taken as aggressive. Who made the complaint?" George asked.

"Richard said it was a guy by the name of Yung. Is he the one you talked to?"

George's forehead wrinkled as he tried to think of the guy he was talking to. "Yung? I don't think I met anyone by that name. I am pretty sure the guy I was talking to was named Gilbert, although he did not give me his last name."

"What did he look like? Was he Chinese?" Kyle asked.

"No. I never saw anyone Chinese. It seems strange that someone named Yung called to complain."

"Speaking of someone Chinese, I have to confess I got the hell scared out of me a few moments ago. When I got off the elevator, a husky Chinese fellow approached me in the hallway. For a moment, I thought they got someone inside the FBI office."

"Oh, yeah. That's Charlie. He is harmless. He was born in the U.S. He is a native Portlander," Laura said.

Kyle added, "Ever since George's encounter, I have been making second-guesses every time I approach a Chinese guy, or one approaches me. I never notice how many lived in the area."

George said, "Back to the subject at hand. You say a fellow named Yung complained to Meisner about me being with you, and he sacked you for that?"

"Yes. I should have thought about it. My employment contract is specific about bringing non-employees onto Meisner or Meisner customer property without prior permission of Meisner Industries. It's perfectly consistent with his effort to protect his proprietary products. I signed the contract, and I could not defend why you were there without disclosing what we discovered. He also got me for using non-Meisner test equipment without permission. He had me dead to rights. I have no reason to complain. The question is what it does to our plans with the FBI?"

"First, we need to think about it, then we need to let Kameron know as soon as he gets back. He will pick up the team from Washington at the airport this morning and take them to the hotel. Kameron told me he would notify me when they were here. Kameron will brief them on the ideas we suggested. When that is done, and they have settled in their motel, he will let me know. I assume, I hope, they will like our idea. Kyle, I have been thinking about this since you called, and I don't think your firing will change anything. In fact, it might help," Laura said.

"How could it help? It sure as hell doesn't help me." Kyle mused.

"Yeah, well, if you are present, it will confuse him. At first, he might think you put the FBI up to the whole thing, be on the defensive, or maybe on the attack. Then when we spring the Chinese thing on him, he will be off guard. He has no idea the Chinese are involved, that his read-heads are manufactured in China, etc. By the way, George, did you get that affidavit from Chao, Tao Li's son, about the parts manufactured in China?"

"I don't know. He said he would be more comfortable sending it through FBI sources in Palo Alto. I told him that would be fine," George responded.

"And what about the missing partner of Tao Li? Did you get a confirmation from the CIA in Taiwan, Laura?" Kyle asked.

"Yes, and finally, do we have information from Clackamas and Washington counties regarding the deaths of Dennis and Stewart?" Laura asked.

George answered, "I called the DA's, and both said they would forward that information to the Portland FBI office, attention Kameron. I don't know, of course, if they did that yet."

Laura observed, "I think that is about all we can do other than show up to the cocktail party, assuming the Washington team is willing to go with the plan. Now, we have to wait." Laura turned her attention to Kyle's situation, "Kyle, what about you. What are you going to do now? How are your finances? How long can you go without a job?"

"I'm good for now. I think I have enough set aside for a few months. I put a lot of my salary into my IRA. Unless Richard puts my name on the blacklist with other employers, there are many possibilities in Portland. I can't do programming for a while. I can always get a bridge job someplace. Right now, it is a seller's market, so I am okay."

Laura poured George and Kyle another cup of coffee and suggested they order in lunch while waiting for a call from Kameron. Pizza was the quickest and easiest, and it was delivered in less than thirty minutes. The day dragged on. For personal reasons, Kam did not tell them that the team from Washington had arrived. Finally, they all had to hit the sack, sequestered for another night at the FBI office.

Everybody was up early the next morning. Laura found enough eggs and bacon to fix the three of them a good breakfast. They were finished with breakfast by eight and just sitting around when Kameron came in and asked the three of them to come to his office. Kam told them the team from D.C. had arrived and would be at the meeting at ten. They waited in a conference room that could seat twenty people. There was a wall-mounted TV screen and cameras, so the room could be used for teleconferences. The equipment was on, and Kyle and George could see another conference room on the screen. It was occupied by three people who were reading iPads. Laura had been pulled off for a brief discussion before they all came into the conference room. Before long, the room had many people besides Kyle and George. It included Laura, Kameron, Uri, Don, Ron, Lark, and a woman who introduced herself as Jane D. Immediately, Kyle thought her last name was probably Doe or Dough, and she used D to avoid wisecracks. He later learned it was Dumley, another good reason to go by Jane D. As Kameron began to speak, the two people on the remote end put their iPads down. They paid attention to what must have been a screen on their end of the link. George assumed the connection must be secure if the FBI relied on it for video conferences.

"Greetings, Bill and Joe, joining us in this conference from Chicago. This morning we want to outline our plans concerning the Meisner investigation. I will assume that all of the agents have read the briefing papers, and I won't spend any time on the events leading up to today. Today, our purpose is to get a sign-off by everybody regarding our plans to try to turn Richard Meisner as a witness in the larger case against Senator Corning. Are there any questions before we continue?"

"Bill from Chicago spoke up, "I assume the psych team has made a risk assessment of a successful outcome."

"That was a question, Bill?" Kameron asked.

"Yes. What chance do they give for success?" Bill continued.

"Before the latest hiccup, it was estimated to be ninety percent."

"What hiccup? There was nothing in the briefing papers about a hiccup." Bill asked.

"I will get to that briefly, Bill. So, if everyone is ready, we can proceed to review the plan and our contingencies for unplanned deviations," Kameron said. He then proceeded to read through the planning document. There were a few questions here and there, but generally, it was agreed to by everyone. Kyle assumed he was the hiccup that Kameron alluded to, so he did not interrupt. Neither did George or Laura.

Chapter 21

~ Cocktail Party ~

Kameron had arranged a smart maroon cocktail dress with a deep cut neckline for Laura. She was wearing a multi-layered gold chain with matching earrings. In high heels, she reached Richard's height, just over six feet. She carried an expensive petite black purse with gold lettering. Each of the FBI agents, men, and women dressed smartly for the occasion. Uri had married money. His wife, who had retained her maiden name, Margaret Olson, was a central figure in the art scene and well known to Richard. Anyone else, and Richard might have declined the party.

Margret had a fair complexion and silver blond hair. Her features were sharp, which gave her a Greek goddess appearance, a standout in every gathering. Richard had met Margret at one of the many cultural events at which Margret was a prominent figure. Richard had not met Uri, her husband. Margret was the one who invited Richard to the cocktail party. Because of her influence in the cultural scene of Portland, Richard could not easily beg off. Margret did not like being used by Uri. Still, she loved him and was willing to do him the favor of setting up this meeting with Richard, even without her knowing its exact purpose. Margret was willing to risk her reputation for Uri, at least on the very few occasions that he asked for a social engagement favor.

Uri had been to lots of social gatherings with Margret. She met Uri when he was investigating a homicide at the Portland Opera fifteen years ago. Although Uri never imagined he would have a chance to be in a relationship with such popularity and money, he was not shy about asking Margret for a dinner date the next time their paths crossed. As they say, the rest is history.

Richard was prompt, as was his reputation. He was dressed in a dark black suit with a dashing red tie and matching handkerchief in the breast pocket of his smartly tailored jacket. Margret introduced him to Uri. Richard had seen Margret at any number of social events, but this was the first time he had met Uri. He recognized him as Margret's companion. Now, he learned he was, in fact, her husband. Margret also introduced Uri to Laura, which they pulled off as though they had never met before, much less worked together in setting up this cocktail party. They arranged for Margret to get a phone call that would require her attention. When the call came, not too long after Richard's arrival, she apologetically excused herself. She did not want to be a party to whatever the FBI had in mind for Richard as she regarded him as a solid cosponsor of any number of humanitarian events in Portland. Uri, faithful to his responsibilities as an agent of the FBI, had not told Margret any of the details of what was planned for the evening. It was the nature of her love and trust of Uri that she required no explanation, and true to her devotion to Uri, she asked no questions.

It was not long after Richard's arrival and Margret's departure that Uri asked that everyone join him in an adjacent room where comfortable chairs had been arranged in a circle. When everyone took a seat, Richard followed suit and took a seat with Laura beside him. There was one empty chair, reserved for Margret when she returned, Richard assumed, but she would not be returning. It was for Kyle when it was time for him to appear. A server who had been managing the bar offered to refresh people's drinks. When several of the group agreed, Richard too requested a refill. Laura declined. Several of the group asked for refills, but unknown to Richard, none of them had alcohol-based drinks, only Richard.

Uri began the conversation, "Richard, I want to tell you how much we appreciate your coming to our little party. Margaret has been so appreciative of your support for the arts in Portland." Richard demurred graciously.

Several of the rest of the group on queue added their agreements. *A good detective, or apparently FBI agent, has to be a good actor,* George thought to himself.

Kameron added, "Richard, I want to tell you right off the bat that you are here because of a serious topic we need to discuss."

How much is this going to cost me? Richard immediately thought. *How much do I have to support the arts in Portland to influence local politics?*

Kameron continued, "You are probably thinking this is a shakedown for the arts. Not so. It is a more serious issue regarding your company."

Richard had always been in control. He was the one to establish how his company and its work were discussed. Now, this person he just met was telling him there was a serious issue related to his company? It was an insult to attack his company in this social setting. However, Richard remained cool and collected. He had weathered criticism all his life and always came out on top. *Let's see what this guy thinks is so serious.*

Kameron continued, "I am confident I know how executives like you think. You want to control elections. You give to the arts. You drop money into various political coffers, all in the hopes of increasing your influence, your control of the environment in which you do business and make money. You like power.

Although Kameron was correct, Richard did not like the way it was blatantly expressed. Richard's fight or flight instincts were immediately on high alert. He was under attack. He had been attacked before, but not by people like Kameron with no political influence in Portland, or Oregon for that matter. Who does this guy think he is? In normal circumstances, he would have stood up, and taken command of the situation giving Kameron a virtual fuck you finger. But he did not know who all these other folks were and what influence they might have. They were sitting there without any

~ 470 ~

objection to Kameron's crass comments. However, he realized he might not be stable if he stood. Drinks did not usually affect him so hard. He thought he should not have skipped dinner. Unbeknownst to him, his drinks had been intentionally strong when everyone else was drinking non-alcoholic beverages. He wanted to be clear-headed, so he focused as clearly as possible on what was being said. He was prepared to win any argument this nobody, piss-ant Kameron could deliver. Kameron had the nerve to wait till Margaret left the room to attack him? *She will defend me when she returns. Why isn't anyone else speaking up in defense. This guy is so out of line.*

"And exactly what have I been brought here to discuss?" Richard ventured to ask even though he realized that he did not want to hear what Kameron had to say. But the first way to win was to get his opposition to express an obvious lie he could easily refute.

"Richard, every person you see sitting here with you, with the exception of George, is an FBI agent."

And except for Laura. Richard thought to himself.

"But Kameron, to drill it in, added, "Even Laura, who you have been friends with for several years."

Could that be true? Richard turned his head to see Laura's reaction. Laura nodded her agreement to Kameron's statement. That she had never disclosed her relationship to the FBI angered Richard. He could not conceal the anger that formed on his face despite his initial resolve not to show how irritated he was by this whole set up. As he turned his head, the room spun. *Have I had that much to drink? No, these guys have spiked my drinks. What the hell is going on?* Richard thought to himself, but he said nothing. Having glared at Laura, he turned to face Kameron again. "FBI—you don't say? I did not know Margret had so many FBI friends," he said, trying to figure out what was going on. Again, he thought about getting up and leaving, but his head was spinning from the drinks.

Kameron continued, "Margret is Uri's wife. They have been married for over fifteen years. Uri works in the local FBI office here in Portland. He reports to me."

"And Margret? Is she a secret agent too?" Richard said with chagrin.

"No, not Margret. And she will not be returning to this gathering, Richard."

It was clear that Kameron was in charge of this conspiracy. Kameron continued to introduce the rest of the FBI. Richard, a quick study, especially with people's names, something he was noted for, in this case, could not keep up with Kameron. He did not know if it was the alcohol, the shock at being cornered, or both, affecting his ability to keep up. Richard wondered what they wanted; why they had set this up. It did not occur to him that Kyle Tredly had anything to do with this until Kyle walked into the room, having heard Kameron make introductions. George Lockit came with him, bringing a folding chair.

"And I am sure you know Mr. Tredly, Richard. Kyle is not an FBI agent. This is his friend from St. Andrew's Texas, Mr. Lockit. Mr. Lockit is a private investigator." Richard's flight or fight emotions were telling his mind to escape whatever was about to happen. His reputation, however, was of the cool, collected, calm manager of a multi-million operation, accustomed to being the one in charge, the one giving directions. He was trying to figure out how to manage the current situation. What did these guys want?

Kameron continued, "Richard, we want to discuss your Meisner Voting Systems. We understand that you have been especially successful in marketing your systems."

Richard wondered: *Did they know about his machine's capability? He had not made any attempt to date to exercise any control over ballot counting, so they could not be trying to accuse him of election tampering. All his other operations were on the up and up. Why bring Kyle in on whatever was going on? Had he caused this by firing Kyle? Was Laura somehow choosing Kyle as her person to defend against him? Maybe they knew about his work with Corning and getting the specifications before anyone else.*

Kameron noticed that Richard was in a state of suspended animation. He knew that Richard was trying to figure out what was going on. Best if he helped answer that question,

"Richard," Kameron addressed him by name as a way to get his attention, "This has nothing to do with Mr. Tredly's termination. That was an unfortunate timing issue. You will recall that the invitation to this meeting was made before you fired Mr. Tredly. However, Mr. Tredly has important information to share with you that will most likely alarm you. Mr. Lockit has assisted with uncovering what we want to share with you. We want to enlist your help with a problem of national significance. Please do not be alarmed and hear us out."

Wait! They want my help? Richard relaxed slightly and gave a non-verbal nod to Kameron to continue. He needed to know what was going on, and the sooner, the better.

"I have asked Mr. Tredly and Mr. Lockit to share what they have learned in the past few months. Mr. Tredly, would you tell Mr. Meisner what you have learned?"

"Richard, first, I want to say I appreciate your trust, assigning me responsibility for the hyperspectral read-heads. Not only did I get an opportunity to apply my knowledge, but to observe a number of great people you have working for you. Of course, my very first meeting with you before I was hired has always made me curious about your intentions. Clever of you to pair me with Laura. You had me hooked from the beginning. I am sorry that I did not share with you the details of what I was doing all the time. Frankly, with all your emphasis on security and leaks, I thought you were aware of what was going on with the read-heads."

Having recovered from his initial shock, Richard felt he might take charge of the conversation, "Kyle, you were always a wild card in my plans. Frankly, I have never fully trusted you, or you too, Laura. I was not surprised that I had to fire you. Don't get me wrong, your technical skills are superb, but your loyalty has always been questionable. I ..."

Kyle interrupted authoritatively, "Richard, now is not the time to speculate on what we each thought and try to justify our actions. Please don't interrupt me until I complete what I have to say. I assure you it will be worth your while."

Richard was taken aback. *Who is this guy to talk to me this way? There is nothing he can tell me that I do not already know. Little worker peons in the company seldom understand the big picture. He may have discovered my plans regarding the hyperspectral read-heads. Still, he does not realize he is dealing with something a lot bigger than his story.* But, having been put in his place, he decided to see what this twerp had to say. He said nothing and therefore left Kyle the chance to continue.

"Richard, I do not believe you know that your hyperspectral read-heads are being manipulated by Chinese intelligence," Kyle let that sink in before saying anything else. The silence was deafening.

Finally, Richard said, "What? Chinese intelligence? How could you possibly know this?" The mere idea sent shivers down his spine. *No way!*

Kyle continued, "Well, you can imagine how much trouble I could be in making this accusation in front of all the FBI agents. I have shared my findings with them, and they understand, as much as anyone, that what I have said is true. Furthermore, I doubt you know that the read-heads were not manufactured by your good friend Tao Li, but by a factory in Shenzhen, China. All the evidence suggests that the factory was infiltrated by the Chinese Ministry of State Security and your specifications for the read-heads altered before they were shipped to you. Tao kept this secret from you. You may know, his partner has disappeared, probably as a result of his knowledge, and sharing of information to an MSS agent spy in Taiwan."

Richard had an ongoing debate with himself. Did he believe Kyle? Why would he make this kind of stuff up? Could this all possibly be true? He could not contain himself. He had to respond, "So, Kyle, if this is all true, how is it that you know this? And why have you kept it a secret from me? So, you knew all along and played along to pull this power play if you were ever terminated?"

"I can see how you might take it that way. But that is not the case. It was the trip to Minnesota that made it all clear. You know, the one you fired me about? The person with me was Mr. Lockit here, my friend. I trust Mr. Lockit with my very life. And in the past week, Mr. Lockit almost lost his life by the people who worked hard to keep you and me from discovering the fact that you have been hacked by one of the most sinister crimes to influence elections in the United States. It has resulted in the murder of two of your company's employees, Dennis Andersen, on my team and Stewart McNally, on a team you had working secretly in Hillsboro."

Richard suddenly felt the trap closing around him. Yes, he knew about Dennis and Stewart, but he thought Stewart's death was a gang's error. But the fact Kyle knew about the secret team meant he probably knew what they were working on. Richard was the one seeking to manipulate elections, not the Chinese. Maybe he could get away with all of this if they thought it was the Chinese, not him wanting to alter election outcomes. But he could not rest yet. Kyle seemed to know a lot. He needed to hear more.

Richard asked, "So, the Chinese have been trying to manipulate our elections. How can I help? What do you want me to do? If we have to re-manufacture the read-heads, we can always replace them all. That should not take too long."

Kameron spoke up, having been quiet up to this point, "Richard, that is a great idea, one that we have already discussed. However, I believe you will have to do a lot more than replace those read-heads. You should begin to think now about how your machines will work without any read-heads at all?"

"I am not sure that is possible," Richard said. He needed these read-heads to accomplish the plans that he and Corning had hatched up, "I think we have to get read-heads that conform to my original specifications."

Kyle jumped back in before Richard could continue, "Richard, I have not finished with my story. I took George, Mr. Lockit, with me to Minneapolis so I could run tests without customer intervention. George's task was to keep the customer out of my hair while I ran my tests. It was in those tests, whose results I believe the FBI will share with you, and for which you paid, that I discovered what was going on. You know that anomaly you have asked me about repeatedly? In Minneapolis, thanks to the equipment that George rented for me, I discovered the anomaly was, in fact, a radio-frequency way for the Chinese to control the read-heads remotely. You can read the test results for yourself. But I also discovered that the read-heads implementation permitted the ballot-counting machines to know information that they should not know if ballots were to, in fact, be secret ballots. Your read-heads, together with your elaborate ballot coating systems, coded ballots in ways that would permit the manipulation of ballot counting. Not only were the Chinese interested in manipulating votes, so were you!"

Richard realized he might be in legal trouble, so he said, "These are serious accusations you are making. Considering the potential implications, I think I should have legal representation here with me. What I am doing is all aboveboard, so I do not want to walk into a trap." Richard stood up and planned to leave. Immediately he realized he was unstable. Whatever he drank, it was stronger than his usual.

Everyone else took the hint and stood as well. Kameron said, "Richard, you can leave if you choose, but I assure you it will be more problematic for you if you do. I guarantee we are not trying to trap you. There are no recordings of these conversations. You are not under arrest. We want you to know that things have not been what they seemed to you. Yes, you were trying to manipulate ballot counting. Yes, that would be a federal crime. But everything we know tells us you have not done that, at least not yet. We are meeting tonight to make sure you understand how foreign agents have compromised your systems without your knowledge. We know that you are a patriot, someone who believes in this country. We need your help. Please let us continue before you decide to leave. We will not force you to make disclosures you do not want to make. Please, listen. Let us finish what we have to say."

Richard did not say anything. He just stood there. Everyone stood there, looking at Richard. It was apparent that Richard was thinking about what Kameron had said. Finally, Richard asked, "You say I just have to listen?"

"Yes, that is all that is required of you. If you decide to say anything or share anything, that will be entirely your choice."

Richard, feeling very unsteady, was not sure he could navigate an exit until the drinks began to clear. He said, "Okay," and sat down.

Kameron continued, "Good choice. Here is the thing, Richard. You are a very successful businessman. Meisner Industries is one of the most successful private companies in the U.S. Without a question, that is true in Portland and in Oregon. It is important to the economy, and we want it to continue to be successful, to employ the many talented folks that work for you. I know you would not like to be used by others to engage in illegal activities that could destroy you and your company. This issue with the Voting Systems has that potential. The voting systems you have created are important to the voting integrity in every jurisdiction they are implemented, and many jurisdictions are buying your systems. I assume this is all-important to you," Kameron said, prompting Richard to say something if he wished to do so. He did.

"Yes, I am proud of Meisner Industries, and it would be devastating, not only to me, but to many people, if it failed," Richard said before he checked himself and stopped talking.

Don Swartz had been quiet up to this point. Now he began, "Richard, Ron, and Lark are agents in Washington, D.C. We have been investigating a friend of yours for several years, Senator Corning."

Richard winced. This conversation had been uncomfortable, but now he felt a queasiness in his stomach. He reached for his drink and gulped down what remained. It did not help. He was not sure he could leave if he wanted to. He would have to ride it out.

Swartz continued, "We think you already know this, but Senator Corning wants to control elections. Secretly, he wants to become the President, and he has a plan to accomplish that. Richard, Corning uses people. He pretends to be a close, dependable friend, but that is not important to him; being elected until he has the power to change the entire system, even to get the term limit on the president repealed, is his goal. He seems like a nice guy, but he has dark ambitions. You, Richard, are a pawn in his plans."

Richard, at first, was resistant to Swartz's description of Corning. Corning has been friendly, supportive. He and Corning have been intimate. Richard did not feel it as love, but he cared for Corning, and he was confident it was reciprocated. He did not believe Swartz. He could not keep quiet, "Don, I don't think I agree with your assessment of Corning. I have spent a lot of time with him. We have discussed the future. I don't believe his ambitions are as sinister as you are describing them."

But Swartz had sowed the seeds of mistrust, and Richard began to recall all the times he had been with Corning. What Swartz described was in the realm of possibility. After all, Corning had gone to considerable effort to make sure no one knew about their relationship. Corning had lent him money, not from his accounts but from offshore accounts. It was possible the accounts were not Corning's, but someone he had not told Richard about. Corning had appealed, not to his civic urges, but to his desire to build his company, impact society, and work things in his favor.

Swartz continued, "Richard, Kameron and his team have done a great job looking into your background and the work you have done. I know you won't like what I am about to say. Still, it looks like you have been manipulated into illegal actions by appealing to the worst inclinations that we all have, that we all have to guard against. You have to decide now who you are. Are you a manipulator of people to achieve your own selfish goals, or are you the decent, honest businessman and contributor to good things in our world? Which are you? Which do you want to be? What will be your legacy in this world?"

His legacy? Suddenly Richard was consumed with guilt. Indeed, he had given in to his dark side. The cat was out of the bag. He was the one being manipulated, first by Corning and now by these FBI agents. Indeed, who was he? Who was he going to be? He began to think of his father, the kindness with which his father had accepted his odd son. He thought of his wish to have a family, a son to whom he could leave his legacy, a son that would make him proud of his accomplishments. Was this the effect of what he had drunk? He blurted out, "What did you put in my drink?"

Kameron replied, "Honestly, Richard, it is nothing other than vodka punch."

Everyone looked at each other to see where this was going next. Laura nodded. It was her turn.

"Richard, I have to confess my role in this. Would that be okay with you?" Richard nodded. "I told you that I knew Kyle in Texas. Of course, I did not tell you how or why. I was assigned to protect him from threats made to his life. When my mom was ill, I transferred to Dallas. You have been under investigation for a long time based on your friendship with Corning. I arranged to meet you, and you took advantage of the offer I made to move to Portland. As I have come to know you, I know you aspire to do good for this world. I have watched you; I have heard your wishes, your desire to do good as a philanthropist, especially here in Portland. I have come to understand your philanthropy not so much as a method to become known, but because you have a good heart, are interested in what is good for Portland, care about the causes you have supported, even the cultural ones like the Opera and Symphony. You supported them because you believed in their value, not as a means of being popular or well known. I know this about you. So, I have not understood why you became involved in the deceptions about the Voting System. I was assigned a role to help investigate you, but in the process, I have come to admire your good intentions. If you have any weakness at all, it was allowing yourself to be manipulated, and that fact is a huge embarrassment. I like you, and you now need to step up to make the correct decision."

Richard liked Laura. He had trusted her, so while he disliked her secret role as an FBI agent, he felt she did know him. So, he asked, "Laura, you have been a great companion for me. What is this right decision you think I should be making?"

Laura was surprised Richard asked her opinion. On the other hand, he often talked to her in private and asked her opinion. Laura asserted, "You must, you have to help us prevent Corning from executing his destructive ambitions to be all-powerful. He will not be good for this country. And, you must realize he will not be good for you or your company either. You, and possibly you alone, can help prevent this."

Richard knew she was right, "Can I help without losing my company?"

Kameron said, and Swartz nodded as he did, "We believe that is possible;" they lied. They did not know what the outcome would be. Their job was to catch Corning. "Give us the word, and we have a plan we think will preserve your ability to continue without disgrace and help us thwart Corning's seriously wrongheaded adventure."

Richard considered things as everyone waited. Kyle felt as if it was taking Richard forever to decide, yet no one said anything. Richard was thinking about his father. His father repeatedly asked him, "Son, what are the three values of life?" and Richard would answer "honesty, integrity, and truthfulness." Richard realized he knew what the right thing to do would be. His father had always been proud of him, something Richard appreciated. He owed his success in life to the moral grounding his father had given him. How had he ended up in this situation? Why had he given in when Corning had initially approached him? Had he gravitated to Corning as a father figure after he had lost his own? Did Corning love him, or use him? He knew the answer. Corning, ten years Richard's senior, had played on Richard's sexual preference, had groomed him, had led him down this path of dishonor.

Chapter 22

~ Closing the Deal ~

Don Swartz had been down the road of getting people to turn state's evidence. After the initial agreement, there were lots of details. Don took charge now that Meisner had agreed to help.

"Richard, there are implications to helping us expose Corning. Because of the risks involved, I think it would be prudent to bring your attorney into the discussion at this point. Before we continue, I need you to affirm your willingness to work with the FBI on this case. I have drafted an agreement that you need to sign, but I need your lawyer to review it before you sign. I assume you do have an attorney on retainer for your personal business as well as one for your company. Is that correct?"

Richard found this suggestion interesting and surprising. He had always heard that people were arrested and put in positions to agree to cooperate before they were allowed to call their attorneys. He replied, "I do have an attorney that I would like to consult. But I thought you guys tried to keep people from calling an attorney until after you had their agreement."

"You watch too much television, Richard. If we tried to commit you to our plans before you had legal counsel, a couple of things could happen. In one case, a good lawyer could argue in court, and probably successfully, that you were trapped and agreed without good representation. We don't want that to happen. Secondly, with the information you likely already know, backing out without counsel could put you in a position of obstruction of justice, a felony.

Do you want to go to jail? Look at it this way. With your lawyer present, it is like negotiating a contract. Both sides need to be clear about what they agree. Does that make sense?"

"Sure. Give me a minute, and I will call my attorney, Karl Rogen. Have you heard of him?"

Kameron spoke up, "I am familiar with him. Don probably is not familiar since his work has been mostly in the D.C. area. Don, Karl is a reputable attorney in good standing. I have worked with him a few times. He is reasonable and provides good representation for his clients. He is not considered a criminal lawyer, but don't let that fool you. He is well versed when it comes to protecting his clients."

Don suggested, "Richard, do you want to call him now? If he is available, we could get on with things right here, tonight."

"I can call him. I was wondering if you have anything that might ease my stomach, Richard requested. This evening, I feel as if I drank too much, although I only had two or three drinks."

Kyle looked at George. George shook his head as if to say, "Don't ask."

Laura got up and went into the other room. It took her only a couple of minutes to return with a cup of coffee and a pill. Laura told him the medicine would help counteract the alcohol he drank. After he swallowed the pill, he took out his cell phone and called Karl. Karl answered after two rings.

"Karl, this is Richard. I have run into a situation, and I need your assistance. Any chance you would be available now to consult with me and representatives of the FBI?" He did not turn the speaker on his cell phone on, so no one else could hear Karl. After a moment, Richard continued, "Well, I am with several FBI agents now. They are the ones that suggested I call you." Richard listened then said, "It might wait," and Richard looked at Don. Don shook his head and pointed to his wristwatch, indicating it needed to be now. Richard continued, "Karl, I don't think it will wait," and he listened again, "No, I am not under arrest, at least not at the moment," and he put his hand over the phone and asked, "Am I?"

"No," Don mouthed as he shook his head involuntarily.

Richard listened a bit, then said, "Fine, that will work. I am going to hand the phone to a Mr. Don Swartz, FBI from Washington. He can give you background. Thanks," and he handed his phone to Don. Don introduced himself and gave Karl a brief description of the situation. Karl let Don know it would be about an hour before he could get there.

While they waited for Karl, Richard began a conversation with George asking him about his work as a private investigator. The conversation gravitated toward his work in Portland, and George was forthcoming within his sense of what would be appropriate at this stage of the general discussion. No one from the FBI team interfered. Richard was beginning to feel better since drinking coffee and taking the pill that Laura gave him. Next, Richard turned to talk to Kyle and offered an apology, of sorts, for terminating him. He asked Kyle if he would consider continuing to work for Meisner Industries.

"Richard, I would have to think about it. Before you offer, you need to determine what your future looks like."

Richard acted humble. There was natural skepticism, given he had always been self-assured. If he had a humble side, neither of them had observed it. Perhaps it was the trouble he was likely facing that was skewing his thinking. Maybe he was a good actor. No one knew for sure how this would play out.

Richard continued, "Fair enough, Kyle. I realize there are lots of questions you need answered. I guess I don't know what my position will be until everything is resolved. At least, I hope it is—soon." Everyone was quiet when Richard spoke up again, "Kyle, I was wondering, how long you have known that Laura was an FBI agent."

Kyle blushed because he had known, and Richard had not. Laura stepped into the conversation and rescued Kyle, and told the story of how George had been the one that told Kyle. Richard continued to ask detailed questions about Kyle, Laura, and Mr. Lockit. Each was patient with the questions and answered truthfully the ones they could, considering current circumstances. About the time that Richard had run out of questions, Karl Rogen showed up. Karl was introduced and shook hands with everyone. Don explained that he had a very early flight back to Washington in the morning to deal with another case he was working. Ron Ableson would follow up with Richard and his attorney.

Ron directed everyone to a round table in the corner of the room. When they were seated, Ron took twenty minutes to outline the situation and bring Karl up-to-date. The rest of the crew were there as witnesses to Richard's agreement to cooperate, and the FBI's commitment not to publicize Richard's situation, provided he did not talk to the press without consultation and approval by the FBI.

Karl asked for a few minutes to talk to Richard privately, so the rest waited in the adjacent room. Twenty minutes later, Karl invited everyone back, and Richard and Ron signed an FBI provided contract with a few handwritten adjustments. All agreed it was too late to make plans for the next step and agreed to meet tomorrow evening over dinner, location to be announced in the morning. Richard was not arrested and was free to leave with his attorney.

After Richard and Karl left, Laura suggested that Kyle and George stay at her apartment until things were resolved. Kameron thought it was a good idea because they still did not know how many Chinese agents were afoot and precisely their intentions. Ron arranged for additional FBI security for Laura's apartment building.

~ Richard asks for Help ~

Richard had been up talking to Karl Rogen until 2:00 AM, but he still managed to come into the office by 10:00 AM the next morning. The first thing he did was call Laura.

"Hello," Laura answered on the third ring.

"Laura, this is Richard. Would you mind coming to my office this morning? I have things to discuss with you."

"Uh ... sure. It will take me at least forty-five minutes. Will that work?"

"Okay. I was wondering if Kyle and George might come too?"

Laura was frowning, but of course, Richard could not see her. Laura was wondering if Richard was still on board to cooperate? Could this possibly be a set up since the three of them were critical to keeping Richard committed? Was this a ploy to change his agreement from last night? She asked, "Why do you want us to come? Did you change your mind?"

Richard did not waste any time answering her, "No, hell no. I am feeling better than I have in a long time. I will be glad to get this behind me."

"Are you sure you are not mad at me? I suppose you have every reason to be pissed off."

"Laura, yes, I am aggravated. I never knew you were FBI. But I understand why you did not tell me. Still, it is frustrating to know I have been on the FBI's list of suspected people for as long as I have known you. I need to talk to you about the next steps. Rogen has suggestions I want to run by you."

Laura asked, "Why Kyle and George?"

"I can make that clear when they get here. Just tell me, can you all come?"

"Give me a moment," and Laura put the phone on mute so Richard could not hear her conversation with Kyle and George. It seemed like an eternity before she came back on the line, "Okay. The three of us will be there in about forty-five minutes." Laura was still hesitant about going with the three of them, so she called Ron Ableson at the FBI office to see if he could join them. Ron agreed.

When the four of them, Laura, Kyle, George, and Ron, arrived at Richard's office, Rogen, Richard's attorney, was also present. In a way, while they had been leery of the meeting, seeing Rogen put them all at ease. As it turned out, Rogen wanted to hear firsthand the same information that Laura, Kyle, and George had shared the night before that led Richard to agree to work with the FBI. Charla knocked on the door during the conversations and came in with box lunches for all six of them. They continued over lunch. Before Rogen gave Richard advice about cooperating with the FBI, he needed to hear the facts. Richard assured them all that there would be no recordings or notes of this meeting. One of the things that particularly interested Rogen was the experience George had when his life was threatened. Around 2:45 PM, Laura, Kyle, and George headed back to Laura's apartment. Ron Ableson remained to review the agreement they had signed, especially as it addressed Richard's future and the future of Meisner Industries. Ron was able to satisfy all of Rogen's questions. Rogen asked Richard again if he was in agreement with the terms of the deal the FBI was offering and if he was still willing to go forward with the meeting with Senator Corning as roughly outlined. Richard reassured Rogen in Ron Ableson's presence.

~ The Set-Up ~

It took a couple of days of back and forth with Ron Ableson from the FBI and Richard, with his attorney, to iron out the details of what would be expected of Richard. Richard would make arrangements to meet Corning as soon as possible at Richard's house in Glendale, Maryland. The FBI was given access to the house and wired it with sound and video capturing equipment in every room that Richard suggested as places he and Corning met, including the bedroom, in case Corning expected a sexual liaison on this trip. The FBI suggested the outline of how to get Corning to own up to his plans and intentions for the Meisner Voting System and how he and Richard planned to influence elections.

The FBI had Richard call Corning and arrange a day to meet. Corning was anxious to hear about implementations, so he readily agreed to a meeting the next weekend. With things all set up, the rest of the D.C. FBI team returned to Washington. Kameron was asked to go with them, which he did. Richard had a nervous feeling in the pit of his stomach. The wait was torturous.

Richard, his pilot, and Ron Ableson flew to Glendale the next Thursday evening. Corning would meet him at his house the following day and would stay overnight. Corning said he had a meeting on Sunday with a lobbyist who arranged substantial contributions to his upcoming campaign.

Before he left Portland, Richard asked accounting and marketing to get him the information about the number of Meisner Voting Systems sold and to whom. He wanted an overall picture of the financial analysis, including the profits. From Marketing, he asked for their projections based on contracts signed and on serious negotiations currently taking place and finally on their forecasts for sales before the end of the year. He got regular reports of Meisner Industries overall, but he wanted details of the Voting Systems that he could share with Corning when they met. Even Richard was astounded when he got the report. Because of Corning's work on setting up tight specifications for voting systems through HAVA, sales far exceeded Richard's expectations. The last report he had seen was two weeks ago. He was sure Corning would be delighted with the report.

Now that Richard had agreed to work with the FBI and had found a new moral grounding, it pained him to continue to send out voting systems that he knew were subject to manipulation by the Chinese. He had provided the FBI with his original specifications. The FBI had specialists pouring over the specs looking for ways to disable the particular feature that allowed manipulation of counts by the ballot counting machine. Richard had also provided them a dozen read-heads that a different team of FBI specialists could reverse engineer.

The FBI specialist had a surprise for Richard. The Chinese manufactured read-heads did not permit the secret code his team had developed for the Meisner Voting System to manipulate vote counts. Richard and Corning's plans would not have worked after all. Only the Chinese adaptations to the read-heads could do that. They double-checked with Richard. Since he had not tried to manipulate votes with code his secret team had written, he was surprised and unaware the secret code would not work. This put the FBI in an interesting position concerning Richard, and possibly Corning as well. As delivered, the machines did not contain features that allowed Richard or Corning to manipulate votes, and indeed, there was no way to prosecute them for a feature they talked about. This put the meeting Richard was about to have with Corning in question. Everything was in the works. The meeting was set up, Corning was coming, and he was still guilty of planning to manipulate votes. Richard was on the hook because of his admissions and agreements. Corning had secrets that a meeting might disclose. They decided the meeting continued to have value if only to gain more data about the scheme to manipulate elections. They quickly modified their plans with Richard in agreement. Richard was pissed, first that he had allowed Corning to drag him into this mess and second that he had spent so much money on code that would not work anyway. Richard did not grasp the fact he might not be in trouble since his secret code would not work. He did not realize the Chinese might have saved his ass.

~ Richard Meisner and Rolfe Corning ~

The meeting with Richard and Corning occurred as scheduled. Corning drove his private car as usual and drove into the garage at Richard's estate in Glendale, avoiding any photo's documenting his presence in Glendale, or so he thought. The FBI was documenting it all. When he came inside, Richard greeted Rolfe as usual. Corning detected a certain reticence on Richard's part.

"Richard, you look pale. You feel okay?"

"I am okay. I have had an upset stomach, but I am feeling a lot better," Richard said to cover his nervousness about the evening. "Let me fix you a drink. What would you like?"

"The usual, Richard."

Richard continued as he added extra vodka in Rolfe's drink. "I have a steak I want to put on the fire for us. Come on in the kitchen with me while I cook dinner."

Rolfe brought his drink in the kitchen as Richard put the steak on his stove's grill and turned on the hood vent. Corning, full of himself, appreciated that Richard was always attentive to his exploits in the politics of Washington, D.C. He bragged about how he had maneuvered the other senators around the HAVA bill, so the specifications were uniquely favorable to Meisner Industries. The FBI listening nodded their heads as this was incriminating enough to cause Corning problems, even if it did not snare him completely.

Richard also had two baked potatoes in the oven that would be ready as soon as the steaks.

Richard realized he needed more incriminating statements from Rolfe, so he asked what other interesting deals he had been making. Corning bristled at the question. He had lots of deals going on, but not any he would share with Richard. He needed Richard for one thing, to influence elections. Richard and he stood to gain substantially from the sale of his machines, but there was a lot Richard did not need to know about Corning's exploits and ambitions. Richard asked Rolfe if he had any elections in mind that he wanted Richard to prepare to influence. Corning ignored his question. Fortunately for Corning, Richard did not understand that people like Richard were tools for powerful people like Corning to exploit. Nevertheless, he needed to keep Richard on the hook, so he told him about how he sabotaged one of the senators who had opposed him on the HAVA bill. Corning had the opponent removed from the budget committee. Otherwise, his stories were more braggadocios. Richard kept him busy telling stories and bragging about his manipulation of other senators to his will. They had to take a break while they fixed their potatoes and carried everything to the dining room. Corning continued to expound on his exploits during the entire meal and then finally asked how things were going with Richard.

As they sat to eat, Meisner poured Corning another drink of vodka laced Gin. During the meal, Richard brought Corning up to date with all the events in his personal life. He avoided discussion of voting machines. Instead, he talked about all the philanthropic projects he supported. Rolfe feigned that he was duly impressed. When they finished, they retired to the study off the kitchen, where Richard poured them more drinks. As instructed, he used a vodka laced drink for Rolfe and a non-alcoholic version for himself. As they drank, Rolfe became more serious.

"You said you had good news?" Rolfe inquired.

"Excellent news. Meisner Industries has sold one-hundred-twenty Voting Systems since HAVA passed. We have orders for fifty more and inquiries from another one-hundred," Richard said.

"That is more than we thought would be in place before this next election. That is good news, very good news, assuming they are going into useful jurisdictions," Rolfe answered with enthusiasm.

"You didn't give me a list of preferential jurisdictions. What are the ones you particularly want to influence? Richard asked.

Rolfe rattled off a half-dozen.

Richard was able to show Rolfe a list and map of where the machines had been purchased. Rolfe was ecstatic to see a number of machines were located in jurisdictions that had not been supportive of his ambitious adventures in the Senate. At this point, Richard began the script the FBI had suggested.

"But something has come up in our project." Richard teased.

"A problem?" Rolfe asked, somewhat deflated from the good news.

"Something like that. You recall me telling you about Stewart McNally, one of the guys writing the special code we discussed? Well, as it turns out, we thought he had been killed in a gang shoot-out. You do remember him, don't you? He is the one I sent you a note about."

"McAlly, you say?"

"No, McNally. M C N A L L Y." Richard spelled out the name for him.

"Okay, McNally. You say he was killed in a shootout? I think you did tell me something about that." Rolfe knew full well about McNally.

"Well, as it turns out, the body they found in his car was not him."

"Interesting, but what does that have to do with the project?" Rolfe had also received a report on McNally from another source that indicated McNally had been eliminated.

"Nothing when we thought it was McNally. Well, not nothing. He was quite a talented coder. The secret team he belonged to was almost finished with the code you wanted, and he wanted to test their code. When they thought McNally had been killed, the rest of the team took some time off."

"So, a delay? That should not be a major problem, should it?" Rolfe asked. A delay was fine with him. He knew their code would never be executed.

"I'm not through with what happened, Rolfe. Well, when we all learned that McNally was not in the car, everybody, including me, was alarmed. Where was he? What was he up to? He had disappeared, and I was alarmed the purpose of the secret team's work would be exposed."

"And was it?" asked Rolfe, who was beginning to show the results of too much vodka in his drinks.

"No. As it turned out, they found McNally's body in a shallow grave in the forest. The body was cut up in parts. Identity was verified with a DNA test."

Rolfe already knew this from the reports he had been secretly sent. He nevertheless acted surprised as best he could, "Oh, no. Mutilated? Do they know who did it?" Rolfe was hoping this was the end of this story, but it was not.

"No, they don't have any suspects, at least not yet. But I am very concerned our scheme might become exposed. They said the body showed signs of being tortured. What were they after? He could have told them very damaging information. I don't know how those medical examiners figure things out, but they say the torture marks were typical of the kind the Chinese use." Richard was presenting the story the way the FBI had instructed. There was no particular Chinese torture method that could be identified postmortem on a dismembered corpse.

"Chinese?" Rolfe asked. He was visibly shaken as hard as he tried not to show alarm. He wondered what Richard knew and where this conversation was headed. If Richard knew too much, he might be holding out for something more than profit on selling machines. Rolfe was in no mood to be manipulated by some cheap business owner.

Richard answered, "Yes, Chinese. They seem sure of it, which is alarming. What were they after?" Rolfe did not respond, so Richard continued, "There was another unusual death. There was a fellow, Dennis Andersen, who worked in my building. He went missing and was found in his car in the Willamette River. At first, we all thought it must have been an accident, but the investigators said "no" after his autopsy. It was clear he had been murdered, but no one knows the motive or who did it."

"Who was this guy?" Rolfe asked and then regretted allowing Richard to think more about it. His scheme worked best if Richard was kept in the dark about what he, Rolfe, was doing.

"Dennis was working on the in-house team. One of his colleagues uncovered the fact that he was murdered. It occurred right after he and Dennis were studying an anomaly in the hyperspectral read-heads."

"Colleague? Do I know him?" Rolfe asked.

"Fellow I recently hired by the name of Kyle Tredly. That name ring a bell?" Richard asked.

Corning did know that name. He had his agents tracking Kyle's work as best they could. His team was prepared to eliminate him if he got too close to discovering how the read-heads worked. But he did not want to let Richard know, so he said, "Tredly, you say. I don't think I know who that is. What was his job?"

"He worked on my in-house team in headquarters, the floor below my office. I brought him on because of his familiarity with hyperspectral analysis. He is a very talented guy. I gave him an undercover assignment because I thought there were technology leaks on his team or somewhere in the company. I had him look into activities in most of the Voting System groups."

"You did what?" Rolfe asked. He was becoming irritated at the direction of this conversation. "We never agreed to that. Don't you realize people might uncover our scheme?" This was the first time Rolfe had made any potentially incriminating statements regarding the vote manipulation scheme.

"Rolfe, I needed someone who knew the whole voting system so we could identify and fix problems that might crop up at customer sites. I swore him to secrecy. Laura McLaughlin knew him from when he was working in Texas and assured me that he was a straight-up guy to help me find the leak. But he did turn out to be a problem."

"Explain!" Rolfe said somewhat like a command. Richard kept his cool.

"Turns out, Tredly was suspicious of me, but I did not know that he was. I wanted to keep tabs on several of my teams' work, so I had used the leak as a cover. Unbeknownst to me, he hired a private detective to help him find the leak."

"Oh, god! A private dick. That's all we need. Do we have a problem?" Rolfe asked. Rolfe knew about George and the attempt to neutralize him that had failed. Things were getting out of hand, and Richard was looking more like a problem than an asset.

"Honestly, yes. But the problem is bigger than I was aware. Fortunately, for the two of us, Kyle and his private eye made a discovery that we need to discuss."

"What problem?" Rolfe asked nervously.

"Well, Lockit, that's the P.I., almost got himself killed investigating things."

"Shit!" Rolfe said involuntarily. The report he got from his Chinese contact had told him all about it. It could be a problem if Richard discovered the real purpose behind their project together. He had to think fast, "What does this Lock guy have to do with anything?" He had to know what Richard knew. He did not want to let Richard in on his plan. He could not be sure how Richard would react.

"Lockit is his name, George Lockit. He began to look into a threat that a friend of a friend of Tredly's got, and determined it was from a Chinese source." Richard continued to spin the web to capture Corning.

"That's the second time you have implied there was a Chinese connection to problems. How confident are you it was Chinese?" The alcohol was beginning to interfere with Corning's ability to think quickly. When Richard offered him another drink, Rolfe declined. He needed to sober up fast before things got out of control. He had several drinks, thinking they might sleep together tonight. He had never considered Richard a threat to his plans, but now he was wondering how much Richard knew.

"Quite sure it was Chinese. There is more you need to know, however. All of this led to a discovery that threatens our plans, Rolfe." and he paused.

"Keep talking. What is the threat? It is the threats you don't know about that can kill you." Corning slurred in an agitated tone revealing his anxiety and frustration about the conversation.

"Well, Tredly discovered an anomaly in the Hyperspectral read-heads that I asked him to delve into. I had no idea where this was going to lead. I think we could be in a real bind. Tredly discovered this anomaly was, in fact, a feature. I won't go into the gory details, but it turns out that the code my secret team wrote could be overridden using this anomaly that Tredly discovered. I took care of it. I fired him for another reason. I think having him out of the picture will help us keep our scheme secret."

"Keep what secret?" Rolfe was sweating now. He was not sure he needed to worry. Richard had been more than willing to engage in voter manipulation.

"The fact that an external source can control the ballot counting," Richard said. "I think it might be the Chinese who can do it. Unless you know something that I don't know."

"Chinese? I think you are delusional."

"No, I am not. I discovered that the read-heads had been manufactured in China, not by my friend in Taiwan. The Chinese modified my specifications. They have introduced a way to impact vote counts, and it might override the code our secret team developed. Do you realize what this means? We are not in control like we planned. I have placed an order for new read-heads that do not contain the anomaly, only the original specifications, so my team's code will work. They will be manufactured in the United States. I will replace all the read-heads in existing and machines currently being built.

"God dammit, Richard. You should have told me what was going on before now." Rolfe said. "Get a grip. We have not lost control. Don't replace the read-heads. That will call attention to a problem we don't want to explain."

"What do you mean, Rolfe?"

"I know about what you are now discovering. You don't need to worry. You don't need to replace the read-heads."

"What? You want the Chinese to have access to the ballot counting?"

"I did not want to get you involved, Richard. At least not more than you already were. I have everything under control. You need to keep your mouth shut and follow my plan."

"Your plan?"

Rolfe realized he goofed, "I meant our plan."

Richard brought the conversation back to the agenda, "Wait a minute. You knew about Chinese involvement?"

"Knew? Knew? Hell yes, I knew. Who do you think arranged all of this? The election fairy? You don't understand Washington. You think you are such a big dog with your little Portland manufacturing company. You are just another cog in the big giant wheel of politics. You don't get ahead by being fair. Politics is war. Politics is about power. Politics is about money."

Corning could not take any more of Richard's stupidity. He thought he had Richard handled. Every once and a while, he ran into a guy he could not compromise. It looked like Richard was one of those. He was glad he managed to get the voting machines completed before all this came up. From his experience with other of his minions, Richard could not afford to back out now. He had Richard by the balls!

Corning continued with a certain disgust, "Frankly, peons like you are not capable of playing in this world of politics. It takes people like me to organize things, to run the system. It is a war. I am the senior general. People like you who think too small are foot soldiers. A General uses all the assets at his command to win. Winning is all that matters. So, what if I used the Chinese to subvert your programmers' game?" This kind of put-down had worked for Corning more than once.

Richard answered, "So I guess I get it. My role is to play along, say yes sir, salute, and do my duty."

"That a question? You need an answer? You keep doing as I tell you, and I will take care of you. That is how it works. You take care of me—I take care of you."

"Got it! So how do the Chinese play into this game of politics?"

Rolfe explained, "Game? Are you kidding? Politics involves life and death issues, and if you are going to be a winner, you have to play big. I hate to tell you this, but your secret team's code is useless. The Chinese have revised the read-heads features so that your code won't see the light of day. It is only the Chinese code that will control the ballot counting. You want to know more?"

Richard said, "Sure. If I am going to be a partner, you can't keep me in the dark. And, come to think of it, why did you have my secret team write code that was never going to be used? That cost me mega-bucks."

"Richard, Richard, you are so naive. Do your employees understand the problems you have as the owner of a company? Similarly, did you expect to be an expert in the world of politics?"

Richard pushed back, "You know the answer to that. I have told you over and over, I have no ambition to be in an elected office."

"Well, there are a lot of parts to politics besides being elected to an office. It takes a team, a big team, to win big elections. It takes money, lots of it, and influence to win elections. You have no power unless you get elected. I thought you were a part of my team."

"And the Chinese are part of the team too? I did not sign on to participate in people's murder. Who all is part of your team? Were you ever going to tell me? How about letting me in on your plans. Don't you realize I could help?"

"Richard, you are an important part of the team? So-what if the Chinese have members on the team? So-what if they are the ones to help us influence elections?" So-what if there are inevitable casualties in the process. As I said, this is war, and war has casualties. So, now I need to know, are you in or out? Do you still want to control elections? Do you still want to be one of the country's wealthiest citizens? You know I can make you a rich man if you continue to work with me?" Rolfe had come prepared. He was always prepared for whatever came up. He had extinguished an opponent before.

Richard said, "I feel an implied threat in what you are saying."

"No implication, Richard. If you are not part of the team, then you are part of the enemy! Sometimes the enemy becomes the casualty."

"You mean you even fucked me to get me to cooperate?"

Rolfe ignored the truth of it, "Think about what you want. That was an extra benefit as far as I am concerned. I need you to make a decision, right here, right now. Then I need to make a phone call."

"I don't know, Rolfe. How can our relationship be based on a bunch of lies? How can I trust you?"

"Trust equals money, Richard. Trust me, and you will be rich."

"And if I don't?"

"That is not something I need to spell out. You assume I am the only one with an interest in this project. The Chinese have an interest too, and I don't control them. They have their methods, and you have seen them used on your employees. I know what is good for me and what would happen if I did not trust them to be successful. I can't protect you if you want out of this project, but I can assure you the project will continue with or without you. And that, dear friend, is a threat you should not ignore. Take the money. Look the other way. You and I can share in the power and wealth that comes with being cooperative with the Chinese. They will not be denied their goals, and their goals have a much longer horizon than either you or me." This back and forth with Richard was getting tedious. Every once and a while, Corning misjudged a person. He assumed that every person could be compromised. Every once and a while he ran into someone who could not be. He always found a way to neutralize his opponents. It was looking more and more like he had misjudged Richard.

"How long, Rolfe? How long have you been dealing with the Chinese?

"I don't have to answer your questions." Rolfe had about had it. "I don't answer to you; you answer to me. You have to decide, right here, and right now, how you want this conversation to end," as Rolfe got up and wobbled over to this coat hanging by the door. It was clear he was drunk. But he surprised Richard by removing a handgun from his jacket hanging over the back of a chair. He held it, not pointing at anything. The implication, however, was clear.

"Jeeze, Rolfe. There is no need for a gun. This is not the wild west." The reference to the wild west was the signal to the

FBI agents that he was in danger. Richard had expected the FBI to rush into the room, but nothing happened. Richard continued, "Wild West? Did I say wild west?" He thought they must not have heard him. Now he was scared shitless.

"What the hell are you jabbering about? I need an answer, Richard. Are you going to take care of things, or do I have to—? Rolfe said as he raised the gun, waving it around.

That alarmed Richard. No one warned him he might be in physical danger. *They never tell you anything!* Rolfe was having trouble keeping the gun pointed at him. Suddenly, there was a gunshot; the picture beside Richard shattered, sending shards of glass into the side of his head. Richard crouched down and started to exit the room through the swinging door to the kitchen when it swung open, hitting him on the head as he bent over, knocking him to the floor. A second gunshot went off, digging into the floor beside Richard. Richard urgently crawled toward the kitchen. An FBI agent was rushing across the room at Rolfe, gun raised. His instructions were to avoid lethal force at all costs. They needed Rolfe alive. They need information from Senator Corning.

Rolfe aimed at the agent and fired another shot, but it missed embedding in the kitchen door an inch over Richard's head as he tried to crawl out of the room. The last thing Richard heard was the agent tackling Rolfe as another shot was fired, and they rolled to the floor. This shot went through a stained-glass window in the dining room as Richard left. At the same time, several other agents entered the room, guns drawn. One agent pulled Richard into the kitchen and gave him a signal to move on through the other kitchen door onto the porch and outside, where another agent signaled for him to get in the car. He did, and the car pulled out. That was the last time Richard saw Rolfe in person until the trial a year later.

~ The Trial ~

Rolfe hired the best lawyers that money could buy. His defense was based on the argument that although he had known the Chinese were involved in a scheme to manipulate elections, he was in the process of trying to lay a trap for them. He claimed that Richard was the one behind the scheme and that he was trying to defend himself. The evidence the prosecution produced, including the testimony of the FBI, made a compelling and convincing case that it was Senator Corning who solicited the aid of the Chinese in Corning's scheme to subvert elections and grant control to a foreign government. A number of Corning's senatorial staff were called to testify about Corning's influence in the legislation that made Meisner Industries Voting Systems practically the only source of voting systems in the U.S. Richard had to testify in the trial under the glaring eyes of his onetime ally. During Richard's cross-examination, he had to confess to working with Corning in a scheme to write legislation favorable to Meisner Industries to give both of them the opportunity to manipulate votes in elections. However, it became clear to everyone, including the jury, that Richard had no participation in the Chinese plan to manipulate elections. Everyone, press included, agreed that Richard's actions since Corning's arrest and his testimony in the trial was instrumental in Senator Rolfe Corning's conviction: thirty years to life. Corning was sent to the Federal Prison in Otisville, New York.

~ And Then ~

During the year between Corning's arrest, and his trial, Richard had adhered to the agreements made on that fateful night when the scheme was exposed. In return, Richard was permitted to retain ownership and position as CEO, provided he expand the Board of Directors to include FBI appointed members for fifteen years. In addition, he agreed to a court-appointed chief financial officer to oversee all financial affairs of the company, make any necessary restitution, and sit on the Board. Richard had to give the CFO veto power over all major decisions of the company for ten years. Since the time Richard experienced his "come to Jesus" inspiration, that turned out not to be a problem.

With FBI supervision, Meisner Industries arranged to have all the hyperspectral read-heads replaced with ones manufactured in the United States using Meisner's original specifications modified by experts appointed by the FBI and paid for by Meisner Industries. In addition, ballot production machines were modified so that the invisible coatings no longer provided any information about the voters. Meisner Industries was obligated to hire external auditors to validate elections for every jurisdiction that requested it. Still, Meisner

Industries managed to do quite well financially, and Richard continued to be a generous philanthropist.

Richard was not told much about how Rolfe's failed attempt to gain control of power in the U.S. was wrapped up. There were ongoing investigations that involved other members of the Senate and their aides. Richard was assured that the Chinese connection was resolved, key agents were rounded up, and his life was not in danger. There were numerous press reports of China's attempt to interfere and gain control of U.S. elections. Significant sanctions were applied by most members of the United Nations even though China vetoed official censure attempts.

Postscript

Portland seemed a lonely place after Laura moved to Washington, D.C. and George returned to St. Andrews in Texas. Given his history with Meisner Industries, Kyle Tredly was not comfortable staying employed. Being financially secure, Kyle decided to move back to Texas. He got a job working as a computer support person for a clinical trial at South Memorial Health System in Houston, Texas. Kyle connected with an old friend, Kat Winshaw, who also worked for SMHS. Kat involves Kyle in his next adventure in the next novel, Magnetics.

~ Magnetics ~

She knocked on the open door of my office. I turned around to see a woman in a floral dress and tan leather flats. She looked to be in her mid-twenties. She had long eyelashes and pale blue shadow that made her eyes look hollow. Her lipstick was a subtle red-orange. Her cheeks were blushing red. It was like a kindergartner applied her makeup.

"Hello? Are you Mr. Tredly?" she timidly said as she hesitated at the door to my office. I motioned for her to come in. "Please call me Kyle," I said; what can I do for you?"

"Mr. Tredly, I mean Kyle," she said with some hesitation, "They told me you might be able to help me." I invited her to take a seat. First, I had to move a stack of research papers. I asked who *they* were. She said it was her friend who worked in the Public Relations Department, Kat Winshaw.

"Ah, Kat and I met when we were in graduate school at the University of Houston," I added, being cordial.

"I don't think you told me your name," I asked as she took a seat in the recently vacated chair.

"Oh yes," she said, blushing as though doing something naughty. "My name is Sylvia Richardson." She offered nothing else, no further information, no detail about what she wanted, so I felt this might be a long conversation.

"Do you mind if I call you Sylvia?" I asked.

"That's fine," she said and added, "Kat said you might help me locate my boyfriend."

Author Biography

Cecil Denney was born in Edinburgh, Scotland, where his father attended the University of Edinburgh. He grew up in Oklahoma, Georgia, and Florida. Denney majored in mathematics at Phillips University in Enid, Oklahoma, and obtained a master's degree in mathematics at Kansas State University in Manhattan, Kansas. Professionally, he taught high school mathematics for eleven years in Overland Park, Kansas, was Director of Marist College's computer center during his eleven years in Poughkeepsie, New York, and Director of Academic Computing for sixteen years at the University of Texas Medical Branch in Galveston, Texas.

Denney uses his life experiences to create mystery novels that involve programmer Kyle Tredly's adventures. He started writing after his retirement. *Intruder*, was published July 2020. *Intrigue,* was publish in March 2021. Three additional stories about Kyle and his adventures are in the works.

Made in the USA
Coppell, TX
08 June 2021

57013021R00308